Lincoln Township Public Library
2099 W. John Beers Rd.
Stevensville, MI 49127
(269) 429-9575

D1435564

The
SWITCH

ALSO BY SANDRA BROWN

Standoff
The Alibi
Unspeakable
Fat Tuesday
Exclusive
The Witness
Charade
Where There's Smoke
French Silk
Breath of Scandal
Mirror Image
Best Kept Secrets
Slow Heat in Heaven

SANDRA BROWN

The SWITCH

Lincoln Township Public Library
2099 W. John Beers Rd.
Stevensville, MI 49127
(269) 429-9575

BOOKSPAN LARGE PRINT EDITION

WARNER BOOKS

A Time Warner Company

This Large Print Edition, prepared especially for Bookspan, contains the complete, unabridged text of the original Publisher's Edition.

This book is a work of fiction. Names, characters, places, and incidents are the product of the author's imagination or are used fictitiously. Any resemblance to actual events, locales, or persons, living or dead, is coincidental.

Copyright © 2000 by Sandra Brown Management, Ltd. All rights reserved.

Warner Books, Inc., 1271 Avenue of the Americas, New York, NY 10020

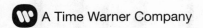 A Time Warner Company

Printed in the United States of America

ISBN 0-7394-1160-8

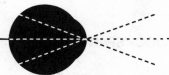

This Large Print Book carries the
Seal of Approval of N.A.V.H.

The SWITCH

C H A P T E R | 1

Kiss, kiss." Melina Lloyd kissed the air in the general direction of her twin sister's cheeks. "I've ordered an Italian white wine. Crisp, light, and not too fruity, according to the waiter who *was*. Fruity, that is. Speaking of, here he comes."

Gillian sat down across from her. The waiter served her glass of Pinot Grigio, spilling some of it over his hand as his shaved head swiveled back and forth between them. "Oh, my goodness gracious!"

"We're identical," Gillian said, sparing him from asking.

"I'm speechless. The resemblance is positively flabbergasting."

Melina gave him a frosty smile. "My sister would like to place a drink order, please. If it's convenient."

Her tone of voice, which had been as crisp as the wine, got his attention. "Certainly," he said, practically clicking his heels. "Forgive, forgive. Madam?"

"Club soda. Lots of ice, wedge of lime, please."

"I'll be back *prontomente* with your drink and to recite today's specials."

"I can hardly wait," Melina muttered as he glided away.

Gillian leaned forward and whispered, "Is *prontomente* a word?"

"Is *flabbergasting?*"

The sisters laughed together. "I'm glad to see you smiling," Gillian remarked. "When I got here you looked grumpy enough to snarl."

"I *am* a little cranky," Melina admitted. "I had to drive an author to the airport this morning in time for a five fifty-eight flight. Five fifty-eight! I know publicists book flights at those ungodly hours just to provoke us media escorts."

"Who was the early bird? Anybody interesting?"

"Forgot her name. First book. *Treating Your Children Like Pets.* Subtitled *With Amazing Results.*"

"Two-year-olds are sitting up and barking on command?"

"I don't know. I didn't read it. But someone is. It's currently number three on the *New York Times* bestseller list."

"You're kidding."

"Swear to God. If it's gimmicky enough, it'll sell. Nowadays even *I* could write a book. It's just that I can't think of anything interesting to write about." She thought it over for a second or two. "Maybe about the famous and infamous I've met and barely tolerated for a day. But then I'd probably be sued."

The waiter returned with Gillian's club soda and a tiny silver basket of bread. He recited his elaborate spiel, which was more about adjectives than food, and retreated in a huff when they ordered avocado halves stuffed with shrimp salad off the printed menu.

Melina offered the basket to Gillian, who broke open a quarter-size biscuit spiked with pecan bits. "What about being an identical twin? You could write about that."

"There's too much material there. The field would need to be narrowed."

"Being dressed alike versus not?"

"Possibly."

"Competing for parental attention?"

"Better. How about connecting through preternatural telepathy?" Melina eyed Gillian over the rim of her wineglass as she sipped from it. "Which leads me to note that my twin seems awfully introspective today. What's up?"

Before answering, Gillian polished off the biscuit and dusted flour from her fingertips. "I did it."

"'It'?"

"You know." Self-consciously she lowered her voice. "What I've been contemplating for the past few months."

Melina nearly strangled on the excellent Italian import. Her eyes, smoke-colored replicas of Gillian's, lowered in the direction of Gillian's lap, but it was out of sight beneath the table.

Gillian laughed. "You can't tell by looking. Not yet, anyway. I came straight here from the clinic."

"You mean today? Just now? I could be an aunt-in-the-making as we speak?"

Again Gillian laughed. "I suppose so. If the little guys are doing what they're supposed to do, going where they're supposed to go, swimming upstream."

"My God, Gillian." She took another quick sip of wine. "You actually did it? You did it. You're acting so . . . normal. So relaxed."

"Then the gynecologist would be pleased. He had the nerve to tell me to relax. As if I could. For one thing, the stirrups were cold as ice, hardly conducive to relaxation. For another, this was the culmination of months of debate. It wasn't a decision I made lightly."

Artificial insemination using donor sperm. Gillian had been weighing the pros and cons for months. Melina was confident that her twin had spent hours soul-searching, but she couldn't help nursing a few ambiguities of her own. "Did you consider it from every angle, Gillian?"

"I think. I hope. Although there are probably angles I didn't think of."

Those unthought-of angles worried Melina, but she kept her concerns to herself.

"Sometimes I became so ambivalent, I

was tempted to reject the idea altogether. I wanted to deny it had ever occurred to me and forget about it. But once the idea took hold, I couldn't shake it."

"That's a good sign. When something grabs us like that, it's usually for a good reason."

"Physically there was no deterrent. I'm in perfect health. I read everything I could get my hands on about alternative methods of conception. The more I read, the more conflicted I became. Honestly, I even tried talking myself out of it."

"And?"

"And I couldn't come up with a reason not to." She grinned happily. "So I did it."

"Did you use the Waters Clinic?"

Gillian nodded. "They have a high success rate, a solid reputation. I liked the doctor. He was very kind. Patient. Explained everything in detail. I made an educated decision."

And it was clear from the glow on her face that she was delighted with it. "I can't believe you didn't tell me. I would have gone with you if you'd asked. Held your hand. Lent some kind of support."

"I know you support me, Melina. You

and Jem were the only two people I discussed it with. I'm sorry I didn't inform you of my decision. But Melina . . ." Her eyes went liquid with appeal. "Please understand. I filtered your and Jem's opinions and viewpoints through your respective biases."

"I—"

"Hear me out, please. When all was said and done, when all the votes were in, I was the one inseminated. If it's successful, I'll carry the fetus and have the child. So the decision was mine to make. Alone. I wanted to tell you. But once my mind was finally made up, I didn't want it—"

"Changed."

"Or even questioned."

"I respect that. I do." She underscored it by reaching for Gillian's hand and giving it a quick squeeze. "Was Jem there?"

"No."

"I still can't believe it," Melina said, taking another quick peek toward her tummy. "How do they . . . ? How is it actually . . . ?"

"Yesterday, a self-administered urine test indicated a hormone surge, meaning that I would be ovulating within twenty-four to thirty-six hours. I called the clinic and booked the appointment. It's very clinical. They use an intrauterine catheter."

Melina listened spellbound as Gillian talked her through the procedure. "Did it hurt?"

"Not at all."

"Where'd the sperm come from?"

"Where do you think?"

Melina grinned. "I meant geographically."

"The Waters Clinic has its own sperm bank, but they'd rather not use a specimen acquired locally on a local patient."

"Good thinking."

"Mine came from a very reputable sperm bank in California. The specimen arrived this morning packed in dry ice. Then it was thawed and washed—"

"Excuse me?"

"That's the term. The semen is mixed with a protein and spun in a centrifuge, so that what is drawn into the catheter is . . ." She laughed. "Sperm concentrate, I guess you could say."

"I can think of a thousand jokes, all of which shall go unvoiced."

"Thanks for that."

"Do you feel any differently?"

"Not at all. I actually dozed afterward. I

had to remain lying down for about half an hour. Next thing I knew, the nurse was back in the examination room, asking me to dress and join the doctor in his office. He gave me a pep talk about their success rate and told me not to get discouraged if it didn't work this time, and then I left and drove straight here."

Satisfied with Gillian's reassurance, Melina sat back in her chair and stared into the face identical to her own. "My, my. It's positively flabbergasting." After they'd shared another laugh at the waiter's expense, she said, "Seems to me the trickiest part would be peeing on that little strip of paper."

"It did require a certain amount of skill. I was getting pretty good at it."

"And frankly . . ." Melina broke off and waved her hands in front of her as though erasing the unfinished sentence. "Never mind. I shouldn't say anything."

Gillian, however, already knew what her sister was thinking. "You were about to say that you prefer the old-fashioned method of insemination."

Melina shot an imaginary pistol at her. "You know me well."

"Daddy always said we share the same brain."

"Call me slutty," Melina said, giving an exaggerated shrug, "but I prefer flesh and blood to catheters and stirrups. Cold metal just doesn't have the same appeal as a warm chest and hairy legs rubbing against mine under the covers. Not to mention the sexual apparatus."

"Please! Don't mention the sexual apparatus."

"Didn't you miss the heavy breathing? That marvelous buildup? That 'Oh, my God, life is beautiful' feeling? Just a little?"

"It's not about sex. I didn't do this for the thrill. I did it to make a baby."

Melina sobered. "I'm just teasing." Folding her arms on the table, she said seriously, "The underlying, fundamental truth of it is that you want a child."

"That's right. That's the underlying, fundamental truth of it."

"Good for you," she said, giving Gillian a fond smile. After a reflective moment, she added, "Too bad Jem is firing blanks. You could have one-stop shopped. Sex and baby-making in one."

The waiter arrived with their order. The

food was garnished with fresh pansies and was almost too pretty to eat. Using her fork, Gillian toyed with the tiny purple blossom atop her scoop of shrimp salad. "Jem had his vasectomy long before he ever met me."

"Which I take as good fortune." Melina raised her wineglass in a silent salute. "He's a stick."

"Melina," Gillian said reprovingly.

"Sorry." But she wasn't, and Gillian knew the apology was insincere. "But he is a dud, Gillian. He doesn't make you happy."

"That's not true. I'm happy."

"Really? You don't seem over-the-moon in love to me. Unless I've missed something. Have I?"

"Apparently. Because I do love Jem."

Melina raised her eyebrow to form a skeptical arch.

"I do," Gillian insisted. "But what relationship is perfect? One can't have everything in a neat and tidy package. It's asking too much of any one person to fulfill all your needs and desires."

"In your case, a baby. You've wanted one since you were a child yourself. You played with dolls while I favored skates."

"Do you still want to be in the Roller Derby?"

"Yes, and I'm pissed because they switched to in-line skates, which is much harder."

Gillian laughed. "Sometimes Mother could tell us apart only by looking at our knees."

"Mine were the ones with the scabs." They laughed at shared memories, but gradually Melina's smile relaxed. "If Jem's sterility is the obstacle to your having a perfect relationship, ask him to have the vasectomy reversed."

"I broached it once. He wouldn't even talk about it."

"Then how has he reacted to your decision?"

"Surprisingly well. In fact, whenever I expressed doubt, he encouraged me to go through with it."

"Hmm." Melina was surprised to hear that. "Well, as I've said many times before, he's a weird duck."

"Let's not talk about Jem. Whenever we talk about Jem, we get into an argument, and I don't want anything to spoil today. On the topic of Jem, let's agree to disagree. Okay?"

"Fine by me."

They ate in silence for a moment before Melina said, "Just one more point." Gillian groaned, but she spoke above it. "If the procedure is successful and you do conceive, it'll be an acid test of Jem's love."

"I've thought of that."

"Beware, Gillian. If a baby comes of this, the reality might not be as rosy as it seemed in theory. Kodak moments don't occur as often as messy diapers. Jem might not be as accepting as he's led you to believe he'll be. And in fairness to him, he probably believes he'll be okay with it."

She paused to sip her wine, then decided to speak aloud her troubling thoughts. She and Gillian had always been candid and brutally honest with each other. "I'm a little concerned that his attitude will change when the baby is actually here. Wouldn't it be hard for any man to accept what is, essentially, another man's child? At the very least, Jem will harbor a few misgivings. Possibly some resentment."

"I anticipate some backlash," Gillian said. "And I took that into account. But I couldn't base my decision on possibilities and speculations. I had to stop asking myself 'what if?' or I'd never have done it. If I was going to do it, I needed to do it sooner rather than later. We'll be thirty-six in a couple of months."

"Don't remind me."

"I was constantly being reminded that my biological clock is ticking. I could no longer ignore it."

"I understand."

Gillian set down her fork. "Do you, Melina? Can you understand?"

They had always sought each other's approval. Melina valued and trusted Gillian's opinion above all others, and she knew the reverse was true. "Yes," Melina answered slowly, "I understand it. I just don't share it. I've never felt the urge to have a child." Smiling ruefully, she added, "It's good that I didn't, isn't it? My life, my future, is all about my business."

She reached across the table to clasp Gillian's hand. "The maternal instinct may be the only difference between us. I think you got both portions, yours and mine. If it's that strong, you would have been wrong to ignore it. You needed to respond to it or you would never have been happy. So the decision you made was the right one for you."

"Oh, God, I hope so." Even knowing how meaningful this experiment was for Gillian, Melina was surprised by the level of emotion in her twin's voice. "I want a child very much, but what if . . . what if the child doesn't want me?"

"Excuse me?"

"What if my maternal instinct is false and I'm no good at mothering?"

"Not a chance."

"You're just saying that because you know that's what I want to hear, Melina."

"Have you ever known me to mince words? I'm saying it because it's true. You'll be an ideal mother."

"I want to be." Gillian's expression, her tone, conveyed her earnestness. Neither of them was given to spontaneous crying, yet Gillian appeared to be on the verge of tears, which could be attributed to that hormonal surge thing, or was still another indication of the depth of her feeling.

She said, "Of all the decisions I've made in my life so far, this is the most important one. Of all the decisions I'm likely to make in the future, it's the most important one. I don't want to fail at something that is this important to me. I simply can't."

"And you won't," Melina stated definitively.

"I want my baby to be as happy with me as I'll be with him. Or her."

"It'll consider itself the luckiest kid alive. And I wish I could be that certain about everything else as I am of that. You'll be a stunning success at parenting, Gillian. So put the improbability of failure out of your mind. Banish it. Bury it. It ain't gonna happen."

Her twin's firm validation of her decision made Gillian smile with relief. She blinked away her unshed tears. "Okay. My doubts are officially banished and buried."

"Well, thank God we got that out of the way."

Again Melina raised her wineglass. "Here's to you and modern medical science. I hope those microscopic tadpoles are doing their thing!"

They clinked glasses. Gillian said, "The success rate—even when all systems are go, as in my case—is only twenty-five percent. It may take more than one time."

"That's not what Mother told us before our first car date."

They laughed at the memory of their mother's painful shyness when it came to discussing sex and her warnings to her daughters of its potential hazards.

"Remember that lecture? I didn't know there were that many euphemisms for body parts and intercourse!" Melina exclaimed. "But the message that came through loud and clear was that it only took one time to make a baby."

"We'll see. The doctor assured me that these were good swimmers."

"He actually called them *swimmers?*"

"I swear."

They giggled like teenagers over a dirty joke. Eventually Melina signaled the waiter to remove their plates and ordered coffee. "What about the donor?"

"He's only a number, selected from the sperm donor's equivalent of a Spiegel's catalogue. Of all the candidates, he best fit my preferences."

"Hair color. Eye color. Body type."

"Those, along with interests, background, and IQ."

"So you just ordered a number out of a catalogue?" Melina asked wryly.

"This is a scientific procedure."

"Biology. Human reproduction boiled down to its most clinical form."

"Exactly."

"But . . ."

Gillian smiled, knowing she'd been trapped. They couldn't hide a thought from each other for long. "*But* I'm a human being, and my body isn't a test tube. I can't be as entirely objective as I should." Staring into near space, she said quietly, "With the help of an unnamed person, I hope to create a new individual. A baby. A personality. A soul. That's heady stuff. Naturally I wonder about the donor, who he is and what he looks like."

"How could you not? Of course you wonder. But you don't have a clue?"

"Nothing. He's probably a med student who needed some extra spending money."

"And who likes to jack off. But then, they all like to jack off, don't they?" Melina winked at the man seated at the next table. He smiled back at her, flattered by her flirtation.

Seeing the exchange, Gillian chided her in a stage whisper. "Behave."

"He doesn't know what I said."

They were different in that way, too. Melina tended to speak her mind, where Gillian was more discreet. Melina said and did things that Gillian thought about but was often too inhibited to say or do. They shared the same impulses, but Melina acted on them: She plunged headfirst off the high diving board. Gillian would stand with her toes curled over the end of it until dared to dive in. Melina admired her twin's circumspection. Gillian claimed to be envious of Melina's courage.

Leaving the gentleman at the next table to think what he wished, Melina asked Gillian how long it would be before she knew if the artificial insemination had worked.

"I go back in a week for a blood test."

"A whole week! Are you under any restrictions?"

"None. I go about my everyday activities."

"Work?"

"I have an appointment this afternoon."

"Sex?"

"Female."

"Very funny. You know what I meant."

"I know what you meant, and no, there's no restriction. In fact, the doctor told me that if I had a partner who would share the child, he would encourage us to have intercourse soon. That's psychologically beneficial for infertile couples who have resorted to using donor sperm when all else has failed. If they have sex on the date of the AI, there's always the outside chance that—"

"The partner's sperm was the one to fertilize the egg."

"Exactly."

Melina pressed her temples with her index fingers. "Jeez, this gets—"

"Deep. I know. There are myriad facets to this issue. Endless factors to consider. Ethical and religious questions to probe and hopefully resolve. But I don't regret doing it. Nor am I going to start second-guessing the decision now that I've acted on it. In fact, if I don't conceive this time, I'll definitely try again.

"Until recently, my fantasies of motherhood were nebulous. They took place in the far-distant future. But now that I've actually taken the step necessary to conceive, those fantasies have crystallized. I want a baby, Melina, dirty diapers and all. I want one very much. A son or daughter to care for. Someone who requires my love. Someone who loves me back."

Melina swallowed hard. "Are you trying to make me cry?"

Gillian blinked back her own tears.

Touching her tummy lightly, she said, "It's going to be a long week."

Melina sniffed, impatient with herself for becoming so sentimental. "What you need is a diversion," she stated. "Something to take your mind off it and make the time go faster."

"Such as?"

"I'm thinking." She tapped her lips with steepled fingers. After a moment, she experienced a burst of brilliant inspiration. But it was immediately followed by exasperation. "Damn!" she exclaimed, slapping the table-top. "I can't believe I'm about to offer this to you."

"What?"

"Oh, what the hell?" she said, making a sudden decision. She leaned across the table and said excitedly, "Go in my place tonight."

"What? Where?"

"Guess who I'm escorting this evening."

"I don't care."

"Sure you do. Christopher Hart."

"The astronaut?"

"Ah-hah! Your eyes lit up when you said his name."

"If they lit up, and I doubt they did, it's because I'm impressed that my sister's been retained to escort such a VIP. Isn't he just back from a space mission?"

"Three months ago. He completed a shuttle mission that salvaged an important military satellite. Crucial to world peace or something like that."

"What's he doing in Dallas?"

"Receiving an award from SMU's alumni association. They're giving him a distinguished something-or-other award at a black-tie banquet at the Adolphus." She smiled wickedly. "Want to meet him?"

"I don't know how to do your job!" Gillian exclaimed. "Any more than you know how to sell commercial real estate."

"Your job is difficult. It involves interest rates and plats and stuff. Mine's a no-brainer. What's to know?"

"Plenty."

"Not so. You pick him up at the start of the evening, you drop him off at the end of it."

Of course, she was grossly simplifying her job description. She had worked as an apprentice for years before her employer retired and sold her the business. Under her management it had expanded.

Essentially, unless a celebrity visiting

Dallas arrived with his or her own entourage, she, or one of her three carefully screened and trained employees, was responsible for that individual until he was safely on his way to his next destination. She served as chauffeur, confidante, shopper—whatever the client needed her to be. She sometimes groused about having to work ridiculous hours, but her complaining was so much hot air, because she loved what she did. Her business had thrived because she was good at it.

But she wasn't worried about Gillian taking over for her for one night. Like her, Gillian had never met a stranger in her life, and she wasn't likely to become tongue-tied in the presence of Colonel Christopher Hart. She'd sold real estate to men more important than he. And it would get her away from Jem Hennings for one night, which in Melina's view was a bonus.

"You know where the Adolphus is, right?"

"Forget it, Melina," Gillian said, enunciating each word.

"He's staying at The Mansion. You pick him up there and get him downtown by—"

"You're not listening."

"I don't listen to lame excuses. You

haven't given me one good reason why you won't go."

"Then how's this? We're no longer children. Adults don't play games like this."

"We could still get away with switching."

"Of course we could, but that's beside the point."

"Why?"

"Because it's crazy."

"Colonel Hart doesn't know me from Adam. What's the harm?"

Gillian continued to ignore her arguments. "I've got my own business to attend to! I'm on the brink of getting a hot new ad agency to sign a contract on a new facility to the tune of three million. I'm meeting with them this afternoon to hammer out the deal points with the seller. In addition to all of the above, Jem's coming over tonight. So, thank you for the thought, but no."

"Christopher Hart is hot, hot, hot," she taunted in a singsong voice.

"You can tell me all about him later."

"Last chance. Going, going . . ."

"No, Melina."

"Gone."

Frowning, and muttering over what a wet blanket Gillian was, she requested the check and insisted on treating. Outside the fashionable restaurant, parking valets brought their cars around. One of the young men was staring so hard at the two of them, he nearly rear-ended another car.

As they exchanged goodbyes, Melina made one final pitch. "You're going to regret passing up this opportunity."

"Thanks anyway."

"Gillian, he's a national hero! You'd be spending the evening with him. This could be the best gift I've given you since introducing you to the Miracle Bra."

"I appreciate the thought."

"Oh, I get it. You're still pouting."

"Pouting?"

"Because I couldn't arrange a meeting between you and Kevin Costner last month. Gillian, I've told you a thousand times that he was on a very tight schedule. There was absolutely no way."

Laughing, Gillian leaned forward and kissed her cheek. "I'm not pouting. I love you, sis."

"Love you."

"Have fun with the astronaut."

She winked, drawling, "You can bet I'll try."

"I want details," Gillian called back to her as she climbed into her car. "The nitty-gritty."

"Promise. I'll call you as soon as I get home."

A strong wind blew across the desert floor, lifting sand and using it to scour the face of the mountain before scattering it among the scrub brush. At the peak where the air was thinner and cooler, the same wind made castanets of the saffron-colored leaves of aspen trees.

The compound, situated in the midst of the aspen grove, blended so well into its setting that it was almost invisible to motorists on the highway that snaked across the desert floor miles below. The buildings were constructed of granite that had been handpicked and imported from Scotland. The rivers of color streaking through its basic gray background perfectly matched the dun and ocher and sienna hues of the surrounding landscape.

The shaded terrace on the third level of the central building served as an outdoor temple for the one presently at prayer. His knees were cushioned by a maroon velvet pillow that was elaborately embroidered. The gold and silver metallic threads glittered in the sunlight that filtered through the trees.

The cushion had been a gift to him from an admirer. It was said to have been brought from Russia by emigrants at the turn of the last century. A family heirloom, it had been the gift-giver's prized possession, and, as such, a supreme sacrifice, an enormous tribute to the one to whom she had given it.

His head was bowed. His thick blond hair appeared almost white, silky in texture, angelic. His eyes were closed. His lips formed silent words of supplication. His hands were folded beneath his chin. He seemed the epitome of piety. God-touched. God-blessed. God-sanctioned.

He wasn't.

A man wearing a severely tailored dark suit emerged from the wide glass door separating the terrace from the vast room inside. Without making a sound, he approached the man at prayer and laid a sheet of paper beside his kneeling form, tucking the corner of it beneath the velvet cushion to prevent it from being swept away by the wind. Then he withdrew just as noiselessly as he had approached.

The man at prayer suspended his petitions to the sky, picked up the note, and saw that it had been stamped with the day and time. Today. Less than an hour ago.

As he read the typed message, a slow smile spread across his handsome features. His long, tapered hands pressed the note against his chest as though its value to him were inestimable. He closed his eyes again. Seemingly enraptured, he angled his face toward the sun.

He didn't invoke God's name, however. Instead, the name he whispered reverently was "Gillian Lloyd."

CHAPTER 2

As unobtrusively as possible, Colonel Christopher Hart checked his wristwatch. But apparently he wasn't as subtle as he had hoped to be. George Abbott, one of the men seated across from him, leaned forward. "More coffee? Or maybe something stronger this round?"

Christopher—or Chief, as he'd been nicknamed by his NASA cohorts—smiled and shook his head. "No, thanks. There's a press conference prior to the banquet tonight. I need to keep a clear head."

"We won't detain you much longer."

This came from Dexter Longtree, a man of few words, who'd left most of the talking to his partner. Longtree's voice was as smooth and cool as polished rock, and it seemed to land on them with as much dead weight. His smile looked forced and out of place on such a stern, sunburned face. The smile was a jarring misfit with the webwork of lines around his deep-set eyes and the parenthetical furrows on either side of his thin, wide mouth. Only his lips were involved in the smile, and they seemed unnaturally stretched.

Since the meeting began, almost an hour earlier, Longtree hadn't moved except to stir a packet of sweetener into his coffee and then to periodically lift the dainty china cup to his mouth. His rough dark hand appeared capable of crushing the cup and saucer with one moderate squeeze. When he wasn't sipping from his cup, his hands were planted solidly on the tops of his thighs.

Abbott, on the other hand, fidgeted constantly. He'd removed the drinking straw from his glass of iced tea and had reshaped it a dozen times or more, finally tying it into a knot. He fiddled with the matchbook in the clean, empty ashtray. He continually repositioned himself in his seat as though experiencing a hemorrhoidal flare-up. He jiggled his knee. And, unlike Longtree, he was all smiles.

Longtree was forbidding. Abbott was ingratiating. It was a toss-up which of the two Chief mistrusted more.

Wishing to conclude the meeting, he said, "I appreciate your interest, gentlemen. You've left me with a lot to think about."

Abbott cleared his throat nervously. "What we'd hoped, Colonel, was that you could give us something to take back."

"Today?" Chief exclaimed. "You want an answer now?"

"Not anything definitive," Abbott rushed to clarify. "Just an inkling, so to speak, of what your final decision might be."

"That's unrealistic." Chief looked at Dexter Longtree, whose gaze remained implacable. "My retirement from NASA won't be official for another few months, and what I'll do then remains a mystery even to me." He forced a laugh. "I'm not even sure where I'll be living."

"Well, naturally we'd love for you to relocate to your home state of New Mexico," Abbott said in a voice that was too boisterous for the sedate cocktail lounge. "You grew up in New Mexico. We still claim you."

"Thank you," Chief said tersely. His memories of childhood weren't all happy.

"We'll be headquartered in Santa Fe. It would be convenient if you lived nearby."

"Convenient but not necessary," Longtree intoned.

"No, of course not," Abbott concurred. He was a toady who deferred to Longtree on every point. "What Dexter is saying, Colonel, is that with this job, you'd have a lot of freedom to do other things. You'd be able to pursue your own interests—so long as they didn't conflict with ours, of course. It'd be a win-win situation for everybody. Simple as that." He sounded like a used car salesman trying to close a sale, and his toothy grin was just as untrustworthy.

"I'm afraid it isn't at all that simple, Mr. Abbott."

Longtree spoke again, his voice reminding Chief of a snake moving through still water. "Colonel Hart, I sense you have some reservations."

"No pun intended," Abbott chortled.

He was the only one who laughed at his

lame joke. Chief's eyes remained on Dexter Longtree, and neither of them smiled.

"I do have some reservations, yes."

"About the organization?"

Chief took his time in answering. He didn't want to offend them, although Chief Dexter Longtree was intimidating. A Jicarilla Apache, he wore waist-length braids that lay like twin plaits of black silk against the lapels of his suit jacket. Except for the occasional blink, he could have been mistaken for a bronze statue in a southwestern art museum. On the other hand, Chief had served under imperious military commanders who could probably curl Longtree's braids.

In response to his question, Chief replied, "My concerns aren't specifically about your proposed NAA."

Native American Advocacy was the name of the group they planned to charter. According to the formal proposal they had sent Chief in advance of this meeting, NAA's services would be available to any tribe or reservation that needed help having its needs met. Those services would run the gamut from legal representation to fund-raising to lobbying for or against congressional bills that would directly affect Native Americans.

The lawyers and other professionals from whom they had already received commitments had agreed to participate without salary on an as-needed basis. NAA was offering Chief an annual retainer to serve as their point man, their official spokesperson to the media and in Washington.

Budgetary considerations aside, his initial reaction was to decline not with a mere *No,* but with a definitive *Hell, no.*

Remaining as noncommittal as possible, he said, "I've heard and read things that I find greatly disturbing."

"Such as?"

"Such as a few Native Americans getting rich off mineral rights, gambling casinos, and other profit centers on the reservations, while many continue to live well below the national poverty level. The wealth isn't evenly distributed. Sometimes it isn't distributed at all. That bothers me. A lot."

Abbott pounced on that. "All the more reason for you to get involved. You could make a difference. Change things. That's our goal, too."

Chief turned to the hyperactive man.

"Aren't there already other organizations that provide similar services?"

"Yes, and they're good. But we hope to be better. The best. You would make us distinctive."

"Why me?"

"Because you're a national hero, the first Native American astronaut. You've walked in space!"

"Which doesn't qualify me to be anybody's advocate."

"On the contrary, Colonel Hart. When you speak, people listen. Particularly the ladies," Abbott added with an offensive wink.

Hart looked at him and shook his head in dismay. "You'd be willing to sign me up before you even know what I'd say in a given forum? Don't my political leanings enter anywhere into your thinking? You haven't even asked me what my personal philosophy is."

"But—"

Longtree halted Abbott's rebuttal simply by raising his hand. The other man fell immediately silent. "Let Mr. Hart say what's on his mind, George."

"Thank you." Further discussions would

be pointless because he'd already made up his mind. They'd just as well know that now. "Before I affiliated myself with any self-appointed public service group or organization, I would have to be convinced first that their interest wasn't self-serving. Secondly, I would have to be convinced that the group was interested in me the man. Not me the Indian."

A long silence ensued.

Finally it was broken by Longtree. "Do you disavow your heritage?"

"I couldn't, even if I wanted to. My nickname comes from it. But I've never exploited my Indian blood, either. I wouldn't accept any position where my qualifications are based strictly on my lineage."

Again Abbott laughed nervously. "It's a tremendous advantage to us that you're a descendant of Quanah Parker."

"Who was half white."

Abbott had no comeback for that. After another awkward silence, Longtree apparently saw the benefit to beating a timely retreat. He came to his feet, and Chief was suddenly cognizant of how short he was. His demeanor had made him seem much taller than he actually was.

He said, "We've given Colonel Hart enough to think about for one afternoon, George. He has an important banquet to attend this evening."

Chief also stood up. Abbott looked confused, as though there'd been a last-minute change in the program and they'd failed to alert him to it. Finally he stood with them.

"I appreciate the vote of confidence," Chief said as he extended his hand to Longtree. "I'm flattered by the offer. But I'm not ready to commit to anything yet."

"Then it's our job to see that you get ready to commit." He squeezed Chief's hand once, quick and hard, then released it. "Would you agree to meet us tomorrow morning so we can continue this discussion?"

"I was planning on returning to Houston fairly early."

"We're early risers. You name the time and place."

Actually, there was nothing else to discuss. Chief had known what his answer would be even before this meeting. He'd agreed to it merely as a courtesy. Listening to their pitch hadn't changed his mind. Longtree looked prosperous, not like an Indian who was barely scraping out a living on the reservation, not like someone who'd be going to bat for the underdog and trying to right all the wrongs heaped on the Indian nations. But the cagey bastard wasn't giving him a graceful way out of a breakfast meeting.

"Oh nine hundred?" Chief asked with military briskness. "Over breakfast here in The Promenade?"

"We'll see you then," the Apache replied. Abbott quickly shook Chief's hand, then trotted after Longtree as he strode from the bar.

Other happy hour patrons had turned to stare. Dexter Longtree cut a distinctive figure, but he didn't exactly blend into the well-heeled crowd of The Mansion's elegant lounge, especially with the beaded and fringed breechcloth he'd worn over his trousers.

"Is he an actor or something?"

Chief turned to the cocktail waitress who had sidled up to him and posed the question. "No, he's the genuine article."

"Really? Wow." Once Abbott and Longtree were out of sight, she smiled up at Chief. "Is there anything else I can get you, Mr. Hart?"

"Not right now, thanks."

"Then I hope you'll drop in again before you leave us."

"Maybe I'll come in for a nightcap."

"I'll look forward to it."

He was accustomed to flirtations. He had received shameless propositions through the mail, sometimes with X-rated photos enclosed. He'd had room numbers scrawled on cocktail napkins in hotel bars across the country. And once, during a formal dinner at the White House, a woman had pressed a pair of panties into his palm as they shook hands.

He more or less took female attention for granted. But this young woman was very attractive. She had mastered the dazzling, Dallas-girl smile, that irresistible combination of coy southern belle and brazen cowgirl. Chief felt himself responding to it.

But damn, she was young! Or maybe he was getting old. In his younger, wilder days, he would have taken her smile for the open invitation it was and accepted it.

But he was no longer young, and some of his wildness had been tamed. In any case, he tipped her generously, then wasted no time returning to his room and getting into the shower. As promised by the hotel staff, his tuxedo had been pressed and was hanging in the closet. The black cowboy boots he wore with it had been shined to a high gloss.

He allowed himself a short bourbon while he dressed, then mercilessly brushed his teeth and gargled mouthwash. It wouldn't do for an Indian to show up at a press conference with firewater on his breath, now, would it?

Chiding himself for the chip on his shoulder, he pulled on the pleated shirt and poked the onyx studs into the buttonholes. Most of the time he kept that chip on his shoulder under wraps. His conversation with Abbott and Longtree was responsible for its present upsurge.

What did he have to prove? Why did he still feel the need to prove himself or to justify himself? He had nothing to apologize for. He had excelled at everything he'd ever tried. Collegiate sports. Air Force flight training. Fighter jets. War. The space program.

He would have accomplished it all despite his heritage. He'd grown up on a reservation. So what? He'd been granted no special favors. He hadn't been catered to because of it. Even so, he realized what a public relations gem he was to the space program. Rationally he knew that NASA wouldn't have entrusted three shuttle missions and their crews to an individual who wasn't qualified to command them.

But another part of him, the Indian part, would always wonder if the skids of the system had been greased for him in order to make his university, the Air Force, and NASA look good. *Let's make allowances for the Indian kid. It'll make for great PR.*

Probably no one within his experience had ever said that or even thought it. But he hated to think that someone might have. Just as he'd told Longtree and Abbott, he had never used his heritage either as a crutch or as a leg up.

If somebody took that as a denial of his origin, then that was their problem and just too damn bad.

He slapped a light cologne onto his face and ran his fingers through his unrelentingly straight black hair. His Native American genes had certainly been the dominant ones. He had Comanche hair, Comanche cheekbones. His mother had been fifteen-sixteenths Comanche. If it weren't for Great-Great-Grandfather, he might look even more Native American than he did.

As it was, a lanky wrangler on a ranch in the Oklahoma panhandle had taken a fancy to Great-Great-Grandmother shortly after the Indian Territory became a state. From him Christopher Hart had inherited a tall, rangy physique and eyes that his first lover had deemed "Paul Newman blue."

His eyes had been one of his old man's excuses for leaving. Unfortunately, he had some of his father's blood, too.

Impatient with the track of his thoughts, he strapped on his wristwatch, shot his cuffs, and he was ready. Before leaving the room, he glanced at the itinerary that had been faxed to his Houston office. He checked the name of his contact and committed it to memory.

Actually, he would have preferred to drive himself from the exclusive Turtle Creek area where The Mansion nestled, largely unseen, on an ultra-private lane. With no more than an address and his reliable sense of direction, he could have located the Hotel Adolphus easily.

But the group bestowing the award had insisted that he have an escort. "She's more than a chauffeur. She's media-savvy and knows all the local reporters," he was told. "You'll appreciate having Melina Lloyd to run interference for you. Otherwise you'd be mobbed."

As he stepped through the doors of the hotel, a woman approached him. "Colonel Hart?"

She was wearing a simple but elegantly cut and very expensive-looking black cocktail dress. Sunlight painted iridescent stripes of color onto her hair, which was almost as dark as his. It was worn straight from a side part. No bangs. She had on sunglasses.

"You must be Ms. Lloyd."

She extended her hand. "Melina."

"Call me Chief."

They smiled at each other as they shook hands. She asked, "How is your room? Satisfactory, I hope?"

"Complete with a basket of fruit and a bottle of champagne. The staff has treated me royally."

"That's what they're famous for."

She nodded toward a late-model Lexus waiting at the end of the canopy-covered walkway. A doorman had the passenger door already open for him. Melina Lloyd tipped the young man handsomely. "Drive safely, Ms. Lloyd," he said to her as he waved them off.

"You must be a regular here," Chief remarked.

She laughed. "Not me. A few of my clients stay here—the really famous ones," she added, giving him a sidelong glance. "When I want to splurge, I love to come here for lunch. It's good people-watching, and they make scrumptious tortilla soup."

"I'll tuck that away for future reference."

"Adjust the air-conditioning to your liking."

The curtain of dark hair swished across her shoulders as she turned her head to check for oncoming traffic before pulling out. He caught a whiff of fragrance.

"I'm comfortable, thanks."

"What time did you arrive in Dallas?"

"About two this afternoon."

"That's good. You've had some time to decompress."

"I went out to the pool."

"It wasn't too cool?"

"Not for me. I swam some laps. Worked on my tan."

She cruised to a stop at a red traffic light and turned her head. "Your tan? That's an Indian-insider's joke, right?"

He laughed, pleased that she got it and even more pleased that it didn't make her uneasy to comment on it. "Right." She smiled back, and he wished she would remove her sunglasses so he could see if her eyes lived up to the rest of her face. Particularly her mouth. Her mouth made him believe in sin.

When she lifted her foot from the brake pedal and applied it to the accelerator, the hem of her dress rode up an inch or so above her knee. The fabric made a sexy rasping sound against her ultra-sheer hosiery. Nice sound. Even nicer knee.

"What would you like?"

His eyes shot from her thigh to her face. "Pardon?"

"I have bottled water and soft drinks in the cooler on the floorboard behind me."

"Oh. Uh, nothing, thanks."

"I was told to prepare you for a large turnout tonight. You know about the press conference beforehand?"

"Second-level lobby."

She nodded. "It's limited to those holding a special pass. Keep in mind that the dinner officially begins at seven-thirty, but the press conference doesn't have to last until then. You're to give me a high sign whenever you're ready to stop, whether it's after five questions or fifty. At your signal I'll make your excuses and hustle you toward the ballroom for the banquet. That way, I'm the bad guy."

"I don't think anyone would believe that."

"That I'm the bad guy?"

"That you're any kind of guy."

She wasn't a fool; she knew flirting when she heard it. She gave him another glance out the side of her sunglasses. "Thank you."

"Gillian?"

"Hi, Jem."

"Darling, I just checked my messages, and I'm delighted. You actually did it."

"Just before lunch."

"And?"

"I'll know the result in a week."

"When did you decide for sure?"

"Yesterday. I had several bouts of cold feet and stomach butterflies, but I went through with it."

"Why didn't you call me? I'd have gone with you. I would have liked being there."

"I'm sorry, Jem. I really wanted it to be private. I didn't call sooner because I met my sister for lunch. It went too long. I almost didn't make my afternoon appointment, and only had time to talk to your home-number voice mail."

"Did you tell Melina?" Before she could respond, he said, "Of course you told Melina. What does she think about it?"

"She's excited that I'm excited."

"I'm excited, too."

"I'm glad. I appreciate you for backing my decision."

"I have something for you. A surprise. I've had it for a while, waiting for you to make up your mind. I'd like to bring it over."

She could hear the smile in his voice and knew he was eager to share his surprise. But she didn't want company. Trying to let him down gently, she said, "Jem, I know we made plans to see each other tonight, but would you take a rain check?"

"Is something wrong? Don't you feel well?"

"I feel fine. Just very tired. It was . . . an extremely emotional experience. More so than I counted on. I didn't realize until afterward how emotionally involving it was going to be."

"In what way? Did you get upset? Cry?"

"Nothing that demonstrative. It's hard to explain."

"You had me convinced that it was a sterile, clinical procedure."

"It was."

"Then I don't understand how it could be so emotionally . . . What was the word? Involving?"

Jem was wont to overanalyze everything. Tonight especially she didn't welcome his analysis. Trying to keep the irritation out of her voice, she said, "I just need some time alone. To think about it. Things. Can't we just leave it at that?"

"Sure, we can leave it at that." By his tone she could tell that he was hurt. "I would think you'd want some loving support on a night as momentous as this. Obviously I was wrong."

Immediately she regretted shutting him

out. Why hadn't she taken the more expedient route and agreed to his coming over and delivering his gift? It would have cost her far less stress.

But before she could extend another invitation, he said brusquely, "I'll call you later, Gillian," and hung up.

CHAPTER 3

Ms. Lloyd, I left your car right over there so you wouldn't have to wait in line."

As soon as Chief and Melina exited the hotel following the banquet, the valet materialized and indicated the Lexus parked nearby. The motor was already running, and Chief was grateful that the air conditioner had been turned on. Officially it was autumn, but the calendar was out of sync with his body's thermostat. He was sweltering inside his tuxedo jacket.

It had been a long banquet. Every

scheduled speaker had taken more than his allocated time at the microphone. By the time it was Chief's turn to make his acceptance speech, even he was bored. He was glad to be escaping and grateful to the valet for enabling him and Melina to avoid further contact with the crowd that was pouring through the exit doors.

As they walked toward her car, the starstruck valet asked, "What's it like in space, Colonel Hart?"

He gave the young man his standard, glib reply: "Out of this world."

"Must've been something."

"It was."

Chief added a five-dollar bill to the one Melina had given him. "Thanks, sir. Y'all take care."

As they buckled their seat belts, Melina complimented him on his speech. "You were excellent. Once you leave the space program, you could have another career in public speaking."

"Lots of former astronauts do."

"Any aspirations in that direction?"

"I'm weighing several options."

"Such as?"

He unfastened the button on his jacket. "Can we talk about something else?"

Looking mortified, she exclaimed, "I'm so sorry. I didn't mean to pry."

"It's not that, it's just—"

"We don't have to talk at all. Feel free to lay your head back, close your eyes, and rest. I should have realized you'd be talked out by now. Probably the last thing you want is conversation."

"Melina." Chief reached across the seat and touched her arm to stop the flow of apologies. "I'm not talked out. In fact, I would enjoy a conversation. Just not about me, okay? I'm tired of talking about me. Can we switch subjects?"

"Of course. To what?"

"Sex?"

"Okay," she replied unflappably. "You want my opinion on the topic?"

"Please."

"Well, for starters, I think everybody should have one."

He grinned. "You're quick."

"So I'm told. Sometimes to my detriment."

"Do you mind if I take off my jacket?"

"Not at all."

He shrugged off the tuxedo coat and

tossed it into the back seat, then undid his bow tie and unbuttoned the collar of his shirt. "Ah! Much better."

"Would you like something to drink?" she offered.

"A stiff bourbon?"

"I was thinking more along the lines of a Diet Coke or springwater."

"I wouldn't mind a splash of either."

"In the bourbon," they said in unison. Then they laughed together.

When the laughter waned, he looked at her with a direct and serious gaze. "Is there someone waiting at home for you?"

She didn't immediately acknowledge the question. Not until she came to a stop sign did she turn her head. He locked gazes with a pair of gray eyes that turned out to be her best feature of all—and they were all damn near spectacular.

"Why?"

"Because I'd like to invite you to join me for a drink. Any reason I shouldn't?"

She shook her head, then returned her eyes to the road and put the car in motion again.

"Okay, then, would you care to join me for a drink?"

"Chief, you do understand the difference between a *media* escort and the other, more prurient type, don't you?"

He would have feared that he'd overstepped his bounds and offended her, except that her question was accompanied by a teasing smile. He laid his hand on his heart. "I didn't mean to imply that you are anything other than a professional." Wincing, he said, "Oh, jeez, that didn't come out right, either, did it?"

"No, it didn't," she said, laughing.

Relaxing, he said, "Explain your job to me."

She gave him the condensed version, then expanded. "Most of the time is spent in the car traversing the metropolitan sprawl, seeing to it that the client gets to all his appointments and media engagements on time, relaxed, and in a positive frame of mind. I try and protect the client from any inherent chaos that might arise at any point along the way."

"Like what?"

"Stalled traffic. Last-minute cancellations. Last-minute additions to the schedule. Illness. Just about anything your imagination can conjure up. Sometimes the schedule is tight and I'm barely allowed travel time. That's why I carry all this stuff with me," she said, tipping her head back to indicate the supplies on the floorboard of the back seat. "I even have a first-aid kit, a sewing box, and Handi Wipes."

"Handi Wipes?"

"I once escorted a TV diva who had a phobia about shaking hands with the general public. She washed after every contact."

"Who?"

She cocked her head and looked at him askance. "Do you want me to divulge your secrets to my other clients?"

"I don't have any secrets." But the mischievous grin he gave her belied the claim.

"Right," she drawled. "Anyway, the Handi Wipes are also good for wiping TV makeup off dark fabrics."

"No kidding? Huh. You learn something every day."

"I've learned by improvising. It's also my job to see that my clients are given their due just for being who they are, and that they receive—whether they deserve it or not—the red carpet treatment everywhere they go."

"I can attest to that."

She smiled at him. "Then I get a gold star for tonight. You were supposed to feel free of all responsibility except for making your speech."

Because he was enjoying listening to her, he continued asking questions. He learned that her job didn't always end with chauffeuring and orchestrating a news conference.

"Say a client wants some company—I provide it. I've become a very good listener. I take them anyplace they want to go. Restaurant, amusement park, concert, movie theater. One repeat client, an author who goes on a book tour every spring, loves to play pool. It's his way of unwinding and clearing out the cobwebs. We play each time he's in town."

"And I suppose you always let him win."

"The hell I do!"

Chief laughed. "You don't resent doing these little extras?"

"Those 'little extras,' as you call them, keep repeat clients coming back and earn me new ones. Word gets around, especially among authors who routinely tour. Of course, we escorts compare notes on the celebs, too. Who's nice, who's weird, who's a terror."

He considered her in profile. He couldn't have been the only man to notice how attractive she was. Riding next to her all day in the confines of a car could prove to be a temptation to a man who was far from hearth and home. "You must draw the line somewhere. To those little extras, I mean."

"Strip joints or topless bars are a no-no. I won't procure a prostitute, male or female. If that's what they're looking for, they're on their own. Anything having to do with controlled substances is out, of course. And . . ." She glanced at him. "Let's put it this way: I once escorted an actor who copped a feel during the drive back to his hotel. I stopped the car, shoved him out, and let him find his own way back."

"Repercussions?"

"Who was he going to complain to? His wife is his manager. It was she who booked me. Besides, his monstrous ego would never have permitted him to tell about a rejection."

Chief laughed with her. "Give me a hint."

She hesitated a moment, then said, "An over-the-hill stud."

"I can think of fifty. Stage, screen, or TV?"

"Screen."

"That narrows it down. What are his initials?"

She shook her head. "Too easy."

"What'd he cop a feel of?"

She shot him a retiring look.

"Above the waist or below? Just tell me that much."

"Chief!"

"Okay, then. I'll just have to give my imagination free rein."

She glared at him, but it was still all in fun. "Above."

"Hmm. Can't blame a guy for trying."

"I did. I'll go out of my way to meet a client's needs and wishes. Within reason."

"Aw, jeez."

"What?"

"Well, I was going to put in a request." When she was looking at him, he added, "I just hope you consider it within reason."

"Jem!"

"Don't be angry because I didn't call first," he said quickly. "I had to see you, Gillian. Especially after our conversation ended on such a sour note."

"I was unhappy about that, too."

"Then can I please come in? Just for a little while. I promise not to stay long."

She wasn't overjoyed to see him, and she resented this unannounced visit. He had a bad habit of dropping in without giving notice, which she secretly considered a violation of privacy. But he was smiling sweetly, beseechingly, and the front door threshold wasn't the ideal spot for a discussion of character flaws. She stepped aside and motioned him in.

"As you can see, I wasn't expecting a gentleman caller."

"You look adorable. I prefer you without makeup."

"Then you should have your eyesight checked."

Laughing softly, he pulled her against him and kissed her lips gently and noninvasively. He was sensitive enough to her mood not to press his luck with a deep kiss. When he pulled away, his eyes moved up to the towel wrapped around her head. "I even like the turban."

"I'm deep-conditioning my hair."

Although it wasn't even nine o'clock yet, she already had on sleepwear—cotton boxer shorts and a matching top. It was a comfy outfit, but not what you'd call fetching. Another blow to her ego was that Jem looked like he had stepped out of a bandbox. Even in khakis and a polo shirt, he was, as usual, well turned out.

Taking her hand, he led her into the living room and pulled her down onto the sofa beside him. "I had to come tonight, Gillian. I didn't want to wait and give you the gift tomorrow. It had to be today. On the actual day you were inseminated." He slipped his hand into his pocket and produced a velvet jewelry box.

"Jem! When you said 'surprise,' I thought you meant something like flowers. Chocolates. But this? Shouldn't you wait until after the blood test, until we know I'm actually pregnant?"

"I want you to know that I'm with you all the way. Whether you conceive this time or have to try again, I want to share this event with you. I want to be involved in the baby's life from the very beginning."

She glanced at the box and for one heart-stopping moment feared that he was about to propose marriage. But the box was oblong, not square like a ring box. When he opened the spring-hinged lid, he took her soft cry of relief to be an exclamation of delight.

"You like it?"

"It's beautiful, Jem."

The gold chain was very slender but sturdy enough to hold the small, heart-shaped pendant of clustered rubies. "I thought it would complement your coloring."

"It's lovely. Truly."

He removed the pendant from the box and placed it around her neck, securing it with the tiny clasp. Then, taking her by the shoulders, he turned her back to face him, looking very pleased with himself. "Perfect. Go look."

He guided her to the mirror above the console table. The pendant was indeed beautiful, reflecting ruby sparks of light off her skin. Turning back to him, she struck a glamour-girl pose. "Am I gorgeous or what?"

"You're gorgeous. And sexy. Even if you do have a towel on your head. You're going to be gorgeous and sexy during the pregnancy, too."

"When I'm ballooned out like a blimp?"

He splayed his hand over her lower abdomen and, with his other arm around her waist, pulled her close. "Even then." He kissed her neck, murmuring, "Gillian, I want you tonight. Please let me stay."

When his hand slid between her thighs, she stopped it with an apologetic smile. "I'm sorry, Jem."

"What's the matter?"

"Don't ask to stay tonight, because I don't want to refuse you."

"Then don't," he said, reaching for her again.

She dug her heels in when he tried to pull her against him, but she cradled his face between her hands. "I just can't be with you tonight. It's hard to explain. I couldn't make you understand over the telephone, and I can't now."

"I can explain it," he said curtly. "You had lunch with Melina today."

"What has Melina got to do with it?" she snapped back.

"You tell me. Every time you see her, I coincidentally turn into poison."

"That's not true."

"Then what's wrong?"

"I can't put it into words."

"Give it a shot."

She took a moment, then said, "It would feel awkward to have sex so soon after the procedure."

"I read that they encourage couples to have sex afterward."

She was surprised that he knew what the experts recommended. He must have been doing his own research on the subject. "That's true. Intimacy soon afterward is encouraged for couples—"

"We're a couple."

"Not a couple who have tried for years to conceive."

"So, we're fudging." Smiling engagingly, he placed his hands at her waist.

"It's a personal thing, Jem," she said, worming free of his hands. "My heart and mind wouldn't be in it tonight, and that wouldn't be fair to you or enjoyable for either of us." When she saw that he was about to offer another argument, she laid her fingers against his lips. "Please? I need you to understand. Indulge me. Let me have a headache tonight."

Grudgingly he kissed her fingertips, then the tip of her nose. "All right. I'd be a heel not to. I'll go home and take a cold shower. Maybe two. I guess I'll have to get accustomed to these hormonal inconsistencies, won't I?"

"I suppose you will," she replied, smiling with him. "We can see each other tomorrow."

"Lunch?"

"Call me in the morning. I'll check my schedule for lunch. But definitely sometime tomorrow."

She saw him to the door, where he kissed her again lightly on the lips. "The pendant is truly beautiful," she told him as she fingered it where it lay against her throat.

"You're beautiful. I love you."

"I love you, too."

*T*acos?"

The picture of innocence, Chief said, "What'd you think I was going to ask you for, Melina?"

She could tell that he was trying hard to contain a wicked smile. "Not tacos."

"I'm a junk-food junkie. Besides, I'm starving."

"You didn't like your dinner?"

"I couldn't eat it for all the people talking to me and the autographs I ended up signing. Would it be out of our way to stop?"

"Tacos are easy to come by."

"Can you find a place open this late?"

"It's not even ten o'clock."

"You sure?" He checked his wristwatch to confirm the time. "Huh. It seemed like the banquet dragged on forever."

A few minutes later, they pulled into the parking lot of a fast-food chain restaurant. Although it was past the normal dinner hour, it was doing a brisk business. "Do you want to drive through or go inside?"

A long line of cars was wrapped around the building awaiting their turn at the window. Inside, the restaurant didn't appear to be as crowded. He said, "I've got nothing to hide, do you?"

She pulled into a vacant parking space. They alighted, and as they moved toward the door, she remarked, "I've got nothing to hide, but we're a little overdressed. I'm sure we'll be gawked at."

"Safety in numbers."

With that he slid his arm around her waist and drew her up against him, so that they were walking hip to hip. Lord, it felt good! Never one to simper and play coy and helpless around men, she now delighted in feeling small, delicate, and intensely feminine. From the instant he stepped through the door of the hotel, she'd been wondering how it would feel to be this close to him. It surpassed her expectations. He was so wonderfully masculine.

Extending the joke, he nuzzled her hair. "I dare anybody to mess with the two of us."

By now they had almost reached the door. At the same time, a man approached it from inside, a take-out order in his free hand. He reached the door first and politely pulled it open for them and stood aside. Chief was still nuzzling her and playfully making aggressive growling noises. Absently, he thanked the man for holding the door.

They had almost moved past when the man suddenly blurted out, "Ms. Lloyd? Gillian Lloyd?" She stopped and turned toward him.

He was dressed in baggy khakis, a sad T-shirt, and rubber flip-flops. His thinning hair was fair and stringy. He pushed a slipping pair of eyeglasses higher onto the bridge of his nose. He said, "I thought it was you."

Chief looked from her to the stranger and, responding in a territorial male fashion, hugged her even closer against his side.

Smiling helplessly, she stammered, "I-I'm sorry, I don't . . ."

Suddenly embarrassed by her failure to recognize him, the man swallowed hard, making his knobby Adam's apple appear even more prominent. "Dale Gordon. I work at Waters."

"Oh, yes, of course. Hi."

He looked from her to Chief. His myopic gaze took notice of Chief's hand at her waist and stayed fixed there for several seconds. Then he looked back at her with something akin to wounded puzzlement.

The situation was fast becoming awkward, and she had no idea why. Brightly, she said, "It appears everyone's hungry for tacos tonight."

"Huh?" Dale Gordon seemed to have forgotten where he was. She indicated the sack he was carrying out. He looked at it in confusion for a moment, then stammered, "Uh, oh, yeah. I wanted a, uh, snack."

"Well, enjoy."

"You, too."

Chief gave her a slight nudge forward. They continued into the restaurant and joined the queue of people waiting to place their order at the counter. "Friend of yours?" he asked. "And what was that he called you?"

"He obviously mistook me for my sister, Gillian. It happens all the time. In this instance, it was easier to pretend that I knew him than to explain that I wasn't her."

"You look that much alike?"

"Identical twins."

His expression went deadpan. "You're kidding."

"No. I'm an identical twin."

He conducted a visual survey of her hair, her face, settling momentarily on her mouth. Her face grew warm under his frank appraisal. When his eyes came back to hers, he murmured, "How could there possibly be two women with eyes that shade of gray?"

Smiling up at him, she asked, "Is there a compliment somewhere in there?"

"Oh, yeah. And just so there's no misunderstanding of my meaning, let me make it clearer, Ms. Lloyd. You're a very attractive woman."

"Thank you, Colonel Hart."

"I find it hard to believe that . . . Gillian?" She nodded. "That she's as attractive as you."

His eyes held hers, and together they sank into a long and evocative stare, which wasn't interrupted until the woman taking orders greeted them. "Hi, folks. What're y'all having tonight?"

Chief seemed to shake off his daze. He cleared his throat. "What would you like, Melina?"

"I'm invited to supper?"

"It was implied."

"Then whatever. I like it all."

While he was placing their order, she glanced back at the door through which they'd entered. The man who'd introduced himself as Dale Gordon was no longer there. But he had left her with a creepy feeling—like she'd walked through a cobweb, like someone with fetid breath was blowing on the back of her neck.

However, by the time Chief unlocked the door to his suite at The Mansion and motioned her to go in ahead of him, she had forgotten the incident. "I'm glad you suggested this because I just realized that I'm famished, too. I didn't eat much of my dinner, either." Making herself right at home, she stepped out of her heels, then went around the suite's sitting room switching on table lamps. "It smells delicious."

They decided to picnic on the coffee table. While she unwrapped the food and divided it, he poured each of them a drink at the bar, which had been stocked with his brand of bourbon in advance of his visit. "Branch water?"

"And ice, please."

He came to the table with a drink in each hand. He passed one of the drinks down to her, then lowered himself to the floor across the low table from her. He raised his glass. "To fat grams and high cholesterol."

She clinked her glass with his and sipped. "Hmm. Add to that good sipping whiskey."

They dug in and were soon laughing over the ravenous way they were consuming the food. The crunchy taco shells fell apart, so they were reduced to scooping up cheese, lettuce, and spicy meat with their fingers.

"You'd think I hadn't eaten in a month," he remarked. "Or that I'd just completed a mission. Soon as I can after leaving the shuttle, I mow some real food."

"Space cuisine isn't that tasty?"

"It's okay, but . . . it . . . you know . . ."

She'd been involved in what he was saying, so until his voice dwindled to nothing she wasn't even aware that she had been sucking hard on the side of her index finger and licking it with her tongue. That's where his focus was. It was that he was concentrating on, not the food the astronauts ate on the space shuttle.

Flushed and self-conscious, she lowered her hand to her lap. "Paper cut," she said gruffly. "From the sack. I think . . . salt . . . or something got . . ."

Then she stopped talking, too, because he wasn't listening. He was watching her lips move, but he wasn't paying attention to the words, and frankly neither was she. She was watching him watching her mouth, and it made her tummy feel weightless despite the amount of food she had gobbled.

Finally his eyes reconnected with hers. "What were we talking about?"

On his way to his car, Dale Gordon tossed his unopened take-out sack of food into a trash receptacle because he was far too upset to eat.

Verging on nausea, he got into his car and slumped in the driver's seat. Folding his hands over the steering wheel, he rested his clammy forehead against them and gulped in air through his mouth to stave off his gag reflex. Tears trickled from his eyes onto the backs of his clenched hands.

He broke a cold sweat. It was a mild night, but not so warm as to warrant his profuse sweating. His T-shirt was soaked through with perspiration by the time Gillian Lloyd and the tall, handsome man came out of the restaurant with their order. They were chatting and laughing as they climbed into a Lexus, which she drove away.

Dale Gordon fumbled his ignition key in his haste to start his car and follow them. It was a short drive to the fancy-schmancy hotel. He'd heard of it, but he'd never been there. The tree trunks in the entry courtyard were covered with lights, even though it wasn't Christmas. The water in the tiered fountain sparkled and splashed.

The Lexus glided into the circular driveway. Dale Gordon cruised past. He drove to the end of the block, executed a three-point turn, and doubled back. He could see them getting out of the car with the assistance of a parking valet and heading for the discreet entrance beneath the white canopy.

Gillian Lloyd was going into a hotel with a man. A man who'd been publicly groping her as though she were his property. She had permitted his manhandling. No, she had seemed to *welcome* it.

This shattered Dale Gordon's world.

"What's it like?" Chief had finished eating and was leaning back against the sofa, one knee raised, one hand draped over it holding his highball glass.

She was looking at his hand, at the casual way his strong fingers held the glass by the rim. Great hands. Rousing herself, she addressed his question. "What's what like?"

"Having an identical twin."

She gathered up the last of the paper wrappers and napkins and stuffed them into the empty sack. "You know how you feel when you're asked what it's like in space?"

"Impossible to answer and you get tired of trying?"

She smiled. "Something like that."

"Sorry."

"It's a common question. I forgive you."

"Good. Because I would forgive you just about anything when you look at me like that."

She lowered her voice to match the intimate pitch of his. "How am I looking at you?"

"The same way you were looking at me during my speech."

"I was being politely attentive."

"You were being pointedly suggestive."

"I wasn't looking at you in any special way."

"Oh, yes, you were."

"Not that I'm conceding the argument, Colonel, but how did you *imagine* that I was looking at you?"

"Like you knew damn well that I could barely keep my mind on my speech for looking at your legs."

"I was assigned that particular seat at that particular table," she retorted. "I didn't select it because it placed me in your direct line of sight."

"But you took full advantage of it."

She gave a noncommittal shrug. "I always sit with my legs crossed."

"In high heels?"

"Usually."

"In a short black skirt?"

"It's not that short."

"Short enough to carry my imagination up to its favorite vacation spot."

She pretended to take umbrage. "I'm a lady, Colonel Hart."

"Every inch of you."

"Your look doesn't make me feel much like a lady."

"Oh, so it's *my* look now."

"Turnabout is only fair."

"Okay. How am I looking at you? How does my look make you feel?"

"Like it's a hot evening in the summertime and I'm an ice-cream cone."

Several seconds laden with sexual undercurrents ticked by before he leaned forward to set his glass on the coffee table. "Melina?"

"Hmm?"

"Are we going to sleep together?"

A dart of excitement found its target and caused her to catch her breath. "I have a reputation to uphold."

"So do I."

She laughed softly. "But your reputation is that of a lady-killer."

"And yours is of fending us off."

Hesitating only a heartbeat, she answered, "No." Then slowly she stood up and stepped around the table to stand directly in front of him. "Ask anybody about

Melina Lloyd, and they'll tell you that she's impulsive. She does whatever seems right at the time."

He remained seated on the floor, but his eyes had followed her up, taking their time to track the terrain of her figure. Huskily he asked, "What seems right?"

Dale Gordon's apartment was only slightly warmer than the temperature outside, but tonight when he let himself in, the single room seemed especially musty and close.

The single-car detached garage had been converted into living quarters a decade before Pearl Harbor, and few improvements had been made since that original renovation. Its one nod toward modernity was an air-conditioning window unit that belched humid cool air in summer and humid warm air in winter. Unfortunately, it fit into the dwelling's single window, which was not only a gross violation of the fire code, but created a ventilation problem. Consequently, the air that Dale Gordon now sucked into his thin body with a high, whistling sound, was stale, dense, and insufficient.

He peeled off his T-shirt and tossed it onto the narrow, unmade bed. He swiped his hands over his bony, almost concave chest, skimming off the sweat that had beaded on his pale skin and prominent ribs. His nipples were erect with a sudden chill. They were very red and sparsely ringed with long, straight blond hairs.

With almost frantic haste, he moved around the cluttered room, lighting candles. His hands shook as he held kitchen matches to wicks that had been relit so many times they were thick with char. Habitually he burned his candles down until there was no more wax to burn.

The heat and smoke from so many candles increased the room's stuffiness, but Dale Gordon didn't notice that as he kicked off his rubber thongs and peeled off his khakis and underwear.

Naked, he dropped to his knees before a crude altar. His kneecaps sounded like cracking walnuts as they struck the bare concrete floor. Dale Gordon was unaware of the sound and unmindful of the pain that accompanied it. His pain was emotional, spiritual, but it was real. To him it felt as though all the demons of hell were inside him trying to claw their way out through his vital organs.

He had waited in his car until the Lexus pulled out of The Mansion's driveway. Gillian Lloyd was alone in the car. She was going home. After hours of fornicating with the tall, dark man who looked Indian except for his brilliant blue eyes.

Dale Gordon didn't care about him. He didn't even need to know his name. It didn't matter who he was. What mattered was what Gillian had done with him. Dale had no sexual experience of his own to serve as a point of reference. Nevertheless, he knew what men and women did together when they were alone. He'd seen pictures. He'd seen movies.

Each time he envisioned Gillian's lustful foreplay and imagined her shapely limbs twined around the man's body as he rutted with her like an animal, he was seized by another bout of uncontrollable weeping.

He wept noisily and wetly as he prayed at his altar. Sobs wracked his skinny torso so violently, they almost rattled the bones within his skin. He prayed earnestly and with contrition because it wasn't Gillian's failure alone. It was also his. He had failed. Miserably.

But prayers of confession weren't enough. In order to atone for his dismal failure, he must be punished.

Lifting up the fringed cloth draping the chest that served as his altar, he opened one of three drawers. Inside was a leather whip with several wide strips. He clasped the sweat-stained handle in his right hand, said a quick prayer, then, reaching over his shoulder, lashed his back with it. He repeatedly lashed himself until blood was running down the sharp ridge of his spine and dripping onto the floor.

He fainted.

Finally he stirred to discover himself on the blood-spattered floor, knees curled up to his chest, shivering. Stiffly, he pulled himself to his feet and staggered into the bathroom, which was separated from the rest of the room only by a threadbare curtain. He took a cool shower. Then, letting his skin air-dry, he carried a towel to the altar and tried to wipe up the blood on the floor.

It was a mess. He had made a bad, bad mess. But the red streaks smeared by the towel also reminded him of Jesus' blood, which had flowed from him as he hung on the cross. Comparing himself to that most revered prophet and martyr was vainglorious, he knew, but he derived comfort from it.

The lashing, however, was only the first stage of his punishment. He must confess to Brother Gabriel. As humiliating as it would be, he must tell Brother Gabriel that he, Dale Gordon, had betrayed his trust and failed at his mission.

With tears streaming from his eyes, he moved to his telephone. He clutched the receiver in his pale hand, dreading what he must do. It was late. Maybe he should wait until morning.

No, the time of day was irrelevant. Brother Gabriel's work never ceased. He was tireless. The phone lines at the Temple were answered twenty-four/seven. Besides, Brother Gabriel had mandated that he be informed of good news immediately. The same went for bad news.

Dale Gordon knew the telephone number by heart. He had called it just that morning. That call had been cause for rejoicing. He had called to report that the mission entrusted to him had been accomplished. Oh, he'd been so proud!

Now . . . now this.

His heart pounded painfully against his rib cage as he listened to the hollow hissing sound in the receiver, signaling him that the call was going through. After five rings, a telephone in the mountaintop compound far away from Dale Gordon's squalid apartment was answered.

"Peace and love. How can I help you?"

C H A P T E R | 5

It promised to be a damp, oppressive day. The temperature was seasonably cool, but the humidity was high. Dale Gordon was sweating copiously again. The salty perspiration caused the abrasions on his back to sting, but he was unmindful of the discomfort.

Undeterred, he marched along the sidewalk like the soldier he was. A good and obedient soldier focused on his mission, not on the obstacles that might prevent him from accomplishing it. In the surrounding predawn silence, his ragged breathing was the only sound. He didn't hear it.

There was nothing to light his way. The moon was a mere sliver lying on its back just above the western horizon. Sunrise was still an hour away. But even in the gloom, Dale Gordon didn't miss a step. Although he'd never been here before, he knew the way.

He attributed his surefootedness to divine guidance. Brother Gabriel had assured him that his path would be made straight and sure, and, as with all things, Brother Gabriel had been right. He could work miracles. He could make miracles happen even in his absence by the sheer power of his mind. He had even caused the neighborhood dogs to remain mute. Not a single one had barked a warning.

Dale Gordon hadn't written down her address because he had committed it to memory. His eyes remained fixed directly ahead of him until he came even with the front of her house, where he slowly executed a military turn to face it.

It was a single-story house. The style was traditional. It had a brick exterior. The wood trim was white, the front door dark. Blue, possibly green, maybe even black. It was hard to tell in the darkness. The yard was well tended.

She really should leave on a porch light as a safety precaution, Dale Gordon thought as he made his way up the front walkway. He didn't fear detection from her or her neighbors. He had been assured invincibility, and he had faith.

Three wide, shallow steps led up to the front door. Pots of flourishing chrysanthemums flanked it. Cupping his hands around his eyes, he peered through the fan-shaped window that formed the top third of the door.

He could see only one bluish white glow coming from the back of the house. The rest was dark. He tested the latch on the front door. It was locked. Stepping off the porch, he methodically checked the windows on the front of the house, trying three before he found one unlocked.

"If there's a home security system and an alarm goes off, you must be prepared to act quickly. Before neighbors or police arrive."

Brother Gabriel thought of everything.

Dale Gordon wiped his sweaty palms on his khakis and took several quick breaths, puffing them in and out of his inflated cheeks like an Olympic weight lifter about to heft the barbell.

But the precaution was unnecessary, because when he hastily raised the window, no alarm was activated. Then for half a minute, he stood very still and listened for movement inside the house. Hearing nothing, he levered himself up and climbed through the window.

His eyes were already accustomed to darkness, so he could see his surroundings fairly well. He was in her living room. It smelled good. Like flowers and spice. He sniffed his way to an end table, where he found a pretty crystal bowl filled with dried flower petals and cinnamon sticks. He bent down and inhaled deeply of the pleasing fragrance. He'd never lived in a place that had such frills as this. He would have liked to tarry, but he'd been instructed to complete his mission before daylight, so he straightened up and glanced around.

He wished he could turn on a light in order to see the other items in the room. He longed to linger among the personal possessions that she touched on a routine basis. Scattered about on the various tables were books and magazines and picture frames, but it was too dark to see who was in the photographs. He was tempted to take one as a keepsake, so he would have something that had belonged to her. But he resisted the temptation. That would be stealing, and he wasn't a thief.

He moved carefully to avoid bumping into furniture. The floor was hardwood, but he trod lightly so none of the boards creaked. He traced the single light he'd seen through the front door to the kitchen. It was the light in the vent above the range. He thought of turning it off but decided it didn't matter that it was on.

He was about to leave the kitchen when he spotted a drinking glass on the counter. It had about two tablespoons of liquid in it. He reached for it, then hesitated. Brother Gabriel had told him not to touch anything that wasn't necessary.

But Brother Gabriel would never know, would he?

Dale Gordon picked up the glass and drank the liquid, which turned out to be plain water. Nevertheless, it made him slightly dizzy. It was intoxicating to know that he was drinking after her, that his lips and tongue were touching a surface that hers had recently touched. The experience was almost religious in its significance. His heart raced as it did when he listened to tapes of Brother Gabriel's sermons.

But it was also a carnal experience for him. He ran his tongue around the rim of the glass, inside and out. The rate of his breathing escalated until he was practically panting. Inside his underwear he felt stirrings he knew were sexual and therefore wrong.

Stop! What was he doing? He mustn't let himself get distracted. Mustn't let himself be ensnared by the wicked whore Gillian Lloyd. He set down the glass and turned his back on it, symbolically turning his back on temptation. Quickly and silently he retraced his steps to the front room of the house, where he paused to calm down and reorient himself.

Extending from the main room in the opposite direction from the dining room and kitchen was a darkened hallway. Three doors opened off it. One must be the bedroom in which she slept. Imagining himself to be just another shadow, Dale Gordon crept down the passageway.

The first room he came to was furnished with a desk and computer terminal, file cabinets, fax machine. On the wall was a corkboard covered with handwritten notes and business cards. Her home office.

The second door opened into a small, neat bedroom. The bed had a pretty pale bedspread and an old-fashioned quilt folded over the foot of it. An easy chair. A round table with a cloth matching the bedspread draped over it. Obviously a guest room. He stepped back into the hallway.

Blessed with a keen sense of smell, Dale Gordon knew before stepping through the door at the end of the hall that he would find her there. He could smell her shampoo. The scent of her skin, warm from sleep, was like a taste inside his mouth.

The room was dark, but his eyes were so accustomed to the darkness by now that he could see her plainly. Either that or the divine guidance that had accompanied him this far was serving him well now and providing enhanced night vision.

His heart thudded, but not from fear or anxiety. From excitement. From the thrill of being this close to her. One of the chosen. One of the select. At least she had been until . . .

But he wouldn't dwell on that or he would get angry. If he thought about the tall man mauling and pawing her, defiling her, desecrating her body, he might become ill again. If he imagined her clutching him and moaning in pleasure and responding to such defilement, he might actually retch.

She was sleeping on her stomach, her head turned to one side on the pillow. One cheek, one eye, one delicate ear were exposed to him. Her breathing was almost silent, but he could smell the flavor of it. Her dark hair was fanned out over the pillow, untangled and silky smooth.

On the floor beside the bed were two articles of clothing. He bent down and picked them up. Pajamas. The short jacket was sleeveless and buttoned up the front. He fondled the soft cotton that had covered her breasts. He lifted it to his face and inhaled deeply. It made him giddy to think about her bare skin rubbing against the fabric, about her breasts reshaping it. The soft cloth would have defined her nipples, nipples from which the baby would suck.

Only now there wouldn't be a baby.

Sadly, he lay the pajama top on the foot of the bed. But he continued to hold the shorts, gently squeezing them between his hands. Even though he knew they couldn't have retained her body heat in the cool room, he imagined the fabric still to be warm. Warm and moist from her womanplace. He turned the shorts inside out, spread them over his crotch, and began rubbing himself.

Even through the layers of clothing, he could feel his arousal. It was a rare sensation for Dale Gordon. Ever since that episode in gym class in junior high school when the other boys had stripped him of his underwear and ridiculed the smallness of his penis, he had denied the nasty thing that lodged between his legs. He resented having to touch it even to urinate. Or to hold it while he scrubbed and scrubbed until it was clean.

He was mortified on those mornings when he woke up to the realization that it had betrayed him in his sleep, that his sheets were stained . . . just as they had been that morning Mother discovered the bad thing he'd been doing in his bed each night. She had made him beat himself for it until he bled and was purged of impure thoughts and deeds.

Brother Gabriel agreed with Mother.

Gratifying the flesh was wrong. He must keep himself pure because the carnal nature was anathema to spiritual men. That's what Brother Gabriel had told him, and Dale Gordon understood that truism now as never before. Because if he wasn't careful, this pleasure he was experiencing was going to overwhelm him, cloud his judgment, and jeopardize his mission.

But it felt good to rub Gillian Lloyd's pajama bottoms against himself. It felt so good, in fact, that he couldn't stop himself from doing it. Nor could he hold back a low groan of animal bliss and saintly shame.

That's what awakened her.

Her eyes came open first, but she didn't move immediately. It was as though she were trying to remember where she was and determining what had awakened her. Then, as though sensing him there, she hastily rolled onto her back.

She screamed.

It wasn't much of a scream. Small. Half formed. As though her throat had been clutched before the scream could completely escape and a good part of it was still trapped inside her throat.

"Hi, Gillian."

She gasped, "What are you doing here?"

She recognized him! She knew him now. She knew his face.

And he gloried in the certainty that it was the last face she would ever see.

CHAPTER | 6

Ms. Melina Lloyd?"

Roused from a deep sleep, she had thrown back the covers, grabbed a robe, and stumbled from the bedroom, making her way to the front door on autopilot, intent on answering the doorbell if for no other reason than to stop the incessant ringing.

Groggy and muddle-headed, it took several seconds for her to register that this wasn't the extension of a dream, that she was indeed awake, standing upright, and facing a pair of uniformed Dallas policemen.

In her bleary peripheral vision, she saw their squad car parked in the driveway.

"Ms. Lloyd?"

She pushed a hank of hair off her face. "Yes. I'm sorry, I was . . . What do you want?"

"I'm Corporal Lewis, this is Corporal Caltrane."

"Is something wrong?"

"May we come in?"

In that instant she was jarred fully awake. Because policemen didn't come to someone's door this early in the morning to sell tickets to their charity ball. If the house were on fire, or a whacked-out sniper had the neighborhood under siege, or any number of other emergencies, the light bar on their car would be flashing and they would be frantically shouting instructions.

No, they hadn't come to warn her of potential disaster. Something disastrous had already occurred. Something tragic had brought them here. Otherwise Corporals Lewis and Caltrane wouldn't be asking to come inside. They wouldn't be so reluctant to look her in the eye.

"What's happened?" She gripped the edge of the door. "Tell me."

Lewis reached for her, but she waved him off and backed into the entry hall. They followed her inside. Caltrane closed the door, while his partner approached her tentatively. "You'd better sit down, Ms. Lloyd."

"I don't want to sit down. I want to know what's going on and why you're here."

She divided a wild look between them, and apparently they saw the wisdom in telling her straight out. Lewis, the spokesman of the team, said, "Your sister . . . There was some, uh, trouble at her house. Either last night or early this morning. We're not sure yet."

"Is she all right?"

Caltrane looked down at the toes of his serviceable shoes. Lewis coughed behind his hand, but at least he had the gumption to maintain eye contact with her. "No, ma'am. I'm afraid not. She was found dead this morning."

It was as though someone had charged her lungs with a battering ram. Her breath gushed out in one loud exhalation. Her knees buckled. Lewis reached for her again, and this time she allowed him to support her as she lowered herself into a chair. The room tilted and her stomach heaved. Her earlobes seemed to catch fire. A curtain of blackness descended over her.

Somehow she managed to keep from fainting, but her breathing was choppy. Lewis ordered Caltrane to get her a glass of water, and he seemed relieved to leave the main room in search of the kitchen.

She covered her mouth with her hand. Her palm was damp, her fingers icy cold and trembling. Tears filled her eyes, but they were tears born of shock, not grief. It was too soon for grief.

What she felt was disbelief. This simply could not be happening. It had to be a bad dream from which she would awaken. Soon, please. Relieved, she would say a quick prayer of thanksgiving that it was only a dream. She might recall it later in the day and shudder, and then she would do something silly to help shake off the grim remnants of it. By tomorrow she would have forgotten it entirely.

Or if it wasn't a nightmare, it was a dreadful mistake. The police had the wrong house, the wrong person. They had made a grave error. She would sue the Dallas Police Department for putting her through this.

No, no, wait. She would send each division of the department a gift basket of fruit and cheese and summer sausages because she would be so glad that they'd been proved wrong.

But when she lifted her watery gaze to the police officer and asked if he was sure, she realized that her fantasies about nightmares and mistakes were just that—fantasies.

"One of your sister's neighbors knows that she's an early riser. She went over to borrow some coffee around seven-thirty this morning. She rang the doorbell several times. Ms. Lloyd's car was there, so the neighbor lady knew she must be at home. She knew where the spare key was hidden and let herself in. She found her in the bedroom."

Caltrane returned with a glass of tap water. Lewis took it from him and passed it to her. Fearing she would throw up if she tried to swallow anything, she set it untouched on the end table next to her chair.

Lewis continued. "The neighbor gave your name to the investigating officer. He sent us over to notify you."

"She's dead?" She shook her head with misapprehension. "How?"

Lewis glanced uneasily at his partner, but neither was brave enough to say anything.

"Answer me," she demanded, her voice cracking. "You said . . . you said there was some trouble. What kind of trouble? With the furnace? Was she asphyxiated? Did she have a heart attack or allergic reaction? What?"

Lewis said, "Uh, no, ma'am. It looks like murder."

Her lungs wheezed on another sudden exhale.

"I'm sorry, Ms. Lloyd. There's just no delicate way to put it. Your sister was killed. Rather viciously."

"Viciously?" she repeated in a thin voice.

"Investigators are already at the scene. A crime scene unit is on its way."

She surged to her feet. "I'm going over there."

"That wouldn't be wise," Lewis said hastily, patting the air between them. "Your sister's body will be taken—"

"I'm going over there."

She rushed into the bedroom and threw off the robe and nightgown. She grabbed a pair of jeans and a shirt from the closet and pulled them on, then shoved her feet into a pair of sneakers. She grabbed her wallet and car keys, and, in under two minutes, rejoined the policemen at the front door.

Seeing the car keys clutched in her hand, Lewis offered to drive her there.

"I'll drive myself," she said, shoving him out of her path.

"I can't let you drive in the state you're in, Ms. Lloyd. You'd be a danger to yourself and other motorists. Maybe a friend could come—"

"Oh, all right. I'll ride there with you. But please, let's go."

"Remember the house is a crime scene," he said. "You might not be allowed to go inside."

"I'd like to see someone try and stop me."

The drive from Melina's house to Gillian's took exactly eleven minutes. They had timed it. But at this time of day, the school zones were activated. The mute Caltrane drove slower than the posted speed limit, so the short trip seemed to take three times longer than usual.

Lewis, who was riding shotgun, consulted her several times along the way. "Are you all right, Ms. Lloyd?"

She didn't respond. Of course she wasn't all right, and he knew it. Why assure him that she was fine when she wasn't? The only reason she wasn't kicking and screaming was that she lacked the energy that hysteria required. She was too numbed by shock to weep, too shocked to do anything really except stare vacantly through the car window and try to sort through what she'd been told had happened, but which she could not grasp. Impossible. It could not be.

To everyone else this was just another day. Mothers were hustling their children off to school. Professional couples were hurriedly coordinating schedules before kissing one another goodbye. Retirees were sharing the morning newspaper or watching the news shows on TV.

Everyone except her was going about their routine, unscathed and unconcerned. She resented their disregard for her personal tragedy. Her life had just undergone a shattering, irreversible event. From this point forward, nothing would ever be the same. The loss of her sister, her twin, was permanent. It would last forever. Didn't anyone realize that? It seemed inherently wrong that the rest of the world hadn't paused to observe this tragic, life-changing episode.

Besides resenting anyone to whom this

was a normal day, she envied their innocence. She desperately wished she could roll back the clock to a time when a scheduling snafu, or a snagged stocking, or a broken fingernail was the crisis of the day. She wanted to return to yesterday, to last night, to an hour ago, when she had been sleeping peacefully, blissfully unaware of the tragedy about to befall her.

But she was lapsing into wishful thinking again. This was all too real, as evinced when they turned the corner onto the block where a murder had taken place. Several emergency and official vehicles were parked haphazardly in the street. Yellow crime scene tape had been strung around the entire perimeter of the house with the smart white shutters and glossy black door. Uniformed men and women were either going about their various tasks or milling around trying to look busy. Along the sidewalks on both sides of the street, neighbors had clustered in small groups. Some were already being questioned by police.

"No witnesses so far," Lewis informed her, noticing the direction of her gaze.

Because of the congestion on the street, the squad car was reduced to a crawl, then

Caltrane brought it to a complete stop. "Can't you honk your horn or something?" she asked impatiently.

"Sorry, Ms. Lloyd. It's unfortunate, but a crime scene always attracts a crowd."

When a kid on a bicycle shot out in front of them and popped a wheelie, her tolerance level maxed out. "Oh, for heaven's sake," she shouted, "let me out of here."

Lewis must have sensed that she was losing control. He motioned Caltrane to pull as close to the curb as possible. Immediately after he got out and opened the rear door, she pushed past him and ran the remainder of the way to the house, ignoring the curious stares of onlookers.

When she ducked beneath the tape, several officers rushed toward her, shouting for her to stop. Heedlessly, she sprinted across the lawn. She made it through the front door and into the entry hall. There, three officers grabbed and restrained her from going farther.

"I must see her. . . . Let go of me!"

Huffing, Lewis ran in. "This is the victim's sister."

"Twin!" she corrected in what sounded to her own ears to be the ragged scream of a deranged woman. "I want to see her. Please let me go in. I must see her."

"Truly, you don't want to, Ms. Lloyd. Not now." A plainclothesman approached and flashed her his badge. "Senior Corporal Lawson, Homicide Division."

"Let me through, please. Please."

"I understand your need to verify that she's dead, Ms. Lloyd. Believe me, I do."

"Then let me see her."

He shook his head decisively but kept his voice even. "The experts are collecting evidence. The fewer people in there," he said, using a quick motion of his head to indicate the bedroom down the hall, "the less contamination of the scene and the better chance we'll have of gathering clues that'll point us to a suspect. You want to know who killed Gillian, don't you? And you want to know why, right?"

The detective's technique was straight out of Psychology 101. Obviously he had experience dealing with the hysterical relatives of violent crime victims. In any case, his calm manner steadied her. She stopped struggling against the officers holding her back.

Lawson's eyes held hers with the power of a hypnotist. Any other time, this man wouldn't have exercised that kind of control over her, but in the saner regions of her mind, she realized that she wanted someone to take control. She wanted someone to restore a semblance of order to her life, which, suddenly and without warning, had been pitched into chaos.

"We're going to work together to get some answers, right?" he asked.

She bobbed her head.

"Right. I want whoever did this caught, prosecuted, and convicted. So it's best if we stay clear of the scene. Otherwise, it could be mucked up and whoever murdered your sister would get away with it."

"I don't want . . ." She stopped to swallow emotionally. "I don't want him to get away with it. I want him captured and punished."

"Then we're in agreement." He motioned brusquely, and the officers cautiously released her and fell back several steps.

She clasped her hands tightly, literally getting a grip on herself. "Do you know what happened?"

He motioned her toward the living room. "Why don't we sit down? I have some questions for you."

Her view into the bedroom was obstructed by a technician dusting the doorframe for fingerprints. Maybe she had deluded herself into believing that she was steeled for whatever she might see in there. Similar scenes on TV and in movies hadn't prepared her for the harsh reality. Being caught in such a circumstance was much worse than she could ever have imagined or any film could have depicted. Every sensory stimulation was vivid and jolting. In addition to the strange sights and sounds was an unfamiliar smell that was making her queasy.

Once she was seated on the sofa, Lawson asked if he could get her anything. She shook her head.

"Nothing to drink?"

"No, thank you."

The detective settled himself on the ottoman in front of the sofa. "Is there someone we should call?"

"My—" The tears came abruptly. One second her eyes were dry; the next, tears were overflowing her eyelids and streaming down her cheeks. Her nose began to run. Lawson motioned for a policewoman to bring her some Kleenex and a box was brought immediately.

She blotted her eyes and blew her nose. "I was about to say you should call my sister. You see, we are—were—very close."

Grimly, he nodded. "Your parents?"

"Deceased."

"Other siblings?"

"No," she said, clearing her throat. "Just us."

The detective frowned his regret. "I know this is tough, Ms. Lloyd. You'll be asked to identify the body."

She swallowed thickly but nodded her understanding.

"The neighbor who found her identified her immediately. And you bear a remarkable resemblance to her."

"What happened to her, Detective?" She couldn't remember his official rank, but he didn't correct her.

Her first impression of Lawson was that he was square in shape. He had a boxy torso that had been squeezed into a jacket that was an inch or two too short and a size too small. His flattop haircut made his head look square. His neck was thick, his eyebrows a straight bushy line across his forehead.

In early life, he'd probably been an athlete.

A football lineman or a wrestler. His bulky appearance made him look mean. His eyes were world-weary and a bit cynical. But his manner toward her was kind and sympathetic.

"I won't spare you, Ms. Lloyd. It was a brutal attack. She was killed with a sharp object, probably a knife."

"She was stabbed?"

"Repeatedly."

A low moan escaped her. She crossed her arms over her middle and bent from the waist, rocking slightly back and forth. She pinched her eyes closed, forcing out fresh tears.

"I'm sorry," the detective murmured. "Are you sure you wouldn't like somebody here with you?"

She nixed the suggestion with a strong shake of her head. "Was she raped?"

"The ME is examining the body now. It's being photographed. Once it's transported to the morgue, a complete autopsy—"

"Detective," she interrupted, "was she raped?"

"I honestly can't tell you. It doesn't appear that she was sexually assaulted, but please understand that at this point in time, we can't be positive."

"Thank you for your honesty."

Lawson shifted his weight on the ottoman and removed a notepad and pen from his breast pocket. "Are you willing to answer a few questions?"

"Of course. I want to help any way I can, but does it have to be right now?"

"The sooner we can establish a motive, the sooner we'll know where to begin looking for a suspect."

"How would I know what the killer's motive was?"

"We'll look first at your sister's routine, her friends, acquaintances, work habits, and so forth. Then work from there."

Nodding understanding, she blotted her eyes, blew her nose, and, with a small hand gesture, indicated for him to proceed.

"Did she have any enemies that you know of?"

"No."

"Jealous ex-husband?"

"She'd never been married."

"Jealous ex-lover or boyfriend?"

"No."

"A former employee, spiteful coworker?"

"She got along with everyone."

"As far as you know."

"Mr. Lawson, if she'd had an enemy, I would have known about it."

"She told you everything?"

"Yes."

"Even details about her personal life?"

"I can't be sure she told me everything, but she couldn't have kept a deep, dark secret from me, any more than I could have kept one from her. We could gauge each other's mood after exchanging a single word, even over the telephone. I would have sensed if she was worried about something or someone. We had this . . . telepathy. I could virtually read her mind. It's a phenomenon common to twins."

"I've heard that. Did she ever mention a stalker?"

She sighed. Wasn't he listening? "No."

"Anyone who made her uneasy? Gave her unwanted attention?"

"No."

"And you can't think of anyone who might have held a grudge against her?"

"Nobody."

He tapped his pen against the pad and gnawed the inside of his cheek.

"What?" she asked.

He shifted his weight on the ottoman.

"Well, we don't think it was a random attack. No ordinary break-in or burglary. Nothing seems to be disturbed or missing, although later you can help us determine that by walking through the rooms and checking. We also found a ruby necklace on the nightstand beside the bed. It's lying in plain sight. Not something a burglar would overlook."

"It was a gift from Jem. He brought it over just last night."

"Jem?"

The detective's ears seemed to peak. He exchanged a significant glance with the other officers standing nearby listening.

"Jem Hennings." She shook her head in dismay. "I can't believe I haven't mentioned him before. I completely forgot him. I wasn't thinking—"

"Who is he?"

"The man she was seeing."

"Boyfriend?"

"Yes."

"Do you have a number where he can be reached?"

She cast an alarmed glance around the group of policemen. "Yes, but . . . but Jem couldn't possibly be involved."

"He should still be notified, though. Right? And if he was here last night, we certainly need to talk to him."

She provided the name of the stockbrokerage firm where Jem Hennings was employed. "He gets there early, before the market opens in New York."

"Then he should be there by now." Lawson dispatched Caltrane to place the call. "Just get him over here. Don't tell him what's happened."

She watched as the uniformed cop withdrew, cell phone in hand. Coming back to Lawson, she said, "That's awfully cruel, isn't it?"

"What happened to your sister was awfully cruel, Ms. Lloyd. That's another reason I don't think burglary was the motive. If caught in the act, a burglar might panic and lash out quickly. He has a knee-jerk response, and somebody winds up dead. No premeditation."

She glanced toward the bedroom and said quietly, "This wasn't like that? You think it was premeditated?"

He nodded grimly. "I think your sister was . . . targeted. And it's more than a gut instinct. Evidence indicates it."

"What evidence?"

Caltrane entered and, speaking for the first time, said, "Hennings is on his way."

Lawson nodded an acknowledgment to the officer's announcement, but his eyes never left hers. "How involved were your sister and Mr. Hennings?"

"They were dating exclusively."

"How long had they been seeing each other on this exclusive basis?"

"Let's see . . ." She did a mental calculation. "Almost a year."

"And the relationship was intimate?"

"Are you asking if they slept together?" she asked testily, and when he nodded, she said, "They had a sexual relationship, yes. Is that relevant, Mr. Lawson?"

"It could be. What kind of guy is Hennings?"

"What kind? Successful. Overachiever. Nice-looking."

"Ethnicity?"

She looked at the detective with puzzlement. "I'm not sure. *Hennings* is Irish or English, isn't it? Frankly, I don't see the relevance," she said with a trace of impatience.

"And you're sure that Hennings was the only man your sister was seeing?"

"What are you getting at?"

"In your opinion, is Hennings the jealous sort?"

"I don't know. Maybe. Why? Detective Lawson—"

She broke off when she heard the wheels of the gurney squeaking along the floor of the hallway. She never remembered standing, never recalled taking several halting steps before gripping the back of an armchair for support. The body had been placed in a zippered bag and then strapped to the gurney.

"I want to see her."

Lawson advised that she let the coroner take the body downtown and prepare it for formal identification.

"I want to see her," she repeated.

After a long hesitation, Lawson gave his reluctant approval. He stood close to her and she moved toward the gurney, which was now crowding the entryway. Lawson nodded to the medic, who unzipped the bag only far enough to reveal the face.

It was so still and pale, it could have been formed of wax. It also could have been her face, except for the brown flecks on the very white skin. Those spatters puzzled her for a moment, and then she realized that they were dried droplets of blood.

Reality hit with the impetus of a freight train.

She felt her knees giving way. "I'm going to be sick."

CHAPTER | 7

Ms. Lloyd?" A policewoman tapped softly on the powder room door. "Are you all right?"

All right? Am I all right? Hell, no, I'm not all right. She didn't speak her sarcastic thoughts aloud. The woman's intentions were good. "I'm okay," she called. "I'll be out in a moment."

She'd had the dry heaves, but the nausea had passed now, and she was left feeling only hollow, emotionally as well as physically. She bathed her face and neck with cold water, rinsed her mouth out, and washed her hands. She looked ghastly, but she couldn't think of a single reason why it mattered.

When she opened the bathroom door, the policewoman smiled sympathetically. "Can I get you anything?"

"Yes. Detective Lawson."

The policewoman accompanied her back into the central room, where the detective was kneeling down in front of a window. Another cop was explaining to him that footprints had been found outside. "We'll dust. Impressions have already been made of the footprints. We're getting soil samples, too."

"The drinking glass in the kitchen?"

"Already bagged."

Lawson nodded as he stood, favoring what appeared to be arthritic knees. The policewoman got his attention. "Ms. Lloyd has asked to speak to you."

"Sure."

As he approached, she geared herself for the argument she knew was coming. "I want to see the bedroom."

He shook his head. "I don't think that's advisable."

"You mentioned evidence that indicates

Gillian was targeted. If I see what you're talking about, I may be able to shed some light."

"We'll have photographs."

"Why wait on them?"

"It's not pretty."

"And I'm not a shrinking violet. I know it'll be bloody. I saw blood splashes on her face. And you said she was stabbed repeatedly. I know what to expect."

"Not entirely." He lowered his gaze for a few seconds before apologetically meeting hers again. "I haven't mentioned this before because you had enough to deal with."

What could he have possibly omitted? How much worse could it get? She stared him down, silently demanding that he hold nothing back.

"There's some writing on the bedroom walls."

"Writing?"

"Apparently he— Based on the size of the footprints we found outside the window, our suspect is male. Looks like he dipped a washcloth in your sister's blood and scrawled some . . . well, some obscenities on the walls."

Her stomach rose and fell like an ocean

swell. But she was resolved to see the worst of it. If she didn't, then years from now her imagination would still be painting the scene for her. She wanted to see it as it actually was, not an image her mind conjured up. It must be real to her, not an abstract. She must see the scene in order to cope with it and, she hoped, eventually file it away in a compartment of her heart and subconscious. If she didn't confront it now and deal with it, she would never be able to lock it away. The frightening unknown would remain with her always, haunting her forever.

"I must see where and how my sister died, Detective."

The crime scene unit had completed their work. They had packed their gear into a van and departed, officially relinquishing the scene to the homicide detective. It was at Lawson's discretion who went in and out of that room now.

The seasoned investigator peered deeply into her eyes, and apparently her steady gaze conveyed her determination. He sighed like a man conceding an argument he was destined to lose.

He motioned her down the hallway, then

paused on the threshold of the bedroom and waited for her to catch up with him. She stepped into the room, braced for the worst.

Actually, it was almost easy to view the scene with detachment. Because nothing in her life prior to this moment was relatable. She had no point of reference for comparison. The carnage was so horribly foreign to her experience that she couldn't connect with it on any level.

It was as shocking to her system as plunging into frigid waters. The quality that made it stupefying was the same quality that provided protection. It wasn't painful because all sensation was instantly frozen. Upon seeing her sister's deathbed, her senses froze. That's the only way her sensibilities could have sustained this assault on them.

After being photographed as they'd been found, the linens had been stripped from the bed, bagged, and sent to the crime lab for testing. But there was a bloodstain in the center of the mattress that hadn't completely dried.

She stared, transfixed by the horror of it.

"We figure he was standing about where you are now," Lawson told her. "There was some loose dirt there on the floor that he must've tracked in from outside. She was probably asleep."

"I hope so." Her remark was only half audible.

"She was found lying on her back. Nude. Was that normal? Is that how she usually slept?"

"I think so. Not always."

"We found a pajama top on the bed, but the bottoms haven't been located."

She looked at him for an elaboration, but he glanced away. "There were no resistance wounds on her arms and hands. Seems it was quick. If that's any comfort."

Her eyes strayed from the mattress to the nightstand. It had been dusted for fingerprints. The powder had left a messy residue on the ruby pendant. She looked over at Lawson, a question in her eyes.

"Yeah, go ahead," he said.

She picked up the pendant and closed a fist around it.

The walls screamed to be noticed. Not that she could have avoided noticing them. The printed letters were large and well formed, except for the ones that had dripped rivulets of blood. The killer had felt comfortable enough to take his time and get his message across.

WHORE. MOTHERCUNT. BREED-FUCKER.

She stared at the writing, wondering first about the sick individual who could have done this, marveling at the unbridled rage or hopeless psychosis that had plunged someone into such depths of depravity.

Then she reread the words, concentrating on their meaning.

In one heart-stopping instant, she deciphered them. Realization struck her like a blinding light. She even covered her eyes and recoiled, crying out, "Oh, my God, oh, my God!"

She spun around and tried to flee the room, but she ran squarely into Lawson. "Ms. Lloyd? What's wrong? What is it?"

"Oh, my God!" she screamed. "It was supposed to be me! It should have been me!"

She tried to fight off his hands as she stumbled into the hallway, but he was stronger and wouldn't let her go. Once outside the room, he propped her against the wall. She closed her eyes, but that didn't stop the tears. She caught her lower lip between her teeth in an attempt to contain the keening sounds issuing from her throat.

Lawson had her by the shoulders, shaking her slightly. "Talk to me. What's with the words? What do they mean?"

Another commotion erupted at the front door. "Let me in. I was told to come here. What's happened? What's going on?" Jem Hennings was trying to push his way through a human barricade of uniformed policemen.

"Are you Hennings?" Detective Lawson barked.

"Who the hell are you?"

The other officers obeyed the abrupt motion of Lawson's hand and stepped aside, allowing Jem Hennings to come in. He strode up to Lawson, who showed him his badge. "Dallas PD."

Clearly baffled, Jem reached past the detective and took her hand. "For God's sake, Gillian, you're as pale as a ghost. Are you all right? What the hell is going on?"

Before she had an opportunity to respond, Lawson said, "Gillian was taken away in an ambulance."

"An ambu— Why?" Jem's gaze swung back to her. "Melina? What's wrong? Has something happened to Gillian?" No one said anything. When next he spoke, his voice was shrill. "Will somebody please tell me what the hell is going on?"

"I'm sorry to have to tell you this, Mr. Hennings." Jem faced the detective. "Gillian is dead. She was found murdered in her bed this morning."

He opened his mouth but didn't emit a sound. He staggered backward a step or two and gaped at them with disbelief. Then he turned toward the other policemen still clustered near the front door, as though willing them to contradict the unbelievable news.

Eventually he managed to gasp, "That's impossible."

Their funereal expressions must have confirmed it for him, because he covered his mouth for several seconds before dragging his hand down his chin.

"Would you like to sit down, Mr. Hennings?"

He shook his head. "You said she was . . . was *murdered?*" His eyes strayed beyond them, then, before either could react, he charged past.

"Wait!"

"Jem!"

Their grasping hands came up empty. Neither could stop him. But he drew up short when he reached the threshold of the bedroom. "Oh, God," he moaned. "'Oh, no." He covered his head with both hands.

"Jem, I'm sorry."

"Melina . . . ? What . . . ?"

She moved up behind him and placed her hands on his shoulders. "Come away, Jem. Sit down with me. I need you beside me. We need each other."

His sobs were painful to listen to. It took some urging, but she managed to turn him around. Leaning into each other, they staggered into the living room, where they sat down side by side on the sofa. He groped for her hand, squeezed it, raised it to his lips, and kissed her knuckles.

"Melina, I'm sorry. God, I'm so sorry. Did you find her?"

"A neighbor who came over early to borrow coffee."

She was moved to see the tears collecting in his eyes.

To Lawson's credit, he gave them several minutes alone to comfort one another. Eventually he sat down on the ottoman as he had before, ungracefully, bulky shoulders hunched, looking like a frog squatting on a lily pad.

Jem had composed himself. He mopped his face with his handkerchief, then addressed Lawson. "What happened?"

He gave Jem a rundown of the known facts. "She sustained multiple stab wounds, several of which could have been fatal. It appears to have been an act of vengeance. Rage for sure."

"Who could have been enraged at Gillian?"

"That's what we're going to find out. Anything you can tell us might help." Jem nodded vaguely and Lawson continued. "When did you last speak to her?"

"Last night. I came over here with a gift. A ruby pendant."

"We found it on the nightstand."

"I have it, Jem." She opened her hand. The piece of jewelry had left a heart-shaped impression in her palm.

Jem lifted it from her hand and smiled wistfully. "It looked beautiful on her. She was wearing it when I left."

"What time was that?" Lawson asked.

"Uh, nine or so, I think," he replied, rubbing a spot on his temple. "Do we have to do this now? I need some time."

"If you would indulge me by answering a

few more questions." Reluctantly Jem signaled for the detective to continue. "How long were you here?"

"Not long. Gillian was ready for bed when I arrived. I gave her the pendant and left."

"Just gave her the gift and left?"

"Basically."

Lawson said nothing for a moment but used the time to take Jem's measure. "That's a valuable piece of jewelry, Mr. Hennings. Was last night a special occasion?"

"Yes."

"Care to share?"

"It was private."

"Private."

"That's right."

Lawson tugged on his lower lip as though mulling over a contradiction. "So you just came and went. Around nine o'clock."

"Yes."

"And you said Ms. Lloyd was ready for bed when you got here?"

"She was very tired. She'd had an eventful day. She was already in pajamas."

"Pajamas."

"Am I not speaking clearly, Detective Lawson? Or is there something wrong with your hearing?" Jem asked testily. "Why are you repeating my answers? Jesus Christ! My fiancée has been found murdered—"

"Fiancée?"

"Fiancée?"

She and Lawson spoke in unison, neither concealing their surprise.

"You were engaged?" the detective asked.

Ignoring him, Jem turned to her, looking chagrined. "This should have been happy news, Melina. I'm sorry you had to hear it under these tragic circumstances."

"You were engaged?" she repeated.

"I know you two confided everything to each other. But Gillian and I made a lover's pact not to tell anyone for a while."

"When did this come about?"

"A few weeks ago."

"Had you set a wedding date?"

"Not yet. We were taking first things first."

He gave her a significant look, and she realized that he was referring to the AI, which he obviously didn't want discussed in front of Lawson. "I see."

"It was tough to keep the secret," he said, smiling sadly. "Especially from you."

"It must have been."

"There was no engagement ring on her finger," Lawson noted. "You're sure that it was official and that Ms. Lloyd had agreed to marry you?"

Jem rounded on the detective. "Of course I'm sure. What do you think? That I'm making it up?"

Lawson shrugged. "Are you?"

"Why would I?"

"Because it might be easier for a homicide investigator to believe a fiancé rather than a boyfriend who drops by at bedtime with an expensive gift but who doesn't spend the night. Were you angry because Gillian sent you packing last night and didn't invite you to stay over?"

Jem sprang to his feet. "You think I did that?" he shouted, angrily pointing toward the bedroom. "I loved her. She was going to be my wife."

"Jem."

"Calm down, Hennings." Lawson was unfazed by Jem's angry outburst. "Nobody's accused you of anything. I'm just tossing out some options."

"Your options stink."

"I just want to make certain I've got your story straight."

"It's not a *story.* It's the truth."

"Fine. Sit down."

Jem was fuming and looked ready to fight, but he resumed his seat. "Did he put you through the third degree, too, Melina?"

"I had to answer some questions, yes."

Lawson continued as though Jem's outburst had never occurred. "You said Ms. Lloyd was wearing pajamas."

"Yes," Jem hissed. "Boxer shorts and a matching top."

"She wasn't wearing any when she was found."

"Then she must've taken them off when she went to bed."

"We found the top. No bottoms."

Jem's posture became rigid. "Your implication is insulting to both Gillian and me."

"I'm not implying anything. Why are you so defensive?" Jem remained mutinously silent. Lawson picked up his questioning. "After you left here, did you go straight home?"

"Yes."

"Can anyone corroborate that?"

"The doorman at my building. I live in a high-rise just off Oak Lawn. I left my car with the parking garage attendant. It remained in the garage until I left for work this morning. You can check it out."

"I will."

"There's no need for you to do that, Detective Lawson. It would be a waste of your time."

Jem jerked his head around to her. "What do you mean, Melina?"

Both he and Lawson had been startled not only by the quiet quality of her voice, but also by the statement. Even the other policemen in the room stopped what they were doing and paused to listen. The policewoman who'd treated her with such kindness was regarding her expectantly.

She addressed the detective. "There's no need for you to check with the personnel at Jem's building. I can corroborate his story."

"Melina, what—"

She shook her head to stop Jem's shocked protest. "I know you were here at nine o'clock last night. You left about nine-fifteen. After . . . after you left, I rinsed the conditioner off my hair."

For several seconds he stared at her with misapprehension. Then his lips parted in wordless surprise. "That was . . ."

"Me," she said gently. "I was the one here

with you last night." He was still too stunned to speak, so she turned to the detective, who was now regarding her with a mix of astonishment and suspicion.

"When we were kids, my sister and I often switched identities," she explained. "We played tricks on babysitters, school-teachers, friends, even relatives. It was a child's game to us, a challenge to see if we could pull it off without being discovered. We always got away with it." She returned to Jem, who was still looking at her with patent disbelief. "I guess we still can."

Finding his voice, he stammered, "But . . . I kissed you."

"And I stopped it before it got too heavy. Remember?"

He was still mystified. "But why? Why last night?"

She took a deep breath. "It was my idea. A silly, frivolous whim. I suggested it yesterday at lunch. Gillian refused, with very good reason. She reminded me that we're no longer children. But I called her later and pressed the point. I told her I wasn't feeling well, which wasn't exactly true, but I wore her down until she finally agreed to switch places last night. I was here with you, Jem. She escorted my client."

"What do you mean, 'escorted'?" Lawson wanted to know.

She explained the nature of her business to the detective. "Last night I was responsible for taking Colonel Christopher Hart—"

"The astronaut?" Jem interjected.

She nodded. "I was to take him to a banquet at the Adolphus, ramrod his press conference, and so forth." Tears began to cloud her eyes. "Gillian went in my place. That's why I reacted so emotionally to the words on the wall."

Lawson pieced it together and slowly nodded his head. "Breed. Christopher Hart. He's part Indian, right?"

"If my sister's murder is somehow linked to him, then it should have been me who was killed."

"Wait a minute." Jem was rattled, angry. "Okay, I get the reference to Hart. That's obvious. But the rest of it, that . . . that filth about Gillian. What's that supposed to signify?"

Lawson snuffled and lowered his eyes to his notepad.

Jem's voice rose an octave. "Melina? What does it signify?"

It was an understandable question. His asking it was justified. But, like the detective, she couldn't comfortably look Jem Hennings in the eye.

CHAPTER | 8

I don't really have anything new to say." Chief nodded thanks to the waiter who re-filled his coffee cup. He needed it. He felt like hell. He'd been out of sorts when he woke up, and his mood hadn't improved. This unwanted and time-wasting meeting with Longtree and Abbott was only making his sour disposition worse.

"Well, I'm disappointed," Abbott said. "I know I speak for Chief Longtree, too."

Although Longtree had said nothing, his unblinking eyes remained on Chief's face. He had to concentrate to keep himself from squirming beneath that implacable glare. "It's not that I don't appreciate your interest in me," he said. "I do. And the goals you've set for NAA are admirable. These are definitely worthy causes, needs that should be addressed and brought to public awareness. It's just that . . ."

Shit. He didn't know how to turn them down without either obligating himself or insulting them, and he resented being placed in a situation that forced him to do one or the other. He also resented having to think about this now, when all he really wanted to think about was last night.

"I haven't made up my mind about anything yet," he stated curtly. "The future is just that. The future. Until my retirement from NASA is official, I see no need for further discussions."

"But as you're making your future plans, will you take our offer into consideration?" Abbott pressed. "Agree to let us make at least one more run at you. Say, in sixty days?"

Again, Chief was forced to hedge. "I think that no matter what course I choose, or what I decide to do, I prefer to remain independent. No offense intended, Mr. Abbott, but I—"

"You don't want to be lumped in with Indians."

Chief turned to Longtree, who'd spoken for the first time in almost half an hour. "I didn't say that."

"But that's what you meant. In so many words."

Chief figured that he'd just as well pull out all the stops. After all, he'd already offended them. Longtree could see that he was mincing words. So why not stop trying to be politically correct? Why not cut through the bullshit and end this thing right here, right now, and save everybody a lot of time? When it came right down to it, he didn't owe them anything. Nothing. Not even tact.

"Yes, Chief Longtree. That's what I meant. In all honesty, joining your new advocacy group doesn't appeal to me. If you're genuine, then you're to be commended. It's a noble effort and a great idea. But it's been years since I was even near a reservation. I'm disassociated and don't wish to become reassociated.

"I've never credited my Indian blood with my achievements, nor blamed it for my failures. I would look like a fraud, especially to the Native Americans I'd be representing, if

I presumed to be their spokesperson. I have nothing in common with the Indian population except some DNA."

"In other words, NAA needs you, but you don't need it," Longtree said.

"I wouldn't be that rude."

"But that's the essence of what you're saying."

The old man seemed determined to piss him off and make him look like a heel. Fine. He was in no mood to pussyfoot around, either. "That's right, Chief Longtree. I won't let my name be exploited by anyone or any organization, especially if I feel that their interest in me is self-serving and one-sided. And frankly, I think such is the case here. If I accepted your offer, it wouldn't be a reciprocal exchange. As you stated so bluntly, you need me more than I need you."

Calmly, Longtree removed the napkin from his lap and folded it beside his plate. Abbott seemed ready to argue for another round, but one stern look from Longtree admonished him to let it drop. "Thank you for seeing us," Longtree said, coming to his feet.

Chief stood up, too, and the two men faced each other. Although he was a head taller than the old chief, Longtree made him feel small. Again, he resented them for not taking his "no, thank you" graciously. They'd forced him into being an asshole. He didn't want to get into bed with these guys, but he hated that they were leaving with a negative impression of him.

In an effort to conciliate, he said, "I respect your position, Chief Longtree. I hope you can respect mine."

Longtree declined to acknowledge the request, but his eyes bore into Chief's as he gripped his hand hard. Chief experienced an irrational urge to pull his hand free of the older man's.

Longtree said, "There will come a time— soon, I predict—when you *will* need us, Colonel Hart."

"Christopher Hart?"

At the sound of his name, Chief turned. A man as solid as a tree stump flashed a badge several inches from his nose. "Senior Corporal Lawson, DPD Homicide."

Longtree released Chief's hand, but he barely noticed. When he'd turned, he had expected an autograph hound, someone who had spotted him having breakfast and recognized him from his recent media exposure. In fact, there had been a write-up about last night's banquet in this morning's edition of the *Dallas Morning News* along with a photograph of him taken as he was delivering his acceptance speech.

But the stocky plainclothesman didn't appear enamored of him. He wasn't even smiling. Neither were the two uniformed policemen flanking him.

The maître d' moved to Chief's side. "I'm dreadfully sorry, Colonel Hart. I suggested that he let me summon you out of the restaurant, but he—"

"It's okay." Chief held up his hand to stop the effusive apology. To the detective he said, "Can I help you?"

"I believe you can."

Chief was thinking that he really should have taken at least one more swig of the strong black coffee. He could've used another kick of caffeine. His head still felt muddled. He'd had only one bourbon last night, but he felt hungover. Probably from too little sleep and too much sex. Well, actually, not too much. If anything, not enough.

"I'm sorry, did you say homicide?"

"That's right."

"Are you sure you've got the right guy?"

"Are you the astronaut?"

"Yes."

"Then I've got the right guy. I need you to answer a few questions."

"Sure. What about?"

"The murder of Gillian Lloyd."

Before Chief could contain it, he blurted a short laugh. So that was it! A practical joke. Those guys!

His eyes swept the occupied tables in the restaurant. All the other diners had stopped eating and were staring, but none of the faces was familiar. They would soon reveal themselves, though. Whoever was responsible for this charade would leap out from behind the furniture and the potted palms, laughing their asses off and mimicking the stupid expression on his face.

Like that Sunday afternoon two years ago, when he'd been home alone, peacefully watching an NFC championship game between Dallas and San Francisco. Steve Young had just thrown a fifty-yard touchdown pass late in the third quarter when Chief's doorbell rang.

On his doorstep stood a woman in the advanced stages of pregnancy, whom he'd never seen before. With her was a cop who looked bigger and meaner than any tackle playing in the game he'd been watching.

The woman began screaming horrible allegations. In a voice that could have shattered glass, she claimed that Christopher Hart had raped her at a party eight months earlier. He had slipped a drug into her drink, forced himself on her, infected her with a sexually transmitted disease, and left her pregnant and traumatized by his threats to kill her if she exposed him for the sexual predator he was.

She was a full two minutes into her diatribe before Chief could find his voice and appeal to the ugly copy, who was brandishing an even uglier billy club. He claimed never to have seen this woman in his life and didn't know what the hell she was talking about.

But she continued to hurl vicious accusations, embellished with such intimate knowledge of him and his physique that he began to doubt his own protestations of innocence.

Then, to his utter dismay, she ripped open the front of her dress and out popped the pillow she'd been using to simulate pregnancy, along with two luscious tits. On one was tattooed HAPPY, and on the other, BIRTH-DAY. Then she winked and cried, "Surprise!"

Some of his rowdier friends at NASA stumbled from their hiding places in his yard, weak with laughter. They had brought with them enough liquor and food to create an instant party. The cop, who was in on the joke, told them before he left to have a good time but to keep the noise at a tolerable level. The girl, an exotic dancer by trade, stayed to give the birthday boy an extraordinary lap dance and to entertain the rest of the troops for as long as they were sober enough to appreciate her talents.

Chief never saw the fourth quarter of that game and didn't learn the outcome until the following day.

Now his first thought was that this was the same kind of practical joke. He and his circle of friends were always trying to outdo one another, devising pranks that made the butt of the joke look like a complete fool or worse. This one was pretty damn good. He had to hand it to the jokesters. This one was going to be hard to top. This one might even make the *Guinness Book.*

Except that his birthday wasn't for another six months.

A surprise retirement party? Not when retirement was still weeks away. Besides, they wouldn't hold a party outside Houston, where most of his friends and associates lived.

And this cop, this Lawson, looked like he'd never quite grasped the concept of humor.

Suddenly he wished he could call back his spontaneous laugh, because he realized now that it was inappropriate. "I'll be right with you."

He turned to extend his apologies to Longtree and Abbott, but they had moved away and were already at the exit. Longtree looked hard at Chief just before stepping through the door.

"Looks like your friends have deserted you."

Chief came back around to the detective, put off by his heavy sarcasm specifically and this crappy morning in general. Assuming his commander's stance and his most brusque military tone, he said, "What's this about? I don't know anything about a homicide."

"Gentlemen, perhaps you'd like to move to a more private area?" The hotel manager had replaced the maître d'. Discretion and the hotel's reputation being his uppermost concerns, he motioned them toward the exit.

Chief followed the hotel manager into an office, where he was left alone with Lawson. Were the uniforms guarding the door from the outside in case he decided to bolt?

He launched an offensive. "You want to tell me what the hell this is about?"

"The murder of Gillian Lloyd."

"Yeah, you said that. I never heard of her, and I resent like hell the Dallas Police Department for needlessly embarrassing me in public."

"You never heard of—"

"Isn't that what I just said? And—" He broke off, suddenly realizing how imprudent it was to be talking to a cop about a murder without a lawyer on hand. "Maybe I should call my office."

"What for?"

"Advice."

"Legal advice? Are you going to need a lawyer, Colonel Hart? Have you got something to hide?"

Chief ground his teeth in order to avoid telling Lawson to go fuck himself, which, until he could correct the mistake that obviously had been made, would be imprudent and inflammatory.

"NASA wouldn't approve of my being questioned about something as serious as a murder without having an attorney present, which doesn't indicate guilt or even knowledge of the crime. It simply makes good sense. NASA is very touchy about the public image of its astronauts."

"I'm sure," Lawson said drolly. "Go ahead, then, call."

Chief reconsidered. Maybe he was overreacting. He'd started off this day in a sulk because he'd awakened alone. Compound that with his breakfast appointment with Longtree. Thank God their business had been concluded. Longtree and Abbott were out of his life forever. But their final meeting had left a bad taste in his mouth, and he couldn't exactly say why. Then he'd been harassed and publicly embarrassed by a cop wearing a jacket that didn't fit. No wonder he was edgy.

Forcing some nonchalance into his posture, he propped his hips against the hotel manager's desk and crossed his ankles. "Okay, Detective Lawson. Who is Juliet—"

"Gillian. Last name Lloyd. Her nude body was found in her bed this morning. She was the victim of multiple stab wounds, most of them to her lower abdomen and pubic region. We think—hope—that most were delivered postmortem because it was a fuckin' bloodbath. In fact, her killer wrote obscenities on her bedroom wall in her blood." He finished snidely. "Do I have your attention now, Colonel?"

He did definitely have Chief's attention. Genuinely sobered and subdued, he said, "I'm sorry. Truly. It's . . . that's terrible. But I still don't understand why you're talking to me. I didn't know this lady. I never met—"

Then it all congealed. Moving slowly, he uncrossed his ankles and came to his full height. "Jesus," he whispered. "I just got it. Lloyd. Melina's sister? Her twin?"

Lawson nodded.

Chief expelled a long breath and ran his hand around the back of his neck. For a moment, he stared into near space, trying to absorb the shocking news and the rippling impact it would have, especially on Melina. Only a few hours ago, he'd been making love to her. Now she was somewhere in this city trying to come to terms with the brutal slaying of her identical twin.

He blinked Lawson back into focus. "Is Melina all right?"

"She's bearing up."

"I'd like to call her." Her number was on the itinerary. He'd already called it twice this morning but had gotten no answer. He had planned on calling it until he reached her, not just a voice mail. But he hadn't planned on calling to extend condolences.

"Not a good idea," Lawson told him as he removed his cell phone from the pocket of his leather jacket. "She's got more distractions than she can handle right now."

He hoped that Melina would look upon a call from him as something other than a distraction. He hoped she would welcome hearing his voice. But he wasn't going to discuss Melina or what had happened between them last night with this detective. Replacing his telephone he mumbled, "I guess you're right."

"What do you know about her?" Lawson asked.

"I only met her yesterday. She'd been retained—"

"Yeah, she explained her job to me."

"She's very good at it. Competent." He smiled at the memory of her at the news conference, bossing the reporters in a way they seemed to adore. The women as well as the men. "She's very capable."

Remembering her smile as she gave in to his pleas that she stay just a little while longer, he wondered if she was blaming herself, wishing that she'd left when she had first tried to go, wishing she hadn't been with him at all last night, castigating herself for not protecting her sister.

It was crazy thinking, of course. But people tended to think irrationally, and often with self-chastisement, when a loved one died unexpectedly, like in an accident. But *murder*? That would thrust someone's guilt into overdrive.

Backing into the edge of the desk again, he said, almost to himself, "God, she must feel awful." He raised his head and looked at Lawson again. "Do you know who did it?"

"Not yet."

"Any clues?"

"A few. The writing on the walls, for instance. That's what linked this crime to you."

"To me?"

Up till now, it hadn't occurred to Chief why the homicide detective had sought him out. Upon hearing the staggering news, his initial concern had been for Melina and how she must be feeling. He hadn't connected all the dots. But Lawson's last statement made the connection. It put him in the picture. He just couldn't yet tell what the picture was.

"I never even met Gillian, Detective. If there's any doubt of that, you can ask Melina."

"In fact, it was Melina who put us on to you."

He shook his head. "I don't get it."

"You will. We'll explain it all."

"We, who?"

"Me. Melina. At a meeting downtown. Two-thirty today."

He felt sorry for Melina, but for the life of him, he couldn't imagine why he was being dragged into her sister's murder investigation. "At two-thirty today, I plan to be in my car somewhere along I-45 between Dallas and Houston."

"I don't recommend that. You'd probably be summoned right back."

Chief gave him a long incisive look. "Cut

to the chase, Lawson. Are you suggesting that I had something to do with this woman's death?"

Lawson merely turned his back on him and headed for the office door. "Two-thirty, third floor of police headquarters downtown. Ask for me." He opened the door. As guessed, the uniformed cops were standing just beyond it. "You might want to call one of those NASA lawyers before the meeting." He started out, then paused and turned back. "You're too recognizable to hide for long, Colonel. Just in case that's what you were considering."

"You've demonstrated your faith and loyalty, Brother Dale. Far beyond my expectations."

Dale Gordon, speaking to Brother Gabriel by phone from his room, shivered with delight. His throat was tight with emotion. "Thank you."

"And you're absolutely sure that Gillian Lloyd has been properly sanctified?"

Brother Gabriel had a real way with words. The reporters on Dallas TV were calling his mission "an act of seemingly unprovoked violence." Gillian Lloyd's sanctification had made all the local mid-day news shows. They showed video of her house with policemen going in and out. They showed the gurney bearing her body being wheeled down the front walk-way toward the waiting ambulance. It had torn a bright yellow blossom off one of the chrysanthemum plants at her front door when it was pushed past.

The reporter standing on Gillian's street with her house in the background had termed his mission a vicious homicide. But the reporter didn't understand. Few would understand that it was necessary for Gillian Lloyd to be ki . . . *sanctified.*

"Yes, Brother Gabriel, she was sanctified."

"Did she suffer?"

"No. I was swift and sure, as you in-structed, as you promised I would be when the time came. I felt the strength and sense of purpose you said I would feel."

"You've done well, my son."

Dale Gordon blushed hotly with pride. No one had ever called him son before. His fa-ther had disappeared before he was born. Mother had called him many things, horrible things. Never son.

"Give me an account, Brother Dale. I want

to share it with the disciples here in the Temple."

The Temple! Brother Gabriel was going to praise him to the disciples who'd actually earned the right to live with him in the Temple!

The words tumbled from him. Never had he spoken so eloquently. With the same precision with which he'd carried out his mission, he briefed Brother Gabriel on it. He enhanced the basic facts with small details so that Brother Gabriel would realize how attentive he'd been to his task.

"To the best of your knowledge, you left no clues?"

"No, Brother Gabriel."

He didn't mention touching the drinking glass in the kitchen. It wouldn't matter anyway because he'd never been fingerprinted by police. Even if they found fingerprints, they couldn't be traced to him.

Nor did he mention writing on the walls. That had been a last-minute inspiration, one he'd thought of all by himself. Mother had always used ugly words. They were very effective to make a person feel low and worthless and deserving of harsh punishment.

He reasoned that Gillian Lloyd deserved to be hurt and insulted with ugly words. After all, she had tempted him beyond his ability to resist. It was her fault he had committed the sinful act of mortifying his flesh. With her so near, lying naked on soft sheets, he couldn't help himself from touching his nasty thing and rubbing it until it got hard. He didn't tell Brother Gabriel about that, either.

"Excellent, excellent." Brother Gabriel's melodic voice was like a soothing hand stroking his head. "Because you've done so well, I'm giving you another assignment."

If Dale Gordon hadn't already been lying in his bed, cradling the knife stained with Gillian Lloyd's blood, he probably would have collapsed from joyful disbelief. "Anything for you and the Program, Brother Gabriel."

"That's the kind of enthusiasm I wish all the disciples had."

Dale Gordon's pale body turned pink with a flush of pleasure. "What do you want me to do for you?"

"Not for me," Brother Gabriel said with his characteristic humility. "For the Program."

"Certainly."

"I caution you to think about it carefully before you accept, Brother Dale. It's a very difficult mission this time. Harder to carry out than the sanctifying of Gillian Lloyd."

Pulsing with a rare sense of power and self-confidence, Dale Gordon boasted, "I can do it, Brother Gabriel. Whatever it is. Give me a mission, and I'll do it. Gladly!"

CHAPTER 9

Can I get you anything, Melina?"

"No, thank you."

Jem looked at her more closely. "Are you tired of everyone asking you that?"

"A little," she admitted with a small smile. "A soft drink isn't going to help. But I appreciate your vigilance and concern for my well-being."

"No one knows what to say or do."

"I understand. Because I don't know what to say or do, either. I'm numb."

They'd arrived shortly before the appointed time and had been instructed to wait for Lawson in a small, cramped room adjacent to the Capers—Crimes Against Persons—Unit of the DPD. Groups of desks were clustered in the large room, but none of the personnel could claim an individual office.

Lawson had arranged for this room to be available to them. The furniture was uncomfortable, the atmosphere claustrophobic, but at least the room afforded some privacy. Already she was weary of people watching her with the covert, careful scrutiny given to someone whose stability is unpredictable.

Jem's eyes were red from weeping, and there were other signs of his distress. Ordinarily his ego and self-image were firmly intact. His air of superiority often put people off. This morning, however, he looked haggard and unsure. In deference to the situation, his conceit was taking a day off.

He reached for her hand and chafed it between his own. "Your hands are cold. Just like Gillian's. Her hands were never warm. I teased her about it all the time."

She swallowed a sob, refusing to let herself fall apart in such a dismal place. "I can't imagine my life without her, Jem."

"I can't, either."

"But she was in your life for only one year. She was with me from the moment the cell divided. She was like a part of me. She *was* a part of me."

"I can imagine how you feel."

Actually he couldn't, but she wasn't going to conduct a contest to see whose grief was more severe.

"Did you notify her office?" he asked.

"Unfortunately, they had already heard it on the news."

"Jeez, that's tough."

"They were devastated, but eager to help. Some of them even beat me back to the house."

Before Lawson left to contact Christopher Hart, he had asked Lewis and Caltrane to drive her home. Jem had offered to take her and stay with her, but she really wished to be alone, so she had accepted a ride in the squad car.

Much to her dismay, however, word of the murder had spread quickly and already so many friends, neighbors, and associates had arrived to offer condolences that there was barely space for Caltrane to park at the curb.

The group of mourners followed her inside, where they congregated in the living room. One of the realtors said, "I don't know if you know this, Melina. Yesterday Gillian secured the biggest deal she'd ever negotiated."

"Actually, she told me about it over lunch. For an ad agency, wasn't it?"

The young woman nodded. "We toasted her with cheap champagne before she left the office yesterday afternoon. She seemed so happy. On top of the world. Invincible. Little did she know . . ." Unable to finish, she collapsed in tears and had to be comforted by a coworker.

The refrain became familiar. Gillian Lloyd was highly respected and well liked. At least it seemed so, judging by the number of people who either came by or called to pay their respects and inquire about funeral arrangements.

Funeral arrangements. How could she even think about it?

Their parents had had the foresight to make those arrangements as part of their wills. Gillian and Melina had chided them for being so obsessed with death, and teased that such a preoccupation was macabre.

But their parents' attention to detail had turned out to be a blessing. They had died within three months of one another, their father's coronary following their mother's pancreatic cancer. In each case, all that was required of the twins was some necessary paperwork. They hadn't been burdened with having to make deadline decisions while grieving.

Now the thought of planning her sister's funeral service was daunting. "I can't make any definite plans until the coroner releases the . . . her body," she told the people who inquired. "I don't know when that will be. And I suppose Jem should have some input."

Gillian's friends and associates seemed as surprised as she to learn of the unannounced engagement, although it was inappropriate to gossip about that in the same discussion with funeral plans. They registered astonishment, but tactfully refrained from fishing for information.

Mainly, it was impressed upon her that, although she was Gillian's twin and her suffering would be incomparable, she wouldn't be suffering alone. She had a support group she could rely on.

"If you need me, Melina, call."

"Melina, please call if you need anything."

"I'm here for you. You know I lost my sister in a car accident last year. The suddenness of it is so cruel. Please call if you want to talk."

For all her friends' good intentions, she didn't know how anyone could possibly make her feel better. She had made them feel better by assigning them small tasks so they would feel useful. While coffee was being brewed and the telephone was being manned, she excused herself to shower and dress. Moving toward the bedroom, she heard them speaking in soft voices about how well she was doing, how admirably she was holding up.

Bullshit. On the outside she might appear to be a citadel of emotional fortitude, but on the inside she was crumbling. She turned the shower on full force. Then, with the hard spray to cover her moans of anguish, she let herself go and sobbed until her chest was sore from the contractions. In the tile enclosure where no one could hear her, she wept bitterly for her loss and for her complicity in the tragedy.

Temporarily spent, she had stepped from

the shower and made a stab at applying makeup, which was futile. She cried it off almost immediately. She dressed mechanically. Each small task was performed by rote. She moved as though obeying the instructions of an invisible hypnotist, automatically doing what she knew needed to be done.

She couldn't fathom having to make even the simplest decision, or reasoning through a problem, or going about the most routine daily business. Would she ever be able to lay her head on a pillow and simply fall asleep, or eat a meal for the pleasure of tasting it, or attend a party, or exercise, or laugh? Would life ever hold any enjoyment for her again?

Not as long as her twin's death went unavenged.

Now, seated in this stuffy room in police headquarters, she silently repeated to herself the vow she had made aloud to her reflection in the bathroom mirror earlier: Her sister's death would be avenged, no matter the cost to herself, even to her last breath.

Hatred for the killer smoldered like a nugget of coal inside her chest. She'd never been a vengeful person. She could honestly say she'd never hated anyone. Disliked, yes. Sometimes intensely. But she'd never hated another person on this level. She had never wanted to watch another human being stop breathing. The enmity she felt for this faceless, unnamed murderer was so fiercely felt it frightened her.

"Did you have a client today?"

Jem's question roused her from her malevolent thoughts. "Luckily, no."

"And you've got people to take over for you?"

"Fortunately. I notified them that I'll probably take several weeks off. They're checking our schedule and making adjustments. It'll be all right. The business won't suffer."

Jem bounced the tips of his fingers together in agitation. "Melina, I can't believe . . ."

"What?"

"I can't believe that Gillian pulled a stunt like that. That she impersonated you and went in your place last night. It doesn't sound like her to be that reckless and impulsive. It sounds like—"

"Like something I would do," she said, finishing for him.

"I didn't mean it in a critical sense."

"It's all right. I blame myself. If I had it to do over again, I never would have suggested it."

"Had Gillian ever done it before?"

"I told you. When we were kids."

"But she'd never taken over a client for you?"

"No, that was a first."

"Why last night?"

"No particular reason, Jem. It was a lark, an idea that occurred to me spontaneously over lunch."

But he wouldn't take her explanation at face value. "Was it so she could meet that Christopher Hart character? Did Gillian want to meet a celebrity? An astronaut? What?"

"It wasn't him. It was—"

"Never mind," he interrupted. "I don't want to talk about it."

"It was a silly, childish notion for which I take full responsibility."

"It might have been your idea, but Gillian was responsible for her own actions. She could have said no."

Her temper snapped. "Don't be angry with her! At the time, it seemed like a harmless prank. How could she know it would get her killed?" She yanked her hand from his and stood up. "Excuse me."

"Now I've upset you."

"I'm not upset, I'm pissed."

"Melina—"

"Her death is just a little too fresh for me to listen to criticism of her, Jem."

Chastened, he ran his fingers through his hair. "You're right, you're right. I'm sorry. I know you blame yourself. I shouldn't have touched that nerve."

"I've got to get out of here."

"Where are you going? You can't leave. We were told to wait here for Lawson."

"I'm not leaving the building. I'm only going to the ladies' room."

"I'll walk with you."

"No," she said, waving him back into his chair. "Stay, in case Lawson comes. Tell him I'll be right back."

"You're sure you're all right?"

"I'm all right."

But of course she wasn't anywhere near all right. In the bathroom she bent at the waist and propped her elbows on the rim of the basin, rubbing her forehead and trying to massage away a blasting headache that had developed after her hard crying jag in the shower.

Several minutes later a policewoman came in. "Ms. Lloyd?"

She straightened and turned around.

"I'm sorry to disturb you, but Detective Lawson wanted you to know that he's here. They're waiting. Whenever you're ready."

"I'm on my way."

"Are you okay?"

She nodded. "Thank you."

"Take an extra few minutes if you need them."

"I'm fine." An extra few minutes weren't going to make any difference. Smiling feebly and falsely, she gathered her handbag and left. At the water fountain, she paused to shake two analgesic tablets from a tin she located in the bottom of her handbag, then leaned over the fountain and washed them down.

When she turned around, she came face-to-face with Christopher Hart. He was standing only a few feet away from her. "Hi."

"Hello."

His half smile was private and sympathetic. He moved toward her but was halted midstride by a man who approached with a writing tablet. "Colonel Hart? Corporal Crow." They shook hands. "Heard you were coming in today. I'm part Indian, too. Choctaw. Could I please get your autograph for my kid? He's nine. A real space nut. What I mean is, he's interested in it and all."

"I'll catch you later, okay, Corporal? Before I leave. Right now, I'm late for a meeting with Detective Lawson."

"Oh, sure thing. Sorry to . . . you know, interrupt."

"No problem. I'll be happy to sign an autograph for your son after our meeting."

The man shuffled off, embarrassed.

Chief turned back to her and shrugged with chagrin. "I'm sorry about that. Sometimes they pick the wrong time."

Then he covered the distance between them in two wide steps and came so close, she could smell fresh autumn air and sunshine on his black leather jacket. He had carried the outdoors in with him. Before she realized what he was about to do, he brushed his thumb across her chin.

Reflexively, she yanked her head back.

"You dribbled some," he said, showing her the drop of water on the pad of his thumb. He rubbed it dry and dropped his hand to his side. "Melina, I . . ." He looked away from her for several seconds, then looked back at her. "Jesus, I don't know what to say to you. I'm sorry about your sister."

"Thank you." She would have ended it there, but he continued in a low, stirring voice.

"After last night, would you have ever guessed that our second meeting would take place in a police station?" He shook his head in perplexity. "I don't understand what's going on here. I don't know why you sent this detective looking for me, or how I fit in. Until I do, I'm making no judgments. But regardless of all that, I want you to know that I'm so sorry for what happened to Gillian. It's horrible." He raised his hands helplessly. "I'm sorry as hell about it. That's all I know to say."

Despite her best efforts not to cry, tears filled her eyes and spilled over.

"God, I'm sorry." Placing his arms around her, he pulled her flush against him and pressed his lips into her hair.

The contact with him caused two distinct involuntary reactions: She caught her breath in a quiet gasp. And her posture stiffened.

But he seemed not to notice either, because, with a suggested intimacy, he tenderly kissed her temple. "This must be awful for you. I hate it, hate it for you."

THE SWITCH |

"Anytime the two of you are ready."

They broke apart and turned. Lawson was there, looking square and rumpled. And curious.

Chief followed Melina into the room, which was already crowded with Lawson; Alan Birchman, who was the attorney NASA had retained to accompany him; and another man, who was introduced to him as Jem Hennings, Gillian Lloyd's fiancé.

Chief murmured his regrets. Hennings acknowledged them with a cool, curt nod that might have puzzled Chief had he not been busy wondering why Melina was acting like a stranger.

Although, under the circumstances, she was entitled to behave any damn way she pleased. She had lost a loved one to a violent and bloody crime. He wouldn't have blamed her if she beat the walls with her fists or tore out her hair. The shocking news she had received this morning justified any mode of behavior. So if her reaction was to withdraw and remain aloof, he could accept it.

On the other hand, he wanted to convey

his sympathy. He wanted her to know how sincerely sorry he was for what had happened. But she seemed determined not to look him in the eye. She hadn't since they'd entered the room.

Lawson was giving Birchman the details the investigators had compiled so far. The lawyer, whom Chief had met only a few minutes earlier, was a distinguished-looking man with silver-rimmed eyeglasses, a three-thousand-dollar suit, and a port-wine-stain birthmark on the left side of his face that spilled down onto his neck. They'd barely had time to shake hands and exchange business cards in the lobby on the first floor before they had boarded the elevator.

On the way up, Chief had thanked him for responding so quickly to the summons. "I'm glad I was available," he replied briskly. No b.s., no chitchat, no small talk. Birchman got down to business. "NASA gave me a rundown. What's your story?"

He didn't like the implication that his version was a contrivance, but he let it drop and matched the quick pace the attorney had set for their interview. "I met Melina Lloyd for the first time last night. She was my media escort to the banquet at the Adolphus."

"What about the murder victim?"

"Never even met her. Unless I'm here to corroborate Melina's alibi or something like that, I don't have a clue as to why I was brought into this."

"Lawson could have had you confirm her alibi when he saw you earlier. Are you sure there's nothing I should know before we go into this meeting? I don't like being blind-sided by the other side. I absolutely will not tolerate it from a client I'm representing."

Chief had curbed his anger and said stiffly, "After you," and stepped aside so Birchman could precede him from the elevator onto the third floor. It was then he'd spotted Melina at the water fountain.

Now Birchman again came straight to the point. "Now that we've all met, the first thing I'd like to know is why Colonel Hart has been asked to come here. If his deposition will assist in solving the crime, he could easily have given it in my office."

"Hold on," Lawson said.

Chief didn't blame the detective for reining in Birchman. This was Lawson's arena. It was his meeting. He planned to conduct it as he saw fit. He wasn't going to be ramrodded by an overbearing lawyer who probably earned more on one case than the detective earned in a year.

Lawson rolled his shoulders, straining the seams of his jacket. "Fact is, Mr. Birchman, all the introductions haven't been made."

"Excuse me?"

Chief shared his lawyer's confusion, and his resentful admiration for Lawson slipped. "You enjoy talking in riddles, don't you, Lawson? Will you, *somebody,*" he added, glancing at Melina, "explain to me why I'm integral to the investigation?"

"I thought you two should become acquainted." Lawson, holding Chief's gaze, hitched his head in Melina's direction.

Chief looked from the detective to her. She gazed back at him, her expression remote, revealing nothing of what she was thinking, and he would have given a million bucks to know what was going on behind those gray eyes.

Then he looked at the detective again and with increasing confusion said, "Melina and I met last night."

"No, you didn't." Chief opened his mouth

to protest, but Lawson, who was obviously enjoying himself immensely, held up a hand to forestall him. "The woman you met last night was Gillian."

It took several moments for the words to sink in, and even then he couldn't make sense of them. "Gillian? No, Detective. I was with Melina." He looked at her for confirmation. "Tell him."

She held his stare for a moment, then slowly shook her head.

When he got it, when all Lawson's snide little hints and Melina's unaccountable aloofness toward him finally coalesced into an explanation, he felt his features go slack. He took in her face, her mouth, her hair, her figure. He peered deeply into her eyes and was convinced that this was the woman he'd been with last night. "It was you," he declared in a raspy voice. "It was you."

"It was Gillian," she said quietly, as though speaking to him alone.

He didn't believe it. It simply couldn't be true. The woman looking back at him now was the woman who . . . who . . . Memories washed over him like a tidal wave. In one instant he recalled every smile, every sigh, every expression and nuance, every touch.

He couldn't mistake that woman for another. It wasn't possible.

She stood and came toward him, extending her hand. "I'm Melina Lloyd, Colonel Hart. I was retained to be your media escort last night, but my twin went in my place."

He stared at her hand as though he didn't know what to do with it. Finally he recovered enough to reach out and take it. It felt the same, dammit. The texture of the skin, the size, the way it fit inside his. "I don't believe it," he said, not even realizing that he'd spoken out loud. "The resemblance is uncanny."

She smiled. "We've been told that since the day we were born."

"But your voice, it—"

"No one could tell our voices apart, either."

Dumbfounded, he continued to stare. The hair, the eyes, the lips, were all the same, except that last night she'd been wearing makeup. Or rather, *Gillian* had been.

Gillian.

Who'd been found murdered that morning.

He sucked in a harsh, painful breath. "She's dead?"

Sadly, her replicate nodded. "I can't believe it, either. But she is."

Suddenly things were clear. Now he understood why Lawson wanted to question him. He was one of the last people to have seen Gillian Lloyd alive. Maybe the very last. Other than her killer.

Realizing that he was still gripping Melina's hand, he let it go and she resumed her place near Jem Hennings. Had they introduced him as Gillian's fiancé? Her *fiancé*?

Chief looked at him with renewed interest. He was glaring back at Chief, and resentment radiated off him like heat waves. He was red in the face and seemed to be vibrating somewhere deep within himself, like a kettle about to boil.

Though only Chief knew it, the man was due an apology. "I'm sorry." Then he added, "For your loss."

"You son of a bitch," Jem snarled.

Then he launched himself at Chief.

CHAPTER | 1 0

No one expected the attack, although, having noticed Hennings's suppressed anger, Chief should have seen it coming. He'd never been one to go looking for trouble, but if it came looking for him, he had never backed down. He'd been in his fair share of fistfights and should have recognized the warning signals.

Melina and Birchman reacted with outcries of astonishment. Lawson grabbed Hennings by the shoulder and tried to pull him back, but the man was throwing wild punches. Chief managed to deflect the first several swings, but Hennings's fist finally connected with his cheekbone. That pissed him off enough to retaliate. He took a swing at the other man, but Lawson yanked Hennings out of the way in the nick of time.

"Cut it out! Now! Hennings, what the hell?" The detective struggled to subdue him and eventually his brute strength won out. Pushing Hennings hard, the detective sent him reeling backward. Off balance, he landed ignominiously in a chair. Lawson yelled at him, "You pull that shit again and you'll be cooling your ass in a holding cell!" Then he tugged on the hem of his ill-fitting jacket, ran his hand over his flattop, and composed himself. "Excuse the rough language, Melina."

"You're excused. I was about to use some much rougher than that." Furiously bearing down on Hennings, she said, "What do you think you're doing, Jem? What's the matter with you?"

"I'll tell you what's the matter with me. If it weren't for him," he cried, jabbing his index finger at Chief, "Gillian would be alive. She was killed on account of him." His voice cracked on the last word. Burying his face in his hands, he began to sob.

Chief rounded on Lawson. "What the hell's he talking about?" he demanded. "And why didn't you explain the situation to me earlier? You could've told me about Melina and Gillian switching. I'd have been prepared—"

"Which is why I didn't tell you. I needed to see your reaction, needed to learn how much you knew."

Chief made no secret of his disgust with Lawson's tactics. "Or you knew it would make one hell of a show. Hope you enjoyed it."

Lawson ignored the insult. "Everything will be explained to you. But maybe we should postpone this until tempers have cooled."

"No."

It was Melina who dismissed the detective's suggestion. Chief saw tears standing in her eyes, but they were also filled with steely determination. Her hands were clenched into fists at her sides.

"I feel like doing what Jem's doing," she said. "I feel like crying my heart out. I don't want to be here. I especially don't want to be here for the reason we are. None of us does. But if this meeting will produce valuable leads, if it will help find my sister's murderer, then I'll cry later. I'd just like to get on with it so we can leave."

"Understood," the detective replied. "I'll make it as brief as I can. Thank you for indulging me."

"Thank me by finding and arresting the person who brought us to this," she said curtly.

The tight skin across Chief's cheekbone had been split open when Hennings hit him. He had stanched the blood with a handkerchief that Birchman had given him. It hadn't hurt at first; he'd been too stunned by Hennings's attack to feel it. Now the numbing shock had worn off. His mind was free to register pain, and that entire side of his face was throbbing.

Over the course of the last few minutes, he'd been bombarded, each volley more stunning than the previous one, leaving him no recovery time in between. The cut on his cheekbone had caused a delayed pain. So had learning that Gillian was dead.

At first he'd been temporarily shell-shocked. The twins' switch. Gillian's murder. It had been too much information to absorb at once. But he was now feeling the loss acutely, and it was far more painful than the bleeding wound on his face.

She was *dead.* That beautiful, exciting woman was gone, lost to him forever. One night. Not even a whole night. Only a few hours. But incredible hours. He wanted them back. He wanted her back.

It would be almost a sacrilege to weep for a woman he hardly knew. He hadn't earned the right to grieve her as Melina was. Or even Hennings. So he released his turbulent emotions in the only way available to him. He lashed out in anger. "What the hell did he mean by saying that it was on account of me that Gillian was killed?" He jutted his chin in the direction of Jem Hennings.

"Need something for your face?" Lawson asked with irritating calm.

"No! Hell, no. Like Melina, I'd like to get this over with sooner rather than later. For starters, tell me why this asshole thinks I'm responsible for Gillian's murder." He was surprised to hear his own voice crack. Maybe he was more bereft than he wanted to acknowledge even to himself.

He glanced at Melina and was surprised to find her watching him closely, as though she were trying to read his mind.

"Colonel, why don't you sit down and talk us through your evening with Gillian?"

Lawson directed him to a chair and gratefully he plopped down into it. The detective asked again if he wanted anything for his face, but he shook his head. "What do you want to know?" he asked dully.

"Before commencing, I'd like a word with my client," Birchman said. "We haven't had a private consultation. I insist on one before he answers any questions."

Lawson considered the attorney's request, then shrugged. "Sure. We could all probably stand a break. Clear the air. Hennings. Melina." He motioned them toward the door and they filed out.

Birchman pulled a chair close to Chief's. "How's the cheek?"

"I'll live. What do you want to talk about?"

The attorney took umbrage at his tone. "I advise you not to cop an attitude with me, Colonel Hart. You might be a top gun in your field, but I am a top gun in mine. You've flown rockets in space and you've been NASA's fair-haired child." He glanced up at Chief's ink-black hair. "In a manner of speaking."

"Get to the point."

"The point is that it won't sit kindly with the astronaut office if you've fucked up."

Chief was surprised by the man's blunt terminology. He was accustomed to foul language. Vulgarities were the second language of most military personnel. But he hadn't expected it from the natty attorney. He assumed that Birchman had used it to get his attention, and the strategy had worked.

"I'm listening."

"The image of a NASA astronaut is squeaky clean. Always has been. Sure, there've been a few renegades over the course of the space program's history, but their shenanigans have been kept under wraps."

Chief didn't offer an editorial comment and apparently none was expected.

"I had time to do minimal research on you before coming here," Birchman continued. "From what I can tell, your record is impeccable. You're popular with your supervisors and crew, male and female. You've got a hot temper, but once it flares, it dies quickly, and you're equally quick to apologize and accept responsibility for your mistakes."

"Please, I'm blushing."

The attorney frowned at Chief's smart-ass remark, but continued without breaking stride. "You're heterosexual. Never married. But you've kept your relationships with women—rumored to be many—private. Your longest-lasting romance has been with the media, which has covered you favorably from the get-go. Every time you appear on TV with your Hollywood good looks, natural charm, and articulate speech, NASA creams. You're their current poster boy. You make them look good, and they want to keep on looking good so taxpayers won't bitch to their congressmen about the big bite the space program, and especially its colossal flops, takes out of the national budget, money that could be spent on programs to house the homeless and save the redwoods."

"You're very thorough, Mr. Birchman, but all of this is moot since I'm retiring from NASA soon."

"Which brings me to what should be your primary concern—your future. Whatever field you intend to enter—"

"Undecided as yet."

"I respect that. Respect me for advising you not to make a mistake now that would obliterate, like that," he said, snapping his fingers loudly, "your image as a national hero. I assume you enjoy all the perks that go with that distinction?"

Chief gave a terse nod.

"You're a talented man, Colonel Hart. Intelligent. A valuable commodity on the open market. But let's be frank. A great part of your allure in the job marketplace will be your previous career as an astronaut. More than your talent and charm, et cetera, that's what you'll be peddling to the highest bidder. Go out with NASA's blessing, and any future you devise for yourself will be secure. Retire under a cloud of scandal, and it'll cost you dearly, every day, for the rest of your life."

Birchman paused to take a deep breath before going on. "Now, I don't know what kind of switcheroo those twins pulled last night. Or why they switched places. Furthermore, I don't care. All I want to know from you—now—is if I should be nervous about this fact-finding mission of Lawson's."

"No."

He studied Chief for a long, careful moment, then leaned back, obviously relieved.

"Excellent. Here are the ground rules. Volunteer nothing. Absolutely nothing. Exercise word economy. Don't elaborate. Don't tell them anything that isn't pertinent to this woman's murder. Got it?"

"Got it."

Birchman moved toward the door but paused before signaling the others back in. "Just to satisfy my own curiosity, did you realize when you walked in here that you'd never met Melina Lloyd?"

Chief shook his head.

"The resemblance between them was that remarkable?"

"You can't imagine."

"Melina, why don't you take this extra chair?"

Lawson held it for her and she accepted with a nod of thanks.

As soon as everyone was settled, he started with Christopher Hart. "You're not a suspect, Colonel." The detective paused, allowing Chief to respond. When he declined to take the bait, Lawson added, "Your footprint is much larger than the one we found outside the victim's house."

Christopher Hart's jaw knotted. Even from where she sat, she could tell he was incensed by Lawson's sly implication that if not for shoe impressions, he could be a viable suspect. But he was too smart to let the detective provoke him.

His attorney's pep talk had changed him. He seemed calmer than before, more contained. And something else—he was detached. Earlier, his disquieting blue eyes had revealed shifting emotions. Now they were inscrutable. Just as vibrant, but cool.

"What we'd like from you, Colonel," Lawson said, "is an account of Gillian Lloyd's last few hours."

Indolently, Chief motioned for Lawson to proceed. "What do you want to know?"

"When did you first see her?"

He explained how they'd met, then talked them through the press conference and banquet. "I never would have guessed that Gillian wasn't the media escort, Ms. Lloyd." Looking over at her, he said, "She handled it like a pro."

"She was very capable. And please call me Melina."

He acknowledged that, then picked up his

account of the evening. "When the banquet concluded, she returned me to my hotel."

"No stops along the way?"

"One. I asked her to stop for take-out tacos. She obliged me, explaining that an escort's job was to see to the needs and requests of the client. Right, Melina?"

"Right."

Jem spoke up for the first time since reentering the room. "For chrissake, can we skip the part about tacos? I want to get to the part that relates to the writing on the wall."

"Writing on the wall?" Chief looked to Lawson for clarification.

The detective was glaring at Jem. "If you don't mind, Mr. Hennings." He reminded Jem that his warning about a jail cell still stood, then turned back to Chief. "You had a take-out order?"

"Yes."

"So where'd you take it?"

"To my room at The Mansion."

"Gillian accompanied you to your room?"

"Yes," he replied evenly. "We'd bought enough for two. She admitted to being hungry. We ate off the coffee table in my suite."

"The taco stand didn't have any vacant tables?"

His exasperation showing, Chief said, "I wanted a drink. There was liquor in the bar. Bourbon, in case you want to know that, too. I had one drink."

"And Gillian?"

"One also."

"How long did she stay in your suite?"

"We finished our meal. I don't remember what time it was when she left."

"Did anyone see her leave?"

"I don't know. I didn't walk her out. Maybe I should have."

She saw Birchman give him a cautionary look, but it was so subtle that it had probably escaped the others' notice.

Lawson was saying, "So you ate. You had one bourbon. What else did you do?"

"Talked."

"Talked." Lawson screwed up his face as though trying to envision the scene. "Talked there at the coffee table?"

"Why don't you just come right out and ask what you're itching to ask, Lawson?"

"Okay. Did you sleep together?"

CHAPTER | 11

His answer was succinct. "No."

"Well, somebody thinks you did."

Lawson removed several glossy eight-by-ten photos from a manila folder he'd brought in with him and passed them to Chief. Unprepared for what he was about to see, he irritably snatched the photographs from the detective. But his pique was short-lived. A single glance at the first photo caused him to grimace. Raising his hand to his forehead, he groaned, "Oh, Jesus."

"May I?" Birchman extended his hand; Chief passed the first photograph to him.

He leafed through them all before passing them to his attorney. For a moment he stared into near space, then he focused on her. "Melina, I . . ." Lost for words, he let his expression speak for him. He raised his opened hands toward her in a gesture of helplessness before lowering them listlessly.

"Well?"

After holding her stare a few moments longer, he looked at Jem, who'd practically snarled the question at him. "Well, what?"

"Did you do what the writing says? Did you fuck my fiancée?"

"Jem!"

"You're offended, Melina?" he shouted. "Be offended by him, not me!"

"Perhaps Mr. Hennings should be removed."

Lawson ignored Birchman's suggestion but addressed Jem. "Final warning, Hennings. One more outburst and you're outta here."

"Oh, no, I'm staying," Jem said, shaking his head vigorously. "I want to hear what the space cadet has to say for himself."

"Anything I have to say, I'm saying to Gillian's sister." Chief's voice vibrated with an intimidating timbre. "Not to you."

"Jem, would you please calm down?" she asked wearily.

"I'll calm down. Because I don't want to miss a word Mr. Astronaut says."

Lawson resumed by asking why someone would write such things. "There must be some basis of truth to it, Hart."

"You're asking me—"

"Colonel." As though to stop Chief from speaking, Birchman put out his hand. Chief swatted it aside.

"That's blood, right?" he said, gesturing toward the photographs, which had been returned to the detective. "You're asking me to make sense of it? You expect me to explain what some sick bastard wrote on a woman's wall in blood after killing her?"

He snorted a scornful laugh. "I'm not a psychiatrist. And I'm not a goddamn detective. So how the hell should I know why he wrote it? How could anybody know? Anybody who could do this," he said, again flinging his hand toward the photographs, "is psychotic. Deranged. How the hell do you expect me to make sense of it?"

"All right, calm down."

"Like hell."

"Did you have sexual relations with Gillian Lloyd last night?"

"What'd I tell you?"

"You told me no."

"So there you have it. She left my room, and—"

"What time?"

"I told you I don't remember."

Lawson swiveled his head toward her. "What time did she return home, Melina?"

"Late. Sometime between two and three I think."

Lawson turned back to Chief, his expression sardonic. "Y'all talked for an awfully long time."

Jem seemed barely able to hold himself together.

But Chief didn't quail. If anything, his demeanor grew more defiant. "I don't remember what time it was when she left. I have no idea why she was murdered. That's it. I'm finished here."

He stood up, but Lawson barked for him to sit down. When Birchman protested, the attorney and the policeman launched into a heated argument. Jem shot Chief a menacing look, then retreated to a corner and put his back to the room.

Meanwhile, the gaze Christopher Hart had fixed on her didn't waver. His eyes were as piercing as laser beams. Whatever he was feeling at the moment—indignation, guilt, despair—he was feeling it passionately.

"Just a few more questions, and then I think we'll be finished with Colonel Hart," Lawson was saying to the attorney.

"These questions had better be pertinent to your murder investigation, Detective."

Lawson turned his attention back to Chief and asked if he had noticed anyone following him and Gillian the night before.

His arms were crossed over his chest. "No. But I wasn't looking. Why would I have been?"

"Did she phone anyone?"

"Not while she was with me."

"Which was for most of the evening."

Chief shrugged. "There were a few times when we were separated, so I suppose she could have called someone. I didn't see her place any calls."

"Or receive any?"

"Or receive any."

"Did she talk to anyone?"

"Sure. To everyone. Doormen. Parking valets. Everyone who attended the press conference. The people seated with her at the banquet."

"Anyone suspicious? Unusual? Someone who looked out of place at the function last night?"

"No."

"Someone she might have bumped into by chance? Former classmate? Old boyfriend? Neighbor or acquaintance?"

Chief was shaking his head. "No, no, and no."

"At any point during the evening, did you exchange cross words with someone? Did she?"

"No. Melina," he said, suddenly turning to her. "I know you were counting on me to provide clues. I'm sorry. I can't."

"If there was something for you to remember, you would remember it." She smiled sadly. "Even if an awkward incident had occurred, as Mr. Lawson suggested, you probably wouldn't have realized it. She would have handled it adroitly."

"Nothing like that—" He broke off abruptly. "Wait a minute."

She sat forward in her chair. "Colonel?"

"I do remember something." He thought on it a few seconds longer, while they all watched him expectantly, then he turned to Lawson. "There was a guy. At the taco restaurant. He was coming out as we were going in. He spoke to her. Called her by name. Called her Gillian."

He looked over at her. "She was damn good at pretending to be you, Melina. This guy used her correct name, but it never flustered her. When I asked her why the guy had called her Gillian, she explained that he had obviously mistaken her for her sister." He ran a quick scan of her features. "I can see how that could happen. Anyway, that's when she told me about you, about her identical twin."

"What was his name?" Lawson asked.

"He said it, but—"

"What was it?"

"Hell, I don't know. I wasn't paying attention to anybody except . . ." His eyes cut to Jem, who was listening from his place in the corner. Chief let his original statement drop and continued with, "I'm not sure that Gillian recognized him even after he said his name. They exchanged pleasantries. She passed it off as a case of mistaken identity, and I didn't give it another thought. But now, thinking back on it . . ."

"What?"

"I could be wrong, Melina, but I think he made her uneasy."

"In what way?" Lawson wanted to know.

Chief shook his head. "I'm not sure. I just get the feeling that he creeped her out. In fact, he kinda creeped me out. Strange character."

"How so?" Lawson had his notepad out, pen poised over it.

"His looks, for one thing."

"Describe him."

"Tall. Pale. Very skinny. Eyeglasses, definitely. Because they were so thick they distorted the shape of his eyes, and they had slipped down on his nose. But it wasn't so much his physical appearance that made him strange as the way he acted. The way he looked at Gillian."

"Which was?"

"Like . . ." He groped for the right words. "Like he was shocked, maybe even a little put off, to see her there. Especially with . . ." He hesitated, but after throwing Jem a glance, he finished. "With me."

Mulling it over, Lawson said, "And you're sure he thought she was Gillian?"

"That's how he addressed her," Chief

replied. "And she never corrected him, never passed herself off as Melina to him."

"If for some reason this man was affronted by seeing Gillian Lloyd with Colonel Hart," Birchman speculated, "I would say you have a suspect, Detective."

"But why would seeing her with me piss him off?" Again, he looked across at Jem. "Unless he was a friend of yours and jumped to the wrong conclusion."

"You're full of shit," Jem sneered. "Don't any of you realize that he's making this up? He's created a boogeyman to take the focus off himself. He's lying!"

In a blink, Chief was out of his chair. "You son of a bitch." Apparently seeing the wisdom in containing his temper and backing down, he turned abruptly to Melina. "Melina, I saw the guy. Talked to him."

She held his stare for several seconds, then looked to Lawson. "It bears checking out, doesn't it? If this man was as strange-looking as Colonel Hart described, maybe someone else remembers seeing him."

"Is that all you can tell us about him, Hart?"

He was pushing his fingers through his hair as though supremely agitated. His temper hadn't yet found a proper outlet. "Yeah. The whole encounter lasted maybe twenty, thirty seconds."

"Did you see his car?"

"No."

"Talk us through it again. Maybe something else will occur to you."

He reacted as though he might argue the necessity of the request, but then he looked across at her and his exasperation diminished. "He held the door for us as we were going into the restaurant. He spoke to Gillian. By name. I don't think she recognized him. It was one of those awkward moments when someone you're supposed to know speaks to you, but you can't place them or recall their name."

"We've all had those moments," she said.

"But he jogged her memory."

"Yeah," Chief said in response to Lawson's prodding. "I think he said his name, but if you held a gun to my head, I wouldn't remember it."

"Try."

"He said he couldn't remember it, Detective," Birchman said testily.

"Birchman, this is my inquiry, okay?"

They may as well have not been speaking

at all, because Chief seemed to have re-treated into himself. She watched as he willed himself to remember. His facial features were strained with his effort to remember forgotten details. His brain was a computer. It contained more information than an average individual could fathom—difficult technical, scientific, and aeronautical data were stored there, data that were required for him to do his job. He merely had to concentrate to call the information up when he needed it, as one would bring up a saved file on his computer screen.

"Even after he gave his name, I don't think Gillian made a connection until he said . . ."

The argument between Lawson and Birchman ceased. Both stopped talking to listen to Chief.

"Dammit, what'd he say?" He squeezed his eyes shut and pinched the bridge of his nose. "He said . . . from . . ." His eyes popped open. "Waters. Waters. That's what he said."

"Waters!"

Lawson looked sharply at her. "That mean something, Melina?"

"The Waters Clinic."

"What's that?"

"Oh, God," Jem moaned, grinding his fist into his palm. "I knew that artificial insemination was a bad idea. I was against it all along."

She shot him a look of angry disbelief but didn't have an opportunity to address his remark because Lawson had picked up on her excitement and was already repeating his question. "The Waters Clinic," she explained. "It specializes in infertility. Gillian was there yesterday."

"Ovulating," Jem muttered.

Lawson was surprised. "Gillian was a patient?"

"Yes."

"What for?"

"I think what is relevant, Detective, is that this strange man recognized her from there."

Lawson frowned concession, then stuffed the ugly photographs back into the manila envelope. "All of you are free to go."

"What are you going to do?" she asked.

"I'm going to check out the place, see if they have a weird-looking dude working there. I'll call when I know something. Hart," he continued, "I'd like for you to stay in town until we get this wrapped."

"You can't ask my client to put his life on hold while you solve a murder case," Birchman protested. "That could take months."

As he moved toward the door, Lawson stopped to address the astronaut. "Birchman here's right. I can't force you to stay. But I would think you'd want to. Not because it's your civic duty to try and catch a woman-killer, and not because you've provided our best lead so far and I might need you to identify this mystery man. I'd think that as a decent human being, a *hero,* you'd want to hang around as a courtesy to the other Ms. Lloyd. The living one. Okay?"

He lumbered out, creating a vacuum in the small room. Birchman was the first to move. He picked up his briefcase and nodded Chief toward the door. "After you."

Instead of following, Chief turned toward her. "Melina. I'm terribly sorry for your loss."

"Thank you. I regret any inconvenience this has caused you."

"By comparison, it's nothing."

"If you don't mind," Jem said rudely. "This has taken far too long already." He crowded up behind her as though trying to herd all of them through the door.

Birchman and Chief wove their way through the warren of desks in the central room toward the corridor and the elevator; she and Jem followed. Just as Birchman depressed the button, the same plainclothes policeman who had approached Chief before sidled up to him again, proffering a writing tablet and nervously asking for his autograph.

The elevator arrived. "I'll be a minute here," Chief said, quickly shaking hands with the attorney. He told him he would call him at his office later. Birchman stepped into the elevator.

Jem nudged her toward the elevator doors.

Making a spontaneous decision, she said, "You go on ahead, Jem. I need the ladies' room first."

"Well, okay," he said as he awkwardly tried to keep the automatic doors from closing and squashing him between them. "I'll be over later."

The elevator doors closed, but she made no move toward the rest rooms.

Chief glanced up and regarded her curiously. He finished signing the tablet for the policeman's son. "Thanks, Chief," the man said, saluting.

"You're welcome. Good luck to your son, to Todd." He shook hands with the cop, who then marched off bearing his prize.

Chief depressed the elevator button. "Going down?"

"Please. I fibbed about needing the ladies' room."

"I see," he said, although clearly he didn't.

They waited, each staring at the seam between the elevator doors. The silence stretched out long enough to grow noticeable and awkward. When the elevator car arrived, she was glad to see that no one else was aboard. He motioned her in and then followed. As they began their descent, she turned to him. "I apologize for Jem."

"It's not your fault."

"I'm embarrassed for him. He behaved like an ass."

"You won't get an argument from me." He grinned faintly, but she didn't return it.

"I also wanted to speak to you privately."

He made a quarter turn toward her. "All right."

"To tell you what a gutless coward you are."

He yanked his head back reflexively. "Excuse me?"

"You're a coward, Colonel Hart."

"I got it the first time," he said tightly. "Mind telling me why you think so?"

"Not at all." The doors opened onto the first floor, but she remained where she was. "Jem was wrong to attack you, but he was right about one thing. You're a liar." Before he could counter, she plunged on. "You were too much of a coward to truthfully answer Lawson's question."

"Which question?"

"The one about sleeping with Gillian. You see, I know you did."

C H A P T E R | 1 2

Chief slammed into his suite at The Mansion, tossed his jacket into a chair, and headed straight for the bar. He was tempted to have a bourbon but settled on a soft drink instead. He carried it with him to the sofa, where he threw himself down among the cushions and emptied half the can before taking a breath.

Not too deep a breath, however. On a deep breath he might smell Gillian's perfume on the sofa cushions and that would be too painful a reminder.

A harsh, choking sound erupted from him

before he could contain it. He sat up and placed the soft drink can on the coffee table, then propped his elbows on his knees and plowed all ten fingers through his hair and held his head. Despair settled on him like a coat of chain mail. He closed his eyes tightly and exhaled slowly.

Christ. How could this have happened to him? Why? What god had he failed to appease?

He wouldn't cry. Astronauts don't cry. People don't cry over the death of someone they knew only for a few hours.

But even though he didn't cry, his throat was tight and, when he opened his eyes, his eyelashes were suspiciously damp.

He retrieved his cold drink can and sipped from it as he reflected on Melina's parting words. He'd tried damned hard to stay angry. She had thrown down her gauntlet, then hightailed it from the elevator, all but carrying a banner of righteous indignation, leaving him with his dick in the dirt, so to speak, and when he'd tried to go after her and challenge her, he'd been waylaid by a man waiting in line to pay his traffic ticket at one of the teller windows the police department kindly provided. By the time he'd shaken hands to acknowledge the man's boisterous greeting, Melina had disappeared.

On the drive back to the hotel, he'd tried to fan the anger she'd sparked. She'd called him a liar and a coward. He'd been ready to throttle Hennings for doing the same. He had every right to be good and pissed. But he'd been unable to stay mad because his conscience wouldn't let him. He knew he was wrong.

Anger was a safe emotion. A burst of temper was familiar. He knew how to handle and control it. But this—whatever *this* was—he didn't know how to handle at all. If he couldn't even identify the emotion that was tearing him up inside, how was he supposed to get a grip on it?

A beautiful woman had been brutally slain. Tragic, certainly. But his involvement with Gillian had been so fleeting, he wasn't sure it merited this gnawing desolation.

Nevertheless, he couldn't simply dust his hands off and forget it. Lawson's lecture about duty and decency wasn't keeping him here. He had an ironclad sense of responsibility, but not necessarily to the Dallas Police Department. The detective's point about staying for Melina's sake was well taken, but even that wasn't enough to stop him from tossing his belongings into his duffel bag and heading back to Houston.

No, there was something else compelling him to stay and see this thing through. Something elusive. Something he hadn't yet figured out.

Finishing his drink, he returned the can to the coffee table, then lay back against the cushions. Consciously setting emotions aside, which tended to clutter any issue, he decided to approach the problem pragmatically, just as he would tackle a problem on the shuttle. He would deal with each element of this conundrum separately. The process of elimination would eventually lead to the source of the trouble, ergo the solution.

Taking it from the top, his anger was, to an extent, justified. He wasn't happy about being involved in a murder investigation for obvious reasons, but also for one reason that wasn't so obvious—it fulfilled a predetermination he had hoped to avoid.

All his life he'd been waiting for something awful like this to happen. He was a member of a minority, and, as all minority youths learn early on, he'd had to work longer, strive harder, be tougher. He had more to prove. He was watched more closely, the implication being that at some point he would probably screw up. So, he'd grown up anticipating and fearing his Fall From Grace—in capital letters. At least now that the Fall had happened, he didn't have to dread it any longer.

Furthermore, Birchman's private remarks to him were right on target. NASA wouldn't look kindly on one of its high-profile boys, who'd had an impeccable record up till now, suddenly being questioned by police about the ruthless murder of a young woman with whom he had spent the last few hours leading up to the murder. No matter the nature of that police questioning, involvement of any kind was bad PR. Very bad.

But dammit, this wasn't his fault. What had he done wrong? He wasn't responsible for how some twisted head case reacted to seeing him with Gillian Lloyd.

"Did you sleep together?"

Yes. They had. They'd fucked, okay?

How had Melina known that he was lying? Had he looked guilty when he answered

Lawson's blunt question with an equally blunt denial? Had she picked up his lie through twin telepathy? Or had Gillian told her?

Or maybe . . . maybe Melina was only guessing and happened to hit it right. Perhaps Gillian had switched places with Melina specifically for the purpose of gaining bragging rights. For all he knew, she had collected men like some women collected coupons. She'd wanted to check "astronaut" off her To Do list.

No. No. His own thoughts sickened him. There were women who racked up sex points, just like some men did. He'd been a trophy to women like that. But Gillian wasn't one of them. He knew better than to even think such thoughts about her.

The truth of it was that the desire between them had been mutual, and it hadn't started when they finished their tacos and had a bourbon buzz going. It had begun the instant they laid eyes on each other. From that first handshake, that first smile, the entire evening had been protracted foreplay that had culminated in them—

Dammit, he was *not* going to think about it. He would not. He refused.

To distract himself, he reached for his cell

phone. He called his voice mail at work and at his home phone, then spent the next fifteen minutes returning only the calls that were absolutely necessary.

When asked when he was coming back, he made up some lame excuse for his delayed return to Houston. They'd learn soon enough the real reason. It was only a matter of time before his name appeared in print in connection with a woman's murder in Dallas. Wouldn't the media have a heyday with that? Receiving an award from the SMU alumni association one day, being questioned by police about a homicide the next. And in between . . .

Hell. If all his thoughts were eventually going to come back to last night, he'd just as well go ahead and think about it. He'd been avoiding it all day, from the moment he woke up and realized that she'd left, until now. He hadn't allowed himself to think about it.

Screw her, he'd thought as he grouchily rolled out of bed. He had things to do, places to go, people to see. They'd had some laughs, some good sex. He was sore that she hadn't stayed through the night, but he would survive.

But after all that male posturing, he'd wound up calling her twice before his breakfast meeting and was irked when he got her voice mail. Then at the conclusion of breakfast Lawson had shown up, precluding thought about anything except the crisis at hand.

Now that he had the time to review it, why not? Maybe that would get it out of his system. Perhaps it would even produce another clue, some significant detail, previously forgotten, that would advance Lawson's investigation.

So your motives for thinking about it are noble? he asked himself sardonically. Bullshit. He wanted to think about it because he wanted to think about it. Period.

Leaning back against the cushions, he closed his eyes, and it was as though she were again standing in front of him where he sat on the floor beside the coffee table.

"What seems right?" he had asked, hoping that she shared his idea of the right thing for them to do at that given moment.

Somehow managing to look both seductive and ladylike, she had reached behind her neck and unfastened the hook at the top of her zipper, then gradually pulled it down. She lowered one shoulder of her dress, then the other, before letting it drop to her waist, sliding it down over her hips, and stepping out of it.

In his fantasy, he heard himself whispering hoarsely, "Damn."

"Should I take that as a yea vote?"

His answer was to place his hands at her waist and pull her toward him. He kissed her just above her bikini line, gently sucking her skin against his teeth and tongue. As she gradually lowered herself to her knees, his mouth worked its way up her body. When her black strapless bra impeded his progress, he reached behind her and un- hooked it, and then her nipple was inside his mouth, and her hands were in his hair.

His memory was cloudy as to how they got from there to the sofa. He just remem- bered wallowing entwined among the cush- ions, his hands trying to touch as much of her as possible in the shortest amount of time, and catching her breasts between his lips each time they got near his mouth, and her whispering against his throat, "One of us has on too many clothes," while her hands reached for the studs on his tuxedo shirt.

She pushed him back onto the cushions and knelt on the floor between his knees. Painstakingly she removed the studs. She chastised him and laughingly pushed his hands aside whenever impatience drove him to try and assist. But when his restless hands occupied themselves by cupping her breasts and stroking her nipples with his thumbs, her eyes grew dark and languid.

Finally all the studs were removed. She spread open his shirt and leaned forward to kiss his chest. The touch of her lips was as light as her breath on his skin. Occasionally he felt the damp brush of her tongue and the delicate scrape of her teeth as she worked her way down to his navel.

He held his breath now, as he had last night when she removed his cummerbund and unzipped his trousers. She slipped her hand inside his shorts. A mischievous smile had played behind her voice when she murmured, "No wonder they call you Chief."

Then he had exhaled on a low moan and had entangled his fingers in her silky hair, while her even silkier mouth had taken him, and he had virtually dissolved.

The telephone rang, jarring him out of the erotic daydream.

He covered his face briefly with his hands, then, cursing, reached for his cell phone. But even after engaging it, the ringing continued. It wasn't until then that he realized it was the room phone that was ringing. He stretched across the sofa to pick up the extension on the end table.

"What?"

"Colonel Hart?"

"Who's this?"

"Dexter Longtree."

"What do you want?"

He was being rude, but he was past caring. He'd said everything he had to say to the old chief this morning. He'd squelched any hope of their ever having a working relationship. At least he thought he had made that clear. Since then, much had happened. None of it good, all of it tragic. If he was in a bad humor, that was just too damn bad.

"Is everything all right?"

"Why wouldn't it be?"

"The last time I saw you, you were having trouble with the police."

"Not trouble, just—"

"If you will recall, I had predicted you might soon find yourself in need of my help."

Chief made a scoffing sound. "What, Longtree, you had a vision or something? Are you a medicine man?"

After a slight pause, the old chief asked, "Are you so scornful of spirituality, Colonel Hart?"

"What I'm scornful of is people who can't take no for an answer and who don't mind their own damn business."

"But you are my business," he stated without a qualm. "You and everything you do and everything that happens to you are of tremendous interest and importance to me."

Chief was growing increasingly irritated. "Then that's your problem. I told you yesterday and again this morning that I want no part of your group, that my interests and those of the NAA are incompatible."

"That we need you more than you need us."

"So you were listening."

"I was listening, Colonel Hart. And you made yourself very clear." He paused for so long that Chief was about to excuse himself and hang up when Longtree added, "I was hoping that perhaps you had changed your mind since this morning. That perhaps unhappy circumstances had urged you to change it."

A sudden chill rippled up Chief's spine. It occurred to him that his life had started its downward spiral into the toilet after his meeting yesterday with Longtree and Abbott. "Listen to me, you son of a bitch, if you—"

"Obviously you're still of the same mind. I'll give you a while longer to think matters over. Do so carefully. Goodbye, Colonel Hart."

"Wait a minute," Chief shouted into the receiver, but Longtree had hung up.

Chief slammed down the telephone and began prowling the room, trying to reason it through. Could there possibly be a link between Longtree and his sidekick Abbott, and what had happened to Gillian? Could they have sacrificed an innocent woman in order to create a scandal from which they would "rescue" him? That would certainly place him in their debt, wouldn't it?

He swore with a capacity that had taken years to develop.

If that was the way it had gone down, if there was even the possibility of a connection between Longtree and the murder, he should notify Lawson immediately. But what would he tell him, that he had a hunch he'd been set up?

Before he could decide on his next course of action, the telephone rang again. The old boy in the braids didn't waste any time, did he? Chief snatched up the receiver. "More threats, Longtree?"

"Who's Longtree and what's he threatening?"

It was Lawson.

"Never mind," Chief mumbled.

"Who—"

"The old man I was having breakfast with. It's . . . business," he said impatiently. "Complicated. Nothing to do with anything else. What do you want?"

"We found him."

"Who?"

"The weirdo you described."

Switching the gears in his mind took a second or two. He lowered himself onto the edge of the sofa and digested this new information.

Lawson continued, "His name is Dale Gordon. He works at the Waters Clinic. I gave the staff there your description, and they identified him."

"Did you question him? What's his story?"

"He wasn't there. Left a message on the office voice mail early this morning that he was sick and wasn't coming to work. I'm on my way to his place now."

"I hope it pans out. Good luck."

"I'd like you to be there."

"Me? Why?"

"Before I question some perfectly innocent sucker, I want to make sure he's the guy who spoke to you and Gillian."

"Isn't that what a lineup is for?"

"That would entail an arrest. This weird duck you described wasn't seen leaving the scene of the murder. At this point, he's not a suspect. Officially."

"In other words, you want me there—*officially*—to cover your ass in case you've got the wrong guy."

"I knew you'd understand. We're pulling into The Mansion's driveway now. You ready?"

"Good afternoon. The Waters Clinic," said the pleasant voice.

"Hello, my name is Melina Lloyd. I need to speak to a Detective Lawson with the Dallas

Police Department. He's supposed to be there. May I speak with him, please?" After a significant silence, she added, "I tried calling his cell phone, but apparently it's malfunctioning. It's very important that I speak with him."

With obvious reluctance, the receptionist said, "He was here with another policeman."

"Was?"

"They left about fifteen minutes ago."

"Did he take Mr. Gordon into custody?"

"What did you say your name was?"

"Melina Lloyd."

"I really don't know anything about this, Ms. Lloyd."

"My sister was the victim of the crime the detective is investigating. Did they take Mr. Gordon into custody or not?"

She had learned one thing today: Grief took different forms in different people. Jem was disconsolate, most of the time moving around as though he were in a mental and emotional fog, but also exhibiting periodic bouts of instability, like his violent attack on Christopher Hart. He seemed to welcome the solace of friends, while she had found it claustrophobic to be constantly surrounded by people wanting to wait on her. To escape, she again had retreated to the bedroom with the excuse of taking a nap.

She had lain down on the bed, but to no avail. Her eyes were gritty from so much crying and even closing them caused discomfort. Sleep was out of the question. Furthermore, her own vow for vengeance compelled her to act, not languish.

But what could she do? Disinclined to rejoin the others in the living room and kitchen, where there was an ever-growing amount of casseroles and congealed salads, she had paced the bedroom until she couldn't stand not knowing what progress, if any, Lawson was making. She knew the detective probably wouldn't welcome her interference, but she hadn't counted on catching flak from a receptionist at the Waters Clinic.

"Well?"

"They didn't take Dale—Mr. Gordon—into custody. He wasn't here. He called in sick this morning. I think that detective was going to his house from here." Lowering her voice, she asked, "What'd he do?"

Ignoring the question, she asked for Dale

Gordon's home address. "It must be in his employee file."

"I'm sorry. I can't give out that information."

"Please." But she was talking to a dead line. "Damn."

She sat down on the edge of the bed and hung her head so low that her chin almost touched her chest. God, she was tired. Exhausted. Between her shoulder blades the muscles burned with tension and fatigue.

Maybe she should heed the advice of friends and take a sleeping pill. Two. Three. However many it took to knock her out. Total forgetfulness would be bliss.

But that was the coward's way out. *Like lying,* she thought sourly. At least she had derived some comfort from Christopher Hart's abashed expression when he knew he'd been trapped in his lie.

But that was an avenue of thought that she didn't wish to explore right now, so she returned to the debate over the sleeping pill. What would drugging herself solve? Nothing. It wouldn't relieve her of having to deal with her sister's death; it would only postpone it. Besides, she hadn't earned a state of oblivion yet. She had much to do before she merited escape. But what could she do?

Then she had an idea. Kneeling in front of the nightstand, she opened the second drawer, found what she was looking for, and dragged the large book onto her lap.

"Gordon?" Lawson tapped again on the man's front door. When he received no answer to the second summons, he asked the officer accompanying him to call Gordon's phone number.

Keating had been newly assigned to Homicide. He was anxious to do well, especially in front of a veteran like Lawson. "I have. Twice. No answer."

"Car's here," Lawson noted. "What'd she say?"

He motioned toward the elderly lady who lived in the larger house to which the garage apartment belonged. She was standing on her back porch, leaning on a walker, watching with curiosity and suspicion while a Pomeranian yapped noisily at her ankles.

"She's his landlady," Keating reported. "Hasn't seen him today. Says he's usually at work during the day and doesn't come home until six or better. He stays home only on weekends. Highly irregular for him to be at home on a weekday."

"He live alone?"

"Yeah, and no friends. She's never seen him with anybody. Says he's quiet, pays his rent on time, only complains when the dog messes too close to his apartment."

"I was him, I'd've shot that goddamn mutt a long time ago."

Chief, who'd been following the conversation from a few feet away, agreed with Lawson. He was an animal lover and certainly didn't advocate inhumane treatment, but the miniature dog's shrill barks were like nails being driven into his eardrums.

Evidently making up his mind, Lawson said, "I'm going in. Get her inside." Keating jogged back to the old lady and, ignoring her protests, ushered her back into her house. Picking up the dog, he practically tossed it inside after her. "Hart, take cover. He might be waiting on us."

Chief moved behind the unmarked police car they'd come in. It was like watching a movie as the two detectives, with weapons drawn, took up positions on either side of the door. Lawson called out Gordon's name again, but when there was no response, he gave the flimsy door one swift kick, and it swung open.

The two detectives rushed in. Chief braced himself to hear a hail of gunshots but heard only the two cops shouting the all-clear to each other. Then for several minutes there was nothing but silence from the garage apartment and the muted barking of the dog from within the main house.

Eventually Lawson appeared in the open doorway. "Hart?" He motioned Chief forward. Chief noted that Lawson's nine-millimeter had been replaced in its holster.

"He's offed himself," Lawson told him. "It's not pretty, but I'd like you to take a look for ID purposes. From the looks of his place here, he was one sick puppy." He turned back into the house, saying over his shoulder, "Don't touch anything." Then he stopped and faced Chief. "You don't have a weak stomach, do you?"

"I survived the Vomit Comet."

"Yeah, well, this'll make that seem like a day at the beach." Under his breath, Lawson added, "I've seen more than my quota of blood today, that's for fucking sure."

The small apartment was stifling inside and smelled like a meat locker. It was soon apparent why. As Lawson had warned, there was a lot of blood.

Dale Gordon lay face up on the floor in front of what appeared to be an altar of some sort. His body formed a cross, with his arms extending straight out from his shoulders, palms up, his feet overlapping. He had slashed his wrists. Near the body, a wicked-looking knife was lying on the floor, along with his eyeglasses, as though he had removed them as an afterthought before assuming the Christ-like position. He was naked.

Lawson looked over at Chief. "That him?"

Chief gave a brusque nod. In the distance he heard a siren, signaling the approach of an ambulance.

"Lawson?" Keating stepped out from behind a curtain partition. He was holding a pair of boxer shorts in his gloved hands. "These match the pajama top you found in the Lloyd woman's bedroom?"

Lawson sighed in disgust. "His souvenir."

Keating extended them so that both

Lawson and Chief could see the dried residue on the fabric.

Chief's stomach clenched. Swearing, he pressed his fingertips into his eye sockets and rubbed them hard, trying to wipe out the image of the soiled garment.

Lawson asked Keating if he'd found anything else.

"Still looking." After bagging the pajamas as evidence, he returned to searching other parts of the apartment.

To divert his mind, Chief asked, "Is that the knife he used on Gillian?"

"The bloodstains on it will be tested against hers. And as soon as I get the ME's report, I'll know if the wounds are consistent with this type blade. I'm betting yes to both. He's our man."

Chief looked across at him, knowing there was more he was holding back. "What?"

"This was one disturbed dude," the detective admitted with a frown. "Before I called you in, we found a whole file of stuff on Gillian Lloyd, along with pictures of her. Inside there." He indicated the chest that had served as Gordon's altar.

"Pictures?"

"Candid shots that she didn't know were

being taken. While she was in the examination room of the clinic."

"Jesus."

"Yeah, that, too," Lawson said wryly. "He was some kind of religious freak. Look at all this stuff. More candles than church. Icons. A whip with blood on it. Ten to one it's his blood. A collection of apocalyptic literature. Real spooky shit. Looks to me like he was a man in conflict. A religious fanatic with a hard-on for Gillian Lloyd. He couldn't handle it."

"Especially after he saw her with me."

"I guess," Lawson mused. "He saw her at the clinic. Became obsessed with her. Built his sexual fantasies around her. Then he spotted her with you last night. Got jealous, freaked out. Solved the problem of not having her for himself by killing her."

A mournful groan brought both men around. Melina Lloyd was standing behind them. By her expression, Chief could tell that she'd heard at least a portion of Lawson's summation.

The detective asked what the hell she was doing there. Chief took her by the shoulders and tried to back her through the door. She resisted. "Is he the one who killed her? Why? Why?"

"You shouldn't have come here," Lawson said sternly.

"Outside. With me," Chief said, taking her arm.

"No!" She took a step toward the corpse, but he blocked her path. "I want to see his face!"

"How'd you get here?" Lawson demanded.

"Oh, it took some real detective work. I looked him up in the telephone directory. Get out of my way!" she cried when Chief again blocked her from advancing any farther into the room. She pushed hard against his chest. "I want to see him. I want to see her killer. I want to know he's dead."

"No question of that." Chief covered her hands with his. "Melina, please." He continued to struggle with her until she seemed to lose her will to fight. At the first sign of her relenting, he hustled her outside, where he gathered her against him. She collapsed onto his chest and began to sob dryly. He wrapped his arms around her for comfort and to protect her from the escalating chaos.

The wail of the siren died as an ambulance pulled into the driveway, where the

Pomeranian was bouncing like an animated powder puff and emitting earsplitting barks. The old woman looked frightened and confused and got in the way of the paramedics as they rushed past her pushing a gurney. "Did something happen to Mr. Gordon?" she called after them.

Neighbors were congregating on the tree-shaded sidewalk. They were mostly retirement age. The real-life drama being played out was more entertaining than the afternoon talk shows on TV. The atmosphere was charged with excitement.

Chief stroked Melina's hair. "You don't need this. You shouldn't be here."

She wrested herself free. "Why shouldn't I? He killed my sister."

"It looks that way."

"Then I belong here." Angry eyes flashed up at him. "But you don't. You made it clear by lying about your involvement with Gillian that you wanted to distance yourself from her. From all this. So what are you doing here?"

He explained that he was there at Lawson's invitation. "More like insistence. He thought he'd be questioning Gordon and wanted me to make a positive identification."

"Did you?"

"Yes. No mistake. It's the guy."

"Then you've served your purpose. Why are you still hanging around?"

Her rebuff shocked and angered him. He was here to help. He could think of a thousand ways he'd rather be spending a mild autumn day than looking at a naked dead man lying in a congealed lake of blood.

With Gordon's suicide and the evidence they'd collected, the case would be closed. He'd done all he could do. Lawson didn't need him anymore. Come to think of it, what *was* he doing here?

"Damned if I know why I'm hanging around," he returned, matching her vituperative tone. "But before I go, I want you to know one thing."

"And that would be . . . ?"

"That I hate what happened to Gillian. I hate it more than you give me credit for, and I hate like hell that I played a part in the tragedy." Moving his face down closer to hers, he added, "But I'm glad it was Gillian who escorted me last night and not you."

CHAPTER | 1 3

Lamesa County was the smallest in New Mexico, but it seemed vast because it was also the most sparsely populated.

Sheriff Max Ritchey liked it that way.

To some, the scenery through his windshield might have looked desolate. Not to him. To him it looked as cozy as the womb. He'd been born and reared in Lamesa County. He'd lived here all his life except for the two years spent at college in Las Cruces, a period of time he did not look back on with fondness, and his stint in the Air Force. He accepted an early retirement from military service, with no rank to speak of, returned to Lamesa County, married a local girl, and had three kids by her, one boy, two girls. He would likely die and be buried here.

Before becoming sheriff, his career history had been as undistinguished as his military service. He'd stocked and clerked in a hardware store, but after being passed up twice for an assistant managerial position, he quit and tried his hand at selling used cars and pickups. Sales wasn't his forte, either. That year had put a financial strain on his family from which they hadn't completely recovered until seven years ago when he landed a job as deputy sheriff.

He had served in that capacity only three years when he was approached and urged to run for the office. His opponent hadn't posed much of a threat, and Ritchey had practically been guaranteed a victory. Voter turnout that year had been at a record-breaking low. Nevertheless, Ritchey was as surprised as anyone when the ballots were tallied in his favor. He hadn't been contested in the past two elections, which he took as a sign that folks were pleased with the job he was doing.

He loved being sheriff, every aspect of it, from the smart brown uniform to the compact office he shared with three unambitious deputies. He liked cruising around in the patrol car and having people wave to him with an attitude of respect. He liked that he was permitted to carry firearms. He'd been taught at an early age how to use guns of all types, and his marksmanship skills were kept well honed by frequent trips out into the desert to shoot at the cans and bottles that his wife thought he collected to be recycled.

His shooting skills had never been tested on the job, however. Not in seven years. There was little crime in Lamesa County. Year before last they'd had a rape. A local teenager had picked up a hitchhiker on the highway. The drifter was long gone by the time she reported it. She was little help in identifying him; he'd never been caught.

A homicide had been committed on the reservation. A man had caught his wife in another man's bed and killed them both. The reservation's independent police force had done most of the investigative work, although there'd been no mystery to solve. It had been a clear-cut double murder, a crime of passion. Ritchey's role had been restricted to paperwork. As a rule, he let the Indians take care of their own business. He had no quarrel with them, and they appreciated his hands-off policy and wished every government official would adopt it.

Last fall some boys had been caught breaking into a rival high school for the purpose of shearing the buffalo-head mascot. Actually, that had been pretty funny, that bald-headed buffalo. The boys had been expelled for a few days, and their parents were forced to buy a replacement buffalo head.

Every now and then Ritchey would lock a drunk in jail until he slept it off, or settle an argument between spouses. That was about the extent of the crime in his county.

So it was with a great deal of excitement that he had taken the call this morning from a Senior Corporal Lawson. "Dallas PD," the man had said in the gravelly voice of a present or former smoker.

"What can I do for you?"

"I've been investigating a homicide. The victim was a white female, thirty-five years old."

Ritchey sipped from a cup of coffee as he listened to the facts of the case. "Writing on the walls? Ugly."

"It was that. We got our perp. A little too late, as it turns out." Lawson went on to describe the bizarre suicide. "Eerie as all get-out," the detective concluded.

"Sounds like. Also sounds like you've got your case wrapped."

"Just tying up a few loose ends. This guy, name o' Gordon, was your classic loner. Weird as hell, but above-average intelligence. Good at his job. He was a lab technician at an infertility clinic."

"You don't say."

"Got along with the other staff okay but kept mainly to himself. Didn't mingle or shoot the shit at the coffee machine, know what I mean? And other than his obsession with the victim, he seemed to have no interests. No bowling league. No computer games. No church groups. And that's what's really odd."

"In what way?"

"Because he was real religious. You know of a Brother Gabriel?"

Sheriff Ritchey laughed. "Doesn't everybody?"

"Well, I didn't. I mean, I'd heard of him, but I'd never watched his TV show or listened to one of his sermons until after I discovered Dale Gordon's body and started going through his stuff."

"What's a killer got to do with Brother Gabriel?"

"That's where you come in, Sheriff Ritchey."

As a consequence of that call, Ritchey was now snaking his way up the narrow mountain road that led to the compound at the peak. As a professional courtesy, he had agreed to Lawson's request that he have a chat with Brother Gabriel to ask why Dale Gordon would have placed ten calls to him this month alone.

"Why don't you call him yourself?" he'd asked.

"I could. But I'd probably get the runaround. People tend to freeze up, get skittish over the telephone, become suspicious and won't tell you squat. They know you. You might get more. Besides, this is only background, follow-up stuff."

Ritchey was savvy enough to know that he couldn't just barge in on the county's celebrity citizen unannounced. Brother

Gabriel owned the whole mountain on which his sprawling compound was situated. The last thing Sheriff Ritchey wanted to do was offend the famous evangelist, although Brother Gabriel took exception to being called such. Other TV preachers had given the word a bad connotation. Besides, he was unlike any other and resented being lumped into the umbrella classification.

Sheriff Ritchey had called ahead. He was expected. When he pulled to a stop at the entrance to the Temple, the guard stepped to his driver's window and said, "Peace and love, Sheriff."

"Peace and love," he said back, feeling a little foolish.

The guard looked him over, checked the back seat, and then returned to his booth and opened the electronic gate. From there it was another half mile (point six, to be exact) to the heart of the compound.

In addition to the main building, there were several outbuildings, among them dormitories for the people who lived and worked there. One building was a dedicated school with a well-equipped playground. The building with the satellite dish on the roof was, of course, the television studio from which Brother Gabriel transmitted his various programs.

The building without windows was the command post for the elaborate security system, which was necessary to protect a world figure like Brother Gabriel. It was said he had recruited his guards from armies and intelligence forces around the world, hand-picking the cream of the crop from soldiers and mercenaries trained to protect heads of state and willing to die if necessary to ensure that protection.

Brother Gabriel had legions of followers. Naturally, a man with that much power and influence over the spiritual lives of men and women had also cultivated many critics. He wasn't paranoid, but he was sensible.

He lived in what he called a "carnal" world, where lost souls were wont to do just about anything, sometimes for the thrill, sometimes for attention, sometimes for reasons that were permanently locked inside their troubled psyches. So the compound's security setup was extensive and state-of-the-art.

This was only the second time Ritchey

had been to the compound. He was a little intimidated. He knew his every move was being monitored by strategically placed video cameras. He felt eyes watching him from deep inside the security building as he alighted from his sheriff's unit and climbed the granite steps to the imposing entrance of the main building.

It was rather like a sinner approaching the Pearly Gates. He wasn't all that confident of being admitted. His heart was pounding with excitement and trepidation as he depressed the button to the right of the wide glass doors.

He could see the guard seated behind a console inside the marble foyer. "Sheriff Ritchey?" The voice came through a speaker directly over Ritchey's head.

"Yes, sir?"

"Could you remove your hat, please?"

"Oh, sure."

He took off his wide-brimmed hat and practically stood at attention. "Come in," the guard said.

He heard the metallic click as the locking mechanism was released. Pulling open the heavy door, he stepped into an oasis of pastel marble. Soft music was playing. The guard was uniformed, spit-and-polished, but he smiled congenially. "They're waiting for you upstairs. Take the elevator to the third floor."

"Thank you."

There were cameras in the ceiling of the elevator, too. Ritchey tried not to let his self-consciousness show. He concentrated on not shifting his weight from one foot to the other, on not clearing his throat.

After a smooth, soundless ascent, the doors opened and he stepped out. A man was standing there to greet him, whom he recognized as Brother Gabriel's right-hand man. Tall, erect, soft-spoken, immaculately groomed, a white carnation in the lapel of his dark suit jacket.

"Hello, Sheriff Ritchey. Nice to see you again. It's been a while."

"Mr. Hancock." Deferentially he shook the manicured hand that was extended to him.

"Brother Gabriel is waiting."

Without further ado, Ritchey was escorted into an enormous chamber that reminded him of the Great Room at Carlsbad Caverns, the one you had to troop miles through the deep, dark cave to reach. But when you got there, it was worth the time and effort. So was this.

Gold everywhere. Molding. Furniture. Doorknobs. Hinges. Everything that could be gold was gold. The wattage of the lighting was kept low, otherwise one might have been blinded by so much brilliance.

The walls of the room were royal blue, a shiny textile he figured was silk. The ceiling was one big painting. Like the churches in Europe that he'd seen pictures of. He didn't want to gawk, but he took a quick glimpse and saw a lot of puffy pink clouds and angels with wings.

The rug seemed larger than a basketball court, the desk bigger than a railroad car; the man seated behind it was larger than life.

Brother Gabriel smiled and motioned him forward. "Sheriff Ritchey. It's always a pleasure to see you. Would you like something to drink?"

"Uh, no, no thanks," he stammered as he took the chair Brother Gabriel indicated. It reminded him of a throne, with a high, knobby back of gilded carved wood. Not that comfortable, actually.

"Well, then." Brother Gabriel linked his

long, slender fingers together and set his hands on his desk. "Why did you request this meeting?"

Max Ritchey had never entertained a homosexual tendency in his life. In fact, he had no use for that kind. But he would have to be blind not to notice that Brother Gabriel was truly beautiful. Broad forehead, piercing green eyes, a thin, straight nose, full lips saved from being pretty by a cleft chin and square jaw. All crowned by thick white-blond hair. He was otherworldly beautiful. If the angel Gabriel came down to earth, he would look like this. Maybe not even this good. And he probably wouldn't be dressed as well, either.

Catching himself in a spellbound stare, Sheriff Ritchey cleared his throat and tried to find a more comfortable position in the chair. "I hate to bother you with this. It's nothing, I'm sure."

Brother Gabriel gazed back at him, mildly inquisitive.

"There's sort of a bond between officers of the law," Ritchey explained. "Like a brotherhood. If one asks a favor, you try to grant it."

"'Blessed are the peacemakers,'" Brother Gabriel quoted. "'For they shall be called the children of God.'"

Ritchey smiled. "Well, I've met more than a few who didn't act much like children of God."

Brother Gabriel returned his smile, showing two rows of dazzling teeth. "I admire keepers of the law. How can I help?"

"I got a call from Texas this morning. Dallas. A homicide detective named Lawson." He related the story as Lawson had told it to him.

Brother Gabriel displayed no reaction until he had finished. Then he shuddered slightly. "Ghastly. I'll pray for the souls of both the victim and the disturbed individual who killed her. Mr. Hancock, please add them to today's prayer list."

Ritchey turned his head, surprised to see Mr. Hancock seated on a divan on the far side of the room. He'd been so quiet, Ritchey hadn't realized he was still with them.

"Of course, Brother Gabriel."

The preacher looked back at Ritchey. "I'm still in the dark as to how this concerns me."

"Well." He shifted uncomfortably because of the chair, as well as Brother Gabriel's penetrating green stare. "According to his telephone records, this Dale Gordon had placed several calls to the Temple. Ten, to be exact. Lawson wanted to know if you could shed any light on that."

"But his case is solved, isn't it?"

"He said he was just tying up loose ends."

"Loose ends?"

"That's what he said."

"I myself detest loose ends."

"I'm sure it's only a technicality."

Brother Gabriel nodded in agreement. "Mr. Hancock, would you please check our telephone log?"

"Certainly."

Hancock moved to a wood cabinet that was as large as a mobile home standing on end. Behind the wide double doors were three computer monitors and an array of equipment. Hancock sat down at the built-in desktop and began typing on one of the keyboards.

"Fortunately for you and your colleague in Dallas, we keep records of all incoming calls," Brother Gabriel explained.

"I didn't figure this would be any big inconvenience to you."

"None at all. You declined something to drink earlier. While we're waiting for Mr.

Hancock to retrieve the records, perhaps I could talk you into changing your mind."

More relaxed now that his official duty had been executed with no unpleasant repercussions, Ritchey said that something cold would be nice. "If it's no trouble."

"No trouble." Brother Gabriel pressed a button on the telephone panel and a feminine voice answered. "Send in a cart of cold drinks, please."

The cart must have been prepared ahead of time. Either that or one was perpetually ready, because barely had Brother Gabriel made the request than Ritchey heard the door behind him open.

"Ah, Mary, bring it over."

When Ritchey turned his head, he did a double-take. Mary was in her late teens. She had a small, petite face surrounded by an abundance of glossy dark curls. She was dressed in the royal blue uniform of the Temple school. The color flattered her fair complexion, rosy cheeks, and dark eyes. She glanced shyly at the sheriff but kept her focus on Brother Gabriel as she rolled the cart toward the massive desk.

"What would you like, Sheriff?" Brother Gabriel asked.

"Uh, anything's fine."

The girl opened a can and poured the fizzy soft drink into a glass of ice. She passed it and a small linen napkin to the sheriff. He tried to keep from staring at her as he took them from her with a mumbled thanks.

Brother Gabriel patted his side. Happily obedient, the girl moved around the desk to stand beside his massive chair. He slid one arm around her waist and pulled her closer. He spread his other hand over her stomach, which was distended by advanced pregnancy.

"Mary is one of our special treasures, Sheriff Ritchey," the preacher boasted. "How long have you been with me, Mary?"

"Since I was ten," she answered in a small voice.

"I renamed her Mary because she reminds me of Renaissance paintings of the Madonna. Isn't she beautiful?"

Ritchey nodded dumbly. His drink remained untasted in his hand.

"She's done exceptionally well," Brother Gabriel said, his hand beginning to stroke her. "She's been an example to other children, a good student, a delight to her teachers. In fact, she's excelled at everything she's been taught. Everything." Playfully he tugged on one of her springy curls and she giggled. Then he leaned forward and laid a kiss on her protruding abdomen. Chuckling, he added, "As you can see, Sheriff, we're exceptionally fond of each other."

Hotly embarrassed, Sheriff Ritchey replied in a gruff voice, "Yes, I can see that."

"I hope to keep Mary with me here at the Temple for a long, long time. Oh, Mr. Hancock, thank you."

The assistant laid the computer printout on the desk. As Brother Gabriel scanned it, he continued to caress Mary's swollen belly, from beneath her voluptuous breasts to the lower point where it met her thighs, in a manner that suggested familiarity and intimacy. The girl gazed at the evangelist's bent head with absolute trust and adoration.

Max Ritchey's pounding heart was in his throat. The drinking glass had begun to sweat in his tight grip. He was appalled but fixated, repelled but fascinated. He couldn't tear his eyes away.

"Oh, yes. Mr. Gordon," Brother Gabriel murmured after a time. "Now my memory is refreshed. A very sad story indeed." He took the girl's hand and laid it on his chest, patting it affectionately. To his dazed guest, he said, "Sheriff Ritchey, when you tell Mr. Gordon's sad story to Lawson of the Dallas Police Department, I'm sure he'll be convinced, as I was, that Dale Gordon was a pathetic pervert and lunatic."

C H A P T E R |1 4

Two days after Gillian Lloyd's murder and Dale Gordon's suicide, Lawson was closing the case file. His last official duty was to bring Melina Lloyd up to date. He opened a can of Dr Pepper, took a pull on it, and placed the call from his littered desk in the Capers Unit.

After a subdued exchange of hellos, he said, "Lab tests confirmed what we assumed. Your sister's blood was on Gordon's knife. His fingerprints were the only ones on the hilt. They matched the ones we lifted from the windowsill and the glass in her kitchen. The semen on the pajama bottoms was his. None on her."

The concentration of bath oil found on her skin indicated that she had bathed recently, probably just prior to going to bed. Even if Hart was lying and they'd had sexual relations, evidence of it had been washed off. In any case, there'd been no evidence of sexual assault. Gordon hadn't raped her. Lawson considered that a small favor from the creep.

Melina said, "I don't question the physical evidence, Detective Lawson. I'm convinced, as you are, that Dale Gordon was the culprit. What I question is his motive. Why did he kill her?"

"I'm afraid the answer to that died with him. I've made an educated guess. Gordon was disturbed, one of those troubled individuals that unfortunately slipped through the system. He didn't have a police record. He'd never been in trouble. He'd had no disputes with neighbors or associates. He had a good job. In fact, when it came to science, he was brilliant. He'd earned a master's degree in biology at UT Arlington.

"But he was a social outcast. According to people we questioned about his back-

ground—teachers and former neighbors—
he had no male role model growing up. We
don't know what happened to his father. His
mother was a real trip. She was a domi-
neering religious fanatic who abused him
emotionally and I guess we can safely assume physically. Whatever she did, she created a sexually repressed misfit. Ever since
she died several years ago, Gordon's lived
alone in that derelict apartment.

"For whatever reason, he obsessed over
Gillian. Maybe she was once polite to him
and he mistook it for a come-on. Who
knows? The guy was delusional on many
levels, or why would he strike that crucifix-
ion pose before he died? Anyway, when he
saw your sister that night with Hart, it triggered his switch. He short-circuited."

"And stabbed her."

"Twenty-two times. The autopsy report is
more or less academic at this point, but I
read the pertinent information. The wounds
were consistent with the length and shape
of the knife blade. The fatal wound was the
one to her throat. It severed her carotid ar-
tery, which accounted for most of the blood.
Another went straight into her heart.
Eighteen of the wounds were delivered

postmortem. She didn't suffer for long if at all."

"It should have been me," she said quietly.

"Can't have you thinking that way, Melina." He shifted the telephone from one ear to the other and took a swig of the Dr Pepper. She would probably carry this guilt around with her for the rest of her life. That wasn't right. Or fair. Then again, switching places was a damned silly thing for grown women to do.

"How'd he get the pictures of her?" she asked.

He hadn't shown them to her, but he'd told her about them. "Through a tiny peephole drilled into the wall between his lab and one of the examination rooms at the clinic. Staff there were mortified."

"As they should be."

"Yeah."

A silence as long as a freight train stretched between them.

He cleared his throat lightly. "Just thought you'd want to know all this before I close the file," he told her.

"It doesn't seem . . ."

A victim's family was always reluctant to close the file. Even in an open-and-shut case like this one, they didn't want to accept that their loved one had died for no other reason than someone wanting them dead. The life of their loved one had been squandered on a fit of jealousy, or greed, or the whim of a wacko. He didn't blame them for rejecting the devaluation of a life they had held dear. All the same, he dreaded hearing the familiar refrain today. He was bone-tired, and there were already three other cases on his desk demanding attention.

But he liked Melina Lloyd. He also respected her. She had shown a lot of guts, and he admired pluck like that. So he heard himself encouraging her to say what was on her mind. "Doesn't seem what?"

"Doesn't seem characteristic of a socially withdrawn man to commit a crime this bold. It doesn't seem like Dale Gordon would have had the courage. The balls, if you'll pardon the expression. Was there anything in his history to suggest a latent violence?"

"No, but I followed up on some phone calls he'd made to a TV preacher."

"Which one?"

"Brother Gabriel."

"Blond hair, lots of teeth?"

"That's the one. Gordon was a fan. Or a follower, as the case may be. Brother Gabriel's headquarters is in New Mexico. The Temple, it's called. Anyhow, Gordon had phoned there numerous times, but there was a concentration of calls over the past month. I had the sheriff out there check on it."

"And?"

"He talked to the preacher himself, who remembered Dale Gordon. Now, this is a man who has thousands of people calling him, but he knew exactly who the sheriff was talking about. Seems Gordon would call at all hours—daytime, middle of the night, early in the morning. His phone bills bear it out."

"What was he calling for?"

"Prayers. Mostly about his lust."

"Sexual lust?"

"I'll spare you the details as related to me by the sheriff, as told to him by Brother Gabriel. Pretty sick stuff. Anyway, Gordon had called in the wee hours of the morning of Gillian's murder. He told the preacher he was going to do a bad thing. Previously, the 'bad thing' had referred to masturbation, followed by self-flagellation."

"Good Lord."

"As I said, the mother had done a real number on him. He equated sexual desire and fantasies about women, in this case Gillian, to sin. He probably resented your sister for arousing him. In his mind, she was his downfall. She was keeping him impure, which was in direct conflict with his religious fervor."

"So he graduated from masturbation to murder."

"It's twisted. Because while he probably resented her, he was obsessed. When he spotted her with Hart, he flipped out. Brother Gabriel regretted hearing about Gordon's suicide, but he admitted that he wasn't surprised. He had counseled Gordon that night but wasn't sure his message had sunk in. He said Gordon was farther 'round the bend that night than usual, so he assigned one of his hotline counselors to call him back a couple hours later. Gordon claimed that he was fine, that he felt much better than before, that his talk with Brother Gabriel had given him renewed hope."

"But he killed himself shortly afterward."

"Yeah."

"I'm glad he did," she stated flatly. "If Dale

Gordon hadn't killed himself, I would have killed him."

Lawson didn't sanction anyone taking the law into their own hands or exacting their personal brand of justice, but he couldn't honestly say he blamed Melina for feeling as she did.

He added the autopsy report to the file and mentally stamped it closed. "I think we've covered everything."

"Thank you for filling me in."

"I understand you had the body cremated."

"Yesterday. As soon as the medical examiner released it. I'd done the necessary paperwork ahead of time. There's a memorial service tomorrow afternoon." She cited the place and time.

He tried never to attend the funeral of a victim of a homicide he was investigating, unless the case was unsolved and he needed to see who among the mourners might be a viable suspect.

"I'm terribly sorry about all this, Melina. You have my personal condolences and those of the department."

"Thank you."

They hung up, but it was almost with regret that he added the file to the stack of others waiting to be stored. Closing the case meant there was no need for further contact with Melina Lloyd. He would have enjoyed meeting her under different circumstances. In a social setting.

Of course, she would never have looked twice at a short, stocky burnout like him. She outclassed him several notches. She'd go more for the Christopher Hart type. Apparently Gillian had.

Hart could fly rockets, but he couldn't lie for shit. The fiancé might have been duped, but Lawson didn't believe for one second that Gillian had left the astronaut's hotel suite without trying out the bed first. A guy like Hart didn't "talk" to a woman until two, three o'clock in the morning. Not a woman who looked like Gillian Lloyd. And Melina.

Reaching for the next unsolved case file, Lawson muttered, "Lucky son of a bitch."

Brother Gabriel was in repose in his palatial bed. His hands were folded over his chest. His eyes were closed.

Had they been opened, he would have been looking at the frescoed ceiling above his bed, which was similar to the one in the outer room. Both depicted his vision of the afterlife. His idea of heaven was more prurient than conventional religion conceived it. With the exception of the rays of sun piercing a bank of clouds, the painting above his bed could have been an oil rendition of a Roman orgy.

The women, captured in blatantly erotic poses, were all beautiful in face and form. Their apparel was diaphanous if there at all. By contrast there were few men, and all were physically inferior, looking more like eunuchs than gladiators.

The Christ figure at the heart of the painting bore a striking resemblance to Brother Gabriel, a.k.a. Alvin Medford Conway.

He'd been born in Arkansas forty-six years earlier, the youngest child of a junkyard owner and his wife who already had seven other children to house, clothe, and feed. Little Alvin didn't get much attention and was more or less free to wander the streets of the small town, looking for mischief or other ways in which to amuse himself.

It was on one such aimless expedition that he found the church.

The quaint little protestant church was located on the edge of town where Main Street merged with the state highway. The white clapboard chapel was set apart from the neat graveyard by a low picket fence. The slender black steeple had a tiny cross on top. Its proudest feature were the six tall, narrow stained-glass windows, three on each side of the sanctuary. Twelve rows of hard wooden pews were divided by a center aisle covered with a runner of ratty red carpet that led to the altar.

Behind the communion rail rose the pulpit, and it was behind this pulpit every Sunday morning that the robed minister stood above the congregation. As they desultorily waved their paper fans provided as a courtesy by the funeral home, the preacher handed down instructions to his flock on how to live. He told them how to tithe their paychecks. How to rear the children by not sparing the rod. How to be charitable to those less fortunate than themselves. How to stop cussing, drinking, gambling, and dancing. How to start witnessing. How not to covet your neighbor's ass, or his ox, or his wife.

If there was an ox in their town, young

Alvin Conway didn't know about it. He wasn't even sure what an ox was, but that point of the message was inconsequential. However, the remainder of that sermon on coveting was monumentally significant. It changed the course of young Alvin Conway's life.

But it was the stained-glass windows that had first attracted the eleven-year-old to the church. That July day, when it was so hot outside the sky was white, and Alvin was looking for something to do to pass the hours till suppertime, he'd happened upon the church. He'd seen it before but had never paid much attention to it. On that airless day, boredom motivated him to stop and take a closer look.

With his dirty feet planted in a patch of dusty weeds, as he idly scratched at the bull-nettle welt he'd gotten the day before, he'd stood across the road from the church and speculated on what would happen if he threw a rock through one of those pretty, sparkly windows.

What a hue and cry that would raise! He'd catch hell and probably the strop from his old man. His mama would bawl and carry on and say he was no 'count and would probably wind up in the pen before he turned twenty-one, like his oldest brother.

But it would be worth any hell he might catch. At least it would distract his folks from their ongoing argument over the shortage of money and over what to do about Sister, whose boyfriend had knocked her up and now was nowhere to be found. If the law dragged Alvin home, his folks would be forced to take some notice of him for a change.

He was still weighing the pros and cons of the vandalism when he heard the strains of organ music coming from inside the church. Bravely, he crossed the road, hardly aware of the hot bubbles of tar that burst against the soles of his feet. He crept up the steps of the church and opened the door, just a crack, causing cooler air to blow against his hot, flushed face.

Inside, a pretty lady was seated at the organ, concentrating on her playing. From an interior side door, Alvin saw a man come into the sanctuary. He began moving up the aisle, distributing books among the pews. Alvin later learned the books were called hymnals and that they had the music and words to songs printed in them.

"You're sure doing some pretty playing this afternoon, Miss Jones," the man remarked.

"Thank you, Pastor."

Pastor noticed Alvin peeking through the door, but he didn't run him off. He spoke to him in a friendly manner, motioned him inside, called him "sonny," clapped him on the shoulder, and invited him to come back for the services on Sunday. "I'll be watching for you."

From that first visit, Alvin attended regularly. He loved to watch the lady at the organ as she played for the group of singers he learned was called a choir. Her hands and feet moved at the same time. He couldn't imagine how she kept track.

The music leader was the pastor's wife. She was a plump, freckled lady who sometimes sang all by herself. She sang so hard and so high it caused her chins to jiggle, but when she stopped singing, all the men shouted, "Amen!"

But usually it was the whole congregation that sang. Alvin didn't know the songs, but he stood up when everybody else did and moved his lips, pretending to sing along. Some people didn't even need the songbook. They knew all the words by heart. When the collection plate went around, they put money in it. Since money was so hard to come by in Alvin's household, that was maybe the most surprising thing of all about church.

His family mocked him for becoming their little "Bible-thumper," but Alvin didn't miss a Sunday all that summer and beyond, when the funeral home fans with the face of Jesus—not the cuss-word Jesus, another one that lived in heaven with God and the Holy Ghost—were replaced by space heaters to ward off the cold inside the sanctuary.

But the pastor's sermons were the real source of heat. They warmed everybody who listened, no matter the season or the temperature. He commanded attention with his voice. When he was talking, the people in the pews seemed not to notice how hard the benches were or how loud their bellies growled when it came on to lunchtime. They listened to every word he preached. Even though he sometimes scolded them for their sinful ways and wicked lusts, they loved him and came back every Sunday for more.

One Sunday not long after Alvin had been baptized into the family of believers, the preacher delivered that blistering sermon on coveting. Coveting, Alvin learned, meant wanting stuff you couldn't have. He was thinking along the lines of a catcher's mitt, or a bicycle, or the deer rifle one of his older brothers had mysteriously come by recently.

But as he listened he realized that coveting extended to lots of things, even women. The preacher really got wound up about some guy named King David and a lady he watched taking a bath. Although Alvin didn't understand all the details, he caught the gist of it: You shouldn't go dipping your wick into pussy that didn't belong to you.

Some things his brothers could say a lot plainer than the preacher could.

The following week, on the last day of May, Alvin Medford Conway turned twelve. The first of June marked the final day of school. He celebrated the start of summer vacation by going fishing. When he reached his favorite spot by the creek, he was disappointed to see a car parked nearby under a large shady elm. Somebody was poaching on his favorite fishing hole.

But then he recognized the car as the one Pastor drove when he visited the sick and needy and backslid. If he must share his fishing hole with anybody, at least it was with Pastor, whom he admired for the power he had over people.

But just as Alvin was about to call out a hello, he heard sounds that he knew had nothing to do with fishing.

CHAPTER | 1 5

Walking quietly, Alvin moved closer until he could see the couple lying on a quilt in the grass, fucking for all they were worth. Alvin knew all about it. One evening when he was about seven years old, he'd noticed his brothers whispering among themselves and knew they were up to something. When they trooped from the house after supper, he'd trailed them to this ol' gal's place and watched through the open window as one after the other took his turn on top of her.

One of his brothers discovered the Peeping Tom, dragged him inside, and clouted him in the head for being a sneak. But the others had laughed and teased him and asked him what he'd thought about what he'd seen them doing, and Alvin grinned and said that it looked okay to him, and they'd laughed even harder and, together with the ol' gal, gave him a demonstration. Since then, he'd known all about fucking.

He hadn't figured on Pastor doing it for fun, though. Not out in the open and in the afternoon. He figured him and his wife would do it in the dark, under the covers, after praying first. But Pastor fucked pretty much the same as his brothers. At first it struck Alvin as funny to see Pastor's white butt pumping up and down.

But then he noticed the shapeliness of the legs wrapped around that white butt. He sure wouldn't have thought that a lady as plump as Pastor's wife would have legs that nice and slender. And then he realized that the arms twined around Pastor's neck weren't freckled.

It wasn't Pastor's wife on the receiving end of that vigorous pumping. It was Miss Jones, the organist.

The discovery upset Alvin so badly that he

didn't fish that day or the next. He found solitude in a wrecked auto, abandoned and forgotten in the far back lot of his old man's junkyard. The bottom of the chassis was rusted out and had johnsongrass growing up through it. The faded wool upholstery was scratchy and hot, but Alvin sat inside that old car half of one day and all the next, feeling angry and betrayed.

Pastor was a stinking fraud. Pastor was doing the very thing he'd hollered and yelled against. Pastor was no better than Alvin's godforsaken brothers, who drank and smoked and cussed and gambled and danced and fornicated and didn't care if they were going to hell or not.

Alvin seriously considered standing up in church come Sunday morning and telling all the faithful about their pastor and Miss Jones and what all he'd watched them doing to each other down at the creek.

But his initial feeling of betrayal was gradually nudged aside by a stronger emotion: admiration.

Pastor had everybody believing that he had a pipeline straight to the Almighty. Pastor preached about fire and brimstone for the wicked of the world, but he hadn't looked too worried about hell when he'd been porking Miss Jones down at the creek in broad daylight. Pastor had the best of both worlds. Pastor had the ticket. He had the key. He'd found the answer to a happy life.

Unknowingly, that fallen man of the cloth directed the course of Alvin Medford Conway's life.

He'd known instinctually that he was destined for greatness. Before, he hadn't known how he was going to achieve it. Now he had direction. He recalled all those people coming back Sunday after Sunday to be upbraided for their sinful ways and lack of faith. He remembered how they couldn't take their eyes off the man in the pulpit, how his passion had kept them riveted to the hard pews, how they hugged him on the steps of the church afterward, telling him how important he was to their lives. They brought him little tokens of appreciation. They entrusted him with their souls.

Pastor smiled and clasped their hands and accepted their gifts and their trust as his due. Pastor had the right idea, brother. Hallelujah and amen.

The following August, Miss Jones left

town suddenly. It was whispered that she was "in trouble" and had gone to live with relatives in Oklahoma. Pastor and his plump wife, pregnant with their fourth child, were transferred to another church in another town. The congregation was disconsolate. They wept on his last Sunday and gave him a generous love offering.

His replacement was older and uglier. His sermons were dry as talcum, and Alvin doubted he could get anybody to diddle him, especially his stick of a wife, who had a face like a prune but a disposition that suggested chronic constipation.

Alvin stopped going to church, but he began to practice preaching in front of his mirror and down at the fishing hole. He worked on eliminating the regional accent from his speech and exercised his voice until he sounded like the men on the TV. He rehearsed hand gestures. He composed stirring prayers and committed key scriptures to memory.

When he was fourteen, he got a chance to audition his skills. A girl in his tenth-grade English class invited him to a revival service at her church. When people in the congregation were invited to give impromptu testimonies, he stood and delivered one that didn't leave a dry eye in the crowd.

That night as they were driving home, Alvin claimed that he'd been moved by the spirit to stop right where they were and pray. So the girl pulled off the road into a grove of trees and they climbed into the bed of her daddy's pickup, which had been loaned to her for the evening, and commenced their spontaneous prayer meeting.

They hadn't been praying long when the spirit moved Alvin to worship at the altar of her body. Which involved putting his face between her thighs. She, in turn, worshiped his body in a similar manner. She went home thinking that God surely did work in mysterious ways. And Alvin went home knowing that he was on to something great.

Thirty-two years later, lying in a bed with a golden headboard, he smiled to himself, remembering the scrawny kid he'd been, with dirty bare feet sticky with black road tar, fighting with his siblings over the last piece of fried chicken.

Now he had personal chefs preparing his meals. He had a physical trainer to see that the rich food didn't go to fat. He had a tailor who fashioned a wardrobe to show off his perfect physique.

He loved his body, loved the implied strength beneath this taut skin. His chest was wide, covered with hair that looked like it had been dipped in gold. Idly, he feathered his fingers across it, enjoying the crisp, virile feel of it.

Luxuriantly, he stretched his long, well-muscled limbs, flexing and relaxing them alternately. He raised his hands toward the ceiling and studied them. They looked strong enough to bend steel, but tender enough to cradle a newborn.

Appropriately, he thought with a slow smile as his hand stole down to his sex. His testicals were as firm as they'd been that night he took the spirit-filled girl in the bed of her daddy's pickup. He stroked his penis and felt it filling with blood, lengthening, hardening.

The woman beside him stirred and came awake. She sat up and smiled down at him. She'd had one child. Her nipples were large and brown. He preferred them smaller and pinker, more virginal, but one had to make some sacrifices.

She came up on her knees and was about

to straddle him, but he stopped her. "Only your mouth this time. Very slowly."

Closing his eyes, he let his mind drift and, again, his mind carried him back to Alvin. What ripple in the Conway gene pool had made him so handsome? he wondered. He could barely remember what any of his family had looked like, but his recollections weren't of a particularly comely brood.

He had left home shortly after high school graduation and had never looked back. He hadn't even told anyone that he was leaving. For a time he had wondered what they'd thought when they awakened one morning to find him gone, or if they'd even noticed. Probably not for a day or two, and then they probably had chalked up his disappearance to drowning or something. One less mouth to feed.

His parents were probably dead by now, but surely he had siblings still living. Had any of them recognized him on TV? No. If they had, they would have come asking him for money by now.

He'd definitely been the best-looking of the litter, but he recalled being constantly teased about his towhead. He'd hated his hair then, but now was glad it hadn't darkened with maturity. The golden white color had become his trademark. It prompted favorable comparisons to Michael the Archangel or Gabriel the Herald, from which he'd taken his name.

But that hadn't come until later, much later, after he'd worked his way through college and seminary. He had enrolled just so he could learn the basics, but as it turned out, he had enjoyed the studies more than he had guessed he would. He had applied himself and spent as much time learning the nonbelievers' credo as the theology. He was going to be crusading for one side. If he wanted to win, he had to know his opponents' strengths.

Straight out of seminary, he accepted a job pastoring a church. It soon became apparent, however, that his talents were wasted on one dreary little congregation. He tired of listening to woes, christening children, visiting the sick, and burying the dead. It was amusingly easy to manipulate people into feeding him Sunday dinners and giving him love offerings. It was only slightly more challenging to deflower their daughters. He was destined for bigger and better. Why limit himself to the small-time?

He moved to a bigger city, a bigger church. The only difference there was the quality of the Sunday dinners and the size of the love offerings. The daughters were pretty much the same everywhere. All loved screwing him, of course. But what they really got off on was bearing the secret that they'd been the pastor's downfall, the one woman who'd brought him to his knees in contrition and almost caused him to give up the ministry. They loved playing Jezebel and Delilah. The more wicked they believed themselves to be, the more enjoyable it was.

The third church he pastored had coffers large enough to broadcast the Sunday morning services on a local channel. Soon they were winning their time slot—in TV vernacular—and went regional. That was so successful that he resigned his pulpit at the church and went into full-time TV evangelism. Why restrict it to statewide? Why not go national? Global?

And the rest, folks, is history.

He wanted to laugh out loud, but it was hard to laugh when you were getting damn good head.

Today Brother Gabriel's ministry was a multimillion-dollar ministry. Alvin Medford

Conway had minions all over the world begging to do his bidding. He exercised mind control over hordes of followers, wielding as much, and maybe more, influence over people's thinking than any head of state.

Last year he'd appeared with the Pope at a worldwide religious conference in Belgium. The old man hadn't received nearly the cheer when he was introduced that Brother Gabriel had. The Pope and every other religious leader represented the past.

Brother Gabriel was the future, the hope of the new millennium. His power was seemingly unlimited. But more important, he had a masterful plan for gaining even more.

"Brother Gabriel?"

He opened his eyes in response to Mr. Hancock's voice coming from the invisible intercom system. "Yes?"

"I apologize for bothering you, but the call you've been expecting has just come in. Do you want to take it?"

"Give me five minutes."

"Certainly."

"Shall I finish, Brother Gabriel?"

He grinned at the woman and guided her head back down. "Certainly."

"Are you collecting?"

"Not tonight."

The waste was selfish, but even men in power couldn't be expected to work all the time.

After blessing the woman and kissing her cheek fondly, he had sent her back to the dormitory where she shared a room with her child. Showered and wrapped in a thick white terrycloth robe, he emerged from his bedchamber and moved to his desk. Precisely five minutes after he'd been informed of the call, he depressed the blinking button on the telephone.

"This is Brother Gabriel."

Even on speaker phone, he wasn't worried about being overheard. The room had been soundproofed and was swept for listening devices three times a day. His computer and telephone systems also had security safeguards that were frequently updated to keep abreast of the advancing technology . . . and constantly monitored to prevent betrayal by anyone inside the compound.

After a brief exchange of pleasantries, the

caller said, "I've got good news and better news, Brother Gabriel."

Mr. Hancock set a brandy snifter in front of him. He acknowledged the favor with a nod. "I'm listening."

"The case on Dale Gordon has been officially closed. As far as DPD is concerned, Gillian Lloyd's murder case is resolved."

"That is good news."

"Dale Gordon served his purpose."

"He served it well. He was obedient to the end. But he can easily be replaced. I'm already working on it. I hate losing Gillian Lloyd, though. She seemed to be a perfect candidate."

"Which brings me to the better news." Brother Gabriel indulged him a dramatic pause. "You seem to have forgotten a fact in Gillian Lloyd's dossier. She has a twin."

"A twin?" In spite of his relaxed posture, Brother Gabriel's heart quickened. He *had* forgotten that. At the time he read the information, it had seemed irrelevant. But now!

"Identical. Melina is her name."

"Melina." He liked the sound of it. It sounded almost biblical. "This should be pursued. What kind of obstacles are we facing?"

"Few, I would think."

"Is she married?"

"No. No significant other at this time, either. The twins were extremely close, so she's despondent over Gillian's death. She's in desperate need of some tender, loving care."

Brother Gabriel chuckled. "How ideal for you."

"That was my thought, too. There is one hitch."

A thousand miles away, Brother Gabriel frowned. Lifting the snifter to his lips, he deeply inhaled its bouquet before sipping. "Hitch?"

"Christopher Hart."

Brother Gabriel's frown was drawn even steeper. "What about him?"

"I think she could be attracted to him."

In a voice vibrating with anger, he said, "This man defiled one of our best candidates. I refuse to lose another to him."

"I could be wrong. I hope I am. But I picked up some vibes. I thought you'd want to know that he could be a hindrance. Possibly our only one."

Brother Gabriel took another sip of brandy and held it in his mouth a long time before swallowing. Quietly, he said, "Then something should be done about it."

"I'll see to it."

"Excellent. You've done well and you will be rewarded, Mr. Hennings."

"Thank you, Brother Gabriel."

"Peace and love."

After disconnecting, Brother Gabriel asked Mr. Hancock to bring him the file on Gillian Lloyd. "It's all on diskette, Brother Gabriel."

"Load it for me, please."

He moved to the computer cabinet and idly sipped his brandy while Mr. Hancock called up the coded file. When her photograph appeared on his computer screen, Mr. Hancock commented on the injustice of losing her. "Do you think her sister will be as desirable?"

"You heard Mr. Hennings, and he should know."

Wishing to be alone with her, he waved Mr. Hancock away. He sat down in front of the screen and read the data gleaned from the files of the Waters Clinic. Having refreshed his memory on Gillian's vital statistics, he was as warmed by the pleasure of knowing she had an identical twin as he was by the expensive brandy.

He touched the screen but imagined the feel of her cheek against his fingertips. "Melina," he whispered seductively, as though speaking to a lover. "You will do me well."

CHAPTER | 16

I'm surprised by the turnout."

The chapel was filled to capacity, with standing room remaining only in the back. Jem Hennings glanced over his shoulder at the growing crowd. "I don't know why you're surprised, Melina. Gillian had a lot of friends. You couldn't have known them all."

"I just meant that she would be gratified by the number of people who came."

"I've never seen so many flowers."

"They're beautiful, aren't they? I'm having them sent to a nursing home following the service. There's no room left for them at the house, and it would be a shame to waste them."

"What surprises me is the religious nature of the service," he said, scanning the printed program.

She looked at him with amazement. "You were Gillian's fiancé, but you didn't know that she had a profound faith?"

"She wasn't a churchgoer."

"But her faith was important to her. I would have thought you'd know that. She—"

Curious to know what had caused her to break off in midsentence, Jem turned to follow the direction of her gaze. "What's he doing here?" he asked scornfully.

"Paying his respects, I suppose."

Christopher Hart was standing with the others at the back of the chapel. She was shocked to see him here, especially after their exchange at the scene of Dale Gordon's suicide. She'd been harsh, and he'd repaid her in kind. She had expected never to see him again.

They made fleeting eye contact, then she faced the front of the chapel again.

"If his being here upsets you, Melina, I have no problem at all with asking him to leave."

She was appalled at the thought of Jem creating a scene here at her sister's memorial service. In a whisper, she exclaimed, "Don't you dare!"

"I'm only trying to protect you."

"Well, don't. I don't need protection."

"Not from the astronaut, from heartache. Gillian would want me to look after you."

Feeling badly for snapping at him, she reached for his hand. "Thank you, Jem. You have been incredibly supportive and sensitive, and I appreciate it more than you know."

He stretched his arm across her shoulders and gave her a brief hug. "If you change your mind about Rocket Man, I'll be more than happy to escort him outside."

Their conversation lapsed, but she was still pondering why Christopher Hart was here, not just at the service, but still in Dallas. Surely Lawson had released him from any further involvement. He should have been back in Houston by now, the memory of his evening with Gillian and its dreadful repercussions being dimmed by his professional responsibilities and busy social calendar.

That he had even remained in Dallas a

moment longer than necessary was surprising. Probably he'd been pressured by guilt to pay his respects to the woman he'd slept with the night before she was killed.

To his credit, he appeared to be appropriately reverential. He wasn't doing anything to call attention to himself. In fact, he seemed to be trying to make himself as inconspicuous as possible. Because of his notoriety, the attempt was futile, but she admired him for trying.

The minister she had asked to officiate approached and asked if she was ready for the service to begin. She hoped to avoid making a public spectacle of herself, but it was difficult to hold back tears when scriptures were read and hymns were sung.

One of Gillian's coworkers who'd been asked to eulogize her spoke eloquently. "It's still hard for us to grasp, much less comprehend, how such a vital and vibrant young woman could have been snatched from us so cruelly. I think Gillian would want us to use this tragedy to remind ourselves daily how valuable and wonderful life is. I think this is the legacy she would wish to leave us."

"Well said. And he's right, Melina," Jem whispered to her, squeezing her hand.

After the benediction, she stood outside under a sky threatening rain. She shook countless hands, and received many hugs, and listened to anecdotes about Gillian that people shared with her. Eventually even the stragglers began making their way toward the parking lot, hoping to beat the rain.

"Ms. Lloyd?" The last person to approach her was a woman in her mid-fifties. She had a stout but compact figure, an air of efficiency, and a kind face. "My name is Linda Croft. I work at the Waters Clinic. Your sister was a lovely person. I only met her a few times, so I hope you don't think it's presumptuous of me to attend her service."

"Not at all, Ms. Croft. I appreciate your coming."

"I can't believe she's dead. I just saw her earlier this week."

"In fact, the day before she was killed she was at the clinic, wasn't she?"

"So you knew that she was our patient?"

"I knew that she'd been artificially inseminated. You're not divulging any confidential information. My twin and I had no secrets."

"The resemblance between you is uncanny," the woman observed. "When I saw you in the chapel, it took my breath. I thought the news about her murder must have been a dreadful mistake."

"If only it were."

Linda Croft reached out and touched her arm. "I'm very sorry for you. It's a dreadful loss."

"Yes, it is." Out of the corner of her eye she spotted Jem. He was waiting impatiently in the parking lot, waving her toward the car. It had begun to sprinkle. He popped open an umbrella. A bright red one. She would never see the color again without thinking about words written in blood. Staving off a sudden chill, she said, "Thank you again for coming, Ms. Croft."

"I thought we'd had our share of tragedy at Waters. After what happened to the Anderson baby. Oh, dear. I hope I haven't been monopolizing you." To explain her abrupt switch of subjects, Linda Croft nodded toward a tall, retreating figure. "I'm afraid I kept him from speaking to you. He'd been hanging back, waiting for me to finish. I shouldn't have rambled on."

Christopher Hart was moving along the sidewalk. He was taking no precaution against the light rain falling on him. In fact, he seemed not to notice it, but was intent only on leaving. Ignoring Jem as he moved past him, he didn't break stride until he reached the drivers' door of a snazzy, sleek, two-seater sports car. He unlocked it with a remote control on his key ring, then slid into the low seat. The engine roared to life and he drove away.

". . . kidnapping a few months ago, Ms. Lloyd?"

"I'm sorry?" She brought the woman back into focus. Christopher Hart had been waiting to speak to her? What would he have said?

"The newborn taken from the hospital?" After having pointed out Christopher Hart to her, Linda Croft had picked back up where she'd left off. "The Andersons were our patients, too. I'm not divulging anything private here, either. It was in the news. The couple had tried to conceive for years and finally resorted to artificial insemination. Our excellent doctors were successful on the second try. I've never seen two people happier. Then a day after their baby was born, he was kidnapped."

"I remember now. Was the child ever found?"

"Not last I heard." Looking worried, Linda Croft said, "I shouldn't have brought it up. You've got enough grief in your own life. God bless you, Ms. Lloyd."

"Who was that?" Jem asked as he assisted her into his car. "I thought she was never going to let you go."

"Her name is Linda Croft."

"Friend of yours?"

"She works at the Waters Clinic. She said she thought highly of Gillian and wanted to come and tell me how sorry she was for my loss."

Jem nodded absently. "Did you see him?"

"Him, meaning Chief?"

He cut his eyes toward her. "So he's 'Chief' now?"

Wearily she rolled her head around her shoulders, trying to work some of the strain from her muscles. "Everybody calls him Chief, Jem. Even the media. I didn't speak to him."

"He was lurking."

"But he gave up and went away, which is probably for the best. We don't have any-thing more to say to one another. The way he tore out of the parking lot, he's probably halfway to Houston by now."

Which was unfortunate. In fact, it had been a crushing disappointment that she hadn't been able to speak to him before he left. She would have liked to apologize for . . . well, for everything, beginning with the switch and including her bitchy behavior the last time they met.

But an apology was only one of the reasons she wished she'd had an opportunity to pass time with him, and she wouldn't allow herself to acknowledge any of the other reasons. So to Jem she said, "No, it was *definitely* for the best that he left without our speaking."

They rode with only the rhythmic slap of the windshield wipers to break the silence. Finally he said, "I got a call from Lawson. I assume you did, too." He waited for her nod, then said, "He told you he'd wrapped up the case?"

"He seems satisfied."

"*He* seems satisfied? You aren't?"

She was disinclined to talk about this now. She was disinclined to talk at all. But Jem was looking at her as though waiting for elaboration, so, with a sigh, she said, "I guess I can't be as objective about my sister's homicide as a veteran detective can be. To him, she was a case number. She represented a pile of paperwork he wished he could get through quickly in order to meet the guys for beer, or watch a football game, or make love to his wife."

"Lawson's married? I got the impression he was a bachelor."

"You get my point," she said crossly. "He maintained a professional detachment I almost envied."

"Why's that?"

"Because I'd like to regard the murder with a practical eye. I wish I could remove all the emotion from the equation and analyze it the way Lawson did."

"To what end, Melina?"

To dispel my doubts. To be convinced that it happened exactly the way Lawson said it had. To be satisfied that there wasn't something more to Dale Gordon's motivation. To be certain that something important hadn't been overlooked.

But she didn't share her troubling thoughts with Jem. "To no end, I suppose. The case is closed."

"Speaking for myself, I'm glad the guy who killed Gillian killed himself."

"That was my initial reaction."

"By slashing his wrists, he saved the tax-payers the cost of a trial and imprisonment and saved us the emotional wear and tear of having to relive it. I'm just sorry I wasn't the one to give Gordon what he had coming to him."

She had made a similar statement to Lawson yesterday. But now she wished she'd had an opportunity to talk to Dale Gordon and ask him why he'd done it. *Why?* Was it only a misplaced sexual obsession, the act of a terribly disturbed individual?

Dale Gordon was dead, but there'd been no accountability. That was at the crux of her discontent. Gordon's motives were still up for speculation. That's why Lawson's summary hadn't given her any closure. It had all been too pat, too neat, and, for her, unanswered questions remained. She wouldn't rest until all had been answered.

As though reading her mind, Jem said, "You should be glad it's over, Melina."

"I am." She smiled weakly. "I'm just very tired."

"I've got a remedy in mind."

"So do I—a sleeping pill."

"Ultimately, by all means," he agreed. "But first a hot meal. One I prepare, not the leftovers of all the food brought to the house. Following a good dinner, a long, hot bath. Then I'll give you one of my famous neck and back rubs. I'm sure Gillian told you about my specialty. Finally the sleeping pill."

"Would you be terribly hurt if I said I could skip all the rest and go straight for the sleeping pill?"

"Yes, because Gillian's ghost would haunt me forever if I didn't take care of you."

"Jem—"

"I won't take no for an answer."

Chief didn't know why he'd felt compelled to attend the memorial service and was a little perturbed with himself because he had. Sure, it was the decent thing to do. He'd even intended to express his condolences to Melina personally. But considering their last conversation, it was probably better that he had changed his mind and left before he had an opportunity to speak to her.

What he couldn't understand now was why he was still here. He'd cooperated with

Lawson's investigation, even providing the lead that had served up Dale Gordon. He had attended the memorial service. Melina had seen him there. He'd fulfilled his moral and social obligations. That should have been the end of it. That *would* be the end of it. That was his resolve as he entered the bar.

"Bourbon and water."

The bartender poured his drink. "Say, aren't you—"

"No, I'm not. But I get that a lot."

It was a happening bar, in a happening neighborhood. It was frequented by professional sports stars, the nouveau riche, and the city's bold and beautiful. The bartender was accustomed to celebrities and honored their privacy when they asked him to. He gave Chief a knowing nod. "Next one's on the house."

"Thanks. But this is it for me."

As it turned out, Chief did have the second drink, wishing the alcohol would have a more anesthetizing effect than it was having. He would gladly take a cab back to The Mansion and retrieve his car later if only he could get a little tight, slightly drunk, reach a level of intoxication where he no longer gave a damn what Melina Lloyd thought of him.

But the only effect the bourbon had on him was to make him feel more of a shit heel than he already felt.

Melina's admonishment outside Gordon's apartment had hit home. He *had* wanted to disassociate himself from the murder investigation. He *had* lied about sleeping with Gillian. Melina had nailed it squarely on the head—he tried not to get too involved. Not just with this, with everything. Especially people. He supposed psychologists would have a field day analyzing why as a rule he kept people at arm's length, why his safety zone was wider than most.

He was hardly a recluse. In fact, he liked being with people. He was social. He was good in a crowd. His knees didn't knock when he had to speak before an audience, and he wasn't camera shy.

But there was a limit to the accessibility he allowed to *himself.* The public persona was one thing; the private person was quite another. He put on the brakes whenever someone probed Chief and began scratching the surface of Christopher.

From a professional standpoint, his detachment was an asset. He'd flown fighter jets with a cool, clear head, never allowing himself to think about the potential destruction they could wreak. A certain neutrality was necessary when commanding a shuttle crew and making hard decisions that could mean the difference between success and failure, even life and death.

But in his private life, that neutrality had caused problems. It was why he'd never had a long-lasting or meaningful relationship with a woman, why he'd never married. To be what it should be, marriage required an emotional susceptibility that he was unwilling to grant. He'd been brutally honest with Longtree and Abbott when he told them that he preferred to remain independent. Anything other than independence was too costly.

He acknowledged the character trait. Some might term it a flaw. But in spite of it, he couldn't possibly feel any worse than he did over what had happened to Gillian, apparently as a consequence of being seen with him. What did Melina think he was made of, stone? His sympathy ran deep. He'd even been repulsed by Alan Birchman's relief after getting the all-clear from Lawson.

"You're off the hook, Mr. Hart," the attorney had told him cheerfully. "You're free to go on your merry way. Your night with Gillian Lloyd could have cost you dearly, but thanks to Mr. Gordon, you can consider it a freebie."

He'd found the lawyer's words distasteful. They were talking about two deaths. One innocent. One pathetic. Both tragic. He was glad to be unencumbered, free of a police investigation and all that it entailed, but he didn't share the attorney's blasé attitude.

Besides, what the lawyer didn't know, what nobody knew, was that his night with Gillian *had* cost him dearly. He wasn't going to forget her. Not for a long time. She'd spent the last few hours of her life with him. That lent their time together a special poignancy.

Although—*okay, let's let it all hang out, Chief. No one can read your thoughts, so for God's sake be honest with yourself*—it already had been meaningful, and not just because of the sex. He'd had terrific sex before, but he'd never begged the woman to stay when she'd tried to leave.

He remembered waking up when Gillian had tried to dislodge him. "I hate to disturb you." He'd fallen asleep with his head tucked beneath her biceps, his cheek on her breast. "I've got to go," she'd whispered, running her fingers through his hair once before trying to lift his head.

He'd mumbled a sleepy protest and burrowed his head closer against her side.

She'd laughed softly. "Chief, I've got to go."

Coming more fully awake, he'd raised his head. "How come?"

"It's late."

"Or early. It all depends on how you look at it." He was looking at her breasts, lying soft and relaxed against her chest. He blew gently on her nipple and it responded. She sighed his name, and, with no more encouragement than that, he stretched out along her incredibly beautiful body so that they were touching collarbone to toes. "I don't want you to go. Stay."

"You wouldn't rather be well rid of me come morning?"

He rocked forward slightly, so she would feel him getting hard between their bodies. Her eyes turned the smoky gray that within hours had become his favorite color. Lowering his head, he whispered, "Stay," as his lips moved against her raised nipple. His tongue caressed it.

She made a low, sexy sound deep in her throat. "You're not playing fair, Chief."

"I'm cheating like hell." Reflexively her body arched up to increase the pressure on his erection, and he growled softly, "But so are you."

"Because I want you to win."

Grinning down at her, he slid his palms up the undersides of her arms until they were stretched far above her head. Her thighs relaxed beneath his and separated. Clasping her hands, he entered her.

"Hmm. I don't guess I'll be going anytime soon."

He pressed forward. "Will you be coming?"

She rolled her hips up to receive his slow thrusts. "No question. I'll definitely be coming."

"Sir?"

Chief roused himself, unsure how many times the bartender had spoken to him. "I'm sorry?"

"Another?"

"Got any coffee?"

"Three hours old."

"Perfect."

The coffee was delivered, and it was horrible. But he'd had worse. Staring into the oily brew, he could see Gillian's smile, and hear her voice, and taste her, and feel her. He could remember it all. Everything.

No, not everything, he reminded himself grimly. There was that *something* that continued to elude him. Something important that niggled and nagged but wouldn't reveal itself. What the hell was it? What was his subconscious clutching that it wouldn't give up?

It had originated during Lawson's conference with them. Something someone said had triggered a bothersome thought that had evaporated almost immediately, but not before casting a shadow on his mind that was still there.

But what was it, and who'd said it? Lawson? Hennings? Melina?

Whatever it was, it was the reason he hadn't left Dallas. It had caused him to stay over for the memorial service. It was the reason he couldn't turn his back on this episode of his life. It was the reason that it had grown into an episode instead of remaining simply an unfortunate incident. It

was a threat to his characteristic nonin-
volvement, and it was damned significant,
and he couldn't figure out what the fuck it
was!

The bar was more crowded now than
when he'd come in. The noise level had increased. Chief was unaware of everything
around him. He concentrated on the tableau
inside that cramped room at police headquarters. As though watching a play, he
tracked everyone's movements and listened
to the dialogue. With near-perfect powers of
recall, he reviewed it once. Then again.

It was during the third performance that
he caught it—that implication that had enormous impact.

When it struck him, it almost knocked him
off the barstool. Sightlessly, he stared at the
myriad shapes, sizes, and colors of the
liquor bottles lined up behind the bar. He
didn't hear the laughter of the woman
seated on the stool next to him. Numbed by
the impact of what his memory had up till
now kept secret, he was unaffected by the
jostling and joking going on around him.

Burying his face in his hands, he muttered
bitterly, "Son of a bitch."

"Chief? Hey, bud, everything okay?"

Slowly Chief raised his head and looked at the young man with misapprehension, then gave him a rueful, self-deprecating smile. "I attended a funeral today. A woman's funeral."

"Hey, man. Sorry."

Chief thanked him with a nod. "Let's settle up."

It was a relief to finally have figured out why he'd felt anchored to this tragedy.

But hell if he knew what he could do about it.

CHAPTER 17

The walls of the room were the greenish white color of mashed potatoes that had been stored in the refrigerator for several days too long. There were no windows. The vinyl tile floor had seen better days. The acoustical tiles in the ceiling were stained, some sagged in the middle.

But the computer was new. Only the keyboard showed excessive wear. Lucy Myrick had refused to part with it when obsolete equipment had been replaced with a newer generation of computer. She had used this particular keyboard so long that she'd worn off the letters and symbols stamped onto the keys. Anyone who didn't know the home keys would have been lost. But the point was moot, because she would sooner loan her toothbrush than her keyboard.

Lucy Myrick did not fit the stereotypical profile of an FBI agent. Her carrot-colored hair expanded exponentially with the percentage of humidity in the atmosphere and had been the bane of her existence all her life. Calories seemed to despise her, because even though she consumed them in the multiple thousands every day, none chose to move in with her. She was "skinny as a rail," to quote her grandmother. Given her above-average height of five foot ten and her bristling halo of fiery hair, she'd been cruelly compared to a struck match.

However, Lucy hadn't let her uncommon appearance deter her from pursing her dream. She was good-natured when teased and resilient when discouraged. Her spirit of determination and acumen had won her acceptance into the FBI. She had graduated from the academy and was licensed to carry a firearm, but her weapon of choice was the computer.

She hadn't even considered fieldwork.

Because of her appearance, she would never have been taken seriously either by cops or robbers. Undercover work was out of the question—she'd stick out like a sore thumb in any setting. But those wouldn't have been her choices anyway. What interested her was intelligence. Combining her computer skills with her interest in criminology had earned her the position of intelligence analyst.

Basically she was a researcher. She reviewed police records from all points of the map, made comparisons of crimes, looked for parallels and similar modus operandi, searched for coincidences that weren't and connections that were seemingly disconnected. Her job was to sniff out serial criminals or groups of criminals that otherwise would never have been brought to justice. Lucy preferred to think of it as "seek and destroy."

It was nearing the end of her workday. She yawned and stretched and glanced at the wall clock. She had a choice of leaving on time and battling Washington's rush-hour traffic or working a little overtime and letting traffic clear. Either way, she'd get home about the same time. But she didn't want to arrive home too late and miss her television programs, which began at eight. Tonight's lineup was her favorite of the whole week. Tonight—

Suddenly she leaned forward and focused on the information that had just come up on her screen. She read it three times, and each time she did, her heart beat a little faster. This was something Tobias had assigned her to watch for. She wanted to please Tobias because he . . . well, he was *Tobias,* and she had a massive crush on him.

Ten minutes later Lucy Myrick was sprinting up the stairs in favor of waiting on the elevator. She could have called Tobias's office and told him not to leave for the day until she saw him, but she fancied the idea of bursting in a bit breathless, her cheeks flushed with excitement, her meager chest heaving.

Which is precisely what she did. He was removing his raincoat from the coat tree. "I'm glad I caught you," she gasped. When he turned toward her, her tummy flip-flopped.

"What's up, Ms. Myrick?"

Ms. Myrick. Not just Myrick, as other colleagues addressed her. And never Lucy. She didn't know if the formality was a good sign or bad. Maybe he didn't even know her first name. Or maybe he didn't trust himself to get too familiar. That's what she liked to think.

Hank Tobias wasn't just the best-looking black man she'd ever seen; he was the best-looking man she'd ever seen, period. He'd played college football. Running back. And, to hear the armchair quarterbacks in the office talk, he'd been good enough to go pro. She could believe it, with that body.

Instead, he'd chosen a career in law enforcement. He was smart. He dressed like a dream. And, best of all, he was single. His love life was the object of constant speculation, but the general consensus was that Hank Tobias didn't have time for a meaningful relationship because he devoted so much of himself to his work. Lucy could live with that explanation.

"Should I put my raincoat on or leave it off?" She'd brought printed materials in with her. He was asking how important they were and approximately how much longer he was likely to be here once he saw them.

"Leave it off."

"I was afraid you were going to say that." He rehung the raincoat and sat down behind his desk. "What have you got there?"

"Infertility clinics." She moved farther into the office. "You told me to watch for any connections between children conceived in them and kidnappings."

"Got something?"

"Only kidnappings? What about other felony crimes?"

"Such as?"

"Homicide."

He reached for the information she'd printed out.

"Dallas," she told him even as he began to scan the sheets. "Gillian Lloyd. Caucasian female, age thirty-five. Found stabbed to death in her bed three days ago. Dallas PD attributed the killing to one Dale Gordon, who was an employee of—"

"Let me guess."

"Right. The Waters Clinic, to be exact, where Gillian Lloyd was a patient."

Tobias glanced up from his perusal. "What kind of patient?"

"No information on that, but it's safe to assume—"

"Never assume."

"Yes, sir." She blushed so hotly her freckles seemed to run together. "I'll follow up on the nature of Gillian Lloyd's visits to the clinic."

"Married?"

"Single." He left his desk and moved to a file cabinet. Lucy gazed longingly at his ass while she summarized the remainder of the information and he rummaged for another case file.

Finding the folder he was looking for, he held it up. "The Anderson baby kidnapping. Also in Dallas." He glanced through the material in the file to refresh his memory. "What do you know? The Waters Clinic again. The couple conceived through artificial insemination. Gave birth to a normal baby boy. Two days later, he's kidnapped from the hospital."

"Just like the couple in Kansas City last year. The Dallas case was more recent, wasn't it?"

"February this year."

"But as I recall," Lucy said, "the clinic in Kansas City wasn't one of the Waters chain."

"No, but it was similar. It provided the gamut of services to infertile couples."

"Or singles wishing to conceive." She'd given some thought to that herself. So far, no Mr. Right had come along. Or a Mr. Not-Even-Close, for that matter. If she wanted a child, having one without a partner wasn't beyond the realm of possibility.

Tobias closed the file with a definitive motion. "Notify the Dallas office that I'm coming down tonight. I want to talk to the homicide detective who investigated the Lloyd murder."

"His name's Lawson."

"Lawson. I want his full cooperation when I question Dale Gordon."

"Oh, I'm sorry, Mr. Tobias. I hadn't gotten to that part yet."

He wasn't pleased to hear that Gordon had committed suicide. "Dammit."

"He killed himself within hours of the murder. Physical evidence was found in his apartment. Victim's blood on the knife that was subsequently determined to be the murder weapon. His fingerprints at the scene. His semen on her pajama shorts."

"How convenient," he said quietly before lapsing into deep thought. Lucy welcomed the moment to admire his stern frown of concentration. "Almost too tidy, isn't it?

Does it remind you of anything, Ms. Myrick?"

Thankfully it did. "The case in Oakland, California. Late 1998, I believe. October or November. Kathleen Asher, single, early thirties, was murdered within days of conceiving through AI. Her killer was found only hours later, dead by a self-inflicted gunshot wound to the head."

"Very good. Do you think a pattern is being established here?"

"I'd like to do more research. Dig deeper. Maybe I've overlooked similar cases. Now that we know the link we're looking for, I'd like to go further back, put out a wider net."

"Good. Drop everything else and concentrate on this. Keep me apprised. If you find something that could have even the most remote connection to these other cases, inform me."

"If I turn up anything, you'll know about it immediately. No matter how remote it may seem."

Unaware of her adoring eyes, he again skimmed the information she'd gleaned about the murder in Dallas. "Memorial service was today. Next of kin, Melina Lloyd, her sister. A talk with her could be very beneficial."

"Would you like me to get her on the telephone?"

"Yes, but I can't talk to her now. Request a meeting with her tomorrow morning. Stress the urgency, but keep the reason for it vague."

"Certainly." Trying to keep the disappointment out of her voice, she said, "So you're going anyway? Couldn't the Dallas office handle the interview with her?"

"I'm sure they could, but I'd have to brief the agents down there beforehand. It's almost more time-effective for me to do it myself. Besides, I want to speak with her personally, get a feel for what Gillian Lloyd was like."

"Poor lady," Lucy said, shaking her head. "I hope she's up to it. She's had to deal with one shock already this week."

"I wonder how she'll handle learning that her sister's murder might have been part of a conspiracy." He was already on the telephone, making arrangements for travel to Dallas.

"What sort of conspiracy?" Lucy asked.

While on hold, he replied grimly, "It's up to us to find out."

• • •

"Melina?" Jem tapped on the bathroom door and repeated her name. "Are you all right?"

She swallowed a sob and forced normalcy and lightness into her voice. "I'm fine."

"Can I bring you anything? Another glass of wine?"

"Nothing, thanks." If he realized that she was crying, he might insist on comforting her, when what she desired most was to be left alone.

"Call me if you need me," he said through the door.

She continued to painfully contain her sobs until she was reasonably sure he had gone away, then she resumed what she'd been doing for the last fifteen minutes— crying her heart out. Tears streamed from her eyes, trickled down her cheeks, and dripped into the chest-high bathwater. Her body shook with sobs that caused violent ripples beneath the surface.

The sense of loss was all-encompassing—mind, body, soul. She felt it keenly in every aspect of her being. And yet, her sister's death sometimes seemed unreal to her. It was impossible to accept in spite of the memorial service that afternoon.

But it was real. She'd seen the body.

When she glimpsed the future, she saw only weeks and months of grieving ahead. She dreaded having to live through them. The prospect of it was daunting, exhausting. Since the loss was real, she wished she could sleep through a year or two and awaken only after the worst of the pain was already behind her.

Eventually her tears abated and her sobs caused only minor ripples in the bathwater. Depleted, she rested her head on the tub's rim and closed her eyes.

The ringing telephone woke her from a light doze. She started to let it ring but then decided she'd just as well take the call now as have to call someone back later. She reached for the cordless she'd brought to the bathtub with her. "Hello?"

Simultaneously Jem answered another extension. "Hello?"

"I'm calling Ms. Melina Lloyd."

"Here. I've got it, Jem." She waited for him to disconnect, then said into the telephone, "I'm Melina Lloyd."

"I apologize for disturbing you, Ms. Lloyd.

I understand you held a memorial service for your sister Gillian today."

"Who is this?"

"My name is Lucy Myrick. I'm with the FBI."

Everything inside her congealed. Lingering tears dried instantly. She became very still, so still there weren't any residual ripples in the bathwater. She could hear the tiny bubbles popping in the fragrant foam surrounding her. She wanted to draw the mound of bubbles closer, like a cloak. The water suddenly felt cold, while only moments before she'd been steeping in its relaxing heat.

But it wasn't shock that had paralyzed and chilled her. Oddly, she'd been expecting this call, or something like it. Somehow she had known that the murder wasn't so easily explained. Even as Lawson was closing the case file, she had known gut-deep that there was more to it, that the detective's investigation was incomplete, that he had only discovered the obvious, that mystery still surrounded her twin's murder.

She swallowed dryly. "What can I do for you, Ms. . . . I'm sorry."

"Myrick. I'm calling on behalf of Special Agent Hank Tobias. He would like to speak with you tomorrow. As early as possible."

"About what?"

"What time would be convenient?"

"It must have to do with my sister's murder."

"Why do you say that?"

"Because my taxes are paid up and I haven't incited any riots. Yet," she snapped. "Don't play coy with me, please, Ms. Myrick. My sister's murder is the only crime I've been affiliated with this week. Why else would the FBI be calling me?"

"I'm sorry for upsetting you. Truly. Yes, Mr. Tobias wants to see you about your sister's murder."

"Detective Lawson of the Dallas police is the investigator assigned to the case. He would have more information than I do, particularly the technical aspects."

"Actually what Mr. Tobias wants to talk to you about is more personal."

"More personal than being stabbed to death with a kitchen knife?"

Ignoring her sarcasm, Myrick continued smoothly. "Your sister was a patient of the Waters Clinic, correct?"

"That's the business of the FBI? Since when?"

"What time tomorrow would be convenient for you, Ms. Lloyd?"

On the verge of snapping again, she stopped herself. Lucy Myrick was only a mouthpiece. Even if she knew the particulars of the meeting Tobias had requested, she wasn't going to divulge them. "Nine o'clock? Here at my house?" She gave her the address.

"He'll be there. Accompanying him will be Agent Patterson from the Dallas office."

"Where is Mr. Tobias coming from?"

"Washington."

"D.C.?"

"That's right. Mr. Tobias will see you tomorrow morning at nine, Ms. Lloyd. Good night."

Thoughtfully she depressed the button to disconnect, then tapped the phone against her forehead. The FBI? All the way from Washington? Curious about the Waters Clinic? "What the hell . . ."

"Melina?" Jem tapped on the bathroom door.

"Be out in a sec."

So much for the relaxing bath, she

thought as she rinsed off and stepped from the tub. Of all Jem's suggestions, the bath was the only one that had appealed to her. She would have preferred to be alone tonight, but he'd poured his heart and soul into babying her.

As promised, he'd made her sip a glass of wine and listen to soft music while he prepared dinner. The wine and music, combined with the hypnotic sound of the rain falling outside, had lulled her. She hadn't thought she was hungry, but the angel-hair pasta dish Jem served was delicious. After dinner, she'd offered to clean up, but he wouldn't hear of it and had insisted she soak in a bubble bath.

But what should have been the most relaxing part of the evening had turned stressful with Lucy Myrick's phone call.

When she left the bathroom, wrapped in a comfy flannel robe, Jem was waiting for her in the adjoining bedroom. To cover her anxiety over the call, she smiled. "You were right. That was just what I needed."

"Who was that?"

"Who?" she asked, playing innocent. Why weren't the lamps on? He'd turned them off and lit candles all around the room. She switched on the nightstand lamp.

"On the telephone."

"Oh. I didn't know her. A client of Gillian's. She'd been out of town and only heard the news this afternoon when she returned."

She hadn't made a conscious decision to lie to him about the telephone call—there wasn't anything to decide. She wasn't going to tell anyone, not even Jem, about the FBI's interest in Gillian's murder until she knew the nature of their interest herself.

"I should have grabbed the phone sooner so your bath wouldn't have been disturbed."

"I was getting pruney anyway. It was time to get out."

"Time now for the grand finale."

"You've been busy," she remarked, taking in the candles and the turned-down bed.

"As long as I was here," he said casually. "Some of the floral arrangements were getting stagnant. I carried them all to the kitchen and would have taken them out except for the rain."

"Thanks. I'll put them in the outside trash can in the morning." *After my visit with Tobias, special agent, FBI.*

He sat down on the edge of the bed and patted the space beside him.

She hesitated. "Don't feel obligated to follow through on your promise, Jem. It's getting late."

"Not that late."

"But you must be as exhausted as I am."

"I'm not going to argue with you, Melina. I said I was going to give you a neck and back rub, and that's what I'm going to do."

Short of engaging in an argument that would create bad feelings and drain her of what small reserve of energy she had left, she sat down near him on the edge of the bed and turned her back. "Five minutes. Then you're outta here and I'm off to beddy-bye."

"After five minutes, you'll be begging for more."

She wasn't entirely comfortable with this situation. In fact, she wasn't comfortable with it at all. It felt wrong. Although he was keeping the mood platonic, he worked the collar of the robe down around her shoulders for better access to the back of her neck. When he laid his hands on her skin, she could tell that they had oil on them.

"Still wearing the pendant, I see."

He'd insisted that she accept it. "Gillian would want you to have it," he'd said.

At first she had refused. But then she relented, and now she was glad she had. The piece of jewelry would serve to remind her of her vow for vengeance. If ever her resolve were to weaken, she could rub the red stones and be reminded of the words scrawled in blood on the bedroom walls. Thinking of them now made her muscles tense, and Jem felt it.

"You need this. Your muscles are tied in knots."

She angled her head away from his lips, which were uncomfortably close to her ear. "That shouldn't come as a surprise, considering."

"You've had hell, all right." After a beat, he added, "But Gillian's dead, Melina. We must learn to deal with it. Relax."

His thumbs dug deeply into the base of her neck. It felt good and she told him so.

He chuckled. "Told you I was good."

"Not a false claim at all."

"Gillian loved my neck rubs."

"I can see why."

"They were often foreplay."

To her mind, the statement was grossly inappropriate. But rather than make an issue of it, she turned it into a joke. "More information than I needed, Jem."

He laughed with her. The kneading motion extended down onto her shoulders. "You know, it's funny, Melina."

"What?"

"That I could fall for the switch you and Gillian pulled the night before she was killed. As her fiancé, you'd think I would be able to tell the difference between you."

"You never suspected it was me who answered the door with a towel on my head?"

"Never had an inkling. Not even when I kissed you."

"I stopped you when you tried to deep-kiss me. I wouldn't have let you deep-kiss me."

"It was deep enough." His hands stopped massaging and rested on her shoulders. "Deep enough to get me excited."

She bolted from the bed and spun around to face him, clutching her robe at her throat. "That's a revolting thing to say."

He laughed. "I was teasing." Extending his hand, he appealed to her. "Melina, please. You didn't think I was serious, did you?"

"What I think is that it's time for you to leave. Past time."

"Melina. Come on. It was a joke."

"It wasn't funny."

He hung his head. "No, I guess it wasn't." When he looked up at her, he was trying to appear boyishly repentant, an expression she found precious and offensive. "I'm sorry."

"Apology accepted. Now please say good night so I can go to bed."

She turned and left the bedroom, her brisk footsteps and posture implying that he should follow. He did, pausing only to retrieve his suit jacket from the back of the sofa where he'd left it earlier. She opened the front door and held it for him. "Thanks again for making dinner," she said stiffly.

"Why do I get the feeling that we're ending this sad day on a sour note?"

"It is a sad day, Jem. A very sad day. I want to spend the remainder of it alone, basking in my sadness. Since those cops showed up on my doorstep, I haven't had a moment alone. I need to grieve."

He nodded. "Some things are too private to share."

"Thank you for understanding."

When he pulled even with her at the door, he paused. "I'll come by in the morning to check on you."

"I'm going to the gym tomorrow morning."

"Are you sure you're up to a workout?"

"The exercise will be good for me."

"Then I'll catch you later in the day."

"Call first." She was finding it increasingly difficult to tolerate him. She just wanted him to be gone. Now.

He leaned forward and kissed her cheek. It was all she could do to keep from recoiling. "Good night."

He stepped out into the rain and jogged to his car. She closed the door, bolted it, then leaned against it and took several deep cleansing breaths. They weren't good enough. Hastily returning to the bathroom, she frantically showered off his touch and the oil he'd used. She scrubbed until all traces of it were off her skin.

"Famous neck rub, my ass," she muttered as she sprinkled body powder across her shoulders.

Suddenly her movements were arrested. Either her ears were playing tricks on her or she had heard a noise coming from another part of the house. She strained to listen.

When the scratching sound came again, she traced it into the bedroom, where she realized that the ominous sound she'd heard was only a tree limb moving against the window screen, driven by a rain-laden wind.

Courtesy of the FBI, she had a bad case of the jitters. And wasn't she entitled? She'd seen more blood in the last few days than she had seen in the rest of her life added together, first her sister's blood at the murder scene, then at Dale Gordon's spooky, squalid apartment.

She moved around her bedroom blowing out the candles that Jem had lit. They reminded her of that horrid place with its hideous altar, threadbare curtain separating the bathroom, and the sick individual who had lived there.

He had pictures, Lawson had said. Gordon had taken pictures of Gillian while she was at her most vulnerable at the Waters Clinic. It was too nauseating to think about. She broke out in gooseflesh and rubbed her arms through her robe.

Sleep, long desired and stubbornly elusive, wouldn't come tonight, either, if she didn't calm down, and the only way she was going to do that was to shut her mind off. Contrary to what she had told Jem, she had no intention of taking a sleeping pill. She didn't want to medicate herself, especially since Tobias would be here at nine o'clock tomorrow morning. That was one meeting for which she wanted to be sharp. He was coming for answers to questions. Little did he know that she had questions of her own.

Wine, she thought. Maybe it would relax her enough to sleep, but not leave her groggy in the morning. She and Jem hadn't emptied the bottle he'd served with dinner.

Leaving the lights off, she moved into the kitchen and took the bottle of wine from the refrigerator. As she was closing the door with her hip and reaching for a wineglass with her free hand, her back door crashed open.

At first all she saw was blood.

More blood.

C H A P T E R | 1 8

She closed the refrigerator door to extinguish the light and at the same time slammed the wine bottle against the countertop. California chardonnay and glass sprayed her and the floor.

She brandished the jagged bottleneck at the bloodied figure slumped against the doorjamb. "Get out of here or I'll hurt you. I'll call the police."

He stumbled inside. Blood trickled from a nasty cut on his cheekbone and another above his eye. The eye was swollen and discolored. "I don't recommend Lawson the wonder cop."

"Chief!"

She dropped the broken bottle and, heedless of the glass on the floor, rushed toward him. First she closed the door to keep the rain outside, then guided him into a chair at the kitchen table. "What happened to you? Were you in an accident?"

"Leave them off," he said as she reached for the light switch.

"Why?"

"Because I can't be sure that I wasn't followed here, and—"

"You drove?" He could barely stand.

"No. Witnesses packed me into a taxi. I had the driver drop me around the corner and walked the rest of the way."

"Did you say witnesses? To what?"

"Later. No lights. If they're after me, they're very possibly after you, and with the light on, we make a better target."

"Target? For who? Who are 'they'? What in the world are you talking about?"

During this disjointed conversation she had been searching for a dish towel. She had momentarily forgotten where they were kept, but she finally found the correct drawer and took out several. A piece of glass had taken root in her bare heel, but she didn't stop to tend it. Instead, she pressed the dish towel against Christopher Hart's bleeding cheekbone.

He winced as she applied pressure. "The son of a bitch reopened the cut Hennings gave me."

"What son of a bitch? Start at the beginning and catch me up. Who did this to you?"

"I was attacked outside a club on Greenville Avenue."

"Attacked? Like a mugging? Did you report it to the police?"

"No."

"Why not?"

"Have you got a pain pill?"

"Uh . . ."

"Anything?"

"Wait here." Favoring the heel where the sliver of glass was embedded, she scurried from the kitchen.

In the bathroom, she frantically searched the shallow medicine cabinet, knocking several over-the-counter medications and outdated prescriptions into the sink. Finally she found what she was looking for.

When she turned with the bottle in her hand, Chief was standing in the open bathroom doorway, supporting himself with one bloody hand on the doorframe and holding the kitchen towel to his cheekbone with the other.

She shook a tablet into her palm. "Root canal. Last year."

"What is it?" When she told him, he nodded and pinched up the pill between two fingers. "I've taken it before. Also for dental work."

"It's a mild dosage, but I don't know whether or not this drug loses its potency like vitamins." She filled the toothbrush glass with tapwater and passed it to him.

He swallowed the tablet and returned the glass to her. "Thanks."

"Take off your jacket and sit here." She lowered the commode lid. Shrugging off his leather jacket, he indicated the bright overhead light. "This is an interior room," she explained. "No one can see the light. But I need to see your face."

He sat down and angled his head back. The gash wasn't that long, but it was deep. "That needs stitches."

"Got a Band-Aid?"

"I think so."

"That'll do. Pour some stuff on it first."

"Are you sure? It could scar. I really think it needs—"

"Just . . ." He motioned toward the open medicine cabinet. "It'll be fine."

There was a bottle of disinfectant in the medicine cabinet. She doused the gash with it, causing him to swear lavishly. "Do they teach you that language in astronaut school?" she asked.

"It's a required course."

"You must've passed with flying colors."

"Aced every test."

Once that wound was cleansed, she passed him a square of gauze soaked with the disinfectant. "For the cut above your eye. It doesn't look as bad, but it needs to be cleaned."

She determined that a plain adhesive bandage would be insufficient for the cut on his cheek, so she assembled the makings of one on the dressing table.

"Do you have a gun, Melina?"

The astonishing question came as she was cutting a strip of adhesive tape off the roll. The metal spool fell from her hands, leaving her with a piece of white tape stuck to the pad of her finger. The spool swung like a pendulum. "Gun? Like a pistol?"

"Do you?"

"Why?"

"Do you?"

"No."

"Finish up. We need to talk."

Working quickly, she dabbed both wounds with an antibiotic salve, then covered the one on his cheek with a gauze pad and tightly secured one side of it with tape. "It'll probably bleed through soon. I'll change it when it does."

It didn't occur to her to ask if he would be there long enough to need a bandage change, or how long he planned on staying, or why, following an attack, he'd chosen to come to her. It seemed a foregone conclusion that she and Chief were in this together—whatever *this* was—and that he was going to be around for a while. Which left her feeling both comforted and conversely unsettled.

Comforted because she welcomed having an ally, someone intelligent and self-controlled, someone who even when bruised and bleeding didn't panic but kept a cool head, and someone who shared her outrage, and possibly some of her guilt, over the murder.

Unsettled because that someone was Chief Hart, whose mere presence in a room caused a tingling awareness within her. When near, as now, he generated other, more embarrassing physical reactions. Like having unsteady fingers that had to try twice before successfully placing an additional strip of tape over the bandage.

This up close and personal, she became far too mindful of standing between his thighs, of bending close to his face, of nearly touching him, of wanting to.

When the tape was secured, she hastily withdrew her hands and stepped away from him. It was all she could do to keep herself from wiping her damp palms on her robe, or clutching the neck of it, or any such nervous gesture that might have signaled her silly, adolescent reaction to him.

"Try to keep some pressure on it," she said.

He stood up and surveyed her handiwork in the mirror, touching the bandage gingerly. "Thanks."

"What about your eye?"

"Maybe some ice."

"I'll be right back."

She hobbled into the kitchen again, tiptoeing around the larger pieces of broken glass and hoping she missed the smaller ones she couldn't see in the dark. His comment about being a target had made her paranoid; she kept the overhead light off. She quickly filled a Ziploc baggie with ice chips from the dispenser in the fridge door and wrapped it in one of the few remaining dish towels that wasn't bloodstained.

As soon as she reentered the bedroom, he said, "Here." He was sprawled in an easy chair in a dim corner of the room, one foot propped on the matching ottoman, the other still on the floor. His jacket was draped over his knee. He looked totally fatigued.

"You feel like hell, right?"

He grinned at her wryly as he reached for the makeshift ice pack and applied it to his eye. "I'd have to start feeling better to feel like hell."

She lifted the jacket off his knee and shook raindrops off it, then hung it on the doorknob. Turning back to him, she asked, "Do you want a towel for your hair?"

"It'll dry."

"Any other injuries not apparent? Bruised or broken ribs? Knot on the head? Concussion? Internal bleeding?"

He shook his head. "Only what's visible."

"Shouldn't you go to the emergency room to make sure?"

"You're tracking blood on your carpet."

Looking down, she saw the spots that marked her path out of the bedroom and back. "I stepped on a piece of glass."

"That's what you get for threatening me with that broken bottle."

"I didn't know it was you. Ordinarily visitors ring my front doorbell, not come crashing through the back door."

"What about your foot?"

"The glass is still in my heel."

"Better see to it."

"But I want to hear . . ."

He wasn't listening. He had closed his eyes. Maybe the pain pill was more potent than either of them thought. Or maybe he was simply exhausted.

In the bathroom, she sat down on the lid of the commode and propped her foot on her knee to examine her heel. The piece of glass was large enough to be visible, and she was able to extract it with tweezers. To be fair, she bathed the bleeding spot with the same antiseptic she'd used on Chief, and it stung like crazy. She covered the puncture with a Band-Aid.

Still favoring that foot, she went back into the bedroom. He was snoring softly. Quietly she sat down on the edge of the bed, near the spot where she had been sitting with Jem Hennings less than an hour ago. Much had happened in that brief period of time.

But out of all the surprises that had been sprung on her since bidding Jem good night—the sudden appearance of Christopher Hart, his being attacked, his injuries, his asking if she had a gun—the most incredible to her was that he could fall asleep and snore peacefully in the midst of a crisis.

For ten minutes she didn't move. She sat silently and watched him sleep. Then, as though programmed to wake up after sleeping exactly six hundred seconds, his eyes came open. Seeing her, he smiled and whispered, "Hey."

"Hey."

Extending a hand toward her, he drawled, "What are you doing way over there?"

"I—" Then, realizing his mistake, she smiled apologetically and reminded him softly, "I'm Melina."

He dropped his hand and, looking chagrined, shifted his position in the chair. He sat up straighter and pushed his fingers up through his hair. Irritably he said, "I knew that."

"For a second there, I don't think you did."

Declining to respond, he asked, "Did I doze off?"

"No, you went comatose."

"Sorry."

"You should try and get about eight more hours of it. Unless you think you have a concussion; then you should stay awake."

"I told you I don't have a concussion."

"Okay." After a short silence, she asked, "How'd you know where I live?"

"Lawson gave me the address. I sent flowers."

"Oh. I haven't read all the card enclosures yet. Thank you."

"You're welcome."

He stared at the toe of his boot. The hems of his jeans were wet, she noticed, but the boots had kept his legs and feet dry. He seemed unconcerned about the drops of blood that had discolored the leather.

Finally he looked across at her. "How'd you know?"

"What?"

"About me and Gillian."

"That you'd slept together?"

He bobbed his head curtly.

"She told me. When she got home that night."

The toe of his boot became his focus again. "I wasn't lying to Lawson when I said I didn't know what time she left. She didn't say goodbye." He shot her a quick glance before resuming the study of his boot. "She sneaked out while I was asleep."

"She thought it would be better to make a clean break. That it might have been awkward if she'd hung around until morning." He looked at her as though waiting for a more complete explanation. "Some men would rather not go through that morning-after scene. Gillian thought you might prefer waking up alone."

"She thought wrong."

"Oh. Well." Several beats separated the words. "She had no way of knowing that. She wasn't that familiar with the protocol for one-night stands." Blue eyes drilled into her. "It's true," she insisted. "In that regard we were different."

"So she said."

"She did?"

"While playing you, she described herself as impulsive. She said Melina Lloyd does whatever feels right at the moment."

She smiled sadly. "That pretty much describes me, but it wasn't Gillian. She was much more circumspect. You should feel flattered, Chief. She compromised her standards to sleep with you. You must've been very special to her."

"Then why'd she—" He ended the question abruptly, angrily.

"I've explained why she left without saying goodbye."

"Yeah, yeah," he muttered. "You say she got here between two and three?"

"She apologized for being so late, but I was waiting up for her."

"To hear how the evening went?"

"Yes."

"Well?" he asked.

She bristled. "What do you want, a grade? A through F? On a scale of one to ten? Or will a simple pass-fail classification be sufficient? Isn't that a little juvenile?"

"And twins switching places isn't?" he asked, raising his voice.

Waving her hands in front of her face, she

stood up. "We've gotten off track here." Forgetting to favor her foot, she came down hard on her heel and grimaced.

"Does your foot hurt?"

"Why did you come here, Chief? What happened tonight that brought you crashing through my door?"

"I was at this club on—"

"Greenville. That much you've told me."

"I was on my way to my car when two guys jumped me."

"And beat the crap out of you."

"They were working on it. They were trying to get me into a van and making promises that they were going to kill me. I think they would have made good on that promise if another car hadn't turned into the parking lot. When it did, they got into the van and sped away.

"The people in the other car realized I was hurt and offered to help, to call 911, the police. I told them it was a family fight and best handled privately. If they could please just get me into a taxi . . . You know the rest."

"Could you describe the men?"

"They were wearing ski masks."

"Masks? Good Lord. Did you see the car tag number on the van?"

He shook his head. "Too dark. Didn't even get the state. The van was a blur of some dark color. I couldn't tell."

"They didn't try to take anything?" she asked, glancing down at his aviator's wristwatch.

"These weren't thieves, Melina. They said right up front that they were going to kill me, and when they said it, I believed it. They weren't messing around. I'm no coward . . ." Remembering that she'd called him just that, he added dryly, "Your opinion to the contrary. But in any case, these guys made a believer out of me. They would have done what they said."

Chief wasn't the kind of man who would exaggerate a fistfight. He didn't need dramatic effect to get attention. He attracted attention when he was standing still doing nothing. He didn't need to invent tales of fire-breathing dragons to look like Prince Charming.

"Why do you think they singled you out?"

"I wasn't singled out of a crowd, Melina," he said with diminishing patience. "They were lying in wait for me. *Me,* not just anybody."

"They called you by name?"

"Aren't you listening?"

"Okay, okay. They knew you. That makes this very serious. Why didn't you notify the police immediately?"

He gnawed on the corner of his lip for a moment, then continued speaking with soft urgency. "Think about it. Three days ago Gillian was murdered in her bed. She was targeted. The words painted on her walls were crude references to me and the fact that we had slept together. It pissed off somebody."

"Dale Gordon."

He made a scoffing sound. "It wasn't any fucking ghost that jumped me tonight. You might believe in coincidence, but I don't. At the very least, I'm skeptical of it. I believe in cause and effect. A bell rings, you look for a cause, a reason for its ringing. It's been drilled into me through my training to watch for warning signs and to heed them immediately.

"Granted, sometimes you can read the signals wrong. Sometimes it can be a false alarm. But you've got to check it out. Warning signals are built in for a purpose, and that purpose is to alert you of danger. I consider one murder, one suicide, and one attempted murder to be warning signs that something is terribly wrong with this picture."

"You think Gillian's murder and this attack on you tonight are connected?"

"Yeah. Furthermore, so do you." He looked at her hard, his eyes reflecting the light from the open bathroom door like blue-tinted mirrors. "Unless I miss my guess about you entirely, you thought Lawson's summation of things was a trifle too pat. You're not in complete agreement that it went down the way he says it did. You are not convinced that Dale Gordon acted alone. Are you?"

They stared at one another through the still semidarkness. Her chest was so tight she found it difficult to breathe. Finally she said, "Would you like some tea?"

CHAPTER | 1 9

"Tea?"

"Sometimes I drink it to relax," Melina explained.

"Ever tried bourbon?"

"With a pain pill?"

"Even better."

"I'll see what I've got." She left the room. While she was out, Chief took in his surroundings. The room was comfortably furnished. Feminine, but not fussy. Neat, but not compulsively so. On the nightstand was a framed snapshot of the twins. He pulled himself out of the chair and picked up the photograph, looking from one smiling face to the other.

"Can you tell which is which?" Melina had carried in two highball glasses.

"No. Thanks."

She hesitated before passing one of the drinks to him. "No thanks?"

He reached for the drink. "No, I can't tell you apart. And thanks for the drink."

"You're welcome."

"You took my suggestion, I see."

"The drinks took less time to fix than tea." She nodded down at the picture. "I'm the one on the right."

He looked at the snapshot again, shook his head, and muttered, "Damn." Returning the frame to the nightstand, he resumed his place in the chair. Melina sat on the bed and propped her back against the headboard, but she continued to gaze at the framed photograph. "I haven't mourned her yet."

"You haven't had time."

"I suppose."

"It'll hit you all at once. Unexpectedly. Like a ton of bricks falling on top of you. You'll realize she's truly gone. That's when you'll grieve."

"Speaking with the voice of experience, Chief? Have you lost someone close to you?"

"My mother. Seven years ago. It was tough."

"When our parents died, one soon after the other, Gillian and I relied heavily on each other to get through."

"So it was just you two? No other brothers or sisters?"

"Just us. Now just me." She ran her finger thoughtfully around the rim of the drinking glass. When she looked up at him, she asked, "What about your father?"

"Still alive." That was all he had to say on that subject, and she must have intuited it because she didn't pursue it. After a lengthy silence that closed the subject of loss, he remarked, "This is a strange situation, Melina."

"How so? I agree with you, but specifically why do you think it's strange?"

"Customarily, when I'm fortunate enough to be sharing a bedroom with a beautiful woman, sipping a drink, we're not talking about death and dying and unsolved mysteries."

She smiled, but there was no humor in it.

"Nothing's normal for me, either. My sister's murder changed everything."

"Then you'll empathize with my saying that since I met Gillian, since the two of you switched places, my life's gone to shit."

She came off the bed like a shot, with a flash of bare leg that eliminated his need to speculate further if she was wearing anything beneath her robe. None too gently she set her drink on the nightstand and confronted him angrily. "You know what just occurred to me? None of this would have happened if not for *you*."

"You're right." His calm statement took her aback. She had expected an argument. When none was forthcoming, she was left with nothing to say. "Temper tantrum over? Ready to listen?"

Huffily she resumed her place on the bed, folding her arms across her chest. He asked politely if he could pour her another drink. She shook her head. "Okay, then," he began, "let's lay it all out, and look at it, and see if we can make sense of it. Agreed?"

"Why are you doing this?" she asked. "You made it clear that day at police headquarters that you resented being involved, that you were an innocent bystander, and that the sooner you could walk away from it, the better."

"Initially I did think that way. I didn't want to be dragged into a mess that wasn't even of my making. And you're right, it was selfish of me to feel that way. I feel differently now."

"Why the sudden change of heart? The threat on your life? A prick of conscience?"

"A prick with a conscience," he said, grinning at her. She didn't return the smile. "Okay, give me a hard time about it, Melina. I deserve it for acting like an asshole."

"You're stalling."

He hesitated, then said quietly, "My reason for being here isn't something I wish to share."

"Does it have to do with Gillian?"

"In part. In major part." He didn't expound, but thankfully she accepted the abbreviated version.

"What else?"

"I think that whoever killed Gillian also tried to kill me tonight." He had her attention now. She was listening. The currents of hostility coming from her weren't as strong as before. "At least I was made to believe that

I was about to be killed. It might have only been a scare tactic."

"So you admit that you're scared."

"Mostly I'm pissed. Maybe it's just my Injun blood coming to a boil, but nobody jumps me in the dark, tries to kidnap me, and tells me I'm about to die without getting a good fight out of me."

She thought about it for a few moments, then raised her hands in a helpless gesture. "But Gillian's murderer is dead, Chief."

"You're satisfied that Dale Gordon was acting alone?"

"It's reasonable."

"Then why were you at his apartment last evening?"

Her lips parted in wordless surprise.

"I drove past his place myself," he confessed. "It still had crime scene tape around it, but I went over there hoping I'd come away convinced that this sick dick was solely responsible for killing Gillian.

"I saw you sitting in your car, staring at that creepy place so hard you didn't even notice when I drove past. Seeing you there supported my feeling that Lawson missed something. There's more to this than that one pathetic wacko."

"I went over there hoping for the same thing," she confessed. "Enlightenment. A sense of closure. Something."

"And came away . . . ?"

"Feeling as you do, Chief. There's got to be more to it. I don't think this sad individual acted on his own. If anything, he was manipulated into doing what he did."

"You think somebody knew about his obsession with Gillian and used it to get him to kill her?"

"Something like that." In frustration she thumped the mattress with her fists. "But who? Why? Gillian had no enemies."

He finished the last of his drink. Neither it nor the pain pill had made a dent in the dull throbbing on the side of his face. He could feel his eye swelling despite the ice pack he'd been holding to it. Since it wasn't helping, he set it aside.

"There are these men, Native Americans, who came to see me." He told her about his two meetings with Dexter Longtree and George Abbott. Melina listened without comment.

"Abbot's a yes-man, but Longtree is a chief and looks it. He holds a seat on an intertribal council, apparently wields a lot of influence, and has a lot of money. They hoped to persuade me to join a group they're forming." He described Native American Advocacy and its goals. "They want me to serve as their official spokesperson."

"That sounds great."

"Like hell."

"It doesn't?"

"I've never been involved in Indian affairs. And I'd never be anybody's talking head, a puppet."

"You think that's what they had in mind?"

Her dubiety annoyed him. "I . . . Yes! They tried to strong-arm me into making a commitment right then and there. I told them to fuck off. Words to that effect. Then Longtree calls within minutes after I'd been questioned by Lawson and makes an obscure reference to 'unhappy circumstances' and 'trouble with the police,' which he thought might have caused me to change my mind."

He had to tell her no more than that for her to catch his drift. Her brow was furrowed with concentration, her lips slightly pursed. "You think the men who attacked you could have been sent by Longtree."

"It crossed my mind."

"Were they Indian?"

"Couldn't tell. Masks, remember."

"But that wouldn't make sense, Chief. They don't want you dead. They want you for their advocate."

"As I said, maybe they were sending me a strong message." Watching her closely he added, "Because I didn't heed the first one."

"First one?" She searched his eyes, then exclaimed softly, "Gillian's murder?"

He moved to the bed and sat down in front of her. "Could they have used her?"

"You mean arranged for her to sleep with you?"

"Something like that."

She laughed shortly. "Have you lost your mind? First of all, she never would have agreed to be a whore for anybody."

"I'm not suggesting—"

"And secondly, it wasn't her idea to switch places that night. It was mine. I explained this to Lawson, but you weren't in on that conversation. I was the one who suggested that Gillian meet you. She scotched the idea. Initially. But I called her later and twisted her arm."

"Why did she ultimately give in?"

"I suppose she wanted to meet you. Or . . ."

"What?"

"Nothing." She averted her eyes. "I don't know why she changed her mind."

"Bullshit," he said angrily. "You two kept no secrets from each other. You've said so repeatedly."

"We didn't betray each other's confidences, either."

"It doesn't matter now. She's dead."

Her temper flared. "I don't need you to remind me of that, thank you very much. In fact, I want you to go. Now."

He hated to see the tears forming in her eyes, but he was pressing her as much for her protection as his own. Through no fault of their own, they had become embroiled in something mysterious and potentially dangerous. He had to know what it was. He had to make it go away, even if it meant temporarily hurting this woman who had already been so badly hurt by her sister's death.

He took her by the shoulders. "Melina, could Longtree or someone have possibly gotten to Gillian between lunch and when she changed her mind about escorting me?"

"Gotten to her?"

"Maybe they threatened her."

"She would have told me. She would have called the police."

"Enticed her with money?"

"You're becoming increasingly insulting."

Chief persisted. "Could they have appealed to her social conscience, persuaded her that she would be doing a minority people a service?"

"No. Gillian had pet charities. She supported numerous causes. But she showed no partiality to Native Americans."

"Not until she fucked me."

"You bastard." She tried to wrestle free, but he didn't release her.

"Melina, why did Gillian change her mind?"

"I don't know!"

"You do," he insisted. "Why did she go with me that night?"

"I told you."

"But you're lying. Why did she change her mind?"

"Because of the AI!"

Her shout left a vacuum filled only by their harsh breathing. "What the hell's that?"

"Artificial insemination. Gillian had been

artificially inseminated that day. Will you please let go of my shoulders?"

He released her immediately. He ran his hand over his mouth, down his chin. "Yeah, I heard that. When we were all at the police station."

"That's a far cry from your Chief Longtree conspiracy theory, isn't it?"

"Why were she and Hennings going to an infertility clinic?"

"Not Jem. It was strictly Gillian's decision to have a child. She was inseminated with donor sperm."

"She wanted a child, but not necessarily with Hennings?"

"That's what she told me over lunch that day."

He stood up and began to pace, hoping that movement would enable him to better organize his thoughts. "I still don't get what that had to do with me."

She dragged her lower lip through her teeth as though weighing the advisability of pursuing this topic.

"What, Melina?"

"I'm guessing. And it's only a *guess,*" she emphasized. "Understood?"

"Understood."

She took a deep breath. "Couples who resort to alternative methods of conception . . ." He nodded, urging her to continue. "Experts recommend that they have intercourse the same day."

He looked at her expectantly, waiting for her to go on. When she didn't, he filled in the blanks for himself. "Okay. I can see that. It would be psychologically healthy. For both partners, but particularly for the man."

"Right."

"So why didn't Gillian stay home that night and sleep with Hennings?"

"He's sterile. Vasectomy."

The significance of what she was telling him made him slightly weak in the knees. He lowered himself onto the ottoman.

Softening her tone, she said, "Gillian didn't escort you that night with the express intention of sleeping with you. She wouldn't use someone that way, especially not without his knowledge and consent. But when she got home that night, she told me how mutually attracted you were. At least it was her impression that the attraction was mutual."

He nodded.

"Maybe in the back of her mind—and I remind you that I'm only surmising and could be so very, very wrong. But maybe, deep in her subconscious, Gillian was thinking that you would make a desirable sperm donor." A second or two passed before she said, "Although if you used something . . ."

He looked up at her, but found it hard to hold her gaze.

"Did you?" she asked.

"Of course."

"I see."

"She didn't tell you?"

"Not about that."

"I had condoms."

"Oh."

He looked away, and for a time neither said anything. Their embarrassed silence was deafening. He'd been talking about rubbers with the guys since junior high school, but he'd never discussed them with a woman, not out of bed anyway.

It came as a vast relief to him when Melina forged ahead. "Gillian had no ulterior motive for going with you, Chief," she assured him softly. "The procedure had been a very emotional experience for her. To release the pressure of that day, she went with you for the fun of it. That's why

I thought of it in the first place and urged her to go. To take her mind off the insemination and the decision making that had led up to it. She went. She met you. The two of you were sexually attracted. You acted on it."

"That about sums it up."

"She wasn't part of a grand scheme. She wasn't acting on behalf of Longtree or anyone else."

"You're right." Sighing, he moved from the ottoman and resettled heavily into the chair. "I know you're right. I never got the impression that she was trying to trick me. I was groping." Absently he pulled his shirttail from his waistband and began to rub his stomach. "So where does that leave us?"

"Are you hungry?"

"What?" Then, realizing she had noticed his subconscious gesture, he said, "No, I'm not hungry. Just sore." He unbuttoned his shirt. An inspection of his torso revealed some dark splotches on his ribs and below.

When he raised his head, he caught her studying him with interest. "You're bruised."

"Not too bad."

"Gillian told me you were beautiful."

"What?"

"She said 'beautiful.' That's exactly the word she used."

He could come up with absolutely no response to that. Nothing. He didn't know what to say.

Her eyes loitered in the vicinity of his belt buckle, which made him uncharacteristically self-conscious. It was discomfiting to know that Gillian had talked to her about being with him. He wished he knew what Gillian had told her, wished he knew how detailed their conversation had been. Surely sisters, even identical twins, drew the line somewhere when it came to exchanging confidences about their sex life.

Even though Melina had called his curiosity juvenile, he would pay to know how he'd rated with Gillian. Great? Bad? Or—the kiss of death when it came to rating sexual performance—nice?

After what seemed like forever, she lifted her gaze from his middle and looked him straight in the eye. He felt his face growing warm. Surely Gillian hadn't told her about *that?* He just couldn't see Gillian saying, "I went down on him."

His mind was tugged toward that erotic memory, the first of many they'd made that night. It was there on the outskirts of his mind, flirting with him, torturing him, arousing him in spite of himself.

But Melina had asked him something, and he knew he needed to respond appropriately.

"Lawson?" What had she said about the detective?

"Earlier you made a tongue-in-cheek comment about his ineptitude."

"I meant it," he said, grateful for the distraction. "He's probably an okay guy and a reasonably good detective. I think he approached the case with good intentions. But he's busy. Overworked and underpaid. The sooner he can close a case, the better. He accepted the evidence at face value."

"Evidence that was a little too evident."

"My thinking exactly. For someone who'd just experienced total psychological meltdown and committed cold-blooded murder, Dale Gordon was awfully organized. It's like he had laid out all the evidence so that a complete imbecile would conclude that he was the murderer."

The ice in the baggie had warmed to a cool slush, but it provided a modicum of relief to his eye when he reapplied it. Then Melina hit him with a verbal uppercut.

"Well, maybe the FBI will shed some light on the mystery."

He dropped the ice pack. "You called the FBI?"

"No. They called me. They'll be here at nine." She glanced at the clock on the nightstand. "You're welcome to stay."

CHAPTER | 2 0

"She lied to me."

Upon hearing those words being blurted through his speaker phone, Brother Gabriel frowned. On principle he disliked a call that came in the middle of the night unless he was expecting it. Ordinarily he slept like a baby, and late-night calls disturbed that peaceful slumber. They also portended bad news. Dale Gordon's recent call being a perfect example.

Gordon had called in near hysteria to report on Gillian Lloyd's assignation with the astronaut. What a long, sleepless night that had been. Everything had turned out all right in the end, and things had continued to go well through the subsequent police investigation.

So now what?

In an attempt to buffer the imminent bad news, Mr. Hancock had served him a cup of hot chocolate. He took a sip. It was just the way he liked it, scalding and laced with peppermint schnapps. As it spread its warmth through his midsection, he said, "I assume you're referring to Melina Lloyd."

"Yes," Jem Hennings replied. "She lied to me."

"What was the nature of her lie?"

"She was contacted by the FBI."

Brother Gabriel set down his cup of hot chocolate with a clatter, his mild aggravation escalating into alarm. "How do you know?"

"I was there and picked up a telephone extension. She thought I had hung up, but I listened in. It was a woman calling on behalf of Special Agent Hank Tobias."

"Dallas office?"

"Washington."

The news got worse. "Devils," Brother Gabriel hissed.

"True. I'm sure they'll spawn the Antichrist."

"Nonsense," Brother Gabriel snapped. "They're not that powerful. Or that clever."

They were pests, that's all. But pests whose lies could cause the faithful to waver. He didn't fear the government agency. He believed in his own capabilities and power of persuasion over theirs. Nonetheless, he had a healthy respect for the monkey wrench they could throw into the smooth operation of his ministry if they took a mind to.

He'd been pastoring his first church when the Jonestown mass suicide took place. The story had fascinated him. Jim Jones had been maligned in the media, condemned by governments, censured by the man-on-the-street. Even Pastor Alvin Conway had led his Sunday morning congregation in a prayer for the souls who had gone so far astray. But secretly, he had held the cult leader in high esteem for wielding that much influence and motivating that many people to do the unthinkable.

Since Jonestown, law enforcement agencies had focused sharply on religious leaders and the followers they amassed. The

Branch Davidian disaster in Waco, Texas, had soured them even more. The FBI, the ATF, didn't want another David Koresh making their guys look bad on CNN for all the world to see. It was like these government agencies were holding a grudge against any spiritual leader who got a firm toehold in the minds and hearts of the people.

He had devoted followers planted in these various agencies. They would alert him to any covert investigation of his ministry. But the best-case scenario was to avoid attracting curiosity or special interest altogether.

"Tobias has an appointment with Melina for nine o'clock tomorrow morning," Hennings told him.

"And she lied about it?"

"When I asked her who had called, she made up a story. She didn't want me to know about her meeting with Agent Tobias."

Brother Gabriel's eyes narrowed fractionally. "Why do you suppose that is?"

"That she lied, you mean? I don't know."

"Have you given her any reason to mistrust you?"

"I've treated her with nothing but loving kindness since Gillian's betrayal."

Jem Hennings had been relocated to

Dallas the day after Gillian's first visit to the Waters Clinic. She'd gone only to consult about the viability of having a child by AI using donor sperm. Upon seeing her there, Dale Gordon had excitedly reported to the Temple that he'd found another ideal candidate for the Program.

Hennings had been dispatched straight to Dallas to begin his new assignment. He infiltrated her life first by making friends with one of her associates in the commercial real estate firm. Eventually he finagled an introduction to her. Hennings was very good at his job and had previous experience. It wasn't long before a dating relationship between him and Gillian was established.

He never broached the subject of children with her, but when she brought it up and asked him his views on single women conceiving through artificial insemination, Hennings encouraged her without being too obviously enthusiastic.

Of course, his parenting her child was never a consideration. A prerequisite of holding Hennings's position in the ministry was mandatory vasectomy. (Brother Gabriel hadn't yet figured out a way to eliminate sexual relations between the soldiers like

Hennings and the handpicked candidates for the Program, but when he did, he would implement that rule as well.)

Gillian Lloyd was Hennings's third candidate to go through with the procedure. The other two had borne children. An excellent success rate. They'd had high hopes for Gillian. Then she had betrayed the Program by giving herself to the astronaut. At least it was to be assumed that she had, and in the Program, there was no place even for an assumption of that sort.

Losing her had been a tremendous letdown. But hope had been resurrected in her twin, Melina.

Hennings was still talking. "Tobias wants to ask Melina some questions about the Waters Clinic."

He didn't raise his voice, but with steely resolve, Brother Gabriel said, "This meeting must not take place. You realize that, of course."

"Of course."

"Can I trust you to handle it?"

"I can handle it."

"This isn't your specialty. I could send someone—"

"I can handle it," Hennings repeated

adamantly. Then, in a softer voice, he added, "With all due respect."

Brother Gabriel grinned and took another satisfying sip of his chocolate. Nothing motivated quite as effectively as a little competition. Hennings would work doubly hard to guarantee that another soldier wasn't sent in to clean up his mess. "What about our other problem in Dallas?"

After a slight hesitation, Hennings replied, "Regrettably it remains a problem."

Brother Gabriel cut his eyes over to Mr. Hancock, who eloquently raised his eyebrows. "It was my understanding that that had been taken care of tonight."

"That was my understanding, too, sir," Hennings said. "An attempt was made. Some damage was inflicted."

"'Damage' wasn't what I had in mind."

"Nor I. I share your desire for elimination."

Was that jealousy he detected in Jem Hennings's voice? Apparently when it came to dealing with Christopher Hart, Hennings wasn't acting strictly on his orders. He was being driven by his own jealousy over the night Gillian had spent with the celebrity astronaut.

He decided to exploit that. "It makes me ill

to think of the two of them together. I've seen the photographs of her. Such skin. A very sensual face. I hate to think of him caressing her. Moving inside her. You were the only one I had entitled to that particular pleasure."

"Yes, sir," Hennings said, his voice tight.

"A bachelor of Colonel Hart's fame must have been with many women. He would know how to give one pleasure."

"I suppose."

Brother Gabriel smiled in secret over his brilliant ability to manipulate people. It was almost too easy. "In any case," he continued, "it's distressing to me that the man who defiled our Gillian has gone unpunished."

"Not for long, Brother Gabriel."

"Satan used him. You realize that, don't you?"

"Yes."

"Restore my faith in you, Jem."

Jem Hennings asked for a blessing, which Brother Gabriel bestowed. Upon disconnecting, he turned to Mr. Hancock, who easily detected his boss's dark mood. "Upsetting business. Most upsetting."

Brother Gabriel drained his cup of hot

chocolate, then angrily pushed it away. "I want this situation in Dallas contained."

"I'm confident it will be."

"What about Gordon's replacement?"

"The clinic has had five applicants for the job. Two are ours."

"See to it that one of them gets the job. That is an active clinic. I want someone there."

"Of course."

Absently, he toyed with a crystal paper-weight on his desk, his mind returning to Melina Lloyd. Christopher Hart had cost him a valuable asset. He wasn't prepared to lose another, yet Hennings had said he'd already detected "vibes" between them.

Brother Gabriel began to worry that Jem Hennings wasn't up to the task of finessing Melina. Perhaps she was more perceptive than her twin had been. If that was the case, Hennings could not make one misstep.

"Can I get you anything else, Brother Gabriel?"

Mr. Hancock could always tell when he was feeling the enormous weight of his responsibilities. "What do you recommend, Mr. Hancock?"

"Leslie," Hancock stated without hesitation. Apparently he'd already given it some thought. "Lovely girl. Blond. She came to us last year from Iowa."

"Ah, yes." He formed a mental image of a tall, sturdy farm girl with freckles on her nose.

"We recently intercepted a letter she wrote to her parents," Mr. Hancock told him. "Unhappily, Leslie is homesick."

His temper erupted. "She lives the life of a princess inside a palace. How can she be homesick for Iowa?" Worse than anything he hated ingratitude.

"According to the letter, she's feeling lonely, unappreciated, and unloved."

"Brother Gabriel left the desk and stormed toward the bedroom. "Summon Leslie, Mr. Hancock. I'm feeling a little lonely, unappreciated, and unloved myself tonight."

"Melina?"

She muttered inarticulately into her pillow.

Chief rocked her shoulder. "Come on. Haul ass. They're here."

She rolled over and blinked him into focus. "What? Who?"

"The FBI guys."

She threw back the covers, scrambled from the bed, and lunged toward the window all in one motion. She raised a louver and peered through the blinds. A navy blue sedan was parked at the curb. Two suited men—one black, one white—were alighting. They paused to look up and down the block as though getting a feel for the neighborhood, then started up the walkway.

Turning back into the room, she looked at the clock on the nightstand. She had set her alarm for eight-thirty. It was eight twenty-five. "They're early."

"I heard the car pull up. That's what woke me up."

Chief had accepted her offer to stay over. He had slept in the guest room, but it had apparently been a rough night. His bruised eye was swollen nearly shut, and the bandage she'd put on his cheekbone had a dark bloodstain in the center of it. He had pulled on his jeans, but he was barefoot and shirtless.

"Hurry and dress." He tossed her a pair of slacks and a T-shirt he had randomly pulled from the closet. "I don't think they should know I'm here."

Although she didn't appreciate his rummaging in the closet and ordering her around, he made sense. She couldn't greet the FBI wearing only her nightie. It was bad enough to be caught without makeup and before her first shot of caffeine.

Evidently Chief wasn't operating with a clear head, either. As though addled, he was staring in the vicinity of her knees. "Chief?" He raised his head, looking bumfuzzled. "I need to dress," she said, indicating the clothes he'd unceremoniously thrown at her.

"Uh, yeah. I'll be in the guest room." Turning quickly, he slipped into the hallway.

"Chief?"

He poked his head back in. "What?"

"Why don't you want them to know that you're here?"

He pointed at his face. "This would call for an explanation. So far we don't have one. Hurry."

He popped back out. She peeled off her short nightgown, dressed in record time, and was working her feet into a pair of sneakers when the doorbell pealed. Passing the guest room, she noticed that the door was opened a crack. She ran her fingers through her hair as she crossed the living room and reached for the deadbolt lock just as the bell sounded a second time.

"Sorry," she said breathlessly as she pulled open the door.

"Ms. Lloyd?"

The federal officer's eyes dropped to the Tweety Bird on her T-shirt. Self-consciously she smoothed her hand over it. "You're half an hour early."

"We apologize. Traffic wasn't as heavy as we anticipated. I'm Special Agent Hank Tobias. This is Agent Patterson." In sync, they proffered their IDs.

She stepped aside and motioned them in. "Have a seat."

Tobias sat down where she'd indicated. Her dishabille hadn't escaped him. "Did we get you up?"

"I confess. I didn't fall asleep until after three. Since my sister's murder, my nights haven't been very restful."

"I can understand why," Patterson said somberly. "Condolences."

"Thank you."

"Don't you have friends or family staying with you?"

She thought about Chief hiding in the guest room. He was neither friend nor family, so she wasn't exactly lying when she said, "I've had friends offer to stay with me, but I value my privacy."

"Probably a wise choice." Tobias smiled, but he didn't impress her as someone who made a habit of it. "Grieving is a very private thing."

"Would you like coffee? I know I could use some."

"Sounds good to me. Mr. Patterson?"

"I'd love some. Nice of you to offer."

"It won't take a minute to put on. Then we'll get down to business. I'm anxious to hear what you have to tell me."

"Likewise," Tobias said.

She left them in the living room and went into the kitchen. Up till then, she had forgotten about the mess. The room could have been declared a disaster area. The floor was still spattered with broken glass, spilled wine, and blood, both hers and Chief's. Bloody dish towels littered the dining table.

Walking across the floor even with shoes on was a safety hazard. Glass crunched beneath the rubber soles of her sneakers. She took the broom and dustpan from the pantry and was about to clear herself a path when Tobias and Patterson wandered in.

"What happened here?" Tobias asked.

She couldn't tell the truth without alerting them to Chief's presence. "I, uh, had a little accident last night."

Tobias, obviously a man accustomed to getting all the facts, continued looking at her.

"The lights flickered out during the thunderstorm," she said, improvising. "The sudden darkness startled me. I dropped a bottle of wine. Stepped on the broken glass." She finished with a self-deprecating shrug. "I was too tired to clean up last night."

Tobias was staring at the blood spots on the floor and the stained kitchen towels. "You cut your feet?"

"My heel came down on a piece of glass."

"Did you go to the hospital?"

"Hospital? No, no, it wasn't that serious. Just a sliver, really."

"And it bled that much?"

She cut her eyes from him to Patterson and then back to Tobias. Laughing nervously, she replied, "You know how tiny punctures like that can be sometimes. I thought it would never stop bleeding."

"You should be more careful, Melina."

"Right. I agree. I should definitely be more

careful." Quickly turning toward the counter, she pulled the coffeemaker from the appliance garage built into the cabinetry. "Did you get breakfast on your flight down from D.C. this morning, Agent Patterson?"

"Juice, coffee, and a muffin, if you want to call that breakfast."

Over her shoulder she smiled at them disarmingly.

That's why neither expected what came next.

The floral arrangement on the counter had peaked days ago. Last night Jem had moved it into the kitchen for disposal. The flowers were wilted, dark, and dry. The water in the bottom of the vase was viscous and had begun to give off an unpleasant odor.

She reached for it now and, with the sympathy card still attached by a thin pink ribbon, turned and swung the heavy glass vase, flowers and all, at Tobias's head. It caught him on the temple and split the skin on impact.

"Bloody hell!" He roared in pain and careened backward into the kitchen table, knocking a wooden bowl of fruit to the floor. Oranges and apples bounced amid the broken glass, now also strewn with dying flowers and splashed with stagnant water.

While Tobias struggled to regain his balance, Patterson lunged for her. She dodged and tried to leap over Tobias to escape through the door, but his hand shot out and caught her ankle. As she pitched forward, her collarbone landed hard against the doorjamb, and she cried out.

Chief, appearing suddenly, shoved her aside as he barged into the kitchen, clutching a golf putter. The two men were stunned to see him, and he used that to his advantage. Putting his entire weight behind the lateral swing, he whacked Patterson in the ribs with the golf club. Patterson bent over double. Chief hit him hard again on the back of his head. He went down with a grunt.

But his back served as a trampoline for Tobias, who launched himself at Chief.

"Melina, get out!"

Chief's warning had barely cleared his lips when Tobias grabbed him and practically threw him, face first, into the wall. He dropped the golf club and should have been knocked out, but miraculously he had enough fight left in him to jam his elbow into Tobias's Adam's apple. The other man stumbled backward, then lowered his head and charged, sending Chief reeling through the door and into the hallway, where he somersaulted backward. Tobias slammed the door shut, then wheeled around and reached for her with one hand while yanking a handgun from a concealed holster with the other.

He'd been quick, but not so quick that Melina couldn't react. She had retrieved the golf putter. Before his hand had completely cleared his jacket, she struck his wrist hard enough to crack bone.

Chief came crashing back in. He executed a karate chop to the back of Tobias's neck. His benumbed hand dropped the pistol, his eyes rolled back, his knees buckled, and he went down like a sack of cement.

Patterson was still out cold.

Chief braced his hands on his knees and hung his head between his shoulders. His breathing was labored and loud. He coughed and wiped his bleeding nose with the back of his hand. "I hope to hell you have a real good reason."

"They weren't FBI."

"You know this with some degree of certainty?"

"He called me Melina."

"He called you Melina."

"Isn't that a little out of character for a hard-ass, button-down FBI agent?"

"Maybe. But it's not what I'd call a real good reason for assaulting a federal officer, *Melina.*"

"That's not all. I was told last night that Patterson was from the Dallas office. When I asked about his flight from D.C. this morning—"

"I heard."

"Why would an FBI agent lie?"

"Fuck," he said, which seemed to sum up his feelings on the entire matter, especially his nose, which continued to drip blood. "I give up. Why?"

"I don't know."

Now that the fight was over, her survival instinct had ebbed and common sense was reasserting itself. Maybe her imagination was working overtime. Given the events of the week, she might have overreacted, might have been looking for bogeymen so hard she hadn't recognized the good guys. Not only would she be in trouble, she'd dragged Chief into it with her.

"I could be wrong," she said apprehensively.

He considered that, then knelt down beside Tobias and fished the small black wallet from his pocket. He looked at it, then flipped it up toward Melina. "Looks real."

The photo ID appeared to be the genuine article. She covered her mouth and whispered, "Oh, shit."

Chief came to his feet and for a long moment they stared hard into each other's eyes.

At last he said, "I'm not buying it."

"Neither am I," she agreed on a soft expulsion of breath.

He hitched his head in the direction of the bedrooms. "Get your keys."

Holy . . . !"

The unfinished exclamation came from FBI Agent Patterson when he joined Special Agent Hank Tobias in Melina Lloyd's kitchen.

For a time both men silently surveyed the damage. Eventually Patterson turned to the agent from the Washington office for his more experienced opinion. "Any ideas?"

Tobias nudged a dead flower petal with the toe of his shoe. "Beyond the obvious that some kind of altercation took place, I haven't the foggiest."

When Melina Lloyd had failed to answer her doorbell, Tobias had tested the front door and found it unlocked. He opened it and called out her name. His voice was absorbed by the hollow silence of an empty house.

Had she intentionally stood him up? That could indicate she had something to hide. Reluctance to be questioned usually signified criminal involvement on some level. Or, if she'd had no choice but to leave her house unattended and unlocked, that could mean any number of things. None he could think of were good. Or—and this possibility filled him with dread—she had met with a fate similar to her sister's and was unable to respond.

Silently, using hand signals, he and Patterson went in. Splitting up, Tobias took the side of the house that included the living area, dining room, and kitchen. Patterson crept down the hallway. Soon they were calling out to each other that the house was empty. Tobias had replaced his handgun in his shoulder holster and stood just inside the kitchen door, trying to figure out just what the hell had happened while he waited for Patterson to rejoin him.

Now he raised his chin toward the other side of the house. "What does it look like back there?"

"Two bedrooms. Both slept in. A bathroom with a bloody handprint and kitchen towel in it. Bandages. Spots of dried blood on the carpet and on the pillowcase in what appears to be the guest room. A baggie filled with water."

"Water?"

"Could be a makeshift ice pack."

"Makes sense. If somebody got hit on the head with that vase."

Patterson nodded. "That's about it. The closet door was open, but nothing had been disturbed in it or in the bureau drawers. Jewelry box was full. No sign of theft. No sign of struggle except in here."

As Tobias mentally sifted through the facts of Patterson's verbal report, he unconsciously smoothed his hand over his expensive silk necktie. Silver in color, it perfectly matched his shirt, which matched the chalk stripe in his navy blue suit. He didn't have a hobby other than daily gym workouts. He didn't take vacations to exciting destinations. He didn't own a boat or a pair of snow skis or a set of golf clubs. He drove a company car, and it was his only vehicle. He lived alone in a small apartment, using the second bedroom as an extra closet. Clothes were his one indulgence, and he wore them like a model.

"So all the action took place in here," he mused out loud.

"Unless I missed something."

"I'll take a look," Tobias said.

"I won't be offended."

But instead of moving in the direction of the bedrooms, Tobias gingerly stepped to the other side of the kitchen, moving along the perimeter of the room so as not to disturb anything that might later become evidence—to what crime, he didn't yet know. He covered the back doorknob with a handkerchief and opened it.

"Garage is empty. Where's her car?" he asked rhetorically.

"Want me to call DPD?"

"I'd say so."

"And report what?"

"Damned if I know. No sign of B and E. No corpse."

"Abduction?"

"Possibly," Tobias agreed absently.

Patterson placed the call.

The senior agent left the kitchen, moved through the undisturbed living room, and down the hallway. He came first to the guest bedroom and studied the bed, where someone had recently slept. As Patterson had noted, there was a smudged bloodstain on the pillowcase. And something else. Tobias leaned in for a closer look. He determined what it was and added it to his database of information, but left it untouched for later collection and cataloguing by DPD.

He went from there into the master bedroom and stood beside the woman's bed. The nightgown appeared to have been thoughtlessly removed, not ripped off in a violent struggle. Only one of the pillows on the bed bore the imprint of a head. She had slept alone.

He noticed the framed snapshot on the nightstand and was looking at it when Patterson rejoined him. "On their way." Then, noticing what held Tobias's attention, he said, "I saw that earlier. Amazing, isn't it?"

Tobias had learned that the Lloyd sisters were twins. Lawson had told him in their meeting earlier that morning. "By all accounts they were interchangeable," the detective had said. "I couldn't have told them apart. Except that Gillian was dead."

At Tobias's request the homicide detective had also provided them with some background information. "Both were successful in their chosen careers. Both single. Neither has ever been married. Although Gillian was engaged."

"What about him?"

"Asshole," Lawson said laconically.

"Can you be more specific?"

"Class-A asshole."

If everything Lawson subsequently told them about Jem Hennings was true, the description fit. Tobias had said, "I'm sure you checked out his alibi."

"He was cleared. Plus he had no motive that we could see. Seemed sincerely shaken."

"And Melina?" Tobias probed.

"In what respect?"

"Did she have a motive?"

The detective firmly shook his head. "Not even a life insurance policy. The twins had agreed to make their favorite charity their beneficiaries. After funeral costs and all her outstanding bills are paid, everything in Gillian's estate goes to it."

"Melina seemed okay with that?"

"I never asked but felt I didn't have to. They donated the inheritance from their parents a few years ago. Wasn't a huge amount, but it was a nice piece of change. Neither touched a cent of it."

At the conclusion of the meeting, Lawson had said, "If my opinion means anything to you, Melina Lloyd's clean as a whistle."

"Wasn't she the last person to see Gillian alive?" Patterson asked.

"Right," the detective said. "Besides the killer. Which wasn't her. If you're looking for a conspiracy, I'd bet my left nut that she's not involved."

Tobias had come away from the meeting with a distinct impression of Melina Lloyd and her late twin. Apparently they'd shared the same values. And, as this photograph attested, the physical resemblance was almost eerie. "Lawson wasn't exaggerating," he remarked as he reached into his jacket for his cell phone.

"You calling Lawson?"

"His case is closed, but, as a courtesy . . ." He dialed. "While I'm talking to him, call DMV and get her car tag number. Let's see if we can locate it. It might be parked at the local supermarket where she's gone to pick up some solvent that works on bloodstained carpet."

"Is that what you think?" Patterson asked. "That she made a mess and it caused her to forget her appointment with us?"

Tobias thought about the murder and kidnapping cases that had triggered his search for a pattern. Women had been viciously slain by strangers with no apparent motive, their murderers committing suicide before they could even be questioned. Babies had disappeared without a trace. The common denominator: infertility clinics where alternative methods of conception were performed on a routine basis. Frightening implications.

Solemnly, Tobias answered Patterson's question. "No. That's not what I think."

Supremely irritated, Jem Hennings rapidly tapped his pen against his desk pad. The market was open, trading was brisk, and what was he doing? Wasting his valuable, revenue-producing time on damage control.

Over the last few days, bad news had been breaking over him like cresting ocean waves. Since Gillian's body had been discovered, he felt as though he'd been holding his breath. It was becoming increasingly difficult to come up for air, and now he felt his lungs were about to burst.

"Okay, what went wrong?" he asked into his cell phone.

"He was there."

"Who?"

"The astronaut."

Jem's pen stopped his rapid tattoo. "Christopher Hart was with Melina? Inside her house?"

Hart had given these bozos the slip last night after they had bungled taking him out for good. It was supposed to have looked like the work of tree huggers with a grudge against the space program for getting funds that would be better spent on conserving planet Earth. Jem had composed the letter that was to have been attached to Hart's body when it was found floating in the Trinity with a bullet in the head.

But Hart had been lucky. When passersby became witnesses, the "tree huggers" in ski masks had fled. When they returned later in another vehicle and without their masks, Hart was nowhere to be found.

Jem had had people looking all over Dallas for him, from the parking lot of the bar where he'd left his car overnight, to The Mansion, and at all points in between. After reporting all that bad news to Brother Gabriel, he'd spent a sleepless night.

Meanwhile, Hart had been playing cozy with Melina.

Resentment for Hart burned deep and hot inside him. Last night, Melina had shooed him out of her house, pleading exhaustion and a desire to be alone. *Apparently her aversion for company hadn't extended to Christopher Hart,* Jem thought bitterly. That was reason enough to hate him.

But Jem's hatred went beyond jealousy. Hart was making him look bad in Brother Gabriel's eyes. Because of Hart, he was at risk of losing Brother Gabriel's trust and respect. That was reason enough to kill him.

Forgetting the stock market and the potential income he was losing for his clients and himself, ignoring the call notes that were continually being thrust beneath his nose by a persistent secretary, and pretending not to see the blinking icon on his computer screen indicating that he had E-mail, he growled into his telephone receiver, "Starting at the beginning and tell me what happened."

It was worse than he had expected. "Melina saw through you?"

"Either that or she doesn't care for the FBI."

The thug had been recruited for service by Brother Gabriel himself, who'd baptized him and enrolled him in the elite army, renaming him Joshua after the Old Testament warrior. Jem didn't know his real name. No one did. The man had lived under so many aliases that even he had probably forgotten which name was authentic.

Joshua had distinguished himself in Haiti doing wet work for Duvalier. He wasn't afraid of bloodletting. In fact, he had a passion for it. His other passion was Brother Gabriel, whom he worshiped. Brother Gabriel had won Joshua's unqualified love and allegiance by liberating his brother, another mercenary, from a prison in Malaysia. Joshua would walk through fire for Brother Gabriel.

Jem understood his loyalty, and he admired the man's lethal skills. He was glad he was playing on their team. But right now, he could throttle him.

Joshua complained of having a knot on his temple as proof of Melina's dislike for the FBI. "I also think my wrist might be broken. I don't know what put her on to us."

"You had to get the IDs done overnight."

"But they're the best money can buy," Joshua argued. "The real Tobias would have a hard time spotting them as fakes."

"Then it must've been something you said." Jem had Joshua recount the meeting step by step, word for word. "That's it, you moron," he hissed when Joshua reached the part about Patterson's flight from D.C. "He was supposed to be from the Dallas office."

"You didn't tell me that."

"Of course I did."

"You didn't," Joshua insisted coldly.

"Well, that's how you tipped her."

Joshua described the fight. "Soon's we regained consciousness, we cleared out."

"And there was no sign of Melina or Hart?"

"They'd split. Her car was gone."

Joshua had failed to neutralize Hart. He'd

let Melina disappear. Maybe so much spiritual indoctrination had softened him. What other explanation could there be for his having botched—and botched badly—his last two assignments?

That's the risk you ran by using malleable people. Those who could be so easily manipulated weren't particularly mental giants. Dale Gordon, for example. He'd been a scientific genius. He was steadfastly devoted to the Program. But once he'd served his purpose, he'd been expendable. Unfortunately, he'd been too stupid to destroy all the collected photos and data on Gillian inside his apartment. That had brought the clinic into the investigation.

Jem Hennings wouldn't have made a mistake like that. It still rankled that Brother Gabriel had ordered Gillian's murder and Gordon's suicide without even consulting him. He'd been genuinely shocked when he arrived at her house and saw her body. The words written on the wall had been his first clue that her suitability for the Program had come into question, but it wasn't until the meeting with Lawson, when he heard Christopher Hart describing Dale Gordon, that he realized what had happened and why.

Brother Gabriel couldn't be faulted. He was perfect. It was Gordon's fault for not thinking it through and being more thorough. *Gordon, you damn idiot,* he thought now. If not for his oversight, Jem wouldn't be having to deal with another incompetent.

"You've disappointed me, Joshua," Jem said in the tone of a hanging judge. "Twice."

"Why couldn't we've just shot the guy? Grabbed the girl when she opened the door? That would've been easier. All this role-playing is for shit," he sneered.

Jem ignored the criticism of his strategy. "I have no choice except to report your failures to Brother Gabriel."

The name evoked fear and respect. Since Brother Gabriel was God's chosen spokesperson, the one person on earth to whom God had entrusted the future of the world, even the strongest of men were humbled by the threat of his disapproval. To cross Brother Gabriel was tantamount to raising your fist to God.

"We haven't failed," Joshua countered,

not sounding as contrite as Jem wished. "We've got it covered. Remember?"

And suddenly Jem did. He'd been so upset over their failure, he'd almost forgotten their backup plan! His head broke the surface, and he took a much-needed breath. "You're sure it works?"

"It works. They can't disappear. What do you want us to do with her and the guy?"

That was a very good question. How much had Melina guessed or managed to piece together? Other than him, who could have known that the FBI was coming to her house this morning? If confronted about that, how would he explain? What if she notified the police or the FBI?

He needed time to think, to sort this out, develop contingencies. "When you locate them, do nothing until you notify me first," he instructed Joshua.

The order didn't sit well with the mercenary and his companion, men of action who now harbored a double grudge against Christopher Hart. Good. Jem could foster that resentment.

"Christopher Hart is an enemy of the Program. He defiled Gillian Lloyd. He might already have defiled Melina as well."

"He must be destroyed."

"That's what we've been called to do." Jem's voice reverberated with righteous fervor. He hoped it conveyed the spiritual overtones that the retribution against Hart should take, while on a personal level, he hoped these guys pulverized the bastard and made him bleed into his cowboy boots. "Stay as close to them as you can without their seeing you. They know your faces now. If you're seen, you're blown."

Joshua took umbrage. "I'm not an idiot."

"All evidence pointing to the contrary," Jem said beneath his breath. "Keep me posted."

The instant he hung up, the secretary was there, waving another memo beneath his nose. "Can't it wait?"

"I don't think so," she replied sweetly, practically cooing. Then she turned and prissily walked away.

"Mr. Hennings?"

Jem swiveled his chair around. Two men had converged on his workstation. One was tall, black, immaculately dressed, no-nonsense. He held Jem's gaze so imperiously that the other man was noticed only in his peripheral vision. His presence seemed inconsequential.

Jem's bowels suddenly felt loose, but he managed to come to his feet, a pleasant but inquisitive smile on his face. "I'm Jem Hennings. What can I do for you?"

The man flipped open a small leather wallet. "Special Agent Tobias, FBI."

C H A P T E R | 2 2

"Personal shopper?" Chief remarked drolly as she ended the call on her cell phone.

"What's wrong with it?"

"Nothing. Actually, Melina, I'm impressed." She shot him a dirty look, and he feigned being afraid. "You're not going to hit me in the head with a vase, are you?"

Ignoring that, she stood. The space between the two double beds was so narrow, he had to angle his knees aside in order to make room for her to pass. "Today I'm glad I have her to do my shopping. I told her what I needed. She'll gather up the merchandise and send it here in a taxi."

"These aren't your usual digs. She didn't ask for an explanation?"

"She probably thinks I'm having an affair. Among her clients are the rich and famous. She wouldn't have them for long if she fished for information and told secrets. Discretion is key."

"The same as with your job. Gillian explained to me that you don't divulge one client's secrets to another."

"Bad for business."

"You still haven't explained the necessity for haute couture."

"Anyone looking for us will watch for credit card purchases, but maybe they won't think of Neiman's. This is the best way I could think of to get a few changes of clothes. You told me to grab my keys. I grabbed my keys. God knows when I'll be able to go home, and this is a little conspicuous," she said of her Tweety Bird shirt.

She looked around at the dreary, impersonal room. After stopping at an ATM and getting enough cash to last for several days, they'd checked into an interstate highway chain motel that had a parking lot full of eighteen-wheelers. The room was standard issue.

Her dejected gaze eventually came back to him. "Chief, listen. This may be home for me for a while, but that doesn't mean it has to be for you."

"How's the collarbone?" he asked, making her aware that she was massaging it.

She dropped her hand. "It's fine. I shouldn't have let on that I knew you had slept with Gillian. If I hadn't called you a liar and a coward, you would have walked away from that meeting with Lawson free and clear."

"Do you think it's broken?"

"My collarbone? No."

"Cracked?"

"No," she said with an impatient shake of her head. "It'll probably bruise, but that'll be the worst of it." Wringing her hands, she said, "I hate myself for dragging you into this mess."

He sighed with resignation. "You insist on talking about it, don't you? Okay, let's talk about it. You didn't drag me in, Melina. I was in it from the start. Unwittingly, maybe, but I was in it. Gillian was killed because of the time she spent with me. Now it seems that

I'm next. On both counts, I want to know why."

"NASA would protect you. Whoever attacked you last night wouldn't be so brave if NASA was looming behind you." She appealed to him to call the FBI.

"And tell them what?"

"That you thought I was being attacked by thieves this morning."

"Thieves!" he exclaimed on a short laugh.

"You jumped to my defense. When you realized your mistake, you were appalled. I escaped before you could detain me."

"You think they would buy that?" he asked scoffingly. "No, they wouldn't. And I refuse to hide behind NASA." Pointing to his battered face, he said, "This is a personal fight."

"How does it feel now?"

"You don't want to know."

His nose had finally stopped bleeding. As soon as they reached the hotel, he had washed up and she had replaced the bandage on his cheekbone. He'd been holding a plastic bag of ice on his eye, and the swelling had gone down appreciably. But he still looked like a has-been prizefighter who'd gone one round too many.

"I'm sorry, Chief."

"Well, at least this time I got a whack at the other guys."

Regardless of his jokes and his insistence that he'd been involved from the start, she still felt responsible. "What about your car?"

"It's sitting there like bait. I can't go back for it."

"They'll be looking for mine now, too. What can we do about that?"

"I'm working on it," he said, tapping his temple.

"Fine pair of outlaws we are." She sat down across from him again and gave a mirthless laugh. "In a million years, I'd never have thought I'd be having a conversation like this."

He smiled. "Neither did I."

"I don't know how to be on the lam."

"I guess we'll pick it up as we go along."

"I guess."

He dug his cell phone out of the pocket of his jacket and placed a call to The Mansion. He explained to the concierge that he'd had to leave unexpectedly and that he wished his belongings to be packed and sent by taxi to his present location. He gave them the address of the motel but didn't identify the place by name. "As soon as possible, please." After disconnecting, he said, "I miss it already."

Barely listening, she thoughtfully tapped her own cell phone against her chin. "I don't believe it."

"What?"

"That Tobias and Patterson were government agents. I know, I know, the IDs looked authentic. But crooks would know how to get good fakes."

"There's one way to find out. Call the FBI."

"Call the FBI." They had spoken the words simultaneously. "That's what my sister and I used to do," she told him as she dialed long-distance information.

Their eyes connected. Any mention of her caused their smiles to slip noticeably. Now was no exception.

"I can forget it, temporarily," he said quietly. "But it always comes back with a jolting reminder."

"Me, too."

She was being cued to press a digit if she wanted her call to be automatically forwarded. She did so, then said to Chief softly, "She had a very good time."

Before he could press her for details, her

call went through. "Yes, I'm trying to reach Special Agent Hank Tobias. Do you have a number for him?"

"I can connect you directly to his office."

She covered the mouthpiece. "Oh, God. He's real."

"So we're toast."

The call was answered in a crisp, businesslike manner. She asked to speak to Tobias but was informed that he was unavailable. "Can someone else help you?"

"Ms. . . ." She strained to remember, and miraculously recalled the name. "Myrick."

"Please hold."

She looked across at Chief and shook her head remorsefully. "I'll take full responsibility. It was my mistake, Chief. I'll make certain they understand—"

A voice she recognized interrupted her. "This is Lucy."

"I saw Melina last night," Jem Hennings answered in reply to Tobias's question. "Why? What's this about? Has something happened to her? Oh, Jesus, don't tell me something's happened to her, too."

"We're not jumping to any conclusions,"

Tobias told him calmly. "I had an appointment with her this morning, and she failed to keep it. I'm just trying to track her down."

"You had an appointment with Melina? What for? What's she done?"

Sidestepping the question, Tobias asked his own. "Do you know where she might have gone this morning? We've checked her office. She hasn't reported in."

"The gym. She told me she was going to work out this morning."

"What gym?"

"I'm sorry, I don't know where her membership is."

After directing Patterson to get someone on that, Tobias turned back to Jem Hennings. "What time did you see her last night?"

Hennings divided a confused gaze between him and Patterson, who was speaking softly into his cell phone. "Uh. Let's see, about ten, ten-thirty. We had dinner at her house. Relaxed for a while. She was beat. After the week she's had. You know about my fiancée, Gillian, right? Melina's sister?"

"We had a lengthy discussion with Senior Corporal Lawson this morning."

"Oh. Then you know. Are you investigating Gillian's murder?"

"We just wanted to ask Ms. Lloyd some questions."

"About what?"

"You haven't heard from her since last night?"

"No. I told her I'd check in on her sometime today, but we didn't make specific plans."

"Was she alone when you left her?"

"Against my better judgment. She'd taken a long bath and was going straight to bed. In fact, she ran me out so she could do just that. Personally, I thought she should have had someone staying with her. At least for the next few days. She's very independent, though. Wouldn't hear of it."

Tobias kept his expression impassive. Patterson ended his call and reported that one of Melina's employees had volunteered to call the gym she frequented.

"It's not like her to skip an appointment," Hennings continued. "She's a professional woman. Her business is keeping appointments. But I guess that after what she's suffered this week, she's not her usual self."

"In what way?"

"Absentminded. Distracted. She'll be mortified when she realizes she forgot your appointment. You might try calling her on her cell," Hennings said, trying ever so hard to be helpful. "I have the number."

"So do I." Tobias had called it several times but always got her voice mail.

"If you've called it, you probably got her voice mail," Hennings said. "It used to annoy Gillian that Melina wouldn't answer. She leaves her phone off so it won't disturb her clients."

"You seem to know her almost as well as you knew your fiancée."

"They were so close, to know one was almost to know the other. It was Gillian I fell in love with, but I'd already come to consider Melina my sister, so I want to help any way I can," Hennings said earnestly. "What's this about? Is she in some sort of trouble?"

Tobias withdrew a business card from his suit jacket pocket and gave it to the stockbroker. "You can help by calling me immediately if you hear from her."

"That's it?"

"For now."

"I'd like to know what's going on."

"We just want to talk to her."

"You'll stay in touch with me?" Hennings asked anxiously.

"You can count on it."

Out in the corridor as they were making their way to the elevator, Patterson said, "Lawson wasn't exaggerating. He is a Class-A asshole."

"Who is tripping all over himself in his eagerness to help."

"You think he was lying about leaving her house last night? Was he there this morning?"

"I don't know about that, but it wasn't him who slept in the guest room bed."

"How do you know?"

"He has light, wavy hair."

"Pardon?"

Tobias's cell phone rang. "Yes?"

"You're gonna love me."

"Why's that, Ms. Myrick?"

"I just spoke to Melina Lloyd."

"Black, six feet two inches tall, dynamite dresser. Her words. Gorgeous. Also her word. A Denzel Washington type." Melina reiterated for Chief the physical traits of Hank Tobias as described to her by Lucy

Myrick. "She doesn't know Patterson because he's from the Dallas office."

"And when you asked your Patterson about his flight down this morning, he lied."

"So maybe I won't be sent to federal prison after all."

"I don't think so," Chief agreed. "Because our Tobias wasn't that tall, and he sure as hell was no Denzel Washington."

"Off-the-rack suit, cheap shoes. Not what I'd describe as a 'dynamite dresser.'"

"As anyone with a personal shopper would know."

"Would you please let up on that?"

"Your shopper knows her business." His eyes were on her butt. "Perfect fit."

The new things had been delivered a half hour earlier. She'd specified casual, so the saleswoman at Neiman's had sent two pairs of slacks, one skirt, and sweaters that would go with them. She had included a lightweight wool jacket, three sets of underwear, two pairs of shoes, and a nightgown. A smaller bag had been filled with cosmetics and toiletries, along with a cheeky note from the shopper that read, "Have fun!" She'd taken a quick shower and put on a pair of the new slacks, exchanging her

Tweety Bird shirt for a silk and cashmere blend pullover sweater.

Disregarding Chief's compliment, she told him that Ms. Myrick had promised to contact Tobias immediately. "She assured me that he would call, so I've left my ringer on."

"What are you going to say?"

"I have no idea. I guess I'll play it by ear."

"Who knew about your appointment with him?"

"No one."

"Someone."

"Lucy Myrick called last night while I was in the bathtub. Jem and I answered—"

Their gazes connected like two magnets. "Hennings was there when the call came in?"

"He asked me later who had called."

"You told him?"

"I made up a story."

Chief's eye spoke volumes, but they didn't have a chance to pursue the conversation because her cell phone rang.

She checked the caller ID but didn't recognize the number. At least it wasn't Jem's. She truly didn't know what she would say to him now. On the fourth ring, she answered. "Hello?"

"Ms. Lloyd? Special Agent Tobias."

"I apologize for missing our appointment."

"I arrived at nine."

"Too late, as it turned out."

"Are you all right?"

"I've been better."

"What happened this morning? I was in your house. I saw the mess, the blood. Are you hurt?"

"No."

"Colonel Hart? Is he injured?"

Her eyes sliced to Chief, who was following her side of the conversation. He questioned her pause by raising his eyebrows inquiringly. She shook her head slightly.

When she failed to respond to the loaded question, Tobias said, "I'd like very much to talk to you. Tell me where you are."

"Not yet. Not until you tell me why you're interested in Gillian's murder case."

"Because she was a patient of the Waters Clinic."

"The clinic has a lot of patients. None except my sister was stabbed to death this week. Why did she win that distinction, Mr. Tobias?"

"That's what I'm trying to find out."

"You must have a hunch."

"Not at this point."

"Something flagged your attention to Gillian's murder."

He hesitated, then said, "A series of other crimes."

"You believe Dale Gordon was a serial killer?"

"No. We checked that out," he answered evenly. "He relates only to your sister's murder."

"Then the common thread is that all the victims were patients of a Waters Clinic? There's your answer, isn't it?"

"It would be, except that they weren't all affiliated with Waters," he explained. "One was a patient of a private physician. One went to another franchise clinic with a reputation as solid as the Waters chain.

"One striking similarity between your twin's case and another in Oakland, California, is that both women had been artificially inseminated within days of their murder, and that the suspects took their own lives before they could even be questioned by the authorities."

"My God," she said, her voice quavering. "How many of these crimes are we talking about?"

He refrained from answering. Neither said anything for a time. Chief's laser blues were telegraphing questions.

Finally Tobias said, "That's all I can say for now, Ms. Lloyd. Meet me and Agent Patterson. Let us—"

"I tried that once. It didn't work out."

"Who came to your house this morning?"

"I don't know who they were. Don't you? Have you asked them?"

"Asked them?"

"When you arrived at my house."

"The house was empty, Ms. Lloyd."

"They were gone?" she exclaimed.

Chief sat up straighter. *Gone?* he mouthed.

Tobias was asking if the imposters were in her house when she left.

"Unconscious. On the kitchen floor," she told him.

He ruminated on that for several seconds, then asked her to describe the pair. She gave him a basic description of both, silently consulting Chief about height and weight. His nods confirmed her assessments.

"I was fooled. At first."

"And then?"

"And then I wasn't. At least I was wary enough to protect myself and get out of there."

"We found one hell of a mess in the kitchen and blood tracks on the carpet in the bedroom."

She explained about cutting her heel the night before.

"Do you sleep with your feet instead of your head on the pillow?" he asked.

"Excuse me?"

"There was blood on the pillow in the guest bedroom. And one straight black hair. I presume both belong to Colonel Hart."

She neither denied nor confirmed his guess.

"I've read Lawson's case file, Ms. Lloyd. I know that Hart spent the evening before her murder with Gillian. Had they met before that night?"

"You have Lawson's case file? I thought he'd officially closed it."

"I officially reopened it."

"I see."

"What's the matter? Do you have a problem with that?"

"I'll be in touch." She disconnected and

flung down the cell phone as though it had burned her hand.

"What's the matter?" Chief looked as tense as a coiled spring.

"They won't let it rest," she said with perhaps more agitation than was warranted. "Thank God I had her body cremated. Otherwise they'd probably be exhuming her. Oh, and by the way, he knows you're with me."

"Who're you calling now?"

She had picked up her phone again and was rapidly punching in numbers. "Clunkers."

"Clunkers?"

CHAPTER | 23

I've relocated her," Jem reported to Mr. Hancock. "My men are tracking her as we speak. Please tell Brother Gabriel that I've got it under control." Jem was a little miffed that he hadn't been put directly through to Brother Gabriel and was having to use Hancock as an intercessor.

"I'll inform him the moment his meeting concludes, although he won't be surprised to learn that things are back on track. He has every confidence in you, Mr. Hennings."

"That's the good news." Jem hoped that

Brother Gabriel's confidant would pick up on his sad tone of voice. He did.

"There's bad?"

"I think it's something Brother Gabriel should be aware of and take into careful consideration before proceeding."

"Go on."

"Christopher Hart is still with her." He let that sink in before adding, "They're presently sharing a room in a tacky truck stop motel. I'm sure Brother Gabriel will reach the same conclusion that I have regarding Melina's unsuitability for the Program."

Sounding befittingly downcast, Mr. Hancock assured him that the information would be passed along.

"Not that I'm questioning Brother Gabriel's judgment," Jem said, doing precisely that, "but I'm wondering if this conservative approach is the right one."

Earlier, he'd had to report on Joshua's second fiasco. He'd also had to impart the unhappy news that the astronaut had spent the night in Melina's house and had engaged in a fight with Joshua to protect her. At that time, he'd been instructed to keep close tabs on them, but Joshua was to take no further action until notified to do so. Because of the FBI's interest, Brother Gabriel was now of the opinion that they should err on the side of caution.

Jem understood Brother Gabriel's desire not to arouse suspicion. But on a personal level he was eager to see Hart punished for sleeping with his fiancée. He was also impatient for Melina to get her comeuppance for rebuffing him last night.

Mr. Hancock responded to his suggestion with a typically noncommittal statement. "As soon as Brother Gabriel makes a decision on how best to proceed to solve this problem, you'll be informed, Mr. Hennings."

"I'll be standing by."

Jem hung up feeling that the score was tied. It wasn't a total victory, but his recommendation hadn't been dismissed out of hand. Hart would be dealt with, just maybe not in as timely a fashion as Jem wished. And he'd planted seeds of doubt about Melina. Plans for her to participate in the Program might be scotched.

Physically, she was ideal. Her moral eligibility was another matter entirely. She had always been more sexually active than Gillian. She hinted at having had many lovers, even among her celebrity clients. If she hadn't already slept with Hart, it was more than likely that she would.

The thought of them together infuriated Jem, especially since Melina had spurned him last night and made it clear that she didn't share Gillian's attraction. She had probably shooed him on his way because she was expecting Hart. Fine. Jem Hennings would certainly survive—thrive, even—without her.

It was, however, his sworn duty to bring her unworthiness to Brother Gabriel's attention.

Brother Gabriel's punishment for moral turpitude was swift and sure. Naturally. The mind and arm of the Almighty was behind it. Both Hart and Melina would eventually get their due.

In the meantime, they couldn't escape.

Chief squinted behind his sunglasses. "How do you know she'll come out?"

"I don't. But the clinic is closed every day from one to two-thirty. I figure that's when the staff takes off for lunch."

He and Melina were seated on an iron

bench beneath a large tree at the height of its autumn color. Its leaves were a brilliant red. Patches of green lawn and mum-filled flower beds were connected by concrete paths that formed geometric patterns within the perfectly square park. The park was situated in the center of a medical complex. It was surrounded on all four sides by identical three-story buildings. The Waters Clinic comprised the second floor of one of them.

His belongings had been delivered to the motel by a cab driver, who couldn't resist making a snide reference to his drastic comedown in accommodations. "Ran out of money, did ya?" Then, noting the cuts and bruises on his face, he asked, "Or did ya get rolled?"

"I've got enough left to pay you."

"Twenty-two bucks."

"Thirty-five and you never saw me."

"Forty and I'd forget my own mother."

After a hot shower and a change of clothes, he felt a trifle better, although every now and then his cheekbone would throb a reminder. Although Melina argued with him, in his opinion the cut had closed enough to make another bandage unnecessary. But the gash wasn't pretty. It looked painful and was. His swollen eye was sensitive to sunlight even behind tinted lenses.

His discomfort was sufficient to account for his mood. He couldn't account for Melina's. Ever since talking to Tobias, she'd looked ready to jump out of her skin. She was intent on covering their tracks. They'd paid for the motel room in cash when they checked in. They left without planning to return, because they were abandoning her car there.

"If you're expecting a high-speed chase, we might be in trouble," Chief had warned her as he stashed their belongings in the back seat of their newly acquired wheels.

The Clunkers she had mentioned earlier turned out to be a low-budget car rental outfit. It leased no car assembled within the last decade, although mechanical soundness and reliability were guaranteed. "Clunkers' owner went to high school with Gillian and me," Melina told him. "We've stayed in touch, and he owes me a favor."

"What'd you do for him?"

"Remember *Playboy*'s Playmate of the Year last year?"

"Vividly."

"I escorted her and her entourage when

they came through Dallas. I got him an autographed copy of the issue."

"That couldn't have been that hard to come by. She must've signed thousands."

"Not where he asked her to sign, along with a 'You are here.'"

"Ah."

When her friend delivered the car, she tried to pay for several days in advance. He refused, saying, "No sweat, Melina. We'll settle up later." He assured her that no one would know they'd conducted business that day.

As they left the motel, Chief took the ignition keys from her. "Better let me drive this heap."

"I drive all the time, and I know where I'm going."

"I drive better and faster. You can tell me where we're going." He got behind the wheel, effectively ending the argument.

Even though any law enforcement officer on the lookout for her license plate would find the Lexus parked between two trailers behind the motel, she kept a careful watch out the cloudy rear window. Now she was suspiciously scrutinizing everyone who crisscrossed the park.

Her jitters were contagious. "In case I have

to enter a plea anytime in the near future," he said, "are we doing something illegal?"

"I'm not sure. Is avoiding the FBI a crime?"

"Fleeing to avoid giving testimony?"

"That's a crime?"

"Obstruction of justice is."

"Is that what we're doing?"

"You wear the same kind of bikinis."

Her head came around quickly. "What?"

He wished he could read the eyes behind the shades. Just like with Gillian. He remembered wishing Gillian would remove her sunglasses so he could see the color of her eyes. He knew the color of Melina's, but he wanted to see the expression in them.

"I noticed when I went into the bathroom to shower. You'd washed out your undies and left them to dry on the shower curtain rod. They're the same kind Gillian wore."

"She used the same personal shopper."

"I figured."

The conversation died. Or he thought it had. After a moment, she said, "Why on earth would you bring that up when we're running for our lives?"

"It was just an observation. To kill time while we're waiting."

"My underwear is the subject you came up with to kill time?"

"It was on my mind. I've never had to remove lingerie from the shower curtain rod before."

"You've never lived with a woman?"

"No."

"I would have thought you had."

He shook his head. "Have you ever lived with a man?"

"No."

"Then for as long as we're roommates, I promise to try and remember to put the seat down."

She laughed. "Thanks. I'll appreciate that."

The sound of her laugh, the angle of her head, the arch of her throat, the smile . . . Looking at her made his heart feel pinched, and it was all he could do to keep from touching her. He was glad she looked like Gillian because he had liked everything about Gillian's looks. Face, form, hair, skin tone, smile, all had appealed to him. From the moment he saw her, he'd wanted to gobble her up.

But he liked Melina, too, and because he liked her so much, he wished she didn't look exactly like Gillian. It was disconcerting and strange, to say the least, liking both women a lot and their looking enough alike to be one and the same. It was messing with his mind.

He had to remind himself constantly that this was not Gillian. Beside him now was Melina, not Gillian, who'd cuddled against him in bed, warm and replete, whispering in a sweet, sleepy voice, "Chief?"

"Hmm?"

"I wouldn't have missed this for the world."

He'd drawn her closer and dropped a kiss on her shoulder, little knowing that those were the last words he would ever hear her say. They'd fallen asleep after that. The following morning he woke up alone but determined to hear that voice and to see that face on his pillow again. Many times. As often as he could.

He was looking at it now. Except it wasn't Gillian. It was Melina. He was finding it increasingly difficult to keep them separate in his mind.

"There she is," Melina said.

A group of people wearing variations of medical scrubs were leaving the building through revolving doors. "The gray-haired lady, right? I remember seeing her talking to you at the memorial service."

As they watched, Linda Croft angled away from the cluster and walked toward the wing of the quadrangle that served as a multilayered parking garage. Melina came off the bench like a shot. "Let's go."

Parking garages were inherently scary, and Hollywood had heightened their malevolent reputation by making them the setting for every kind of wickedness imaginable. Except for Linda Croft, the orange level was deserted. She was unlocking her car door when he and Melina closed in. Chief didn't wonder that the woman was startled.

"Ms. Croft, I'm Melina Lloyd. Remember?"

One plump hand was pressed against her bosom as though to contain a pounding heart. "Of course. Ms. Lloyd."

Melina removed her sunglasses. "I'm sorry we frightened you."

"I'm just glad it's you and not a slasher." Her eyes moved to him.

"This is Christopher Hart," Melina said. "Colonel Hart, Linda Croft."

"I saw you at the memorial service and recognized you from the news," she said. "It's a pleasure, Colonel Hart."

"Likewise."

"What happened to your face? If you don't mind my asking."

"I got mugged last night."

"How awful! Did he get anything?"

"Some of my pride." She returned his smile. "Are we keeping you from something?"

"I go home for lunch so I can watch my program. I feed my cats then, too."

"We won't detain you for long," Melina assured her. "I just need to ask you about something. Something you said to me at Gillian's service." Linda Croft tilted her head inquisitively. Melina plunged ahead. "You remarked on how sad it was that two of the clinic's patients had been victims of crime. Gillian was murdered. A couple's child was kidnapped."

"The Andersons."

"Colonel Hart and I find that coincidence very interesting."

Linda Croft's eyes bounced back and forth between them. "How do you mean, interesting?"

She was becoming wary. They were going to get nowhere fast with her unless Melina sensed her apprehension. Apparently she did because she instantly changed her tactic.

"The Andersons must have been devastated. I want to contact them and extend my condolences for what they experienced. Only now can I fully appreciate how heartbroken they must've been when their baby was snatched. I can relate to their loss."

"Oh, well . . ."

"So I was wondering if you could tell me how to reach them."

"You mean their address?"

"Or telephone number. I'd look it up for myself, but I can't remember Mr. Anderson's first name."

Chief placed his arm across Melina's shoulders and drew her close to his side. "I think we've unintentionally placed Ms. Croft in an awkward situation, Melina."

Picking up his cue, she said, "Oh, Lord, I didn't think of it that way. Are we asking you to do something you shouldn't?"

"I'm afraid so," the woman replied, clearly distressed by her inability to help. "We're not supposed to discuss our patients or give out any information. To violate their privacy would be a breach of ethics. The service we provide is of such a personal nature, I'm sure you can understand the need for confidentiality."

"Of course." Chief felt Melina's body sag against his as though she'd suffered a major letdown. "I assumed that since the Anderson baby kidnapping had been the focus of so much media attention, it was a matter of public knowledge."

"No, the Andersons were adamant about keeping their address and first names out of the news."

"Under the circumstances, I can understand why. I wish Gillian's murder hadn't been widely publicized." She smiled sadly. "It's just that so few people understand my double loss, Gillian and the child she might have had. When she died, my hope of having a niece or nephew died with her. I thought someone who had suffered similarly would . . ."

She pretended to run out of steam and paused to take a deep breath. "I'm sorry to have bothered you, Ms. Croft. Forgive me for placing you in such an awkward position. You were very kind to come to Gillian's memorial. We won't keep you any longer. I'd hate for you to miss your program. Thank you."

"Goodbye, Ms. Croft," Chief said, briefly touching the woman's hand. "A pleasure to have met you."

He was turning Melina about when Linda Croft blurted out, "I send them cards periodically."

They came around slowly.

Before continuing, Linda Croft nervously moistened her lips. "Little pick-me-up notes. You know the kind. Thinking of you. Take heart. Good things are yet to come. Things like that. The Andersons are kind enough to acknowledge them, so they're still at the address I have. It's in my address book at home. You could follow me."

Her house was in an area of Dallas called the "M streets," so named because for several blocks all the street names began with that letter. It was an older residential neighborhood, but in recent years it had become fashionable again. As retirees sold out or died off, single professionals and young families bought the old houses for renovation. Situated between two houses recently redone, Linda Croft's cottage looked like an outdated dowager trying to hold on to her dignity.

"Snow White's house," Melina remarked

absently as he pulled to a stop at the curb. Linda Croft waved to them from the small porch, then unlocked the arched front door that was set between two mullioned windows. "You go. You handle her better than I do."

"It's that male-female thing," he said.

"It's *your* male-female thing. The chemistry doesn't work that well for everybody."

He got out and jogged up the walk. Linda Croft had already disappeared inside, calling out to her cats that Mama was home. "Come on in, Colonel Hart."

He stepped directly into the living area. It was filled with family photographs, needlepoint cushions, and the scent of cat boxes. While he waited, the cats, half a dozen at least, wove their way around and in between his feet, curling their tails up around his shins. Linda Croft returned from the back rooms, extending to him a lined sheet of notepaper with an address written in purple ink.

"This is against the rules, but Ms. Lloyd's heart is breaking over her sister's death. To my way of thinking, people are more important than rules. Maybe a talk with those who've been there will help her."

"Melina appreciates this. So do I. Thank you."

He shook her hand. She held on to his maybe a second or two longer than politeness required. "You remind me of my late husband."

"He was a lucky man."

She blushed becomingly. "He was very handsome. He had some Indian blood. A drop or two of Cherokee," she added with a smile. "I never dreamed I'd have such a celebrity inside my house."

"It's my honor."

He said a final goodbye. As he was going down the walk, she called after him, "Take care of that cut so it doesn't scar."

He got in the car and passed Melina the note, then sat for a moment staring directly ahead through the windshield across the dull, dented hood. "What?" she asked.

"I feel like crap."

"Do you need another aspirin?"

"Not physically. I feel bad over the way we manipulated her."

"I know what you mean," she sighed. "Sort of like we just screwed over Cinderella's fairy godmother."

"Oh, thanks. That makes me feel a lot better."

He pulled away from the curb. The club where he'd been forced to abandon his car was only a few blocks away. The sports model he owned was an automobile, and this clunker was an automobile, but there the similarities ended. He longed for the maneuverability and speed of his car and was tempted to drive past the parking lot just to see if it was still there and intact. He doubted anyone lying in wait for them would recognize them in this car, but he couldn't take the chance. Resisting the temptation, he circled a block and headed back toward the expressway.

"Look at it this way," Melina said, evidently still on the subject of manipulating Linda Croft. "By doing this, we could prevent another woman from being killed or keep another couple's child from being kidnapped."

"That's your motivation for doing all this investigative work yourself? Crime prevention?"

"Isn't that motivation enough?"

"Very noble." He glanced at her. "But are

you sure there's no vengeance lurking in there somewhere?"

In a voice made husky by steely determination, she said, "That, too. Definitely."

"What is this garbage?" Tobias frowned with distaste. He'd sifted through hovels before, many a lot more derelict and dirty than Dale Gordon's apartment. Few, however, had rated this high on the creep factor.

"Doomsday stuff," Detective Lawson explained as Tobias thumbed through the low-grade paperback booklet. It was filled with graphic illustrations depicting the tribulation to come in the end days. Decapitations. Disembowelments. Babies impaled on swords. "Gordon was big into the apocalypse. I told you about his calls to that Brother Gabriel character."

After leaving Hennings's brokerage firm, Tobias and Patterson had met the detective at Melina Lloyd's house and recounted for him her story about the two imposters. Chagrined, Lawson had admitted that even though Dale Gordon was Gillian Lloyd's killer, it seemed the case wasn't as open-and-shut as he had originally believed. He'd suggested that the two federal agents see Gordon's apartment, in the hope that out of the rubble they would find a direction to take their further investigation. Leaving other detectives to collect evidence, the three drove to Gordon's apartment together.

At the mention of the TV preacher, Tobias conjured up a mental image. "Brother Gabriel makes some orthodox religious leaders nervous. They claim his ministry is a cult."

"Could be," Lawson surmised. "Or maybe established churches are just jealous of the following he's enlisted. Europe. Asia. Africa. He's not just here. He's everywhere."

"You've researched this." Tobias was impressed with the background work Lawson had done. He looked like an aged hoodlum, but apparently he was more astute than his appearance implied.

"I followed up on Gordon's fascination with Brother Gabriel," he explained. "Telephone counselors out at the Temple in New Mexico told me Gordon called so often he made a pest of himself, although they put it more tactfully. They're too much into peace and love to speak ill of a disciple. Especially a dead one. Anyway, they said Gordon seemed to be preoccupied with Armageddon."

"I'm not an expert on cults, but we have specialists who are," Tobias related. "I read their reports regularly. Dale Gordon fits the profile of a cult member. Low self-esteem. Social outcast. Brother Gabriel would have represented both a father figure and a savior, somebody who loved and accepted him, warts and all."

"When he joined, he became part and parcel of a large family of believers."

"Which gave Gordon instant identity, something he'd lacked. His devotion to Brother Gabriel became his life to the exclusion of everything else."

"Not everything else," said Patterson from the other side of the dim room.

The younger FBI agent came forward with a stack of what appeared to be snapshots. "Found these beneath some loose boards under the bed. Your guys must've missed them," he said to Lawson.

Lawson harrumphed. He had almost as many years of investigative experience as

Patterson was old. Local law enforcement officers typically resented the FBI when they came in and took over their case—especially one already closed. Hoping to keep that resentment at a tolerable level, Tobias exercised some diplomacy. "Easy to overlook something in a dump like this. What've you got?"

He reached for the photos. To his credit, Patterson exercised a little diplomacy himself by dividing the stack of pictures between him and Lawson. "Ladies. Naked ladies."

Tobias leafed through them, his anger for the dead man mounting. "Not your average porno, is it?" It was obvious that the women didn't know they were being photographed. Some were wearing short robes, the kind one donned for a medical examination. Others were completely nude. All were young and appeared healthy.

"He took them at the clinic." Lawson told them about the peephole they'd discovered. "These must've been other patients. We found a couple of snapshots of Gillian Lloyd like this," Lawson said. "Over there on the altar."

"Altar, my ass," Patterson said. "I hope God wasn't in a forgiving mood when this fucker died."

Tobias frowned at the younger agent's editorial comment, but he didn't rebuke him for it. "Does this mean that Gillian Lloyd wasn't Gordon's only obsession?"

Lawson raised his beefy shoulders.

"What was Gordon's job at the clinic?" Patterson asked.

"Here goes your dinner." That was Lawson's way of warning them that what they were about to hear wasn't going to be pleasant.

"Gordon was an andrologist. I'd never heard the word. Had to look it up. They're the lab techs who work with semen specimens at sperm banks and infertility clinics. They perform all the procedures on it. Storing, freezing, washing. Everything required to prepare it for artificial insemination of one kind or another. Intrauterine or in vitro." He sighed, giving them an opportunity to paint their own mind pictures. "Knowing what I know about him, makes me kinda sick to think about him handling . . . it. Ya know?"

"Yeah, I know." After a thoughtful moment, Tobias said, "Know what else I know?"

"We gotta toss that clinic."

He looked across at Patterson. "Go to the head of the class."

As George Abbott paced, he was brutalizing a fingernail already gnawed down to the quick. "I don't understand why."

"I've explained why." Dexter Longtree was measuring the width of the empty office, using his boots as his measuring stick. Toe to heel, heel to toe, he counted off the yardage.

"Well, forgive me, Dexter," Abbott said with a nervous laugh. "Maybe I'm not as in touch with my spiritual self as you are. I don't believe in dreams and visions. I leave that kind of crap to the old men of the tribe."

Longtree raised his head and gave Abbott a hard look.

"No offense," he muttered.

"None taken." Longtree continued pacing off the yardage until he had covered the distance to the far wall. Removing a pencil and paper from the breast pocket of his shirt, he wrote down the measurement. It was only an approximation, but it would serve to plan the layout of NAA's first headquarters.

"All I'm suggesting," Abbott continued, "is that we should push him a little harder."

"There's no need to push."

"We're fresh in his mind. If too much time goes by, he'll forget he ever heard about NAA. Now's the time to move in, apply some pressure."

"We said everything we needed to say."

"Guys like Hart, he's got people coming at him left and right wanting favors, asking for this, asking for that. Write a book. Give a speech. Visit a school. Sign an autograph. He can't do everything, so his stock answer to every request is no." Abbott slapped his palm with the back of his other hand. "I'm telling you, Dexter, only the persistent are going to get anywhere with him."

Longtree finished counting the electrical outlets and made a notation on his paper. "Hart doesn't want to be wooed."

"Hell, everybody wants to be wooed," Abbott argued as he attacked another fingernail. "We could go down to Houston. Leave tomorrow. Or the day after at the latest. We'd have to drive. There's no budget for airfare. Maybe spend one night on the road each way. We'll take him to lunch. Someplace nice. White tablecloths, white wine, the whole nine yards. Convince him we're not savages. Then we'll make our appeal." He glanced at Longtree. "I don't suppose you'd think about cutting your hair?"

Longtree had listened to George's plan with barely contained amusement. "It would be a wasted trip, George. Christopher Hart will come to us."

Abbott dropped his hand from his mouth. "Come to us? Come to *us*? Are we talking about the same guy?" His voice rose to a shrill note. "He couldn't wait to get rid of us."

Longtree could read Abbott's mind. He was thinking that what people said about Dexter Longtree was probably true, that the gossip had some basis of truth. Most of the time, Chief Longtree was a force to be reckoned with. Strong. Passionate. Determined. Intimidating.

But occasionally he went a little soft in the head. He would become one feather short of a full war bonnet. One arrow shy of a full quiver. They'd tap their temples and shake their heads sorrowfully.

"It's the tragedy," the old-timers explained. "Sometimes it still affects him."

Although Abbott had been in grade school when it happened, he'd heard the story about how Longtree had gone crazy. He had made a painstaking and gradual recovery, but he was prone to relapses. No doubt Abbott thought that he was suffering one now.

That was all right. Let him think what he wished. "George, nothing we say will convince Christopher Hart to join us. He'll make the decision when he's ready. On his own. It will come from something within himself."

But Abbott wasn't listening. He was already on to another thought. "We could up the ante. Increase the amount of his retainer."

"Our offer was reasonable and fair."

"Maybe we should give him a signing bonus like they do professional athletes. I don't know where the money will come from. The deposit on this place will just about empty our account. Maybe we should hold off renting the space."

"The issue with Hart isn't money."

"No, the issue with Hart is that he doesn't want to be an Indian." Abbott spat a sliver of fingernail off the tip of his tongue. "His looks might say Indian, but he's white as they come on the inside. What I'd like to do is tell the smug bastard to go fuck himself."

Longtree showed a ghost of a smile. "Good idea, George. Very persuasive. I'm sure that would bring him around."

Irritated, Abbott kicked an empty soft drink can that a former tenant had left behind. It rattled across the bare floor. "You're right. We need the cock-strut. Which brings me back to my original point. We push. Push hard. Work on his conscience."

"Christopher Hart is a conscientious man."

Again, Abbott wasn't heeding a word he said. "How about this? We'll build in an incentive that wouldn't cost us any cash right now. A housing allowance. Or a car. That's it! A car. Maybe we can talk Fred Eagle into donating a new car from his dealership."

"Would you want someone working as our spokesperson who'd had to be bribed?" Corruption on the reservations regarding gaming and construction contracts was one of the issues the advocacy group planned to address. "Besides, Hart couldn't be bribed."

Abbott threw up his hands in frustration. "Then what do you suggest?"

"I suggest that we go straight from here to the rental office and put down the deposit on this space before someone else grabs it."

"Without a commitment from Hart? You're willing to go forward without him?"

"We've got him, George."

"How do you know?"

"I know."

"One of your visions?"

Ignoring the man's scorn, Longtree moved toward the exit. "I know. It's Colonel Hart who doesn't know. But he will. Soon."

Jem Hennings alighted from his car, barely acknowledging the parking valet. The uniformed doorman stepped forward to hold the door for him. Jem gave him a cursory nod of thanks, then did a double-take. "Who're you? Are you new?"

"First day, sir. Harry Clemmet."

"Jem Hennings. Seventeen D."

"Yes, sir, Mr. Hennings. Anything I can do for you, please let me know."

Already buttering me up for a large Christmas tip, Jem thought as he continued across the foyer. He was halfway to the elevator bank when Harry called out to him. "You're a mighty lucky man, Mr. Hennings."

Jem wasn't feeling particularly lucky today. In fact, his day hadn't been at all pleasant. He was preoccupied and in no mood to interact with the hired help. But he never knew when he might need a favor from one of them. He turned. The doorman was grinning at him sappily. "Lucky?"

"Yes, sir. I met your fiancée."

Hadn't Harry the sappy grinner just told him that this was his first day on the job? Jem slowly retraced his steps across the lobby. "How could you have met her? When did you meet her, Harry?"

Sensing that something was amiss, the

new doorman stuttered, "Th-this afternoon. When she came by to pick up those things for you."

Upon leaving Jem's high-rise, Chief announced that they must come to a meeting of the minds.

"Over what?" she asked.

"Accommodations. I've had my fill of fleabag motels, Melina."

"You've only been in one."

"Which is one too many."

"And it was clean."

"Which I don't consider an amenity."

He checked them into a suite hotel that was still modest by his standards but several rungs up from the motel on the interstate. "You didn't use a credit card, did you?" she asked when he returned to the car from the lobby.

"Cash. The clerk asked for the license plate number on the car."

"You knew it?"

"No, I made one up, but he didn't check. He winked and told me to have a pleasant stay. He thinks we're here for some afternoon delight. A hasty-tasty."

Apparently. Because the clerk assigned them a room with one king bed. Neither remarked on it. Depending on how the evening went, they might not be here long enough to spend the night. If they were, there was always the sofa bed in the parlor. She would sleep there. Because spending the night in the same room with Chief would be unnerving for a number of reasons, most of which made her uneasy to think about. Under the circumstances, even a suggestion of intimacy with him would feel inappropriate. Ironically, those same circumstances were responsible for their togetherness.

Who could deny his appeal? Even matronly Linda Croft had responded to his effortless charm. Any woman who shared space with him—small, private space—over an extended period of time would be entertaining a few romantic notions, even though the probability of their being acted on was nil.

Of course, intimacy between her and Chief was out of the question. At this time. In this situation. And given who they were.

"I'm going to freshen up." She went into the bathroom.

When she came out several minutes later, Chief was sitting on the end of the bed, watching TV. He motioned her over and turned up the volume. "Isn't that the guy?"

She sat down beside him. "That's him."

The visage of Brother Gabriel filled the TV screen. He was shown in his very best light, literally. Dressed in a suit the color of heavy cream, a baby blue shirt, and matching tie, he seemed to radiate purity of body and soul. He seemed to glow from within through the peridot-colored eyes.

"Handsome, isn't he?"

"I guess. If you're into that blond Anglo type."

She frowned at Chief derisively, then turned her attention to what Brother Gabriel was saying. "You're feeling lost and alone even around people who profess to love you. I understand that feeling of alienation. Your parents are never satisfied with you. Your boss's demands on you are unreasonable. Your children disrespect you. People who call themselves friends revile and betray you. Maybe even your spouse ridicules you and makes you feel insignificant.

"Listen to me," he said, reducing his soft-spoken voice to an even lower, more confidential pitch. "Are you listening, my child? If you are within the sound of my voice, you are hearing the voice of the one who *really* cares for you. Listen to what I say, because your future in eternity depends on it."

He paused for dramatic effect, then said emphatically, "You are not insignificant to me. I love you. I want to protect you from the disdain you feel from others. From the parents, from the boss, from the teacher, the friend, the wife, the husband, whose claims of love are false. False," he stressed.

"I want to take you unto myself and adopt you into my family. It's large, yes. It has millions of members already. But I've reserved a place for you. Just for you. Your special place will go unoccupied if you don't accept it.

"I know what you're thinking. How would Brother Gabriel know me? Hear me now. Those doubts are spawned by the devil. Don't entertain them. Deny them. Daughter, son, beloved," he said softly, "I know you. I want you with me in the new world order."

"'New world order'? What does that mean?" Chief asked.

"Shh." She waved her hand for quiet.

They listened through the conclusion of the broadcast, when Brother Gabriel offered a flowery prayer of benediction. A mailing address and website address were super-imposed over a photograph of the Temple with a blazing sunset in the background. Viewers were urged to request literature.

"Which I'm sure has the answers to all life's problems."

"Yeah. Wonder where he got them," Chief added as he muted the sound.

"He appeals to the Dale Gordons of the world."

"And to a lot of others, too, Melina. There are a few people in the space program who claim he turned their lives around."

"You're kidding!"

"One of my colleagues has her daughter enrolled in his school."

"How can intelligent people buy in to the notion that one man has all the answers?"

"Easy," he said, shrugging. "He tells them what they want to hear. He appeals to their worst fears—rejection and nonacceptance. He alone can see their worth. He values them when no one else does. If they join ranks with him, they'll become one of the elite."

"Unbelievable. Frightening."

"Not really unbelievable, but definitely frightening. A lot of people thought that Hitler had the right idea. He's the quintessential example of the sway that one man can hold over the minds of many. But think of all the lesser cult leaders who've risen to prominence since him."

She chafed her arms, and it wasn't because Chief had adjusted the air-conditioning thermostat as low as it would go. "This guy doesn't see himself as a prophet, a minister. *He's* the deity of his dogma. He has the secret of life, and if you follow him, you'll have an inside track." She scoffed at the notion. "Somewhere along the way, he totally bypassed God."

"Are you a believer, Melina?"

The quiet quality of his voice arrested her. She replied solemnly, "Yes. Aren't you?"

"I believe in science."

After pondering that for a moment, she asked if he'd always wanted to be an astronaut. "Even when you were growing up."

"I was always fascinated by space, wanted to learn about the planets and the moon, the constellations. When I was old enough, I'd sneak out of the house at night and ride my bike past the outskirts of town where the sky was dark. I'd study the stars for hours, hoping to spot a meteor, or weather balloon, or satellite. The early astronauts were my heroes. So, yeah, I guess you could say that in the back of my mind I always wanted to be one. But I thought it was hopeless."

"Why?"

"Until I graduated from high school, I lived on a reservation."

"So?"

"So, the opportunities are limited."

"Then why don't you do something about it?"

He looked at her sharply. "Like what?"

"Sign on with that advocacy group." He frowned. "Well, what's keeping you from it? That Longbush?"

"Longtree."

"Do you question his integrity?"

"Partially." He rolled his shoulders as though trying to unburden himself of her questions. "I don't know."

"If you don't know, maybe you should find out."

"It's not just him."

"Then what? Not enough money?"

"No. They said I'd be free to do other things as long as my outside interests didn't conflict with their policies."

"To me it sounds like a win-win situation."

"Why are we talking about this?" he asked querulously. "My mind's made up. I've turned them down."

"But you're not content with your decision."

"What makes you say that?"

"Because you're snapping my head off. Why so testy, Chief? If you've made up your mind and you're easy with it, why are you scowling at me for talking about it?" She challenged him with a stare, and it was he who looked away first. "Are you afraid they'll disappoint you, let you down?" Then, in a softer voice, she asked, "Or are you afraid that you won't live up to their expectations of you?"

He raised his eyebrow and whistled softly. "Ouch. You're shooting wicked arrows, Melina."

"Ha-ha. Some Indian humor." She studied him for a long moment. "That's it, isn't it?"

"What's it?"

"You're an overachiever who despises failure, Chief," she said, chiding softly. "You must allow yourself a few small failures and develop the capacity to forgive yourself when you make a mistake."

He sat forward, bringing their faces close. "Have *you*?"

"What?"

"Forgiven yourself."

She sucked in a quick breath. "For switching places that night?"

"Have you?"

After a time, she said, "I'm working on it. But it's tough, and so far the guilt is winning."

"I admire your honesty."

"Thank you."

"It deserves a turnabout."

"Go ahead."

He sat back slightly. "When I was up there on this last mission, I said a prayer." She remained very still, listening, giving him time. He shrugged self-consciously. "It wasn't much of a prayer, I guess. Not anything like his," he said, nodding toward the TV. "Nothing like you'd hear in church.

"The rest of the crew was asleep. I was just looking out, you know. At everything. And it's so vast, so . . ." He paused, momentarily at a loss for words to describe the scope of the universe. "It's so beautiful, Melina. It made me feel superfluous by comparison. Small and inconsequential.

"But at the same time . . . connected. Connected to something greater than all of it, connected to something even more awe-inspiring than space itself. Like God, I guess. So I, uh, just sort of thought, you know, in my mind, a little prayer of thanks that it was there, and that I'd been selected to get a solitary, rarefied look at it." After a moment, he lifted his gaze to hers. "That's it."

"That's enough." She blinked threatened tears from her eyes and swallowed the lump in her throat. The last thing she wanted to do was embarrass him after he'd bared his soul. She wanted to tell him that she was honored he had confided such a private moment to her, but she didn't. She wanted to touch his hard cheek and tell him that he shouldn't feel ashamed for experiencing a spiritual awakening, but she didn't say that, either. And touching him would be risky on several accounts.

Instead she said softly, "You can believe in science and still have faith in God, Chief. They aren't mutually exclusive."

"Yeah. I guess."

He cleared his throat and stood up, moved to the side of the bed, then propped himself against the headboard and stretched out on top of the bedspread, boots and all. Using his cell phone, he placed calls to his office and residence voice mails in Houston but returned none of the messages.

He placed another call to The Mansion and asked if they were holding any messages for him. He listened. Feeling his eyes on her, she glanced at him over her shoulder.

He clicked off the phone. "Tobias."

"Called you?"

"Lawson must have told him where I'd been staying. He left a message for me to call him as soon as possible. Said it was urgent."

"Are you going to call?"

He shook his head no. "If I do, I become

officially involved in an FBI investigation. Sooner or later the media would get wind of it. I'd rather stay unofficially involved. But maybe we should hang on to the number he left. Just in case."

When he recited the number to her, she said, "That's his cell."

"You remember the number?"

"I have a knack. Which reminds me, there were several numbers programmed into Jem's autodial function. Some were labeled. Some weren't. I jotted them down, just in case my memory fails me. We can check them out later. Maybe one will provide a clue as to why he sicced goons on me."

"So you think Hennings eavesdropped on your conversation when you made the appointment with Tobias?"

"It couldn't have been anyone else. It had to have been Jem."

"Unless your telephone had been tapped."

That was an alarming thought. "By whom? Why?"

"I'm not saying it was. I'm playing devil's advocate here, throwing out a few options."

She thought about it for a moment, then shook her head stubbornly. "Jem's involved. I know it. I feel it."

"Woman's intuition?"

"Maybe it is just that, but it's strong. From the morning the body was discovered, he's been behaving in a very peculiar way. Remember in Lawson's office, he claimed he'd been against the artificial insemination all along? Gillian had told me just the opposite. She said that Jem had actually urged her to have a child. So either he was lying to her or to us." She stared into near space until Chief prodded her to share all her thoughts.

"Something else?"

Her eyes found and focused on his. "He's lying about the engagement. Gillian would have told me if they had decided to marry. I'm absolutely positive she would have. Jem gave me some flimsy excuses for why they had sworn each other to secrecy, but he was lying."

"If he's lying about an engagement, what else has he lied about?"

"That's what's been worrying me."

"Is it even conceivable that he is in some way responsible for her murder?"

"I hate to even think it, but it has occurred to me," she admitted.

The expression that came over Chief's face made her glad that she wasn't his enemy. She hoped she never would be. The skin seemed to stretch taut over his facial bones, emphasizing the cuts and bruises. "Does your face hurt?"

"I'm okay."

"Are you sure?"

"Yes." He gave her an appraising look. "Maybe you missed your calling."

"Nurse?"

"Investigator. Should I alert Tobias to your qualifications?"

"Whatever." She lay down on the opposite side of the bed and bunched the pillow beneath her head. "Lord, I'm tired."

"Snooping's tiring work."

Inside Jem's apartment, she'd been as nervous as a cat, waiting for either him or the police to show up. She had risked arrest in order to get in there, but it had proved to be an unproductive waste of time, effort, and nerves.

"I just wish I had more to show for it. If Jem Hennings has a dark side, he's hiding it well. There was certainly nothing inside his condo to indicate an alliance with hit men, or whoever those guys were who came to my house this morning."

"Reading matter?"

"*Forbes, Money, Robb Report,* magazines you would expect a stockbroker to read. No calendar, date book, address roster, telephone list. No receipts, no notes. In fact, there wasn't a scrap of paper in the place. Not even in the trash. It was virtually sterile."

"Sounds like him. A bachelor pad should look like a bachelor pad."

"I'd gone there once with Gillian for dinner. Jem cooked. I noticed then that the place was spotless. His kitchen was like a laboratory. I thought it was because he was having company. Apparently he lives like that all the time."

She paused and shook her head ruefully. "I always thought he was uptight and anal-retentive, but now that I'm learning more about him, I can't imagine Gillian ever being the slightest bit attracted to him."

"Was she in love with him?"

She mulled it over before answering, choosing her words carefully. "I think she talked herself into believing she was."

"Why?"

"Frankly, Chief, I'm a little uncomfortable discussing Gillian's love life with you."

"Aren't I entitled? She spent the night with me. What happened between us didn't feel sordid. I don't like to think of it as cheating."

"Guilty conscience?"

"Because of Hennings? No. If Gillian had been truly in love with him, then yes. But I don't think she was, so no," he said definitively.

"She was approaching the big four-oh, which, let's face it, for a woman is a wake-up call. Time to take stock. I think Gillian was afraid that Jem might be her last chance to have a meaningful relationship."

"Not a very good reason to enter a relationship."

"A very bad reason, in fact."

"Did you share your reservations about Hennings with her?" he asked.

"Frequently. Including that day during lunch."

"I'd like to know what was in her mind that night," he said quietly. "When she got home, did she express any regrets?"

She turned her head toward him. His blue

eyes bore into hers. "I can't tell you her secrets, Chief."

"They wouldn't be secrets. I was there."

"Then you—"

"But I want to hear what she said. You told me earlier that she'd had a very good time. Did she tell you about us showering together?"

"No. In fact, she wanted to shower as soon as she got home."

"We didn't shower together."

She looked at him with angry dismay. "Oh, I see. That was a trap. To see how much I really knew."

"I'm sorry."

"Go to hell." She made to get up, but he grabbed her hand and held her on the bed.

"Please, Melina. Talk to me. Tell me what she was thinking. Please."

He wanted to know how Gillian had felt about that night, but she also discerned his *need* to know. Maybe it had something to do with his motivation to remain involved when, at any point along the way, he could have deserted her to research the murder alone. For that, she supposed he deserved to know some of what she and her twin had talked about.

But she couldn't discuss it and look at him at the same time, so she pulled her hand free and returned her head to the pillow, looking straight up at the ceiling. "She told me that she wasn't seduced, that she initiated it. Is that how you remember it?" She felt his nod. "She was afraid that might have put you off. That you might have thought less of her because of it."

She sensed him shaking his head before he spoke a rough, "Hardly."

"That's good, then."

He waited for more. When her reluctance to continue became obvious, he probed. "What else, Melina?"

"Chief."

"Please."

She drew a deep breath and then released it in a gust. "Men . . . might . . ."

"Go on. Men might . . ."

"Boast."

"About?"

She laughed softly. "Everything."

"Specifically?"

"You know." She cut her eyes toward him, then back to the ceiling. "The number of times he . . ."

"Oh." Then, after a small pause, "Gillian told you how many times?"

"Not precisely."

"Several."

"I gathered."

"So how could she have been in love with Hennings?" Quickly she looked over at him. "I mean, a person might slip once, Melina. Do something in the heat of the moment and instantly regret it. Think, *Oh, my God, what have I done?* and leave feeling remorse. It wasn't like that. Did Gillian tell you how—"

"Chief, please stop this."

"—intense it was? How I couldn't get enough of her?"

His eyes were hot as they looked at her across the expanse of the king-size bed, and suddenly it wasn't quite expansive enough for her.

Flustered, she sat up, planting her feet on the floor and putting her back to him. She checked her wristwatch. "He's probably home from work by now. We should go." She left the bed and began gathering her things. "Take your stuff. Depending on what the immediate future holds, we may not be coming back."

As they collected their belongings, the silence between them teemed with undercurrents of the sensitive topics they had discussed and of the many things they'd left unsaid.

When she had everything, she glanced around to make certain she hadn't missed something, then approached the door with both hands full.

"I'll get it." Chief moved up behind her. Close. Reaching around her, he took hold of the doorknob but didn't turn it. "Melina?"

His breath was in her hair, his body heat against her back.

"You knew Gillian better than anyone."

She gave a small nod.

"How could she have loved Hennings and slept with me?"

It was a long time before she found enough voice to speak, and even then it was thready. "She couldn't. That evening wasn't about Jem. Or the insemination. Or having a child. It wasn't about anything except you. It was all about you."

Imperceptibly he leaned forward, until it was more than his body heat she felt against her back—it was him. "I needed to hear you say that."

"Don't, Chief," she implored in a hoarse whisper.

"What?"

"Don't forget that I'm Melina. I'm not Gillian."

Tony and Candace Anderson lived in an upscale neighborhood in north Dallas. The lawns were well maintained. Each garage had at least two vehicles, one of which was a minivan or SUV. Homeowners here could afford private schools for the kids, ski vacations in Vail, and a membership to the nearby country club.

"Nice area," Chief remarked.

"Hmm." Melina probably hadn't noticed. She was apprehensive about the reception the publicity-shy Andersons might give them. They had waited until late in the day to come, when it was more likely that they'd find both at home.

Their house was situated at the end of a short cul-de-sac. It was contemporary in design. The walkway brought Chief and Melina up to a front door that was constructed largely of panes of beveled glass, so that they could see Tony Anderson's approach before he opened the door. A dog inside the house barked once, but it was a halfhearted, nonthreatening bark.

"Mr. Anderson?" Melina asked.

"That's right." He was of average height and better-than-average looks. His tan suggested a lot of time spent outdoors; his trim, athletic build implied tennis over golf. Friendly but cautious, he evenly divided his inquisitive regard between them.

"My name is Melina Lloyd. This is Christopher Hart."

Anderson looked Chief's way, showing surprised recognition and curiosity over his battered face. "The astronaut?"

"Tony?"

Candace Anderson might have been a Dallas Cowboys cheerleader. She had the figure and the face for it, a mane of sun-streaked blond hair, and eyes as large as a doe's. She was wearing old blue jeans with split knees and a knit top that was cropped at her narrow waist. But for all her beauty, her face bore the imprint of sadness and her doe-eyes had a wounded look. She sidled up to her husband and stood close to him, as though for shelter and support.

"I thought you looked familiar," Tony Anderson said to him.

"Nice to meet you."

Tony looked pleased to be shaking hands with him, but also perplexed. "Uh, this is my wife, Candace. Candace, Christopher Hart. And Miss . . . Sorry."

"Lloyd. Melina Lloyd. Could we have a few minutes of your time? It's dreadful of us to show up without calling first. But I was afraid you wouldn't agree to see us if I called ahead."

"See you about what?" Tony Anderson's voice took on a distinct edge that indicated he already knew what they wished to see him about. He placed a protective arm around Candace.

Melina said, "Your son's abduction."

Candace's chin lowered nearly to her chest. Every trace of friendliness vanished from Tony's demeanor. He turned hostile. "Are you a reporter, Miss Lloyd?"

"No, I'm a victim. Or at least my sister was. She was murdered just a few days ago."

"I read about it in the newspaper." Candace raised her head and looked at Melina. "She was your twin."

"Yes. I think your son's kidnapping and her murder are connected." Candace looked at her quizzically. "Gillian was also a patient at the Waters Clinic."

"That's it? That's the connection?" Tony said harshly. He reached for the door. "I don't think so."

Chief stepped forward. "Could we please come in?"

Celebrity had its benefits. He rarely exploited his fame, but this instance warranted it. "Please. It's very important to Melina. Possibly to you, too."

"We won't stay long," she added.

Tony looked down at Candace, who gave a slight nod.

The couple showed them into a room off the kitchen. They'd apparently just finished dinner. Dishes were still on the dining table. The den was a lived-in room with a large-screen TV, shelves full of books, and a golden retriever who lay curled up on the hearth of the fireplace. The dog gave Melina and Chief a lazy glance, then resettled into his nap. As they took seats, Tony politely muted the TV.

He sat down on the sofa near his wife and took her hand, sandwiching it between his own. Trustingly, she tucked her shoulder beneath his. Plainly they were devoted to one another.

Except for the visible pain of their loss, Chief envied them. He liked this cozy room, the dog, the obvious physical and emotional intimacy the Andersons shared. For every move she made, he made a harmonious countermove, as though their bodies were accustomed to adjusting comfortably against one another. They could communicate with a look. A touch spoke volumes. Their relationship was indeed enviable.

And costly, Chief reminded himself. In order to coalesce with another person on that level, one had to let down all his defenses.

Tony began by saying, "We really don't like talking to strangers about Anthony's kidnapping. Not unless a person has information that might help us find him."

"Unfortunately, I'm here seeking more information than I'm able to divulge," Melina admitted.

"I don't know how we can help you."

"My sister Gillian had been artificially inseminated at the Waters Clinic less than twenty-four hours prior to her murder. Colonel Hart and I think there's a link between her murder and the clinic."

Tony turned to him. "Where do you fit in?"

"Fair question. I spent most of the night with Gillian. She left my room in the wee hours and was killed shortly before dawn."

Tony looked abashed for asking, but Candace asked, "Were you her sperm donor, Colonel Hart?"

"Call me Chief. And no, I wasn't."

"My sister used an anonymous donor," Melina explained. "Forgive my bluntness, but I must ask. Was your sperm used to conceive Anthony?"

"I don't mind your asking," Tony replied. "I lost all sense of shame a long time ago. The day a couple enters a clinic that specializes in infertility, they should check their pride and modesty at the door. Because of the techniques you use in order to conceive, the tests you're put through, the frankness with which you must answer the most personal questions about your sex life and private habits, you are eventually desensitized.

"In answer to your question, no. I'm sterile. They believe because of medication I was given as a child. But in any case, I have such a low sperm count as to be negligible. I had no qualms about using donor sperm. In fact, when all our other options had been exhausted, I was the one who suggested it.

"The donor's physical traits and interests were matched as closely to mine as possible, although at that point, neither I nor Candace really cared. We just wanted a healthy baby. Except for that one biological technicality, Anthony was my child. My son."

Both Chief and Melina pretended not to hear the emotional creakiness in his voice. The tears in Candace's eyes were more difficult to ignore. "I'm very sorry to put you through this," Melina said earnestly. "If it wasn't terribly important, I wouldn't."

"It's all right," Candace said. "After Anthony was taken, we sought answers, too. I understand your needing and wanting to know exactly what happened to your twin."

Then she recounted for them what they already knew. On his second day of life, the healthy and perfectly formed seven-pound eight-ounce baby was kidnapped from the hospital.

"We were in a private birthing room," she explained. "Tony had gone out for some lunch. Anthony was asleep in a crib beside my bed. It was almost time for a feeding, so I decided to use the rest room before he woke up. I went into the toilet. I wasn't in there for more than two or three minutes. When I came out, the crib was empty."

The last four words were barely audible. She was holding on to her composure by a mere thread. Chief noticed that Melina was also having a difficult time keeping her emotions in check. Her throat was working with the need to cry, and she had pressed her fingers against her lips as though to keep them from quivering.

Tony picked up the story. "Security cameras recorded a woman dressed in scrubs going into the room and carrying out a bundle of what looked like soiled laundry. We assume she had Anthony wrapped up in those linens. She was smart enough to keep her face averted from the cameras, like she knew where they were positioned. But enough of her face could be seen to determine that she wasn't someone on staff.

"The FBI ran the photos of her through all their databases. They did computer analyses that could determine race, approximate age, and so forth. But nothing came of it. She didn't match the description of any other abduction suspects."

"Also, anyone that clever and audacious could easily have altered her appearance," Candace interjected.

"None of the cars parked in the hospital lots that day provided leads. Local and federal investigators followed up each one. It was surmised that someone picked her up at or within walking distance of the hospital and drove off with her and Anthony. It would have looked so normal that no one paid any attention. In any case, there were no witnesses to anything unusual on the hospital campus."

"You never received a demand for ransom?" Melina asked.

"Whoever took him wanted the baby, not money."

Chief leaned forward and asked kindly, "What makes you say that, Candace?"

"Because I know he's alive. I know it."

"There was an extensive search for his . . . his body," Tony said with difficulty. "They thought somebody might have a grudge against me, or that maybe some radial group who protested AI were behind it. Not a trace of him was ever found. No hospital blanket, diaper, identification bracelet, nothing. Candace and I feel that he was taken for the purpose of acquiring a baby. Someone's got our baby."

Again his voice cracked, and this time it was Candace who comforted him. She pulled her hand from his and placed her slender arm across his shoulders, hugging him against her and shushing him tenderly.

Chief saw that Melina had given up her effort not to cry and was allowing tears to flow freely down her cheeks. She looked extremely vulnerable just then, crying silently but copiously, her heart breaking for the Andersons and probably a little for herself, too.

In the short time he'd known her, she had demonstrated extraordinary bravery, determination, self-control, and just plain guts. It was easy to admire a woman with that much strength. It was even easier to admire one whose compassion could move her to tears without any evidence of self-conciousness.

For a time no one spoke. The dog got up and ambled over to the couple. As though accustomed to these emotional outbreaks, he whined and propped his large head on Tony's thigh. Reflexively, Tony rubbed the dog's head and scratched him behind the ears. Then the dog returned to the hearth and lay back down, resting his head on his front paws and dolefully watching his owners.

Saddened, Chief's eyes moved from the loyal animal to the flickering TV screen. A house fire with three casualties was the lead story on the muted newscast.

Melina eventually wiped away her tears and broke the awkward silence. "The man who killed my sister was named Dale Gordon. He was an employee at the Waters Clinic."

"I read that," Candace said. "But I don't remember anyone by that name working there."

"Tall, skinny guy," Chief told them, remembering how Gordon had looked as he and Gillian entered the taco restaurant that night. "Thinning blond hair. Thick eye-glasses. Kind of gawky."

"Oh."

Candace's exclamation brought all eyes to her. Her face showed more animation than it had since they'd arrived. "Him! I remember him. He made a point of speaking to me whenever I had an appointment at the clinic." Turning to her husband, she said, "You remember, honey. He brought the teddy bear to the hospital?"

Tony registered sudden recall. "That guy?"

Chief exchanged a quick look with Melina. "Gordon came to the hospital with a gift for the baby? He was in your room?"

"Yes. He was very sweet. He took a pic-ture of me holding Anthony. From the start, when I first became a patient, he seemed to express a genuine interest in . . ." Candace Anderson's face paled almost to stark white. On a filament of breath, she finished her thought. "A genuine interest in me."

"In Gillian, too," Chief said, noticing that Melina looked incapable of speaking at the moment. She was hugging herself as though chilled. He told the Andersons about his and Gillian's encounter with Gordon and how strange the man had acted. "Apparently he got upset when he saw her with me. He wound up killing her for what he must've perceived as her unfaithfulness. He had assumed some kind of proprietary claim on her."

"I got that same impression," Candace said. "Except that he seemed overjoyed when the AI worked and I conceived."

"He got very emotional when he saw Anthony," Tony said. "Like he was about to cry. It was embarrassing for us."

"I felt sorry for him," Candace continued. "I thought he was just a lonely man who took a personal interest in the clinic's success stories because he had no family of his own."

Tony cut to the chase. "Do you think he had something to do with Anthony's kidnapping?"

"It's feasible, isn't it?" Melina replied.

"But he committed suicide, didn't he?" Her distress growing, Candace gripped her husband's hand. "If he knew where Anthony is, the information died with him."

"Not necessarily," Chief said somberly. "That clinic holds the key to all this."

"What are you talking about?"

"How do you know?"

Melina looked at him with puzzlement.

"Tony," Chief said, "disengage the muting on the TV, please. We need to hear this."

Anderson reached for the remote, and they caught the voice track in midsentence.

". . . body was discovered this evening when she failed to join friends for a weekly bridge game." A tearful woman blubbered into the microphone poked into her face. "She never missed. When she didn't show up this evening, we knew something was wrong. We came over and found her."

Turning back to face the camera, the newswoman reported that no motive for the killing had been established. "Investigating homicide detectives have said that the victim appeared to have been bludgeoned to death, probably with the ordinary household hammer found near her body."

The camera pulled back from a close-up of the reporter's face to a wider shot that showed activity in the background. A gurney with a body bag strapped to it was being wheeled toward an ambulance. "Police are still investigating and questioning neighbors, but no one claims to have seen . . ."

Suddenly Melina gasped, seeing what had drawn Chief's attention to the story—a house that looked like Snow White's. Linda Croft's cottage with the mullioned windows and arched front door.

Melina turned to him, her expression one of horror and disbelief. The tears now making her eyes shine were tears of outrage. "Those bastards!"

He came to his feet and reached down for her hand. He pulled her up beside him and said to the Andersons, "You don't know us. For all you know, we're a couple of fruitcakes. But I assure you we're not. That murder victim . . ." he said, pointing to the TV. "We visited her today. She worked at the Waters Clinic. She's the one who breached professional ethics to tell us how to locate you. Someone didn't want us to get together and compare notes."

Candace pressed her fingers against her colorless lips. "Which means Dale Gordon wasn't the end of it."

Chief bobbed his head. "Whoever is behind all this is bigger than that pathetic pervert. I suggest you get out of here tonight. Get your dog and clear out."

"What about the police?" Candace asked. "Shouldn't we call them? Notify the FBI?"

"Good idea, but I'd do it from another location. Agent Tobias is—"

"From Washington? We know him," Tony said. "He questioned us once."

"You'd recognize him, then?"

"Sure. Handsome guy."

"Good." He gave them a condensed version of what happened at Melina's house that morning.

"Tony?" Candace clutched her husband's arm in fear.

But he was already convinced. He moved to a desk across the room and scribbled something on a Post-It, then tore it from the pad and handed it to Chief. "My cell phone number. Only Candace knows it. Wherever we are, we'll have it with us. Keep us informed."

He gripped Chief's hand to shake it, but he was looking at Melina as he said, "If you find out anything about our son, whatever it is and no matter how bad, we want to know."

"You have my word."

Once they were in the car and under way, Chief said, "Thank God they trusted us enough to get the hell out of Dodge. I liked them."

"So did I. Very much. I liked Linda Croft, too. Why didn't we warn her of potential danger?" She covered her face with her hands and sobbed, "Oh, God, Chief. We got her killed."

"We didn't kill her, Melina. Not me. Not you." He reached across the front seat of the car and gripped her knee. "I feel as badly as you do about it, but we didn't kill her any more than we killed Gillian. Somebody else went into her house and hit her with a hammer."

"Our FBI imposters?"

"They'd be my first guess."

Thinking of how helpless and afraid Linda Croft would have been against the two men, she lost it and began to wail. "She was so sweet and guileless. That's what makes this all so confounding," she cried out in frustration. "It's innocent women and children who are the victims of these crimes. My sister. Slaughtered while she was sleeping, when she was most defenseless. The Andersons' little boy snatched like an . . . an apple from the street market. Who could do that? What kind of monster could deliberately cause so much heartache?" She clenched her hands into fists and pounded them on her thighs.

"Melina—"

"Those poor people. Those poor, beautiful, young, healthy people are miserable! And it isn't as if they're being punished for some terrible wrong. Their only sin was wanting a baby," she cried, her voice tearing.

"Melina, stop this!"

"I can't, I can't," she sobbed.

"Yes, you can. You can."

Whether it was the calm strength of his voice or the tight, almost painful pressure he applied to her knee, she gradually came to her senses. The hysteria and wild fury abated, and after several deep breaths, she looked across at him and nodded to let him know that she was once again in control.

"Okay now?" he asked.

"I'm sorry."

"Don't be," he said, smiling crookedly. "If it's any comfort to you, I feel like pitching a billy fit, too."

But he hadn't, and she had, and that's probably why he flew rockets and she had no desire to command a crew of astronauts. Candace Anderson's story had brought her emotions to the surface. Learning of Linda Croft's murder had inflamed them. Never had she experienced such a roiling combination of rage and despair, heightened by her own sense of uselessness. She only wished she knew to what or to whom to direct this all-consuming anger.

She scrubbed her face with her hands in an attempt to eliminate any vestiges of her uncharacteristic outburst. She smoothed back her hair. Fully composed, she said, "Chief, I want to know why this happened to Gillian. I want to know why the Andersons' baby was taken. I want to know who is behind it."

"The clinic."

"To what end? Their service is based on helping women and making babies. Besides, Tobias told me that not all the clinics connected to the crimes are part of the Waters chain. The commonality seems to be the patients, not the institutions."

"The commonality is artificial insemination."

"Like Gillian."

"Like Gillian."

The name fell like a curtain between them. She wondered if the mention of Gillian's name had anything to do with his removing his hand from her knee. Not that she could dwell on that now. She had much more important things to think about.

Using her cell phone, she placed a call. It was answered midway into the second ring. "Tobias."

"Melina Lloyd."

C H A P T E R | 2 6

The search warrant had been served at the Waters Clinic shortly before closing time. The staff on duty had been requested to stay. Individually they were being questioned by police, Tobias, and Patterson. All seemed to be concerned professionals and law-abiding citizens, including the four doctors on staff and the andrologist who'd been hired the day before to take Dale Gordon's place.

The nationwide chain of clinics was headquartered in Atlanta. The corporate top brass were flying to Dallas that evening. A search of your premises by a law enforcement agency was a PR problem for any business. When your business was creating human life, the stakes rose dramatically.

Tobias was overseeing the search when Melina's call came through. He demanded to know where she was.

"Is Detective Lawson with you?" she asked.

"Why?"

"Is he?"

"Yes."

"Tell him he should look into the homicide on McCommas Street."

"What homicide?"

"He'll know. Or somebody in his division will. It's already been on the news. The victim's name was Linda Croft. She was an employee of the Waters Clinic. I spoke with her today."

"Jesus," Tobias muttered. "Hold on. Don't hang up." He cupped the mouthpiece and called out to Lawson, who joined him from another room of the clinic. "Know anything about a homicide on McCommas Street?"

"Heard about it."

"The victim worked here. Melina Lloyd talked to her today."

He didn't have to spell it out for the detective. "I'll get on it," he said, then did an about-face and left the room.

Tobias returned to his phone call. "Lawson's on it. Where are you, Ms. Lloyd? Is Colonel Hart still with you?"

"Take down this address." She reeled off a house number.

"Hold on. What is it?"

"The home address for Tony and Candace Anderson. Remember them? They remember you."

"The couple whose baby was kidnapped. I questioned them."

"But you failed to ask if they'd had any unusual visitors at the hospital."

"Unusual?"

"Other than the expected family members and close friends, guess who came to the birthing room to see them, bearing gifts and taking pictures of mother and child? Dale Gordon."

Tobias ran a hand over his close-cropped hair. He couldn't remember if he'd specifically asked the distraught couple about their visitors. Strangers, yes. *Have you seen anyone lurking in the hallway? Or outside your room? Has anyone threatened you recently?*

At the time, he hadn't been looking at Gordon or anyone affiliated with the clinic. He'd been trying to establish a pattern in the outbreak of newborn kidnappings, believing the culprits to be part of a baby-selling ring.

"The Andersons won't be at home," Melina Lloyd told him. "They've run for cover, just as I've done, as I should have advised Linda Croft to do, since the authorities seem incapable of protecting the good guys from the bad."

He let her have that shot for free.

"However," she continued, "if you dispatch someone to the Andersons' address, you might catch the men who came to my house this morning and the ones who, more than likely, killed Linda Croft. Just a suggestion, of course. I wouldn't presume to tell you how to do your job, Agent Tobias. But your office called me last night, and this morning I'm running for my life. I talked to Linda Croft, and within hours she gets bludgeoned to death. If this course continues, Tony and Candace Anderson will be next on your list of casualties."

Tobias didn't let pride stand in his way. He jotted down the address, confirmed it with her, then passed it to a police officer with instructions to send a patrol car over there ASAP.

"Where are you, Tobias?" Melina Lloyd asked.

He told her. "We're searching the place, although we can't get into the medical records without a court order, and that's going to take a while. Hopefully tomorrow."

"What are you looking for specifically?"

"We're searching the lab."

"Gordon's area."

"That's right."

"What did he do there? Besides some sneak photography through a hole in the wall."

He hesitated before reluctantly answering, "He prepared the frozen sperm specimens."

"For insemination."

"And in vitro. I've asked the doctors to suspend all inseminations using frozen sperm until we can conduct a more thorough investigation."

"What kind of more thorough investigation?"

"This particular Waters is a full-service facility. Besides receiving specimens from other sperm banks, they have their own. I want to interrogate every donor."

"Won't they perceive that as an invasion of privacy?"

"Probably. But I want to match each specimen catalogued and stored here against a specimen that's obtained in a controlled environment and DNA-tested immediately."

During the ensuing pause, he knew she was reasoning it through. Finally she said, "In order to determine if every specimen in the bank actually came from the donor specified on the label."

Evasively he replied, "I can't move this investigation forward until I know what we're dealing with here."

"In other words, you need to test each specimen to see if sperm labeled Donor XYZ actually came from Donor XYZ and not Donor ABC."

She was too smart for her own good. Certainly she was too smart for *his* good, because she'd nailed it on the first try. He had a bad feeling about Dale Gordon, especially after seeing the photographs found hidden in the man's apartment. Since when did a lab technician take such a personal interest in patients? Was he just a pervert who sneaked pictures of naked women? Or did it go beyond that?

Tobias feared the latter. At least that was the supposition he was acting on until it was proved false. If donor sperm was being switched or substituted at the time of artificial insemination, the unthinkable implications were far-reaching. The possibility of such an atrocity being visited on an unsuspecting woman or couple was horrendous.

As though reading his thoughts, Melina Lloyd said, "You think the sperm was being switched, don't you?"

Not wishing to start a public panic, he said, "I don't know."

"But it's possible."

"It's happened before," he admitted reluctantly. "A few years ago a gynecologist—"

"Populated a whole county with his offspring. He used his sperm in place of partner or donor sperm. I remember. And you think Dale Gordon was doing the same thing?"

"His is the first we'll test."

"From the residue on the pajamas."

"Yes. We'll test that against the specimens stored here."

"He was in a position to make the substitutions," she observed quietly. "Without anyone knowing or suspecting."

"Please don't jump to conclusions, Ms. Lloyd. Let me point out that Gordon doesn't fit the profile of an egomaniac who would do such a thing. Just the opposite, in fact. His colleagues here claim that he was a meticulous scientist. Kept excellent records. Resented any intrusion that distracted him from his work.

"The andrologist who was hired to take over for him says she's never seen a lab so well maintained. According to everyone here, he appeared to be a dedicated scientist who took pride in his work and felt he was edifying humankind by performing such a life-giving service."

"So did Dr. Frankenstein."

"This is only one theory I'm playing with," Tobias stressed. "I could be way off base. I admit to being wrong before."

"But I don't think you are. This exemplary, society-edifying scientist killed my sister, and I am going to know why."

The statement made him extremely uncomfortable. "Ms. Lloyd, where are you? You're a material witness to several crimes. If you don't come forward with information that could help solve these crimes, you could be charged with obstruction of justice."

"Yes, someone mentioned that to me."

"Then you'll—Shit!" he swore. He was talking into a dead phone.

Melina repeated to Chief the half of the conversation that he hadn't overheard. Her voice quavered when she told him about Gordon. "Jesus. He was switching out sperm?"

"Tobias hypothesizes several variations of that theme, but basically that's the crux of it."

"Does that mean that Gillian . . . Could she have got . . ."

Burying her face in her hands, Melina groaned, "Oh, God!"

"Are you all right?"

She shook her head violently and signaled for him to pull over. The car wasn't even at a complete stop before she shoved open the door and stumbled out. By the time he got out on the driver's side and came around, she was vomiting.

He placed one hand on the back of her

neck and supported her forehead with his other palm. She tried to wave him off, but he stood firm. Several more spasms seized her. When the retching stopped, he assisted her to stand upright and backed her into the car fender for additional support.

"Better?" Gently he brushed a strand of hair off her clammy cheek.

Keeping her eyes averted, she replied, "Embarrassed."

"As many times as I've hurled in the simulator? As many times as I've been hurled upon in the simulator? Don't be silly." He removed a handkerchief from his rear pocket and dabbed her lips.

"Thanks. I think this is a first, vomiting in front of a man."

"You had good reason to be sick."

When she looked up at him, he could see tears sparkling in her eyes. They reflected the headlights of oncoming cars as they whizzed past on the boulevard. "Gillian was so excited, so hopeful for success," she said. "She wanted a baby. Was that so wrong? Was she being punished for something?"

"Melina." He put his arms around her and

hugged her close. "You know that's not the way it works."

"Then how could something that wonderful and beautiful be contaminated and turned into something that revolting?"

"You can't be certain that Gillian—"

"No, I can't be certain." She shuddered. "I really can't even bear to think that Gordon used his own semen. The thought of it is nauseating."

He continued holding her, stroking her hair, then finally set her away and helped her into the car. "Where to now?" he asked as he pulled back into traffic.

"Home." He looked at her with surprise, and she smiled wryly. "That's where I *want* to go. My bathtub. My bed. My pillow."

"But you're afraid."

"I wish I had warned Linda Croft to be. If I had, she might have taken precautions."

He started driving with no particular destination in mind. "I'm sure Lawson or Tobias would provide you with protection."

"Not an option," she said without hesitation. "If they had me under lock and key, I couldn't maneuver. They would tell me only what they wanted me to know. I'd be powerless. I wouldn't get first crack at—"

When she broke off, he asked, "At what?"

"Nothing."

"At whoever ordered Gillian killed?" When she looked at him directly, words were superfluous. He could read the answer there in her eyes.

"You don't have to go along, Chief," she said quietly. "I haven't mentioned your name to Tobias. He's guessing you're with me, but I haven't confirmed it."

"Thanks for that."

"You're not involved."

"What are you talking about?" he asked angrily. "I'm involved up to my eyebrows. I wouldn't mind having first crack at the responsible party myself."

"It could blow up in our faces."

"I'm willing to take that chance."

"It could become a big news story that would impact your future and nullify your entire career with NASA."

"That's what that lawyer told me, too. But he couldn't talk me out of this, and neither can you. If it becomes an issue, I'll just have to deal with it, won't I?"

"Deal with it," she murmured. "Jem said that to me last night. 'Gillian's dead, Melina. We're just going to have to deal with it.'"

"You know, the more I hear about that prick, the more I hate him."

She fished a slip of paper from her purse and palmed her cell phone. "Let's see who Jem calls routinely."

"While you're doing that, I've got to have something to eat." He pulled into a Burger King and got in line for the drive-through.

"Just a Coke for me, please."

"With sugar and caffeine?"

"Absolutely."

He ordered a cheeseburger and fries and two large drinks. By the time he'd picked up the food at the window, Melina had called two of the numbers on Hennings's autodial, which had turned out to be the retrieval numbers for his office and home voice mail boxes. After dialing the third sequence of numbers, she clicked off quickly and clutched the phone to her chest.

He took a bite of burger. "What?"

"Gillian's number. I got her recording."

He was tempted to ask Melina to redial so that he could hear her voice but decided against it. It would have disconcerted him as much as it obviously had her. She stared vacantly into near space for a long moment, then doggedly dialed the next number on the list. Waiting for it to ring, she took a sip of her cold drink.

When the phone was answered, Chief noticed that she swallowed hard, forcing down the Coke. "Pardon?" she said.

Quickly she reached across the seat and pressed the phone against his ear so that he could hear the female voice on the other end of the line when she repeated, "You've reached the Temple. Peace and love."

Decisively Melina depressed the end button.

Chief said, "That's the name of that preacher's—"

"Brother Gabriel."

"His outfit in New Mexico."

"The number is on Jem's autodial. He calls it frequently."

Chief cranked the ignition key, and the car clattered to life. He threw the shift stick into reverse, and the car shot from the parking space. Tires squealed and smoked when he stopped at a trash receptacle only long enough to heave the remainder of his food into it before stamping the accelerator and wheeling the car into the fast flow of traffic.

"Is Hennings overtly religious?" he asked as he took the entrance ramp onto the tollway.

"Not at all. He even expressed surprise over the spiritual tone of Gillian's memorial service."

"I suppose it could be a coincidence that both he and Dale Gordon had an interest in Brother Gabriel's ministry."

"I don't believe that. If it were a coincidence, Jem would have mentioned it."

"I don't believe it, either. I'm just thinking out loud."

"Having the telephone number programmed into his autodial indicates more than a passing interest. It signifies devotion."

"What do you know about Hennings?" he asked. "Family?"

"His parents are deceased, no brothers or sisters. Some distant cousins living in London."

"Which could be convenient lies for a man wanting to cover tracks. Where'd he come from originally?"

"He says Oregon."

"But you're not sure?"

"I'm not sure of anything. It's frightening, isn't it? That you can be close to someone and not know them at all."

"He would have been your brother-in-law."

"Never. Sooner or later Gillian would have come to her senses."

By the time they reached the exit and slowed down to pay the toll, they had concluded that, to some degree, Jem was involved in all of it. The murder. Dale Gordon. The attack on Chief. The men at Melina's house. Linda Croft.

"He's more than just a sideline participant," Chief said tightly, his lips barely moving. "I think the son of a bitch is a key player."

"But in what? How does it all fit together?" Melina asked in consternation. "Jem's sterile."

"Or so he's claimed."

"What man would claim to be who wasn't? And how does all of this tie in to Brother Gabriel?"

They had many more questions than answers. They hoped to scare them out of Jem.

"You're a white-knuckle passenger, Melina," Chief remarked when he was forced to stop for a red light.

"And you're a maniac behind the wheel."

"You said to hurry. I hurried. Just wish I'd had my own car."

"God forbid. For once I'm grateful for the clunker."

Actually she was glad that Chief was driving. She was a competent driver who had little patience with poky motorists, but she never would have taken the chances that he did. He drove well, but far too fast and with a derring-do that more than once had caused her heart to lurch. But if his driving shaved minutes off the trip, all the better. She was eager to confront Jem.

"They're on their way here now." Jem was relieved to report this to Mr. Hancock. The last few previous reports hadn't been this positive.

"You're sure?"

"They've taken the most direct route from north Dallas. They could be going somewhere else, but it appears that they're on their way to see me."

He purposefully omitted mentioning Melina and Hart's visit to the Andersons. By the time Joshua and his friend had reached the suburban home, the Andersons had split and a police car was parked out front. An unhappy setback, but not disastrous. The couple would eventually resurface.

In the meantime, what purpose would be served by bringing it to Brother Gabriel's attention? It would only be something else for him to worry about.

Nor had he reported on Linda Croft. He had given that order himself. As soon as Joshua had reported to him what Melina had been up to when she wasn't breaking into his apartment, he had instructed Joshua to permanently silence the nurse. It was doubtful that she was privy to anything that might prove harmful, but he favored eliminating even the possibility.

It had been a stressful, eventful day. Thanks to Melina and her Indian friend, Brother Gabriel was burdened with all sorts of unpleasantness. Why make things worse by telling him about Linda Croft and the Andersons? He was doing Brother Gabriel a favor by sparing him more concern.

"They're minutes away," he told Hancock now. "By last report, they were at the cross-street intersection. They'll be here— Ah, there's my buzzer now. Please hold on, Mr. Hancock."

He moved to the intercom near his door and picked up the telephone receiver. "Yes?"

"You have guests, Mr. Hennings."

"Oh, who?"

"The young lady who identified herself as your fiancée earlier today." He'd given Harry the new doorman a blistering lecture for admitting his *fiancée* into his apartment when his *fiancée* had been dead for four days. The man's tone was suitably deferential now. "There's a gentleman with her."

"Send them up, please."

"Yes, sir, Mr. Hennings."

"And Harry, there'll be two other gentlemen arriving shortly. When they do, send them up as well. No need to ring me back."

"Sure thing, sir."

"Don't mention those later arrivals to Ms. Lloyd."

"No, sir."

Jem resumed his telephone conversation with Hancock. "They're here, on their way up. Joshua won't be far behind."

"The woman is not to be harmed, Mr. Hennings."

"As you've told me already."

"Brother Gabriel was very specific about

that. He does not want her injured. Not severely, anyway."

"I understand," he said, although he
didn't. Why didn't Brother Gabriel just cut
his losses? Why preserve Melina? The
Program didn't need her. There were thousands of other women in the world who
would do just as well as she and be much
less trouble to manage.

He supposed that Brother Gabriel couldn't
view her as "the one who got away," as an
ordinary man would. He wasn't an ordinary
man. To Brother Gabriel, Melina was a
stumbling block to a divinely inspired mission. As such, she needed spiritual guidance, indoctrination, and discipline. It was
admirable of him to want to redeem her and
not to take her defiance personally.

Jem wasn't that high-minded. He was
finding it increasingly difficult to be forgiving. He couldn't regard her repeated insults
as spiritual shortcomings. They were blatant, personal affronts that he simply
couldn't overlook and forgive.

"Don't worry, Mr. Hancock," he said
smoothly. "These men are professionals.
Joshua understands the delicacy of the situation. He knows what to do."

"Yes, I'm certain he does."

Hancock hung up first. Jem determined then that the next time he called in a report, he would demand—not request—to speak directly to Brother Gabriel. He resented his conversations being filtered through Hancock, who, in his opinion, was no more than a glorified secretary.

However, with Melina and Christopher Hart on their way up, thoughts of the haughty Mr. Hancock gave way to more imperative matters.

C H A P T E R | 2 7

When they entered, the doorman had greeted them sourly. He was no friendlier after speaking with Jem. "He says you can go up, Ms. Lloyd."

"Thank you."

"You got me into a lot of trouble with Mr. Hennings. Why'd you lie to me about being his fiancée?"

"So . . . Mr. Hennings knows that I went into his apartment earlier?"

"Yes, ma'am."

"Great," Chief muttered. As they made their way to the elevator, he nervously glanced over his shoulder. She did likewise and saw that the parking valet was driving the clunker into the cavernous garage. She would have preferred it be left out front and wished too late that they had thought to request that.

But her paranoia was no more alive than Chief's. When they got into the elevator, he punched the button for every floor. She looked at him quizzically.

"Humor me."

"Do you think we're being followed?"

"I'm not sure. I haven't noticed that we are, but . . ." After a slight pause, he said, "I can't explain it, but I get the feeling we're never truly alone."

"I get the same feeling."

"If somebody is tailing us, I want to make it as difficult as possible," he said, motioning toward the lighted disks on the panel.

"Take all the precautions you want. Now that I think about it, Jem should be irate that I went snooping in his apartment. He hasn't even called to ask why I would do such a thing."

"Not good," Chief remarked as the elevator began its ascent.

They waited anxiously as it stopped on

each floor, feeling dangerously exposed while the doors were open. There were two other elevators, so they didn't worry about inconveniencing other occupants of the exclusive building. In any case, no one was waiting for their elevator car on any of the floors.

When they stopped at the fifteenth, Chief nudged her out.

"Jem's apartment is on seventeen."

"I know."

She didn't argue and preceded him out. He motioned her in the direction of the softly glowing exit sign at the end of the corridor. When they reached it, Chief pulled open the door that led into the stairwell. Before the door closed, he glanced over his shoulder. The corridor behind them was clear.

The lighting in the corridor had been subtle and indirect. Although its primary purpose was to provide enough illumination for one to see where he was going, it also had an aesthetic quality. However, in the stairwell, the lighting was strictly functional. The blue-white fluorescents made her and Chief feel as though they were in a spotlight. A few concealing shadows would have been welcomed.

Chief held up his hand for quiet. The only sound she could hear was the soft soughing of their breathing. After at least sixty seconds had ticked by, Melina looked up at Chief with a silent question. He shook his head and motioned for her to remain still and silent awhile longer. She passed the time by staring into his open shirt collar and watching his pulse beat in the hollow of his throat.

Finally, he hitched his chin upward. Treading lightly, they climbed the two flights up to the seventeenth floor. At the door, Chief paused and looked down at her. *Okay?* he mouthed. She raised her shoulders in an indecisive shrug, then changed her mind and nodded emphatically.

Chief opened the door. The corridor was empty, silent except for the muted sound of a TV coming from within one of the apartments. As they hesitated there, a door opened at the end of the hallway and Jem Hennings stepped out. With a mix of expectation and irritation, he looked toward the elevators. He checked his wristwatch.

On the verge of stepping back into his condo, he happened to glance down the corridor and did a double-take when he spotted them. "What are you doing on the stairs?"

"Getting our exercise."

Walking side by side, she and Chief cautiously moved down the hall toward him.

"I wondered what was taking you so long. The doorman called me five minutes ago. The elevators rarely take that long." His gaze shifted from her to Chief. "The proverbial bad penny."

"Happy to see you, too, Hennings. Are you going to invite us in, or should we discuss out here in the hallway, where your neighbors might overhear, how you set up Melina to be killed this morning?"

"Killed?" he repeated on a laugh. "Shows how much you know." With a sweeping motion of his hand, he motioned them into the apartment. As she was about to step forward, Chief laid a cautionary hand on her arm. "After you, Hennings."

Again Jem laughed as though what Chief had said were funny. Nevertheless, he went into the apartment ahead of them. Chief pulled the door to, but she noticed that he didn't allow the latch to catch. She guessed he wanted an unimpeded escape route, although in any kind of physical contest with

Chief, Jem was certain to come out the loser.

"Can I get you something to drink?" Jem asked cordially.

"This isn't a social call."

"No, Kemo Sabe," he replied with another amused smirk for Chief. "I didn't think it was. You two have been busy sleuthing all day, haven't you?" When he turned toward her, his smile disappeared along with his phony cordiality. "You didn't cover your tracks very well when you broke into my apartment, Melina."

"I didn't care if my tracks were covered or not. I got what I came for."

"Which was?"

"A clue. I just don't know how to interpret it."

Jem propped himself against the back of his sofa and raised his arms to his sides as though to say that he was at her disposal.

"Dale Gordon, Jem," she said without preamble.

"What about him?"

"You knew him."

"Yes."

She could tell that Chief, like her, was somewhat taken aback by his candor. They hadn't expected him to be this forthcoming. In fact, Chief had expressed a desire to beat the truth out of Jem Hennings if he gave them evasive answers to their questions.

Jem's straightforwardness made her increasingly wary. He wouldn't admit to knowing his fiancée's murderer unless he felt confident that he was under someone's protection and that this truth would never come to the attention of the authorities.

"In what context did you know him, Jem? I know you weren't friends with him."

"Perish the thought." He shivered delicately. "Actually, he gave me the creeping willies. Our acquaintance was strictly professional. Gordon and I work for the same entity."

"The Waters Clinic?" Chief asked.

"No, Chief." She was a step ahead of him. "They work for Brother Gabriel."

"You know, Melina," Jem said, casually crossing his ankles and arms, "of the two of you, I always thought you were much brighter than Gillian. More prickly. Less malleable and trusting. But a shade more intelligent."

She wouldn't let herself be sidetracked by his provoking statements. "What do you do for Brother Gabriel?"

"You haven't figured it out yet?" He *tsked* her. "Being the Nancy Drew you've become lately, I'd have thought you would have the mystery solved by now. Especially since you've talked to the Croft woman and to the Andersons. You've got all the puzzle pieces, you just haven't formed the big picture with them yet."

She was certain that Chief shared her curiosity over how Jem knew about their meetings with Linda Croft and the Andersons, but again she refused to be led off the subject. "Did Gordon substitute his sperm—"

"*His* sperm? God, no! What a hideous thought."

"Then yours."

He laughed. "I'm sterile. Remember?"

"So that much is true?"

"Yes, Melina, that much is true. I had a vasectomy years ago. It's compulsory," he stated matter-of-factly. "I was sterilized in order to accept this job."

Chief, giving in to his temper, reached out and grabbed Jem by the front of his shirt and shook him roughly. "I've had enough of this fucking around. What is your job, Hennings?"

"I'm a monitor. I provide watch care over the select."

"Select?"

"Like Gillian. Like Melina is soon to be." He turned his head and gave her a smile that caused gooseflesh to break out on her arms. "I won't continue with my explanation until this savage lets go of me."

She gave Chief a brusque nod. He released Jem but appeared to be holding on to his temper by a thread.

Jem remained unruffled. With maddening complacency, he straightened his shirt, realigned his collar, shot his cuffs. Only then did he continue. "If the woman is married or in a monogamous relationship, her monitor might be a neighbor or coworker. Someone near to keep an eye on her. As was the case with Candace Anderson. Her monitor was actually the woman who cleaned her house three days a week. But for a single woman like Gillian, they bring men like me in to be their partners."

"You were assigned to her?"

"From the day she first consulted the clinic."

"So your meeting was by design?"

"Yes, Melina," he replied in a patient and

patronizing manner. "I was sent to her. Like a guardian angel. She was waffling over whether or not to be artificially inseminated, so I gave her encouragement. I reassured her that it was a sound idea and that I, as her partner, was one hundred percent supportive of her having a child.

"From the day she was inseminated, I would have showered her with affection. But I didn't have an opportunity to do that, did I? As it turns out, when I went over that night to celebrate the event, I wasted my affection on you instead."

"Why was Gillian killed, Jem?"

Rather than giving a straight answer, he continued his explanation in his own way. "If Gillian hadn't conceived on the first try, I would have urged her to try again. If the first try was successful, well, then I would have nurtured her for the duration of her pregnancy. I would have treated her like a princess, for indeed, she was chosen to be royalty.

"Gillian would have been elevated, revered. I would have seen to it that she received everything she desired or needed. I would have supervised her, making certain she did nothing to imperil the child she carried and that she didn't stray from a straight and moral path." At that point, he glared at Chief. "But, of course, she did. With you. You tainted her. You spoiled her for the Program."

Chief's hands balled into fists at his sides. "So it's true. You had Gillian killed because she spent the night with me?"

He took a threatening step toward Jem, but she extended her arm to bar him. "No, Chief. I want to hear this. Difficult as it is to listen to, I want to hear it."

"Thank you, Melina." Jem looked at Chief with contempt, then addressed her again. "The select aren't allowed to be intimate with anyone other than their partners or their monitors."

"Because they're sterile," she said.

"Ah!" he exclaimed. "I think you've experienced a breakthrough."

As it all began to come together in her mind, she nodded slowly. "The women are chosen. Gillian. Candace Anderson. Healthy young women."

Jem smiled. "Superior in every way."

A light came on behind Chief's eyes. "You're genetically engineering babies."

"Candace Anderson is a beautiful woman,

isn't she?" Jem asked rhetorically. "A perfect physical specimen. And extremely intelligent. Blessed with a natural talent for music. We hope to use her again. Just as we'll use you, Melina. Now. Since we were deprived of Gillian. She was sacrificed to her own lust, so you've been selected to take her place."

His voice adapted an eerie singsong quality. "Gillian would have been perfect. Dale Gordon recognized that immediately. That was his job, you see, to spot prospective candidates, then to screen them. Easily done, with their medical histories at his disposal. Gillian was physically ideal. Mentally superior. She was also unencumbered by a relationship, which can prove to be tiresome.

"All told, she was a most desirable candidate for the Program. The Program needed her. Now it needs you, Melina." He clasped her hands, hotly, moistly pressing them between his. Smiling rapturously, he said, "I'm so happy for you."

Then his head exploded.

CHAPTER | 2 8

Chief executed a full-body tackle that sent Melina to the floor and knocked the wind out of her. He landed on top of her. Inches away lay Jem Hennings. There was little left of him above his shoulders. The large window overlooking the Dallas skyline had been shattered.

All this took a nanosecond for Chief to register.

He rolled off Melina and reached for the electrical cord attached to the table lamp. He jerked it from the floor plug. The apartment went dark.

"Who . . . where . . ."

"From the roof of the building across the street would be my guess," he said in answer to Melina's stammering. He had to give her credit. Anyone else spattered with blood and gore might have gone hysterical on him by now. She was either one hell of a brave woman or she was in shock. Which meant that she could come apart at the seams at any moment.

"Are you okay?"

She stared at him wordlessly until he repeated the question and spoke her name sharply. "Yes. Yes."

"Don't move."

"Chief—"

"Hold on."

He duckwalked into the kitchen and returned with a roll of paper towels. "Wipe off your face. Hurry." She did as she was told, making hasty swipes across her face. He spat on the corner of a towel and rubbed off spots she missed. "Take off your jacket." She did that without argument, too. He was glad to see her sweater beneath the jacket was clean.

"Any on me?"

She looked closely at him. "I can't . . . can't . . . I don't think so."

How much time had gone by? Twenty seconds? Thirty? Forty? "We've got to get out of here."

"Are we next?"

"Not you. They need you for the Program," he returned sarcastically.

"I'd rather die."

"I'd rather live. Come on."

He helped her to her feet. At a crouch, they ran toward the door. When they reached it, he snatched the intercom receiver from the cradle. "What's the doorman's name?"

"Uh, Henry. Harry," she corrected just as the man answered.

"Help! They're crazy!" Chief yelled into the receiver. "They've started a fire up here. Harry, can you hear me? Help! Fire! Fire!"

Then he dropped the receiver and let it bang against the wall. Grabbing Melina's hand, he charged into the hallway. Before they'd reached the exit door at the end of the corridor, the fire alarm began to blare at an ear-shattering volume. Behind them, doors began to open.

Human nature being what it is, he was afraid people would hesitate to leave the comfort of their apartments and interrupt their quiet evening until the emergency was confirmed. He also counted on modern society's reluctance to get too chummy with neighbors. He doubted anyone would recognize him as a nonresident.

Waving his arms wildly, he shouted. "Hurry, everybody. Get downstairs. There's a fire in apartment D and it's spreading quickly."

A resident on a lower floor, who had responded to the alarm and ventured into the stairwell, shouted up, "Is there really a fire?"

"Seventeen D," Melina called back. "Get everyone on your floor out!"

By the time they had loped down several flights, they became part of the throng rushing into the stairwell, which was exactly what Chief had hoped to accomplish when he raised the alarm.

"What do we do when we get to the bottom?" Melina asked beneath her breath.

"Hell if I know. I'm hoping there'll be so much confusion, we'll be able to sneak away. No matter what, don't let go of my hand." He received an answering squeeze even though she was helping a woman in a sari hustle two sleepy children down the steps.

Even before they reached the lobby, Chief could hear sirens wailing. By the time they got to the lower floor and entered the lobby, rent-a-cops who provided building security were herding people through an emergency side exit. Two fire trucks had already arrived. Firemen in full garb leapt from them and raced toward the entrance where Harry was babbling frantically. Chief was glad the doorman was occupied and didn't see him and Melina as they were caught up in the crowd that moved en masse toward the bottleneck at the emergency exit.

"Keep your head down," he instructed as they wiggled through the door. They moved along with their eyes on their feet. Once they were clear of the door, he tugged her toward the edge of the gathering crowd but purposefully kept them in shadows as security personnel shepherded them across the street into the parking lot of the building from which he guessed the shots had been fired.

He pulled up short when he recognized two familiar faces in the crowd of condo dwellers. The two men were looking wildly about, but not because they feared fire.

They were scanning the faces of everyone who had exited the building.

Chief spun Melina about and reversed their direction. "Don't look back. Two o'clock. Our FBI impersonators. I'd bet good money they were the shooters."

"But why'd they shoot Jem? They were under his orders, weren't they?"

"He thought so."

Anxiously she pulled her lower lip through her teeth. "What do we do?"

"Well, we could try reasoning with these guys."

"Right," she said caustically.

"Or we could call Tobias. Lawson. Either would help us."

"They'd also contain us."

Privately Chief acknowledged that he and Melina were fools for not taking advantage of the protection that the FBI and the local police department could afford them. Their lives were at risk—at least his. Now that Hennings had been dispatched, the next hollow-tip bullet probably had his name on it. They'd already made two unsuccessful attempts to punish him for "tainting" Gillian and making her unsuitable for the Program. And he didn't like the sound of Melina's being pegged to take her place.

Of course, everything Hennings had said could be nothing more than the blather of a madman. He and his pal Gordon, the sexual deviate, could have been zealots who had twisted Brother Gabriel's well-meaning message to justify their own aberrant agenda.

But maybe not, and that was a terrifying prospect. If Brother Gabriel had authored this program of genetic engineering, the implications were horrifying and had the potential of being globally catastrophic. Chief recognized that he had to be crazy not to call in the cavalry.

On the other hand, he didn't have all the facts yet. At this point it was still a personal fight, and he didn't cotton to anyone else fighting his battles for him. Maybe that misplaced pride, or downright orneriness, was a legacy from his forefathers that was only now manifesting itself. Maybe his inclinations were more Native American than he'd been willing to accept.

Whatever, he chose to rely on his gut instinct.

"I say we go for broke, but it's your call,

Melina," he said quietly, barely making himself heard above the din surrounding them. "Gillian was your sister."

"She was my *twin.* This is personal."

"For me, too."

"Then there's your answer."

"Okay."

But now that the decision had been made, they were stuck in their immediate dilemma, and it was dangerous. He had created chaos in the hope of their getting out of the building unseen. But his strategy wasn't without a few major hitches. For one, they were now afoot. There was no way they could retrieve the clunker from the parking garage because it was blocked by emergency vehicles. Furthermore, it would soon be determined that the fire alarm had been a ruse to cover Jem Hennings's murder.

Following his train of thought, Melina said, "We've got to get away."

"Soon. When they discover Hennings's body, everyone with a badge will be after us for questioning. Harry the doorman isn't going to forget us. Particularly you." He glanced down at her flat-soled shoes. "If we have to, can you run?"

"I do. Three times a week."

"Where's the nearest commercial area? Lots of traffic. People."

"Oak Lawn Street. That way," she said, subtly motioning with her head.

"I'm right behind you. Start out slow, walking. Try not to attract attention."

He placed his hands loosely on her waist. They shuffled through the crowd of milling people, some of whom were already expressing skepticism about the fire and grumbling about the unreliable technology that set off false alarms more often than not.

They had almost reached the fringes of the crowd when Chief turned his head to check and see if they were being followed. He spotted Tobias's impersonator standing no more than twenty yards away. His neck was stretched up from his shoulders as he swiveled his head back and forth, surveying the crowd of men, women, and children who'd evacuated the high-rise.

Suddenly he turned. Chief had no warning. He couldn't avert his head in time. Their eyes connected.

"Go!" he told Melina, giving her a light push, just as he heard a shout behind them.

She didn't hesitate or stop to ask questions, but broke into a sprint across the parking lot. She didn't falter when they reached the low hedge of shrubbery, but hurdled it like an Olympian and kept running full-out. The street was clear. They raced across it. He heard tires squeal behind them and turned his head only long enough to see that the men in pursuit had nearly been struck by an oncoming minivan.

The near miss diverted them just long enough for Melina to plunge through a high, dense hedge that bordered a vacant lot. They were away from streetlights now. It was dark and the ground was uneven. Chief nearly collided with a metal real estate sign planted in the ground, but he managed to avoid its doing no more damage than glancing his kneecap.

"Through here," Melina gasped when they reached the far side of the lot. She led him through a bank annex's drive-through bay and then into another darkened lot that had a vacant house in the center. When they rounded the house, he reached for her hand and pulled her to a stop. They flattened themselves against the frame exterior. The wood smelled old and mildewed and gave off the odor of animal decomposition.

"You okay?" he huffed, trying to catch his breath.

"Are they still chasing us?"

"I'm taking no chances. How much farther?"

"Two, three blocks. See the lights?"

Above roofs and treetops he saw the glow of commercial lighting. "Take off."

Many of the older houses in the area had been converted into businesses—antique shops, hair salons, law offices—which were closed at this hour. They kept to the shadows and used trees, fences, and shrubbery as shields.

Over her shoulder, she asked, "When we get there . . . ?"

"Hail the first taxi you see."

Taxis weren't easily come by in a city like Dallas, where the number of cars nearly outnumbered the population. He reasoned that their best chance of finding one would be near restaurants and clubs where people were drinking alcohol and hopefully opting to take a taxi home rather than risk a DUI charge.

They wove their way through a congested parking lot that served several restaurants. Curious looks were thrown to them by people who were either returning from or going to dinner. Chief didn't resent the passersby. He was glad to see that the sidewalks were crowded and that the street was jammed with traffic.

"Try and blend in," he said, taking Melina's arm. If not for the sweat pouring down their faces, they might have been any other couple out on a date. "There," he said, spying a taxi pulling up to the entrance of one of the restaurants.

They dodged the crawling traffic and jogged across the street, climbing into the back seat as soon as a trio of Japanese tourists alighted. "Where to?" the driver called back.

"Head south out Interstate 45. I'll give you directions as we go along."

Chief pulled Melina back against the seat. She didn't have to be told to keep her head low. "There," she whispered. "Under the R in the restaurant sign."

Tobias's imposter and his partner looked out of place in the yuppie crowd, sweating, their chests heaving with exertion, frustrated. Chief kept his eyes on the pair until the taxi was well away.

"They never saw us," he reported as he

flopped back against the seat, exhausted. For a time, he kept his eyes closed and concentrated on sucking in oxygen. Eventually he asked, "How're you doing?"

She had pulled up the hem of her sweater and was using it like a towel. Her face was buried in it. Then he noticed that her shoulders were shaking. "Melina?"

He stretched his arm across her shoulders and pulled her closer against him.

"Were y'all in some kinda race?" the driver asked.

"Yeah. A fucking marathon. Now mind your own goddamn business and drive."

"Jeez. Bite my head off, why don'tcha?"

Dismissing the nosy driver, Chief threaded his fingers through Melina's sweat-damp hair. "It's okay. Don't cry. You're safe."

When she raised her head, he was amazed to see that she wasn't crying at all. She was laughing. "I don't know what's wrong with me!" she exclaimed in a whisper. "I just saw a man's head disintegrate. We falsely reported a fire. I was chased by bad guys intent on killing one or both of us. I am avoiding the FBI. And I'm *laughing*?"

No sooner had she said that, however,

than her features crumpled and tears spurted from her eyes.

Cupping the back of her head in his palm, Chief pressed it against his chest and continued to massage her scalp while she hiccupped hard sobs into the front of his shirt.

He hated being anywhere in the vicinity of a weeping woman. Tears represented emotions that were best avoided—fear, frustration, heartbreak, disappointment, anger. When a woman began to cry, you wished you were anywhere else but there, especially if you were the one responsible for her tears.

But he didn't mind Melina's crying. He felt if anyone deserved a good cry, it was she. Up till now, she'd demonstrated unusual bravery. He would sign her up to be a member of his crew any day of the week. She had proved that she could be relied on not to unravel during a crisis situation.

Now that the crisis was past, however, he felt she was entitled to an all-too-human crack-up.

He held her close, with his chin propped on the crown of her head, one hand stroking her back, the other still cupping her head. He let her cry until she ran dry. He didn't move until he was sure she was finished. Then he placed his finger beneath her chin and tilted her face up. "Better?"

"I barf and I bawl. Fine confederate I am."

"You don't hear me complaining, do you?" He smiled and she smiled back.

Her neck was resting in the crook of his elbow. Her face was tilted up and back, exposing her throat. After brushing away a tear with the pad of his thumb, he kept his hand there against her cheek. His other moved to that bare strip of skin between her raised top and the waistband of her slacks.

Her lips separated on a quick intake of breath.

He wouldn't have disengaged his eyes from hers just then if someone had told him that the sun had burned out. Without looking, he felt her hand, which had been clutching fistfuls of his shirt moments ago, now resting somewhere just below his belt buckle, collecting heat.

His throat was tight, but he managed to breathe her name. "Melina . . . ?"

"Say, uh, don't get pissed or nothing," said the driver from the front seat, "but I need to know how far south we're goin' before turning off I-45."

She was the first to move. Regrettably, she sat up and put space between them. She smoothed down her sweater, made swipes across her tear-streaked cheeks with the backs of her hands, and tucked her hair behind her ears.

Chief told the driver which exit to take. "Go east."

He was still watching Melina as she unsuccessfully pretended that the moment—he wasn't sure what else you'd call it—hadn't happened, and that, had they not been interrupted, it might have ended with him pressing his mouth against the indentation in her throat where a ruby pendant nestled.

She fidgeted nervously. It seemed her eyes didn't know where to rest. Finally, after running out of self-conscious gestures to occupy her, she looked at him. "Where are we going?"

"You're not afraid of flying, are you?"

Brother Gabriel was at prayer.

Ritualistically he prayed three times a day—before breakfast, before dinner, and before bed. His prayers this evening were effusive because it had been a productive day. The sermon he'd taped this afternoon for his television show had been particularly inspired.

The subject had been tribulation. Not the Tribulation with a capital *T* as described in the New Testament's Book of Revelations, but the minor annoyances that occur in everyday life. He shared with his followers the solution to handling those persistent, nagging nuisances.

"Give them to me," he'd implored in his sincerest voice. "Lay them on my shoulders." He went on to explain that this transference was possible only if the burdened one had absolute faith in him and his ability to improve one's quality of life.

Actually, it wasn't that hard for him to sell the idea because he believed it.

He could improve lives. He demonstrated a perfection to which his followers should aspire. He bestowed love on the unloved. His promise of a new world order gave hope to the hopeless. He was benevolence personified.

Benevolence personified. Hmm. Catchy phrase. He must remember it.

In the courtyard below his balcony, the children were at play. Each evening for thirty minutes following their dinner, they were free to do anything they liked. Except watch TV.

With the single exception of his telecasts, television programming was banned from the compound. So were newspapers, radio, and books, unless he had personally approved them. He wanted nothing to pollute the minds of these who had achieved a level of worthiness that qualified them to live in the Temple and work directly for the ministry.

On clear, clement evenings like this, the children were allowed to play in the courtyard, which was an ideal opportunity for them to see him at prayer. There must never be a doubt in their minds as to the level of his dedication. He hoped to cultivate in each a desire to attain that level for himself or herself.

The children were supervised by their mothers or surrogates, but he insisted that each child be given free rein to pursue the kind of play that interested him or her. How else was he to learn what that particular child's strengths and talents were? Was that boy a scientist? Was that girl a healer? Joel was a natural athlete, Margaret an intellectual. William had a talent for attracting loyal friends as a magnet attracts metal shavings. Sarah was a comedienne but also a diplomat when disputes arose. Did he see in David entrepreneurial skills? Did Jennifer possess outstanding leadership qualities?

Naturally, the boys interested him more than the girls. The girls would become women, and the main function of women was obvious. But Brother Gabriel was a realist. Women had wormed their way into industry, politics, commerce, every area of society, particularly in North America and Western Europe. Until that trend changed, he must plan accordingly. The girls must be prepared to enter fields of endeavor just as the boys would. In fact, there were areas that they could permeate probably better than their male counterparts.

He studied them all, watched their patterns of behavior, looked for weaknesses that might eliminate them from the Program. Only a very few of the children failed to meet his standards, which spoke well of the selection process he had designed.

On his knees, head bowed in prayer, he used his time in the evenings to plan a future for each child. He considered all the mind-boggling changes that would take place when they were turned out into the world to do what they'd been created to do. Just to think about it made him giddy.

"Amen."

He stood and picked up his Russian prayer cushion. Someone below noticed that he had concluded his prayers and called up a greeting. He waved. Soon all eyes in the courtyard were focused on him. They vied for his attention.

"Watch me, Brother Gabriel."

Joel shot a basketball that swished through the goal. An NBA star in the making? If that were to come about, think how many young men would look upon him as a role model. Imagine how many lives he could influence, make converts of. He made a mental note to bring in a coach to hone Joel's natural skills.

He applauded enthusiastically. "Good job," he called down to the boy.

Leslie, the Iowa farm girl, was looking up at him with unabashed adoration. Since her visit with him, her attitude had notably improved. It had been reported that she was no longer forlorn and homesick. She had applied herself to her studies and chores with renewed rigor.

He winked at her, and she blushed becomingly. As she should. In bed, she demonstrated an earthy sensuality that bespoke her rural upbringing. What an incredible fuck she was.

But it was too soon to summon her again. The others would get jealous.

Mary, the girl with the beautiful dark curly hair, was using both hands to cradle her pregnant belly. She looked as luscious as a piece of fruit so ripe it was on the verge of bursting. Beneath her clothing, her projecting nipples looked as large as thumbs, ready for the infant to suck.

Instantly Brother Gabriel swelled with desire for her. Her pregnancy was too far advanced for intercourse, but there were other ways to achieve pleasure. He resolved to send for her later.

He waved one final time and turned to go inside.

Benevolence personified. The words popped into his head again. The slogan would look good on a billboard written in gold script beneath a picture of him with his arms extended in a gesture of encompassing love.

Mr. Hancock was waiting for him with a predinner drink made just the way he liked it. Exchanging the prayer cushion for the drink, Hancock said, "You have a call from Dallas."

Brother Gabriel gave his assistant a meaningful look, and Mr. Hancock nodded subtly. "Brother Gabriel took a sip of his drink, then lifted the receiver. "Yes, Joshua?"

"Your problem has been taken care of."

"I'm listening."

Because of the sensitive nature of this call, he had not engaged the speaker phone. Nor would he ask any questions or make any statements that could later be incriminating. He had every confidence in his various security measures and their backups. But there was always an outside chance that they weren't as foolproof as they should be. Technology wasn't entirely trustworthy. People certainly weren't.

Joshua said, "He thought we were taking orders from him. Never occurred to him that as of this afternoon we started getting our orders directly from you. Cocky little prick."

Brother Gabriel knew from experience that people yearned to please him. The less he commended them, the harder they tried to curry his favor. For example, if he wanted optimum performance from a woman in bed, he acted bored and distracted. She would then go to all lengths to inflame his passions. The same could be said for men. If he appeared unimpressed, they would boast about their feats, and he would learn what he needed to know without having to draw it out a bit at a time.

Sure enough, after a short silence, Joshua continued. "It was a slam dunk. No chance of resuscitation."

Brother Gabriel regretted losing Jem Hennings. For the past few years, Hennings had been a valuable commodity. But he had suddenly turned into a liability. He was dangerously close to the Gillian Lloyd murder investigation. Dale Gordon had been easy to pass off as a psychotic. But the authorities would have looked more thoroughly into Hennings's involvement, which might have led them to the gates of the Temple.

Moreover, Hennings had taken the matter of Linda Croft into his own hands, issuing orders without receiving approval. Of course, he agreed with Hennings's course of action. He would have issued the same order. But how dare a mere follower be so presumptuous as to make a decision of that magnitude on his own?

Hennings had performed his job well, but he wasn't irreplaceable. There were others who'd been trained to do his type of work and were anxiously awaiting a commission. Jem Hennings deserved no further contemplation. Brother Gabriel dismissed him from his mind.

"What about the other matter?"

Joshua's reluctance to answer spoke volumes. Brother Gabriel sipped his drink in an attempt to curb his temper.

Finally Joshua grumbled, "I guess you could say we're batting five hundred."

So Christopher Hart was still alive, and Melina Lloyd hadn't been taken. A tide of fury washed through him. "Why is that?"

"We're not dealing with dummies, you know."

"I am," Brother Gabriel snapped. "How difficult can it be?" His grip on the highball glass threatened to shatter the crystal. "You do not want to disappoint me," he said, enunciating each sinister word. "The gentleman tonight . . . ?"

"Yes, sir."

"He had disappointed me. You do not want to do that."

Joshua wasn't exceptionally bright, but he picked up on the reference to Jem Hennings. "No, sir."

"Then I suggest you bring me good news by morning." He ended the call abruptly and angrily quaffed the remainder of his drink.

"Another?" Hancock asked.

"Yes. Then I want Mary sent to me."

"The—"

"Mary, Mary," he repeated impatiently. "You know the one."

"But Brother Gabriel, she's eight and a half months into her pregnancy."

"I know how far along she is!" he shouted. "Why is everyone arguing with me tonight?"

He could feel the blood vessels in his head and neck straining against his skin. He rarely lost his temper. Even rarer did he lose it in Mr. Hancock's presence. He turned away so he wouldn't have to see the man's wounded expression. Nor did he want Mr. Hancock to witness his loss of self-control. Losing one's temper was a human weakness. But for Brother Gabriel any form of weakness was an anathema.

It's that woman, he thought bitterly. Gillian Lloyd was to blame. His temper tantrum, every mishap that had occurred over the past several days, could be attributed to her and her night with the astronaut. Now her twin sister was proving to be equally as vexing.

"Mr. Hancock," he said abruptly.

"Yes, sir?"

"Have you completed your background check of Melina Lloyd?"

"I'm still researching her, sir. I didn't want to bring the report to your attention until I was satisfied that it was complete."

"I appreciate your thoroughness," he said, throwing Hancock a bone to make amends. "But as soon as you're satisfied that you have everything, I want to see it immediately. I want to know everything there is to know about this woman, beginning on the day she was born."

"Absolutely, sir. I understand. I'll get back on it immediately after summoning Mary. Would you like your dinner now or later?"

"I'll ring when I'm hungry."

"Yes, sir."

He went into his bedroom and closed the door behind him. As he waited for the girl, he paced, his mind not on her but on Melina. She was probably every bit the whore Gillian had been, he thought contemptuously.

No woman, no matter how desirable, was worth all the trouble she had caused. In the grand scheme of things, she was a blip. No more significant than a gnat is to a summer evening. It was laughable to think that the Program would suffer if Melina Lloyd didn't participate. It was bigger than she. It was bigger than all of womankind. One woman couldn't stop its progress or even impede it.

But his pride wouldn't let him simply write her off and forget about her. It had become a contest of wills, an undeclared war between them. If he gave in, what message would that send? What kind of example would that set for the soldiers in the field who were confronted by obstacles every day as they carried out their missions? They would lose faith in him if word got out that he'd been bested by a mere female. Heads of state all over the world called him for advice and encouragement. A man with the power he wielded couldn't have it said that he'd been stymied by a woman. The negative impact of such a surrender would be monstrous. It simply couldn't happen.

Melina Lloyd had refused to accept her sister's self-imposed fate and had allied herself with the FBI. She had cost him Jem Hennings, who had been a valuable asset to the ministry. She'd formed an attachment to the same man who had contaminated Gillian. For these transgressions, she must be brought before him to receive her punishment.

Only then, when she was humbled and repentant, would he consider forgiving her, blessing her, embracing her, and making her a member of his family. Ultimately she would accept the gift of his benevolence. Of course she would. Who wouldn't want to be among his chosen?

He was going to rule the world.

"What is this place?"

Chief had paid the taxi driver, who'd dropped them seemingly in the middle of nowhere. The skyline of Dallas was nothing more than a glow against the northern horizon far off in the distance.

The area was so remote it had made the taxi driver skittish. He'd been in such a hurry to leave, his tires had spun in the gravel as he had executed a sharp U-turn and sped off in the direction from which they'd come. The road they'd taken off the interstate highway had come to a dead end at the spot in which she and Chief now stood.

He took her hand and half dragged her toward a corrugated tin building. "Leave all the talking to me."

"Fine. I'm at a loss for words anyway."

The building was like a tin can that had been halved lengthwise and then laid flat side down. One industrial-strength floodlight shone down from the midway point of the arc. It lighted the concrete apron that extended for several yards in front of the building.

To their left, she noticed, was a landing strip.

Behind them, total darkness.

In front of them was a German shepherd with its teeth bared.

"Chief!" She jerked hard on his hand, pulling him to a stop.

Just then a man came out of the narrow door cut into the tin. Wiping his hands on a faded red shop cloth, he squinted against the glare of the floodlight overhead. Apparently they didn't look very threatening because he commanded the dog to "cool it." Then, "Can I help you folks?"

"It's Christopher Hart."

The greasy hands holding the rag became still. The man's bristled jaw went slack. Chief stepped into the fan of light so the man could see them better. "Well, I'll be damned."

"I didn't know if you were still here and open for business."

"Open. Not much business. What happened to your face?"

Chief provided no explanation. Not even a lie. The two men stared at one another for several moments, then Chief introduced her. "Melina, this is Pax Royston. Pax, Melina."

The man gave her a cursory nod. "Ma'am."

"How do you do?" Under the circumstances, the civility sounded ridiculous. This was hardly a tea party, and between the two men was an underlying tension of unknown origin.

As Pax studied them, she studied Pax. He was dressed in grease-stained overalls that zipped up the front. His face had the deep etchings of a longtime smoker, making him look older than he probably was.

He glanced beyond them, apparently looking for the means of transportation that had brought them there. "Y'all parachute in?"

"Taxi."

"Taxi," he repeated, as though the concept were alien. "From Dallas?"

"Are you here alone?"

"Just me and Bandit." He divided a curious look between them. "You want to come in?"

The interior was dim in contrast to the floodlight. It took a moment for her eyes to adjust. A hockey game was being telecast on a black and white TV sitting atop a fifty-gallon oil drum. Pax turned down the sound but left the snowy picture on. Bandit sniffed her hand curiously, then, obviously approving of her, trotted over to a water bowl and began slurping noisily.

Pax said, "He scares the shit out of people, but the truth of it is that he's a sorry excuse for a guard dog."

"Lucky for us." She smiled at Pax, and he smiled back.

"Y'all want some coffee?"

"A plane," said Chief, bringing the small talk to an abrupt close. "I need an airplane."

The only airplanes parked inside the hangar were in various stages of disembowelment. It was obvious that Pax had been working on one when they arrived. A lightbulb encased in a metal basket was hanging directly above a disassembled engine. Parts were scattered over a piece of salvaged carpet that was unraveling around the edges.

"Single-engine," Chief continued. "Nothing fancy."

"Where're you going?"

"Do you have one or don't you?" he asked, ignoring Pax's curiosity.

"Yeah, I got one. Out back."

"Flyable?"

"You a flyer?"

Chief shot him a retiring look.

Pax shrugged. "Then it's flyable."

She still couldn't account for the unspoken animosity between the two, but it was palpable and thick. Chief asked Pax for the keys to the airplane. "I want to check it out." Pax ambled off in the direction of a glass-enclosed office. Chief turned to her. "Maybe he has a few snacks around he'll sell you. Canned drinks, anything you think you might need. Last thing you do, use the rest room. We'll have to stop to refuel, but there'll be long stretches in between."

"We're going to New Mexico, aren't we?"

Pax returned with the key and a slip of paper with the airplane's tail number printed on it. "Just outside the back door to your right. It's a nice little craft. Recently overhauled."

"Thanks."

She and Pax watched Chief wend his way through the hangar, past the airplanes and the puddles of oil and grease. The back door banged shut behind him. Pax then turned to her. "How about that coffee?"

"No, thank you. But I could use some things for the trip. Snacks and drinks, if you have them."

He led her to a pair of vintage vending machines. "The drinks are cold, but I can't vouch for how fresh that stuff is," he said, pointing to the cellophane packages suspended on hooks inside the machine. "Can't remember when the vendor was last here to restock."

She began digging in her handbag for coins.

"Don't bother." Using a key, Pax opened the two machines. "Help yourself."

As she was making her choices, she said, "I've never flown with Chief."

"You don't have anything to worry about. He's an excellent pilot. Best instincts I ever saw."

"Were you in the military together?"

"You might say."

"Before going into business for yourself, did you also work for NASA?"

He snorted at that notion. "No, ma'am. Not me."

"But you two go way back?"

"Until we had our falling out." He pointed into the vending machine. "Those little pecan pies are pretty good."

"This is plenty," she told him, disappointed that he hadn't expanded on his "falling out" with Chief. What had been the cause of it? A woman? An airplane? Had there been a competition between them over who was the better pilot? Maybe Pax had been turned down for the astronaut program and was jealous that Chief had been accepted.

Considerately, Pax rummaged around for a sack and finally located one in the trash can. "Bought groceries yesterday," he explained as he loaded her selected snacks and soft drinks into the plastic bag. "Mostly dog food. Damn dog eats like a horse."

They heard the back door open and Chief's boot heels striking the concrete as he made his way back through the cavernous hangar. "It looks okay," he said to Pax.

"Told you."

Turning to her, Chief asked if she'd been

to the rest room yet. She shook her head. "Go. I've got some calls to make, then we're outta here."

"Through there." Pax pointed her toward a door. "But I gotta warn you, it's not exactly a powder room."

It wasn't. Not by a long shot. The sink and commode were water-stained. The floor was covered with greasy grime. The poster thumbtacked to the wall featured not just one naked woman, but a chorus line of them striking the same crude pose. Even cruder was the saying on the bumper sticker stuck to the paper towel dispenser.

She used the toilet, then washed her face and hands with the discolored sliver of bar soap. When she took a disinterested glimpse of herself in the cracked mirror above the sink, she gasped. Dark spots dotted her face and neck. She leaned in for a closer look. Blood. Jem's blood. There were also traces of it in her hair.

Tamping down a rising panic, she took a deep breath and plunged her head beneath the faucet. The water was icy, but she held her head beneath the sputtering stream until the water ran clear, with no trace of pink.

Using paper towels, she squeezed the

water from her hair, then combed it as best she could with her fingers. She didn't linger to primp. Any attempt to improve her looks would be futile. She needed to start from scratch. It seemed ages since she had showered and shampooed in the truck stop motel that morning. Besides, she had none of her things. Their bags had been left behind in the clunker in the parking garage of Jem's building.

Chief was still talking on his cell phone when she came out. He noted her wet hair but probably knew why she'd rinsed it. She ventured into the cluttered office where Pax was seated in a rolling desk chair. Bandit was standing beside it, his head on Pax's thigh. Pax was stroking the dog's head.

"I guess this is why he's no man-killer," he remarked with a fond smile for the German shepherd. "I've spoiled him rotten. Made a wuss out of him."

"You seem to have formed a partnership that works for both of you."

He motioned toward her wet hair. "I could probably rustle up a towel from somewhere around here."

"It'll dry before too long."

Her eyes roved the office, coming to rest

on a photograph of Pax and a woman with the neon sign of the Golden Nugget Casino rising up behind them. "Is that Mrs. Royston?"

"Girlfriend."

"Do you go to Vegas often?"

"Louisiana's closer," he said, referring to the casinos in Bossier City. "We go over there every chance we get. I shoot craps. She likes the slots." All the while he was talking, he was watching Chief through the cloudy glass that enclosed the office. "Are y'all . . . ?"

Following his thought, she shook her head. "He was involved with my sister."

He cocked his head in surprise. "Is that right?"

"Hmm."

"I would've thought—"

"No."

Pax grunted a noncomment. His skeptical regard was hard to stare down, so, at the risk of giving herself away, she turned aside. His question had evoked memories of the near kiss in the back seat of the taxi. A very dangerous, very wrong, very foolish near kiss that she had very much wanted.

Their small talk ended with that discomfiting exchange. She pretended to study a Texas state map tacked to the wall, while Pax continued to pet Bandit.

Several minutes later, Chief concluded his calls and came into the office but only as far as the threshold. He fished into his jeans pocket and came up with three one-hundred-dollar bills, which he tossed onto Pax's desk. "That's all the cash I can spare, and I don't want to put these charges on a credit card."

Finding that surprising, Pax sliced a glance at her, but she offered no explanation. Heeding Chief's request, she was leaving the talking to him. Something was out of joint here. She didn't know what, but for fear of saying the wrong thing and upsetting a delicate balance, she thought it best to say nothing.

"You know I'm good for the rest of the charges," Chief told the mechanic. "I'll pay you when I bring the plane back."

"I trust you."

"I hope so, because what I'm about to say is important." He paused to make certain he had Pax's full attention. "Take your dog and your girlfriend and leave town tonight. Go to

Bossier City. Vegas. Go somewhere. Just get away."

It surprised her that Chief had been eavesdropping on their conversation while he'd been on the telephone.

Pax frowned querulously. "Are you gonna tell me what the hell's going on?"

"No," Chief replied evenly. "You said you trust me. I hope you do. Don't ask questions, just do this. Leave. Immediately. Chances are real good that a couple of guys are gonna show up here in a while, and when they do, you want to be long gone."

Pax studied him a moment, then said, "I haven't seen you in years. Not a word from you. Then you drop out of freaking nowhere in the middle of the night, looking like a poster child for assault and battery, with a beautiful woman in tow, who also looks like a little worse for wear—you'll excuse me for noticing, Melina. You stomp through my place acting like God Hisself, then you rent a plane you can't pay for. Lastly, you tell me to desert my place of business and get out of town, and I'm not allowed one little 'how come?'"

"No. You're not."

"Well, that's bullshit, is what that is. Tell

me why I should pay any attention to one goddamn thing you say to me."

Chief wrestled with his answer, then said tightly, "Because you're my father, and I don't want to be responsible for anything bad happening to you."

C H A P T E R | 3 0

Tobias stared down at Jem Hennings's corpse and allowed himself the second expletive of the evening, the first being when Melina Lloyd hung up on him.

Lawson said, "I need a drink."

The FBI agent smiled grimly. "I'll buy. Soon as we get some answers."

If the two were to spend much time together, they probably would wind up disliking each other immensely. Lawson was as poor a dresser as Tobias had ever met. Lawson thought Tobias was a peacock. Tobias was a health nut who had eliminated refined sugar and fat from his diet; Lawson thrived on fast food, the greasier the better. Tobias was an aficionado of all the performing arts and held season tickets to the ballet, symphony, and opera. Lawson had attended only one live concert in his entire life. Willie Nelson. Outdoors. He'd come home covered in chigger bites.

They had spent only one day together, but it had been quite a day, and during that time, for all their differences, they had formed a grudging respect for each other.

They left the corpse to the ME and moved out of the condo into the hallway, where Lawson picked up the conversation. "I have a few answers for you. The doorman described Melina Lloyd and Christopher Hart to a tee. They came to see Hennings no more than fifteen minutes before the false fire alarm." He consulted his notepad. "That was at nine-oh-eight. Estimated time of death is somewhere between nine o'clock and nine-fifteen."

"You're not suggesting—"

"Anything. I'm just telling you how it is."

"Sorry for the interruption. Go on."

"People who live on this floor remember a couple—matching the descriptions of guess who—yelling at them from the stair-well that there was a fire in apartment D."

"They created a distraction."

"That would be my guess," Lawson said. "We'll get an expert to determine the trajectory of the bullets, but unless the shooter had wings, he had to have fired from the building across the street. I've got guys over there combing the roof and all the rooms with windows on this side for evidence, but I'd put money on it turning up clean."

"Professional sniper?"

"Well, it wasn't your ordinary crime of passion. Only a dumdum could do that much damage to a skull," he said, referring to a bullet that would mushroom upon impact. "Two were fired in rapid succession. One of the tenants here said he heard a crack. Possibly two. But they'd have come so close together they could have sounded like one.

"The first shattered the window. We've recovered it. It's distorted so badly it's doubtful it could ever be connected to a weapon, even if we recovered the weapon, which I seriously doubt we will. The other bullet is still in the goo that was once doing

Hennings's thinking for him. Whoever did him is experienced. He knew what he was doing and had the balls to do it. Bold as brass and no fear of being caught."

Tiredly Tobias rubbed his eye sockets. "This just gets better and better, doesn't it? Do you think Melina Lloyd and Christopher Hart saw the shooter?"

"Again doubtful. But they were here when Hennings bought it. The table lamp was unplugged," the detective explained. "There's no overhead lighting in the apartment. Even an expert marksman with a night-vision scope would have had difficulty getting off a shot that precise, less than a second after the glass shattered, if the apartment was dark. It's doubtful they—Melina, Hart, and Hennings—would've been visiting in the dark, anyway. So somebody unplugged the lamp, and it sure as hell wasn't Hennings. He didn't clean himself up with paper towels, either."

Tobias ruminated on it a moment. "The window blows out, Hennings is shot, one of them extinguishes the light, then they create a distraction so they can safely get out of the building."

Lawson said, "Looks like. A few people remember seeing them outside, but after that, zilch. They vanished."

"Neither is answering their cell phone."

"They left a car in the garage here. Two bags were in the trunk, one obviously belonging to Hart, the other to her. The clothes were new. Still had tags attached." He told Tobias that they'd tracked down a personal shopper at Neiman's who admitted to having the clothes delivered to Melina Lloyd earlier that day. "I described the jacket we found here near Hennings's body. It's one she sent. It ain't so new-looking anymore."

"They're traveling light."

"Lighter now than before. We're running leads on the car they arrived in. It's not hers. Hart's has been impounded by the city off a nightclub parking lot."

Tobias ran a hand down his face. Their preliminary search of the Waters Clinic had turned up nothing substantive about Dale Gordon other than that he had the know-how and the opportunity to tinker with sperm specimens. There was no proof that he had. Tobias had put Patterson in charge of rounding up sperm donors.

The assignment caused Patterson to grimace. "I don't have to watch them while they jerk off, do I?"

Tobias sighed. "Samples will be collected in a clinical environment with medical personnel supervising. Your job is to contact the donors and get them there. Okay?"

"Yes, sir," the young agent had said, looking relieved.

"Anything on him?" Tobias asked now, drawing Lawson's attention to the gurney bearing Hennings's body as it was being wheeled into the elevator.

"Nothing. Not even a parking ticket. Last purchase on his credit card was the pendant he gave to Gillian—actually Melina—the night before the murder."

"Hey, Lawson." One of the other detectives poked his head through the door and motioned him into the apartment.

Tobias would have followed, but his cell phone rang.

Lucy Myrick felt as though she'd been born inside the windowless room with the ugly walls. Actually the normally sick color had taken on a rosy tint, but that was because it was being viewed through bloodshot eyes.

She had gas from subsisting on fast food and not getting her daily requirement of roughage. Caffeine had her nerves clawing at her skin from the inside, while at the same time her head was muzzy from lack of sleep. She needed a shower.

"But I can't regret what I did for love, what I did for love," she warbled.

Love for her work, love for Tobias, had kept her here for two days, working straight through and nonstop, searching for the link that connected the Lloyd twins, Dale Gordon, and the Andersons. Recently Tobias had thrown a new name into the mix. Jem Hennings. Caucasian male. DOB 10-2-60, as it appeared on his Texas driver's license issued only thirteen months ago. Five feet eleven inches tall. Weight, one sixty-eight.

Fine and dandy.

Except that Social Security didn't have him in their records under the number he'd given the firm with which he was presently—until tonight—affiliated. Nor had that Social Security number ever filed a tax return with the IRS.

"Something's rotten in the state of Denmark," Lucy mused aloud.

Actually, it turned out to be the state of South Dakota.

She read the information three times before calling Tobias. "It's Lucy."

"It's one o'clock in the morning in Washington."

"You owe me massive overtime and a weekend on the Chesapeake. You may even consider throwing in a bottle or two of fine wine."

"You've got something."

"South Dakota. Seven years ago. One Janine Hennings, age fifteen. Poor grades in school, in with a bad crowd, rebellious at home. Generally running amok. Taken under wing by a school nurse named Dorothy Pugh. Dorothy's all heart, goodness, and light. Within months Janine has done a one-eighty. Gets religion. Prays all the time. Peace and love, the whole nine yards.

"End of the school year rolls around. Dorothy Pugh resigns her post to relocate in New Mexico. Janine is disconsolate and runs away to join her. The parents freak out. Janine's swung too far the other way. Their daughter is still lost to them. They suspect Dorothy Pugh to be a member of a religious cult. They retain the services of a cult-buster—"

"A what?"

"I coined the term," Lucy said proudly. "A shrink that detoxes a mind that's been brainwashed?"

"Got it. Go on."

"Mr. and Mrs. Hennings and the shrink leave South Dakota to rescue Janine."

"And?"

"And they never made it. The RV they'd rented for the trip was found at a campground in Colorado with everything inside intact. But the people were gone."

"Foul play?"

"Indubitably. But not a single clue. No bodies. No blood. No sign of struggle. No nothing. Another family was camping nearby, but they'd gone into town to have dinner. They left early the following morning without noticing that there wasn't any activity around the other RV. Rain that night ruined any chance of identifying tire tracks. There was absolutely nothing for investigators to go on. It was as though the three people had been beamed up by aliens. Nary a trace of them was ever found."

"Who filed the missing persons report?"

"Thought you'd never ask. Jameson, a.k.a. Jem Hennings, the son and older brother. He got worried when his folks failed to call and report in, which they'd promised to do each evening along the way."

"Was he considered a suspect in the disappearance?"

"Ironclad alibi. He was at work both days his parents were away and had dinner with friends both evenings. He couldn't have possibly made a round trip to Colorado. But following the tragedy, he liquidates all assets, relocates, and starts using a phony Social Security number."

"I smell conspiracy."

"Only one friend ever heard from him after he left South Dakota," Lucy continued enthusiastically. "Guess where he wrote from. Drumroll, please. Oakland, California."

"Kathleen Asher."

"No connection so far, but I'd bet that weekend on the Chesapeake that I find one. Meanwhile, the disappearance of Mr. and Mrs. Hennings and the shrink remains an unsolved case in Colorado. When it happened, Hennings grieved publicly. Anguished over it to reporters. 'Woe is me. My parents have vanished. My little sister has

run away to join a religious community.'
Yaddah, yaddah. Note, he never referred to
this religious organization as a cult."

"I don't need to ask, do I?"

"The Temple of Brother Gabriel."

"Lucy?"

"What?"

"Will you have my children?" Before she
could recover enough to speak, he'd already hung up. "Lawson!"

The detective came barreling through the
door of the condo, more animated than
Tobias had ever seen him. "You're gonna
shit when you hear who's on Hennings's autodial."

Tobias grinned. "Way ahead of you."

"You could have told me."

Since taking off, Chief had been subject to
Melina's accusatory stare. He'd given Love
Field and Dallas–Fort Worth Airport wide
berth, swinging out far to the east and then
flying well north of the metropolitan area before banking to the west.

They flew for half an hour before they were
past the glittering suburban sprawl. Now
small towns showed up as patches of light

against a black blanket. The night was perfectly clear. The moon was so slender as to
be negligible, and because it gave off virtually no light, stars shone brightly.

While he was busy navigating, it had been
easy to pretend he didn't notice her stare. It
wasn't so easy to ignore a blatant admonishment. "Could have told you what?"

"Don't play dumb, Chief."

"It wasn't relevant."

"Maybe not relevant, but it's interesting."

"Tell me one reason why."

"For starters, your father is Anglo."

"You knew I was half. Even Dale Gordon
knew I was a breed. Have you ever seen a
full-blood Indian with blue eyes?"

"Why are you so damn prickly?"

"Why are you so damn curious?"

"Why don't you like him?"

"Jesus, you never let up."

"Have some chips."

"Huh?"

"Potato chips." She ripped open a bag
and offered it to him. When he looked at her
with puzzlement, she smiled insipidly. "I'm
letting up."

He plunged his hand into the bag and
crammed the chips into his mouth. He'd

burned off a lot of energy since gulping down a few bites of cheeseburger.

Melina was munching alternately on the potato chips and a box of animal crackers. "Interesting combination," he remarked.

"I'm hungry."

"Fine. But if you have to hurl again, remember I can't pull over this time."

"No barf bags?"

"This is a no-frills flight." They smiled at one another. He pointed toward her mouth. "You have a crumb." Her tongue dabbed tentatively at one corner of her lips. "Other side." She picked up the potato chip crumb with the tip of her tongue, and it struck him as an intensely erotic gesture.

He looked away. Checked the gauges. Checked the sky. Searched for something to distract him from his disturbing awareness of her. "What else have we got by way of cuisine?"

"Let's see. Sour-cream-and-chive-flavored popcorn."

"Good God."

"You'll pass?"

"I'd rather have shuttle food."

"We're fresh out of that." She dug deeper into the plastic sack. "Chee●tos. Chocolate-covered peanuts, which I don't recommend. They've gone a little gray. Lorna Doones. And barbecue-flavored corn chips. Believe me, this was the best of the lot."

"I believe you. I'd settle for a few of your animal crackers."

She passed the box to him. When he thanked her, their eyes met again. "What did Pax do to make you dislike him?"

"I don't dislike him."

"Ah. So I was imagining all that crackling hostility."

"He disliked us."

Melina waited him out. She didn't ask another question, but she assumed a listening aspect that he found himself responding to. Reluctantly, but responding all the same. "Pax was in the Air Force. Stationed at Holloman. My mother was a civilian employee on the base. She was pretty. Petite. I suppose she was a novelty for him, a pretty little Indian girl. Anyway, they married within months of meeting, and I was born before their first anniversary. For a while we were a happy family.

"My earliest memory is of an air show. It was there on the base. I remember my dad showing me off to his friends. One of them gave me chewing gum, the first I remember having. You know, the candy-coated square kind you get out of machines? He let me pick which color I wanted. Then my dad took me around to all the planes and explained how high they could fly, how fast they could travel. I remember thinking that to know all that stuff, my dad must be the smartest person in the whole world.

"He carried me on his shoulders so I could see over the crowd. I was scared at first, but he put his hands on my knees to secure me. He told me to hold on to his hair. No matter how tight I grabbed hold, he didn't complain. I knew he wouldn't drop me. I thought he loved me. Loved her."

He stopped just in time to avoid making a complete fool of himself. He didn't like taking strolls down memory lane, particularly this lane. Melina was forcing him to call forth memories he had deliberately left far behind.

His work had made it easy to take a hard-ass stance against sentimentality. He'd spent years training to respond mechanically to difficult situations, a response technique that he supposed had carried over into his personal life. He performed exclusively on cerebral impulse without allowing any emotional interference to cloud his judgment.

Letting your head govern was easy. It was this heart stuff that was tough. Dealing with emotional issues wasn't for sissies. "Is there another drink in there?" he asked crossly.

She opened a can of Mountain Dew and handed it to him. "What happened to change your mind? About Pax loving you, I mean."

"And here I thought you were different."

"From what?"

"Other women. Women love to talk. Review. Analyze. Discuss. Dissect. They love to see what makes people tick—particularly men."

"Because you're so fascinating."

"Why, thank you, ma'am," he drawled.

"Relax, cowboy. I meant *you* plural. Men. How you think, how you react to things is interesting. I guess because it's generally different from how women react. The difference intrigues me."

"So you like us?"

"Very much."

"Yeah?" He turned to her. "When's your favorite time to make love?"

"When I'm in the mood."

"No go, huh?"

To say no, she shot him a wry frown.

"Okay, then," he said, "let's talk politics. What do you think of the Kuwaiti position?"

"Old joke, Chief."

"You've heard it?"

"'I like it, but my partner says it burns his elbows,'" she said, quoting the punch line.

"I thought it was a military joke."

"It got around."

"So what *is* your favorite position?"

She kept her expression impassive. He bobbed his eyebrows, doing his best to coax a smile from her, but she didn't relent. She wasn't going to blush on a bet, and she wasn't going to be sidetracked with flirtatious chatter, either.

He sighed with resignation. "What was the last question?"

"What made you think Pax stopped loving you?"

"I guess the novelty wore off. He was an airplane mechanic. Couldn't fly himself because of an inner ear problem, but he worked on the bomber jets they tested out there in the desert. His job required him to be away for long stretches of time.

Classified stuff. Top secret. At least that's the excuse he gave for being unreachable more of the time than not.

"One night when he happened to be home I heard my mother crying. She accused him of having a girlfriend. Whether he did or didn't at that point, I don't know, but they never slept in the same room after that, so I guess he probably did.

"The marriage went from bad to worse. Probably to salve his own conscience, he started making sly comments about my eyes. You might have noticed that his are brown. How could two brown-eyed parents have a blue-eyed kid, especially with all that Indian blood?

"Those veiled accusations of adultery, which were totally unfounded, devastated my mother. Completely demoralized her, as I'm sure they were designed to. Anyway, they divorced. When his stint was up, he returned to Texas where he'd grown up. He came back to New Mexico to see me when he could.

"But by the time I reached adolescence, his visits had become noticeably infrequent. He was trying to get that private charter business off the ground—literally—and said it was hard for him to get away, even for a few days. Of course, he always found time to go to Las Vegas.

"During one summer vacation my mother suggested that I go to Dallas and spend a couple of weeks with him. She probably had to twist his arm, but he issued an invitation, and I went.

"By then, he'd had a succession of girlfriends, but the current one lived in. Naturally I harbored the dream of all children from broken homes. I was waiting on a miracle that would get my parents back together. I resented the hell out of Betsy, or Becky, or Betty, whatever her name was.

"In her defense, I behaved like a brat. I was thirteen or so. Very full of myself. Surly. Sarcastic. One afternoon she got pissed because I had put my feet up on the coffee table after she'd repeatedly asked me not to. When Pax came in, she ranted and raved about it. She said, 'Sure his mother's an Indian, but for god's sake couldn't she have taught him *some* manners?'

"I went ape shit and started yelling at her, 'You shut up!' I looked to Pax for support. 'Tell her. Tell her to shut up about my mother.' And he just shrugged and said, 'Well, Chris, she is an Indian.'

"And I realized then that he no longer paraded me around to his friends. He didn't show me off anymore like he had all those years ago at the air show. I was a star athlete at my school, on the honor roll, student council, a Boy Scout, but there wasn't a single picture of me in his house. It was as though he wanted no tangible reminders that my mother and I existed.

"So I told them to fuck themselves, packed my belongings, and left that night. I spent hours in the downtown bus terminal before I could get on one going west. For seven hundred miles I vowed to deny him just as he had denied me. I even had my name legally changed to my mother's maiden name. I wanted nothing to do with him. Still don't. If I hadn't been desperate tonight, I would never have gone to him asking for a favor."

Melina had listened quietly, offering no comments or lame platitudes, which he would have deplored. He looked over at her to gauge her reaction to the story. All the while he'd been talking, she hadn't moved, not a muscle. Now she took an uneven breath, let it go, swallowed.

"That's the last time you saw him?" she asked softly. "That day you left his house?"

He nodded. "He tried to call me several times after that, but I refused to talk to him. He sent Christmas gifts for a couple of years, then gave up when I sent them back unopened. I received a hundred-dollar bill when I graduated from high school, which I kept because I needed the money for college. But from that day to this, we've had no personal contact."

"Your mother never remarried?"

He laughed shortly. "She died loving him. Can you believe that? And I suspect that she sneaked news about me to him until the day she died."

"He recognized you instantly."

"He's got a TV."

"He's followed your career."

"I guess."

"I know."

He looked at her sharply.

"There was a newspaper clipping about your last mission right there on his desk," she told him in a quiet voice. "I thought it was awfully sweet that a former buddy was so proud of his now-famous friend that he had cut an article out of the newspaper. I didn't comment on it because I didn't want to embarrass him. Of course the keepsake makes more sense now, knowing that Pax is your father."

"Don't get misty, Melina. It was only a newspaper clipping."

"Hmm, maybe. But the way he talked about your piloting skills . . ."

Her pause was calculated. She was using it to bait him. Even recognizing that, he couldn't resist turning toward her and silently urging her to go on.

"He assured me that I'd be safe flying with you because you're an excellent pilot. The best instincts he's ever seen."

"He's never seen me fly."

"Not that you know about."

"Well, it doesn't matter because—" He broke off suddenly and, leaning forward, peered hard through the windshield.

"What?" Melina asked anxiously. "What do you see?"

He thought it through for a moment, then muttered, "Son of a bitch."

"Chief, *what*?"

"I just figured out how they're tracking us."

Our two bogus FBI agents?" Melina asked.

"Yeah. Remember how I said I got the feeling we were never alone? Well, we haven't been. They've been tracking us the twenty-first century way. Look up there. Ten o'clock. See it?"

Almost immediately she spotted the bright, moving object. "It's a satellite."

"Exactly. A transceiver sends out data that can be continually tracked by—"

"A satellite. You can know where you are at any given time. It's called PGA, something like that?"

He smiled. "GPS. Global positioning satellite."

"Police forces use them. I've seen stories. But now they've gone mainstream. Gillian wanted one. Another realtor in her office used one all the time to locate addresses."

"Well, these guys have their own application," he muttered. "If they planted a transceiver on you, they can locate you anywhere in the world."

"Aren't the transceivers bulky things strapped to an ankle or wrist?"

"The technology has advanced beyond that. They're much smaller."

"Chief, I would have known if someone had planted something on me."

"Hennings?"

She thought over the possibility, then shook her head. "No. The only time he touched me, other than to hold my hand or to pat my shoulder in consolation, was last night when he gave me a neck rub."

"He gave you a neck rub?"

"Before you came crashing in. That's another story," she said, absently, gnawing her lower lip as she concentrated. "He couldn't have put it in my clothing. All I had on was a robe. Besides, I left the house without anything this morning. You know that." Suddenly her hand flew to her throat. "The pendant."

He'd never seen her without the piece of jewelry. She'd been wearing it the morning they met in Lawson's office. "Hennings gave you that?"

"The night before the murder, thinking I was Gillian. We covered this with Lawson at the crime scene, but you weren't there. It was a gift to commemorate the insemination. Jem insisted that I keep it."

"Hennings was Gillian's . . . What term did he use? Monitor?"

"*Spy* is more like it," she said scornfully. Reaching behind her neck, she hurriedly unclasped the slender gold chain and studied the ruby heart.

"Does it open?" he asked.

"No. There's no back on it. If there were, light couldn't shine through the stones."

"I don't know anything about gems."

She studied the fretwork mounting that held the stones in place, then sighed with disappointment. "Nothing."

"Damn." He was stumped. The necklace had seemed a likely culprit. "Check your handbag."

"Jem would have had access to it numerous times."

She dumped the entire contents into her lap and began sifting through it. There was a wallet containing credit cards, a few coins, and the currency she'd gotten from the ATM that morning. She checked each compartment, running her finger around the lining.

"Nothing. And anyway, I could have changed handbags. Not a good hiding place if constant vigilance was his goal."

"What do you keep with you at all times? Something you would carry in any handbag."

"My cell phone."

"Just to be safe, we'll pitch it. What else?"

Her miniature address book had no pockets or anyplace else in which to hide something. All that was inside her eyeglasses case was a pair of sunglasses. She even checked the hinges that connected the stems to the frames. "Jem was sneaky, but he was no James Bond."

Chief remained stubborn. "It's there."

She held out a sterling silver pillbox that had belonged to her mother. "I'm never without it. But it's solid, no lining, and all it's got in it is two aspirin tablets." She shook them out to prove her point.

"Crush them." She did, and by doing so wasted two perfectly good analgesics. "How about the compact?" he asked.

She opened it and squeezed the small round puff to see if anything solid had been sewn inside. "It's not in here unless something is stuck beneath the mirror."

Chief gave her a meaningful look and, after a slight hesitation, she ground the mirror beneath her heel and shook the broken glass onto the floor of the plane. "You owe me a new compact."

"It is refillable?"

She pried out the pressed powder refill. "Nothing there, either."

"Key chain?"

"With my car, remember?"

"Oh, right, right. Hairpin?"

"Never use one."

"Tampons?"

"No."

"Lipsticks?"

She had two with her. She rolled them out, but they were smooth and undisturbed. She checked the empty cap of each. "Nope."

"Ballpoint pen?"

"Never. I'm notorious for being without and having to borrow."

He thought on it a moment longer, then said, "Besides the pillbox, is there anything in the handbag you can't part with?"

"No. All my addresses and phone numbers can be replicated. I keep them on computer."

"When we land—"

"I'll toss everything, including my phone."

He nodded. "Then if they can still track us, we'll know we're dealing with something bigger than the both of us."

"Such as?"

He relieved her wariness none by saying, "I hazard to guess."

"Melina?"

"Hmm?" There was pressure on her thigh, and it felt so good, so warm, she reached down to increase it.

"We're almost there. Wake up."

Reluctantly she opened her eyes. The pressure she'd felt was Chief's right hand. Hers was massaging the back of it. She quickly removed her hand so that he could remove his. She sat up straighter and blinked her eyes into focus.

They'd landed somewhere in the Texas panhandle only long enough to refuel and use the rest room. The wind had been strong and frigid. Chief had insisted that she wear his leather jacket as they made their way across a desolate tarmac into a shed that wasn't nearly as upscale as Pax's hangar. They left her cell phone, her handbag, and all its contents in a wire trash bin.

She remembered little after takeoff. Now, yawning behind her hand, she asked, "How long was I asleep?"

"About an hour."

She groaned. "I don't remember when I last had a full night's sleep."

Not since the two Dallas policemen had wakened her with the news that her sister's body had been discovered. Her previous life, the one she'd been living prior to that morning a few days ago, had had very few bumps. There'd been some surprises, both happy and sad. But, basically, it had been well ordered. She had known more or less what to expect with each sunrise.

Flying off to New Mexico in the middle of the night, in a two-passenger airplane that had recently needed overhauling, would have seemed crazy. But for all this craziness to make sense, she had only to remind herself of the reason behind it: Her twin had been murdered.

Who had ordained that killing? Brother Gabriel? Was the so-called man of God behind the program, as Jem had alleged? Was it a network of genetic engineering? Were they using unsuspecting women as breeders, human incubators?

It was too evil to contemplate, and yet nothing was really beyond imagination, was it? How many women and their babies had been sacrificed to this "program"? The Andersons' baby? Probably. Jem had said, "We'd like to use her again," referring to Candace Anderson.

She shivered each time she thought of Jem smiling at her with chilling complacency and saying that the Program needed her now that Gillian wasn't available. With that statement, this quest for answers had gone beyond avenging her sister's murder. While that was still paramount, she was now also acting in self-defense.

Bringing her out of her reverie, Chief said, "I'm running on very few Z's myself."

"Not a very reassuring thing to tell your passenger when you're about to land an airplane."

He grinned at her. "Piece of cake."

"Want your jacket back?"

"You keep it."

She was glad she didn't have to give it up. She liked snuggling inside it, liked the feel of the glove-soft leather, liked the smell of him that it exuded.

They'd gained an hour when they crossed into the mountain time zone, so it was still dark beyond the windows of the airplane. There were no lights below, no landmarks, no point of reference with which she could orient herself. "Chief, you said we were almost there. Where?"

"Up ahead."

"There's a town?"

"A landing strip."

"Like Pax's?"

"Not as sophisticated as Pax's."

That wasn't very reassuring, either. "Does somebody know we're coming?"

"I filed a flight plan. Somebody will be there to meet us. I was making arrangements over my cell phone while you were schmoozing Pax."

"I wasn't . . . You see that mountain, right?"

"What mountain? Melina, I'm kidding," he said when she looked at him with bald terror. "I see the mountain. I know what I'm doing, okay?"

"Of course you do. I'm sorry."

Even so, when the small plane seemingly skimmed the crest of the mountaintop, she curbed the impulse to raise her feet as though that would help the craft clear the summit. She exhaled with relief when they did. Then the plane banked sharply to the left. "Chief!"

"It's a little too steep for a direct approach. I'm only circling down. Think of a hawk."

She tried to picture a bird of prey gliding on currents of air, but all she could really think about was the rocky wall of the mountain face that appeared close enough to reach out and touch.

"There are the lights," Chief remarked.

Two rows of lights flashed on below to delineate a narrow runway. "Lights are good," she agreed.

Calmly and competently, Chief executed two lazy spirals within the steep bowl formed by the mountains. Gradually he reduced their altitude so that by the time he went in on his final approach, the plane seemed to graze the tops of the sparse vegetation. The runway slid beneath them and seconds later he set the airplane down. It was the smoothest landing Melina had ever experienced in any aircraft of any size. "Good job," she said tightly.

"Thanks."

They taxied to the small hangar. He cut off the engine. The propeller wound down to a soft, rhythmic clap, then to silence. He looked across at her. In a hushed voice, he confessed, "I was showing off a little."

"I realize that."

"I wanted to impress you."

"And you did."

"Rest assured there was never any reason for you to be afraid."

"I wasn't. Not really."

"You're safe with me, Melina."

She studied his face for a long moment, then whispered, "No, Chief. With you, I'm in danger."

"Of?"

"Of—"

Her reply was interrupted by someone sharply rapping on the window. Neither had noticed that someone had stepped onto the wing in order to reach the door, which was on the passenger side. Caught off guard, she turned her head quickly, and it was all she could do not to recoil from the face peering in at her. It was illuminated by a flashlight, making it all the more frightening.

Pockmarked skin was stretched tightly across a pair of cheekbones that looked sharp enough to chop wood. The eyes were mere slits, the mouth a narrow slash between two deep furrows extending downward from a beaked nose. The center part of the man's hair was half an inch wide. His gray braids extended almost to his waist.

He looked past her to Chief. "Hart?"

She followed the Indian's gaze, turning her head and looking at Chief herself. He must have read the incredulity in her expression, because he said, "Relax, Melina. He doesn't take scalps." Then he added grimly, "I'm fairly certain."

But five minutes later, Chief was convinced that somewhere along the way wires had been crossed, that signals had been scrambled, or that the entity in charge of directing fate was having one hell of a good time at his expense. Never at any time during his three missions into space had he felt this surreal.

Their escort was taciturn to the point of being mute. He never introduced himself. After verifying they were the couple he'd been sent to meet, he had grunted instructions for them to disembark. He had backed down the steps built into the wing of the craft, then ambled into the shed to turn off the runway lights. He hadn't assisted Melina as she climbed out, nor did he offer them the use of his flashlight. He was waiting behind the wheel of a pickup truck with the motor running by the time they reached it.

The terrain was rugged, remote, and desolate. Wind whistled in through various cracks in the pickup, including the hole in the floorboard, which Melina avoided falling through by keeping her legs far to one side, nearly overlapping his. She sat hunched down between him and their driver, shivering against the biting cold that his leather jacket was no defense against. The driver seemed to deliberately target every rut in the road. The truck jounced over stones, sending splinters of pain into Chief's spine.

His jaw ached from keeping it tightly clenched against teeth-jarring jolts.

An attempt at conversation would have been futile and exhausting. They'd have had to shout to make themselves heard over the worrisome racket of the pickup's engine and the roaring of the wind that gusted through the cab. They rode in miserable silence.

After what seemed like hours, although it was only forty minutes, the truck topped a rise, and in the meager gray predawn light they spotted a structure in the recession below. Chief's optimism soared; but then it plummeted just as abruptly. This couldn't be their destination. The house was too modest. The pickup parked in front was too old.

However, their driver pumped the brake pedal to slow the truck down and turned into a dirt driveway bordered by stones, which were a sad attempt at beautifying the entrance to the place, which was anything but beautiful.

He leaned across Melina and shouted at the driver, "Are you sure you got your instructions right? Do you know where you're supposed to take us?"

"Here."

Chief cast a glace at Melina and shrugged, repeating laconically, "Here."

The truck came to a grinding, shuddering stop inches from the front steps leading up to the door of the house. The driver put it in park and let the engine idle.

"I guess we get out," Melina said.

"I guess we do." Chief stepped from the cab and offered his hand to her. She climbed down. "Thanks," he said to the driver, who engaged the gears, let off the brake, and accelerated before Chief could even close the door.

"Mr. Personality," he muttered, waving away exhaust and dust as the truck chugged off.

"Jed is a man of few words."

In unison they turned toward the voice. Dexter Longtree was standing in silhouette, framed by the open front door.

CHAPTER | 3 2

Chief nudged Melina forward. She climbed the steps, her stare fixed on Longtree. "Melina Lloyd, this is Chief Dexter Longtree."

"Chief Longtree."

"Welcome, Ms. Lloyd."

"Please call me Melina."

"Come in." He stood aside and she preceded them into the house. Chief paused on the threshold to shake hands with Longtree. "Thank you for this. When I called, you had every right to tell me to go to hell."

A smile flitted over the older man's stern lips. "Well, the day is young."

He ushered Chief inside. A ceiling fixture provided a circle of light for the center of the room but left the corners dark. From what Chief could tell, the furnishings were old, well-used, borderline shabby. The most appealing feature of the room was the fireplace, where a low fire was smoldering. Melina made a beeline for it and extended her hands toward the warmth.

"Hmm. That feels good." Turning around, she put her back to the hearth and chafed her arms.

"On these chilly mornings, I wake up with stiff joints," Longtree said. "A fire helps."

Melina smiled at Longtree, and he smiled back at her, and Chief felt a pang of irrational and juvenile jealousy, the same as he had when she had made so chummy with Pax. "We hate to impose," he said, moving to stand nearer the fire. And Melina.

"It's no imposition, Colonel Hart," Longtree told him. "We were destined to meet again. I've been expecting you."

"Expecting me? I didn't know until a few hours ago that I was coming anywhere near New Mexico. How could you have known?"

Longtree gave him a long, indecipherable look, then asked if they were hungry.

"Very," Melina replied candidly.

He signaled for them to follow him. Melina did so without hesitation; Chief hung back. He was reluctant to get too friendly with Longtree. When it became apparent that they needed to come to New Mexico and find out what they could about Brother Gabriel and his ministry, and that they needed to arrive in a hurry and as clandestinely as possible, he had asked himself who in the area he knew who could facilitate them.

He had no relatives. His mother's family had died out years ago. He hadn't stayed in contact with his friends on the reservation. Once he graduated from high school, he'd left that part of his life behind without a trace of nostalgia.

A former astronaut with whom he'd flown his first shuttle mission had retired to Albuquerque, but Chief was disinclined to ask him for assistance. He still wanted NASA to know nothing about all this. Not that his former crewmate would betray his confidence, but he was reluctant to tap into that resource unless it became absolutely necessary. More than his reputation was at stake now. His and Melina's lives were in jeopardy. The last thing they needed was a media spotlight aimed at them.

Knowing full well that it would obligate him, he'd called Longtree. He briefly outlined what he needed, then summed up by asking, "Can you help me?"

Longtree had agreed to make arrangements at the airstrip and had promised that someone would be there to meet them with transportation. Chief had insisted on paying him for these services, that it be a business transaction with no strings attached. Longtree demurred. He didn't want to take money for what he considered a favor. Chief had been persistent. Finally Longtree had agreed to accept monetary compensation for his time and trouble.

But Chief wasn't that naive. He realized that he might ultimately be presented a bill higher than he was willing to pay. Unfortunately, he'd seen no alternative.

The kitchen was brighter and warmer than the living room. Melina was asking what she could do to help, but Longtree was holding a 1950s-vintage chrome chair for her. With a thank-you smile for him, she sat down at the table. He offered her something to drink and she asked for tea.

"Colonel Hart?"

"Call me Chief." He sat down across from Melina. "I'll take coffee if you have some made."

Soon there was a steaming mug in Chief's hand. As Longtree went about preparing them a meal, Chief took note of the kitchen. The appliances were old, the plaster walls cracked and scarred, the pattern in the linoleum eroded in heavily trafficked spots.

Longtree was dressed in Levi's and boots that had seen years of wear. His flannel shirt had a fraying hole in the bottom of the breast pocket, and, although his bearing and demeanor were as intimidating and regal as before, this was not the affluent-looking man he'd met in the bar of The Mansion.

As Melina steeped her tea, she asked where the nearest reservation was, and Longtree informed her that she'd been on a reservation since she'd landed.

"I had no idea. I guess I thought a reservation was more . . . contained. I apologize for my ignorance."

"I wish all misconceptions about Indians

were that harmless," he told her with another of his rare smiles.

He set plates of food in front of them, then served his own plate and joined them at the table. Melina sighed around her first bite. "Delicious."

It was only scrambled eggs, bacon, and toast, but Chief's mouth had started watering as soon as the aromas of cooking food had filled the kitchen. He had to force himself not to gobble and added his compliments to the cook.

Longtree said, "I had to teach myself to cook when my wife died."

"Was this recently?" Melina asked softly.

"A long time ago."

"Children?"

He hesitated, then replied, "No."

They ate the rest of their meal in silence. When they finished, Longtree collected the plates and carried them to the counter, then refilled Chief's coffee and her tea and sat back down. "Tell me why you're here."

Chief looked across at Melina. "It's your story."

She told Longtree an abbreviated version, which covered the facts and provided a fairly accurate overview of everything that had transpired since her last lunch with Gillian. After telling him how much she regretted switching places with her twin, she paused as though waiting for him to hand down a judgment. His stony features didn't flinch.

She continued, concluding with, "Maybe Chief and I are being a little paranoid about tracking devices and such, but we don't think so. We've seen these people—whoever they are and whomever they represent—in action. As sure as I'm sitting here, they murdered Linda Croft and Jem Hennings."

"Hennings admitted to us that he facilitated some kind of genetic engineering scheme," Chief said. "He referred to it as the 'Program.' The implication is unthinkable, especially when you consider the extent of Brother Gabriel's ministry."

During the entire telling, Longtree had sat as motionless and silent as a mountain. Then he spoke for the first time. "And you have little doubt that he's behind this plot?"

"We don't know," Melina answered honestly. "I hate to incriminate anyone of something so heinous if it's not true. But Jem admitted that he and Dale Gordon worked for

Brother Gabriel. Patients of the clinic, who meet a certain criteria, are inseminated with sperm that may not be from the donor of their choosing. That was Gordon's job. If the woman conceives, someone like Jem nurtures her through the pregnancy to see that nothing goes awry."

"Like sleeping with me," Chief added bitterly. "Brother Gabriel preaches about establishing a new world order. In my opinion, that fits with the baby-making scenario and explains why he wants the conception of these children to be controlled and remain pure."

"I'm convinced that if Gillian had conceived and stayed with Jem for the duration of her pregnancy, the baby would have been kidnapped just like the Andersons' baby," Melina told Longtree. "We know Jem didn't want me to talk to the FBI."

"I started out thinking the orders to shut us up came from Hennings," Chief said. "But after seeing what happened to him . . . Because of my military training, I would guess the orders are coming straight from the top."

After a time of reflection, Longtree asked,

"These kidnapped children, where are they taken? For what purpose?"

"That's what we came here to determine," Chief said. "Brother Gabriel's compound isn't far from here, relatively speaking. What do you know about it?"

"The Temple is about a hundred miles as the crow flies. What I know about him isn't good." Longtree's expression turned even more grim than usual. "He, or rather his ministry, rooked one of the tribes out of some land. He wanted their mountain. They wouldn't sell. I think he coerced a tribal leader into selling the land out from under his own people."

"How?"

"What I know for fact, apart from rumor, is that the chief had two daughters. Beautiful, accomplished young women. One allegedly committed suicide just before the chief relented and sold the property."

Melina pounced. " 'Allegedly'?"

Longtree's shrug was eloquent. "That was the ruling. Some questioned it. The chief's other daughter severed all ties with her family and friends and ran away to join Brother Gabriel's ministry. The last I heard, she was living in the Temple, which is built on property that once belonged to the people she has denounced. There was a lot of speculation over the level of Brother Gabriel's involvement in the dual tragedy. But the coincidence is too compelling to ignore."

Chief looked across at Melina. "I think the son of a bitch is more diabolical than we've given him credit for."

She asked Longtree if he thought people were being held in the compound against their will.

"I doubt they're held in chains. But mind control can be an even stronger shackle."

"Has Brother Gabriel ever been investigated?" Chief asked.

"By law enforcement, you mean?" The older man shook his head. "Not to my knowledge. State and local police leave him alone. He's a taxpaying, law-abiding citizen. The federal bureaus don't want another Waco."

"Besides, Brother Gabriel preaches good citizenship," Melina observed. "He's not anti-government. At least not overtly."

Chief noticed that even as she was speaking, her eyes were closed and she was massaging her forehead. She looked as though sitting up required more energy than she had. "Before we storm the Temple, we've got to get some rest."

She looked over at him. "I'm fine."

"Well, I'm not. Is there someplace we can get a few hours' sleep?" he asked Longtree.

Chief remained in the kitchen while Longtree showed Melina where she could bunk down. He was at the sink running hot water over their dirty dishes when Longtree returned. "Don't bother, Colonel Hart."

"Chief. And it's the least I can do."

They worked together for several minutes until all the things had been cleared from the table and the dishes were soaking in soapy water. "I'll finish them later," Longtree said. "Would you like another cup of coffee?"

"No, thanks. I've got to try and get some shut-eye myself." But he made no move toward the door leading to the other rooms of the house. Instead, he returned to the table. Longtree took the chair across from him and waited him out.

Chief found it uncomfortable to meet the other man's eyes. "This isn't what I expected."

"This?"

Chief looked around the kitchen. "I expected . . ."

One side of Longtree's narrow lips tilted up into a half smile. "Something nicer."

"I thought you were wealthy."

"George Abbott's idea."

"I see," Chief said, although he didn't.

"George wanted to make a good impression on you. He thought you'd be won over more easily if we didn't appear quite so needy. We pooled our resources to buy me the new suit. Waste of money. Where am I going to wear it?" He smiled again. "I guess I can be buried in it."

"What do you do for a living?"

"I have a law degree, but my clients are poor. I run a very small herd of beef cattle."

"You live here alone?"

"My wife died twenty-six years ago."

Chief lowered his gaze, chagrined over bringing up something that caused Longtree such obvious pain. He didn't expect him to expound and was surprised when he did.

"She was pregnant with our first child. It had been a happy, uncomplicated pregnancy. She went into labor. I got her to the reservation clinic in time, but it turned out to be a difficult delivery. The clinic was ill-equipped and understaffed to handle that kind of emergency. For years the council had been petitioning for funds to improve and update it, but our request had been repeatedly denied.

"My wife's condition rapidly worsened. There was no time to take her to another facility or to get an obstetric doctor here. As I watched, helpless to do anything, she bled to death. My son was cut out of her, but the cord was wrapped around his neck. He never drew a breath. I buried them together."

The wall clock ticked abnormally loud in the resulting silence. Chief eventually stirred. "I'm sorry I made you think about it."

"Don't be. I went a little crazy for a while, but I recovered. Eventually. Since then, even to now, whenever I think about it my resolve to improve life on the reservations is revived. I think the spirits use their deaths to keep my determination alive."

Chief looked hard at Longtree and saw a man of conviction. Why hadn't he recognized it before? Why hadn't he seen past the expensive suit into the heart of the man wearing it? "Why did you let me go on believing in the pretense?"

"It served our purpose, although not in the way George planned. Afterward, I was glad I had agreed to the slight deception, because your reaction to it revealed the character I had hoped to see in you. It was evident that you're a man of integrity."

Chief gave a soft, self-deprecating laugh. "You touched some sensitive spots. You started me thinking."

Longtree nodded approval. "I'd hate for your opinion of me, good or bad, to be the basis of your decision. I happen to think that you were sent to us. To our advocacy group. To help. To work toward bringing Native Americans into the twenty-first century with our pride, dignity, *and* heritage intact.

"Some feel that we can't achieve the former without forsaking the latter. I don't. I do not believe that our heritage must be sacrificed in order for us to move ahead and join the rest of the modern world.

"Regrettably, many of our people have victimized themselves. They've used being Indian as an excuse for their personal weaknesses. Alcoholism, depression, a lack of ambition.

"I qualify that by stating that the underlying cause for these weaknesses is very real. We're still subject to flagrant and hateful racial prejudice. Did you know that Indians are victims of violent crimes at twice the rate of other Americans? Crimes that are inflicted on us by members of other races, not by other Indians. That's not just my opinion. The statistics are there. We have enemies. We're self-defeating. On both fronts, there's much that needs to be done."

"I'm not the man to do it, Chief Longtree," Chief said earnestly.

"You wouldn't have asked for help last night if you didn't feel a kinship with us."

"I'm only half, you know."

"So was Quanah Parker."

Chief smiled fondly at the memory of his mother's stories about their famous ancestor. Like a language, Chief didn't remember a time when he didn't know about nine-year-old Cynthia Ann Parker being kidnapped from Parker's Fort, Texas, in 1836 by raiding Comanche. By the time she was a teenager, she had learned their language and adapted their customs. She married Chief Peta Nacona and bore him three children, two sons and a daughter.

She lived with the Comanche for twenty-four years before being recaptured by Texas Rangers and, along with her daughter, restored to her family. She never readjusted, however, and died shortly after the death of her daughter. Legend maintained that she died of a broken heart over the separation from her husband and sons.

Quanah was in his teens when his mother was recaptured. He succeeded his father as chief and became a feared warrior. For years he waged vicious warfare against the Army, to which he never lost a single battle.

But in 1875, with his provisions depleted, he surrendered and moved his people to Fort Sill in present-day Oklahoma. Greatly influenced by his mother and the way in which she had adopted the Comanche life, Quanah did the reverse. He took her surname and encouraged his people to acclimate to Anglo culture. They learned to farm. The English-speaking Chief Quanah Parker established schools and was appointed a reservation judge. He counted President Theodore Roosevelt as a friend. The once-ferocious warrior became a statesman. He still waged war on behalf of his people, but his battlefield was the floor of Congress.

"Some Comanche distrusted Quanah for being half-white, you know," Longtree said. "He was resented for adopting the white man's way of life. Should you join us, you won't be without your critics among Native Americans. But who in the public eye doesn't have opponents? Speaking strictly for myself, I see your mixed blood as an advantage. As it was for Quanah Parker."

After a moment of reflection, Chief said, "I'll think about it."

"That's the only promise I ask of you."

"No strings for your hospitality today?"

"I wouldn't trust you if such a small favor could so easily sway an important decision." They sat for a time with only the ticking clock to break the ponderous silence. When Longtree spoke again, he switched subjects. "Gillian, the twin, you liked her?"

The old man's eyes seemed to drill straight into him, demanding undiluted honesty. Chief heard himself saying, "Yes. I liked her a lot."

Longtree nodded sagely, then switched the subject again. "What is your strategy from here?"

"To go to the Temple and confront Brother Gabriel."

Longtree frowned. "I don't think it'll be that simple. There are guarded security gates, I'm told. Cameras and such. How do you intend to get in?"

"Any suggestions?"

"The sheriff up there is a man named Max Ritchey. He cooperates with the reservation police force. Seems like a reasonable man. You could start with him."

"I appreciate the tip." Chief stood and stretched. "I'm beat. If you'll excuse me, I've got to get some sleep. Would you mind if I showered?"

"You'll have to ask Melina. The bathroom is attached to the bedroom."

"Okay."

"I'll be leaving soon to attend to some business and won't be back until midafternoon. Make yourselves at home."

Knowing that Longtree would be uncomfortable with an effusive display of gratitude, Chief said simply, "Thanks for everything."

"You're welcome."

He was on his way through the door when Longtree called him back, for the first time addressing him as Chief instead of colonel. He turned. "Yeah?"

The older man said, "Quanah Parker didn't relinquish every aspect of Comanche life. To the consternation of the BIA, he practiced polygamy."

Chief raised one shoulder in a half shrug of misapprehension.

Longtree said, "Apparently your kinsman thought it was possible to be in love with two women at the same time. I thought it might relieve you to know that."

CHAPTER | 3 3

He knocked.

"Come in."

Melina was bending from the waist, head upside down, toweling her hair dry. She was in bra and panties, nothing else, and the sight of so much flesh stopped Chief in his tracks. "Sorry. I thought you said to come in."

In one fluid motion, she stood up straight and flung her damp hair away from her face. "Where's the mystery? I figured that since you'd seen Gillian—"

"I've seen you."

"Essentially. And you've seen my under-wear."

Right. He had. But it looked a hell of a lot different on her than it had hanging on the shower curtain rod. He was gawking like a schoolboy. Her breasts swelled above the cups of her brassiere, the nipples dusky shadows beneath ivory lace. And there, on that spot just below her navel, was where he'd first touched her with his lips.

No, not *her,* dammit. Gillian.

"Chief? Are you all right?"

No, he was not all right. His heart was thumping like a son of a bitch and his mouth felt cottony. "Sure."

"I'm flesh and blood, you know."

"No argument there."

"But you look like you're seeing a ghost."

It was true. He was experiencing a bad case of *déjà vu.* Or, more to the point, *déjà hard-on,* pardon the French. Except for the bruise discoloring her collarbone where she'd caught the doorjamb in her struggle with Tobias's imposter, she was identical to Gillian. Identical in every way. So much like her that he relived a thou-sand erotic memories in the span of a few seconds.

That curve of hip perfectly fit his palm. That patch of skin had a light dusting of peach fuzz. That hollow was particularly sensitive to nibbling. When touched there, she gave a little whimper of arousal.

"Sorry." He curbed the impulse to vigorously rub his eyes like a cartoon character confronted with a phantasm. But he did avert his eyes. A bit crossly, he said, "It could've been Longtree who knocked. How'd you know it was me?"

"By your tread. I first noticed it when you walked through Pax's airplane hangar. You have a very distinctive gait."

"Oh."

He knew his face must look stiff and strained because she was still regarding him with uncertainty. "Look, Chief, if I've made you uncomfortable, I apologize. Gillian was the modest twin."

Recalling how she had stood up and seductively slipped out of her dress that night, he said thickly, "Not very."

"Really?"

"Hmm."

"Oh." For a moment she considered that thoughtfully, then said, "But she was pretending to be me, remember?"

"Right."

Still looking at him uneasily, she said, "If you'd rather I dress—"

"Of course not."

"It's just that I'm exhausted. The thought of sleeping in clothes that I've been wearing since—"

"No explanation necessary, Melina. I was just startled to see you like this. It's not every day a man is lucky enough to walk in on a half-naked woman."

He tried to grin but wasn't sure he succeeded in making it appear genuine. In fact, he was pretty sure it wasn't convincing at all. Even so, she took his statement at face value and acknowledged it only with a huge yawn.

She sat down on the edge of the bed and reapplied the towel to her hair, briskly rubbing strands of it between the faded terrycloth. He groped for something intelligent to say. "Longtree suggested that we start with the sheriff up there near the Temple."

"That's probably a good idea."

"With the local law on our side, we might have a better shot at getting into the compound. It's guarded, he said."

"How will we convince the sheriff that we're not a couple of nutcases?"

"We'll have a hundred-mile drive to think up something to say."

"Drive? I assumed we would fly."

"It's your call, but if you want my opinion . . ."

When he paused, she glanced over at him. "Shoot."

"This morning we were able to sneak in because we had Longtree making arrangements and that landing strip was private and remote. But if two out-of-towners land at a public airfield, it could attract attention."

"You're right. I'd rather our arrival not be announced. I'd also like to get there before dark, if possible, so we'll have a chance to look around."

"There is one major problem with the plan to drive. We don't have wheels."

"I'm sure Chief Longtree would find us a vehicle."

"I'm sure he would if you ask him," he said, partially beneath his breath.

"He's a very distinguished gentleman, isn't he?"

Her glowing review of their host irked him. He agreed that Longtree seemed like a decent man, but he wasn't as carried away as Melina obviously was. "He's okay, I guess."

"I love his face."

"You love his face?"

"His appearance. The way he looks."

"He looks like a wrinkled old Indian."

She shot him a reproving frown. "But the wrinkles are an enhancement. His features are so proud, so . . ." She paused to search for the proper adjective and finally came up with one. "Noble."

Chief had a sour comeback for that, but he settled on a noncommittal harrumph. Out of fairness, he said, "He's had his share of tragedy." He then related the story of Longtree's loss.

"How horrible," she said when he was finished. "His wife and his baby."

"Yeah, that's rough."

She stared into near space for a time, then looked over at him. "He reminds me of you."

"What?" he exclaimed.

"Not physically. Obviously. But the way you hold yourselves . . . intact. That rigid self-control."

"Part of being an Indian, I guess. Aren't we supposed to be a stoic people?"

He'd said it half in jest, but she addressed it seriously. "Maybe. But maybe you and Chief Longtree have even more than that in common."

Before he could pursue the topic, she dropped the damp towel onto the floor and lay down, pulling the covers up to her chin. "Lord, I don't remember ever being this tired." She adjusted her head on the pillow. Her eyes closed instantly.

"You don't mind if I use the shower, do you?"

"It's not my shower," she mumbled. Then she rolled onto her side and brought her knees up even with her waist.

Chief went into the bathroom. As soon as he closed the door, he unbuttoned his jeans to relieve the pressure on his own proud and noble feature. He remained there with his forehead and palms pressed hard against the wood, his eyes closed, breathing slowly and deeply to maintain the rigid self-control Melina had erroneously attributed to him.

When after several minutes he turned into the room, he noticed that the tub had been wiped dry. She'd neatly hung her used towel on the bar. The room smelled of soap and toothpaste and damp skin. Female skin. Soft, bare female skin. Gillian's skin. Melina's skin.

Chief turned on the faucets and stripped

off his clothes. His motions were jerky and angry. At the very least irritable. He soaped and shampooed and when he got out of the tub, he availed himself of the tube of toothpaste and washed his teeth with his index finger, as Melina must have done because they hadn't even carried toothbrushes with them when they left Dallas.

And all that while Chief wondered what the hell Longtree was implying with that irrelevant crack about Quanah Parker's ability to be in love with more than one woman at a time.

He dismissed it as ancient Apache mumbo jumbo. Hocus-pocus. Part of that mystical stuff about visions and crap, which he'd never bought into. Among his mother's tribe there had been old men with stringy gray hair and weatherbeaten faces who'd scared the hell out of him when he was a kid. During ceremonies, their low, guttural chanting had frightened him. In adolescence, he'd ridiculed them for being such fools.

Dexter Longtree hadn't lapsed into any chants, but about half of everything he said was cloaked in innuendo and riddles. Chief was certain the old man talked like that to sound wiser than he was, to make it seem as though he were tapped into the spirit realm. Longtree wanted to come across as the wise old medicine man who could read omens and such.

"Bullshit," Chief muttered as he reluctantly pulled on his jeans again. He was a scientist. He believed in what had been proved or what he had seen and experienced for himself. For all he knew, Longtree's ramblings were peyote-inspired. Or maybe he wasn't altogether there. He'd admitted to going a little crazy when his wife and baby died. Maybe he'd stayed crazy as a bedbug all these years.

Whatever. Colonel Christopher Hart put no credence in any revelations expressed by an old man with a proud and noble face that Melina loved.

He was in a pissy mood when he left the bathroom. He even let the door swing open wide enough to bang loudly against the wall. Melina didn't stir. He'd put his jeans back on in case she made an issue of his climbing into bed beside her.

But why shouldn't he?

He'd flown the frigging airplane while she napped in her seat. The past couple of days his life had been in just as much danger as hers. Why should he settle for the lumpy-looking sofa in that drab living room when the nice, comfy-looking bed was big enough for both of them?

But when he lay down beside her, she didn't utter a peep of protest. Her breathing remained even and deep. There was no re-action from her when he plumped his pillow several times. She gave no indication of knowing, or caring, that he was anywhere near her.

He didn't know whether to be relieved or annoyed.

"Have a seat, gentlemen." Sheriff Max Ritchey motioned the two men into chairs on the opposite side of his desk. "Can I of-fer you a soft drink?"

"No, thanks," Lawson replied. "We just had lunch. Green chile stew."

"How'd you like it?"

"Delicious."

"Good. Good." By settling his butt more comfortably into the seat of his desk chair, the sheriff signaled that the pleasantries were over now and that he was ready to get down to business. "You didn't come all the way from Dallas to eat our regional specialty. What can I do for you?"

"You remember speaking to me on the phone a few days ago?" Lawson asked.

"Sure. Homicide case."

"Gillian Lloyd."

"I was under the impression the case was solved. You knew the identity of the culprit, right? When you phoned me, you were just tying up some loose ends."

"That's true." The detective recounted the facts for him, although Ritchey remembered them.

"As I reported back to you, Detective Lawson, I went up to the Temple and made inquiries about this Dale Gordon. They remembered him because he called frequently and was obviously a mental case. Way over the edge. I think his suicide proves that." Baffled, the sheriff raised his arms. "So what's the problem? Unless there's more to this homicide and suicide than you originally thought."

"Significantly more, Sheriff Ritchey." In somber tones and with little elaboration, Special Agent Tobias brought him up to speed.

As Ritchey listened, his dread increased. Each sentence was like a stone added to a pile, until they had formed a mound of worries he must contend with. When these two men showed up at his department unannounced, he'd recognized them as heralds of bad news. A homicide detective from out of state didn't come to Lamesa County accompanied by an FBI agent out of Washington unless they were investigating a case of national importance.

Instinctively, Max Ritchey knew that his virtually uneventful, well-organized, well-balanced life was about to be drastically rocked. He hoped he could prevent it from being completely toppled.

"We're testing the bullet that killed Jem Hennings," Tobias was saying. "But chances of tracing it are next to nil. We're fairly certain it was fired by a professional."

"Like a hired assassin?" Ritchey asked.

"That's one possibility," Tobias replied evasively.

Lawson picked it up from there. "Hennings was Gillian Lloyd's fiancé. Dale Gordon worked in the clinic where she was artificially inseminated the day before her murder. Hennings had connections to Brother Gabriel's ministry, which we're investigating further. It's been confirmed that Dale Gordon had direct contact with the Temple on a routine basis." He raised his shoulders in an implicit shrug. "You add it up."

Ritchey recoiled with astonishment, exclaiming, "You're not suggesting that Brother Gabriel had anything to do with these three deaths."

"Not at all."

Ritchey didn't believe the FBI agent's smooth denial. "Then why are you here?"

"Because someone else does believe that Brother Gabriel is involved," Lawson told him. "Gillian Lloyd's sister. A twin. A dead ringer. Her name is Melina Lloyd. She was with Hennings when he was shot."

Ritchey thoughtfully tugged on his lower lip. "If this Hennings was romancing her sister for some illicit purpose, she's got motive," he said, quoting a line he'd recently heard on his favorite detective show. "I'm sure you've thought of that."

"We thought of it, but it doesn't hold. Hennings was shot through a window from across the street. She didn't do it, but she's a material witness. We want to question her before she does something crazy."

"Such as?"

"Such as storm the gates of Brother Gabriel's castle. She wants answers same as us," Lawson told him.

"We—Mr. Lawson and I; and you, Sheriff—are constrained to get answers by going through proper channels," Tobias explained. "Unfortunately, Ms. Lloyd feels no such constraint. She's proven herself to be a very resourceful individual. She's managed to elude us, and she's motivated by the strongest motivation there is. Revenge."

"Sounds to me like she's gone around the bend, too. She might be as unstable as Dale Gordon."

Tobias denied that with a firm shake of his head. "No doubt she's emotionally reactive, but her reasoning is sound. Another employee of the Waters Clinic was murdered yesterday afternoon. Within hours of speaking with Ms. Lloyd," he added after a significant pause for emphasis.

"I see you're shocked, Sheriff. Rightfully so. Ms. Lloyd knows she's on to something, and I don't think she'll stop until she gets some answers. She won't quit until she knows for certain why her twin was killed.

Detective Lawson and I are reasonably sure that she'll turn up here."

"Sooner rather than later," the detective added.

Ritchey released a long breath. "I'll notify the Temple immediately, but if she or anyone had tried to barge into the compound, I would have heard about it. The security up there is tight."

"Why's that?" Lawson asked.

"Ask John Lennon. Ask that designer fellow in Florida. Brother Gabriel is an international celebrity. High-profile people make good targets for nobodies who want to get their names in the news."

Tobias frowned thoughtfully. "Are you sure that's the only reason the Temple security is so tight?"

"Why else?"

The FBI agent leaned forward in his chair. Ritchey noticed that the French cuffs of his shirt were monogrammed with his initials. "Sheriff Ritchey, have you ever been inside the compound?"

"Only twice. Last time was three days ago when I questioned Brother Gabriel about Dale Gordon."

"How did it strike you?"

"I'm not sure I catch your meaning." Tobias reacted with impatience to his reply, and Lawson looked ready to shake information out of him with his square, blunt hands. "What I mean is, in what way? My impressions of the place? The grounds are spotless. The buildings are—"

"The general mood. The people," Lawson said, cutting him off. "Did you see any evidence of people being held there against their will?"

Ritchey barked a dry laugh. "You're kidding, right?"

The two men stared back at him with all the levity of hooded executioners.

Nervously he recalled his smile and cleared his throat. "My understanding is that it's an honor for Brother Gabriel's followers to live and work there. People apply for the opportunity. There's a merit system. You do some special work for the ministry, you earn a place in the Temple. Something like that."

"What kind of special work?"

"Pardon?"

"You said if a follower did some special work for the ministry . . ."

"Good deeds. Fund-raising. Proselytizing.

Isn't that what most churches are about? Earning points?"

Tobias asked, "Have you ever known anyone who lived at the Temple but left?"

"No," he replied honestly. "That's not to say it doesn't happen. I just don't know about it." He looked at them quizzically. "And why would someone who'd worked hard to earn admittance want to leave? Wouldn't that be like checking out of heaven?"

They left the sheriff's office and climbed back into the agency car. Tobias got behind the wheel. Lawson was impressed by the authority the man wielded. He had arranged for them to be met at the Albuquerque airport, where the car had been designated for their use. They'd driven from there to Lamesa, the county seat. With a single phone call, Tobias could make things happen. Lawson couldn't get a Bic pen without filling out a requisition form.

"What do you think of Ritchey?" Lawson asked the agent as they pulled away.

"Hard to read, but I'd say he was being about half truthful."

"My impression, too. Everything he said was filtered."

"Maybe through pride. He resents outsiders snooping around his county, looking for a criminal element. It suggests that he's not doing an adequate job. Or . . . ."

"Yeah?"

"Maybe the man was telling the unvarnished truth and we're just getting paranoid."

"Could be," Lawson agreed. "I'm looking for ulterior motives behind every fence post." After several moments had elapsed, he said, "On the other hand, Ritchey could be a devoted follower. Maybe he accounts to a higher jurisdiction than the county, state, or federal laws."

"You mean that Brother Gabriel may have Ritchey and other local law enforcement in his back pocket?"

"Who's to say where his influence stops? We know it extended as far as Big D."

"And South Dakota. That's where Hennings became involved."

"Do you think Hennings and his little sister got converted by the school nurse, and that when their parents raised a ruckus, they were eliminated?"

"Someone made them disappear."

"You suspect Brother Gabriel?"

"Or a zealous follower working on his behalf."

"With his sanction?"

"Frightening prospect, isn't it?"

"If he's got followers willing to kill for him . . ." Turning to look at Tobias, he spoke his thoughts out loud. "That means that when Dale Gordon killed Gillian Lloyd, he could've been acting on orders from the Temple."

"I've thought of that."

Lawson's face turned ugly. "I want to meet this bleached-blond preacher eyeball to eyeball. I want to know what he's all about, and I'll bet you a steak dinner against a bottle of scotch that he's not as saintly as his pretty face and sweet smile suggest."

"You're on. But I don't eat red meat."

Lawson snorted.

Chuckling over Lawson's derision, Tobias answered his ringing cell phone. "Yeah, Lucy, what?" He listened, thanked her for the update, and then, as he clicked off, he turned to Lawson and smiled. "That eyeball-to-eyeball thing . . . you'll get your chance tomorrow morning. We have an audience with the main man."

"Why tomorrow morning? Why don't we just go up there now—"

"No probable cause. No direct link to either Gillian Lloyd, or Dale Gordon—except the phone calls, and he's already explained those—or Jem Hennings. He's granting us an audience as a courtesy, and that's how we must conduct the interview.

"Until we get those sperm specimens from the Waters Clinic donors and run DNA tests to prove that Gordon was switching them, then all we've got is a pile of supposition. At this point, we don't even know with certainty that the sperm was being switched. And even if we do prove that the specimens were being switched, we've got nothing that links the tampering to Brother Gabriel except a dead disciple, who proved himself to be deranged. So, in summation, we've got no probable cause for which to question an eminent man of God."

"My ass." Vexed, Lawson ran a hand over his burr haircut. "I know you're right. From a legal standpoint, you're playing it by the book. But my gut tells me that Brother Gabriel is the source of all this." Lawson gnawed on it for a full minute. "What about Melina Lloyd? What do you think?"

"That she'll come here to confront him."

"I think so, too." After a moment, he said, "Damn! Timing is everything, isn't it?"

"How so, specifically?"

"I was just thinking. If I'd had this lead on the Waters Clinic early on, I would've had smears taken from Gillian Lloyd's body. She'd been artificially inseminated less than twenty-four hours prior to her death."

"If DNA testing had proved that the smears didn't belong to her designated donor—"

"Or to Christopher Hart."

"—then you would have had proof that there was tampering being done at the clinic."

"But we already had our killer," Lawson said morosely. "There was no sign of semen externally. The stab wounds were so conclusive as to how she died, there was no reason not to release the body to Melina for cremation."

Tobias told him he was in the process of getting a court order for the remains of the woman in Oakland, California, to be exhumed. "When it is, we'll DNA-test the embryo inside Kathleen Asher against her designated donor. Of course, all of this takes time. A smear from Gillian Lloyd would have been much more expeditious."

"Sorry," Lawson grumbled.

"Well, as you said, you didn't know then what you know now."

It was gracious of Tobias to let him off the hook. He was gracious in return. "I brought along the case file, if you want to review any of it."

"I might," Tobias said. "It's going to be a long night, and I've got nothing better to do."

Melina?"

"Hmm?"

"It's almost three."

With a heavy sigh, she rolled onto her back and scowled up at Chief through eyes only half open. "Why are you always waking me up?"

"Because you're always oversleeping."

"I was dreaming."

"About what?"

"I don't remember."

"Good dream?"

"I think so." She stretched luxuriantly. "What time is it?"

"I just told you."

"I wasn't listening," she admitted with a sleepy smile. "Tell me again."

But he didn't repeat the time. In fact, he didn't say anything, and it only took her a few seconds to appreciate, as he obviously already had, the intimacy of the moment. His fists were planted on either side of her head, buried in the pillow up to his second knuckles. His arms were bearing much of his weight, so each muscle was well defined.

His face had lost all trace of a smile. The blue of his eyes seemed to have intensified, as the color of the sky deepens immediately after sunset, changing from violet to indigo, undiscernibly but definitely.

Acting on impulse, she reached up and touched his face. First she smoothed down his eyebrows in turn. Then she sighed sympathetically and with regret when she delicately touched the wound on his cheekbone. Her finger traced the length of his slender nose and finally outlined the shape of his lips. She lingered over each feature as though her fingertips were committing them to memory.

Gaining confidence, she lowered her hand

and touched him just below his right breast. His skin radiated a warmth she longed to feel against her. Her eyes tracked her fingertips as they skimmed downward over several lean ribs, then moved back up to the sculpted undercurve of his breast. She whisked the nipple with her thumb.

Emboldened by his quick intake of breath, she did something she would never have dared to do otherwise. She raised her head high enough to flick her tongue over the distended tip.

Cursing softly, he threw back the covers, lowered himself over her, and pressed his face into her cleavage. He pushed her breasts up from her rib cage. Hungrily he kissed the slopes of them where they swelled above the cups of her bra. His stubble rasped her skin, but it was an erotic sensation, and, without any instruction from her, she felt her hips lifting off the bed to nudge the fly of his jeans.

He rubbed his lips against her nipples until they were thrusting hard against the lace that contained them, and just when she was on the brink of begging him, he peeled the lace away and covered her with his open mouth. Each sweet tug of his mouth was felt deep within. She clutched handfuls of his hair and moaned with pleasure.

In a low, gravelly voice he urged her to unbutton him.

Blindly she fumbled with fabric and stubborn metal buttons. The top one was already undone, but when she tried to undo the rest, she met with resistance. The hardness beneath was unyielding. He grunted with discomfort, and they both laughed lightly. Finally she managed to unbutton them all and pushed the jeans down over his hips.

He guided her hand to his erection and folded her fingers around it. When she began a rhythmic massage, he closed his eyes and grimaced with pleasure enough to bare his teeth. "Slower." When she complied, he pressed his forehead against hers. "Oh, Jesus, that's good. You'd better tell me now if you're not okay with this."

"I'm okay with this."

"Arch your back."

She pressed her shoulders into the mattress and lifted herself so that he could slide his hands beneath her and unfasten her bra. When it was unclasped, he pulled it off and raised his head to gaze down at her, then squeezed her breasts together and kissed the nipples, laving them with his tongue and plucking at them with his lips.

"Chief," she gasped.

"I know. Me, too. But I don't want to rush it. You'd better stop that," he said, moving her hand aside.

He hooked his thumbs into the elastic waist of her bikinis and pulled them all the way down past the tips of her toes. Then, wrapping his hands around her ankles and kneeling between them, he slowly opened her legs. Her initial reaction was to resist, or to cover herself with her hand, or to bashfully turn her head aside.

But his ardent stare was sweet, tender. It made her feel elevated, not humiliated. Gradually his eyes traveled up her body until they magnetically connected to hers. They remained locked onto one another's gaze as his hands slid up her shins. They rotated to the undersides of her legs so that her calves were cupped in his palms. Gently he massaged them with his strong fingers.

Then back to the topside, his hands glided upward to lightly squeeze the ticklish area just above her knees. They stayed on course up her thighs until his fingers were splayed over her lower abdomen and his thumbs met at her center.

And still his eyes remained fixed on hers.

Alternately his thumbs stroked her. Became slippery. Found the treasured spot. Caressed it with the merest touch. Sparks of sensation shot through her. She caught her lower lip between her teeth. Her breathing became choppy and quick. Her eyelids fluttered and his image began to blur. "If you don't stop," she panted, "I'm going to come."

"That's the point, isn't it?"

"But I want you inside me."

He thrust into her. Possessively, his hands slid beneath her hips and lifted her to him so that it would have been impossible for him to be any deeper. Nevertheless, she pushed her hands into his jeans and gripped his ass tightly, pulling him into her.

Each stroke was greedy but also giving. She sensed behind every push a wildness that he barely kept harnessed. Strangely, she wasn't afraid of it. Rather than shrink from it, she responded with a complete lack of inhibition and a ferocity of her own.

His breathing became rough, and he

buried his face in her neck and groaned, "You . . . fuck . . . like . . ."

And then he climaxed, calling a name.

"Hey, Tobias, want to hear something really weird?"

"Don't you ever go home?"

"I am home," Lucy Myrick replied from approximately two thousand miles away. "This info came in just as I was leaving the office, so I printed it out and brought it home with me. I fed my goldfish, barely in time to prevent an outbreak of cannibalism. I treated myself to a long bubble bath, nuked a frozen lasagna, opened a bottle of cheap wine, and only now am looking over the material."

Earlier, in the café attached to the motel, Tobias had eaten a grilled cheese sandwich in the time it took Lawson to scarf down two chili cheeseburgers with extra onions. They had then parted company with plans to reconvene at breakfast. Tobias had showered and was now reclining against the faux wood headboard of the motel bed, a pillow bunched beneath his head, a drink from the honor bar in his hand.

He didn't imbibe often, but he felt he owed himself one scotch and soda tonight. He was in alien territory. Without the familiar sounds of traffic outside, the silence of the desert was deafening. He couldn't relate to the paint-by-number artwork decorating the paneled walls of his room, nor to the Pueblo Indian life it depicted.

Despite his request for a nonsmoking room, an ashtray shaped like a rattlesnake was coiled and ready to strike on the dresser. It had red glass eyes that glittered in the light from the TV.

It was good to hear Lucy's familiar voice with her clipped northeastern accent instead of a southwestern twang. "What material?"

Lucy began her explanation by saying, "This Brother Gabriel is creeping me out! I watched his show last night on the TV I keep in my office. 'New world order' sounds a little too Hitleresque to sit right with me. My question to him would be, 'Who would establish this new world order?' Although, I have a sneaking suspicion of who he has in mind.

"Anyway, I did some research today and was staggered by the scope of his so-called ministry. He's not your ordinary TV preacher. His sermons are simultaneously translated into thirty or so languages. He has devotees in countries that are predominately Jewish, Catholic, Moslem, or Buddhist. The religious leaders of each are alarmed by his growing number of converts.

"His doctrine isn't exactly Christian. In fact, it isn't even scriptural. He rarely mentions Jesus Christ except as an example of humility. But that shortage of a specific dogma hasn't hampered his appeal, which seems to be universal." She took a deep breath. "Which brought me to Interpol."

Interested, Tobias set his drink on the nightstand. "I'm sure there's some logic behind that decision."

"Well, we stumbled onto Jem Hennings's connection when we—"

"When *you,*" Tobias corrected.

"Thank you kindly," she said cheekily. "When I started looking for similar crimes on a national basis, we turned up several cases that bore a striking resemblance to Gillian Lloyd's murder and the Anderson baby's kidnapping. Only today did I think about stretching my investigation abroad. And guess what?"

"I'm all ears."

"Five European women over the course of the past two years have died violently—read murder or accidental death—after having been impregnated by artificial insemination. All were single, healthy, of superior good looks and intelligence. Moreover, in the same time period, three children conceived either in vitro or by AI—using donor sperm—were kidnapped shortly after birth. Two from their cribs at home, one from the hospital."

"But statistically, Lucy—"

"I already checked," she said, interrupting his argument before he could even verbalize it. "Only one other pregnant woman—in Portugal, I believe—was murdered during the same time period. She was married and had conceived naturally, and the assault on her was motivated by robbery. The perp was caught and admitted to choosing her at random because of the jewelry she was wearing.

"All the other kidnappings, except for these three, were for ransom. One was a child molestation case by a repeat offender. All those cases were solved. The children were either returned to their families alive or their bodies were subsequently found."

He should have known that Lucy would have checked out all her facts before sharing the information with him. "And the three involving children conceived in a fertility clinic?"

"I don't really have to tell you, do I?"

"Never a trace," he guessed. "Just like the Andersons' baby."

"Precisely like that." She let him mull it over for a full thirty seconds, seeming to sense that he wanted to organize his thoughts about this new data. "I'm going to dig deeper," she told him. "See if I can find any Brother Gabriel disciples connected to these cases."

"Good, but get some rest first."

"Thanks. Is that what you're doing tonight?"

"In a manner of speaking."

He glanced at the thick black notebook containing the file on Gillian Lloyd's murder. He'd taken Lawson up on his offer to loan it to him for the evening, but it remained untouched on the nightstand. He was saturated with this case and was dreading having to review information he already knew.

"Where are you anyway?" Lucy asked.

"In the shadow of Brother Gabriel's Temple."

"Liar."

"No, I swear. I can see the lights of it from my motel room bed."

"Wish I were there with you. In the area, I mean," she clarified hastily. "I'd like to ask Brother Gabriel when God died and left him in charge."

"Let me know what you get tomorrow."

"Quick as a bunny. What's it like?"

"What?"

"Your motel room."

"Your basic stop-over-but-don't-stay-too-long. The sheets are clean, but the pillows are hard." He described the vicious-looking ashtray.

"You're kidding. I'd have nightmares. Aren't there any amenities? Coin-operated vibrating bed? Pay-per-view X-rated movies?"

"There's a brochure on top of the TV that lists the movies for adults only," he admitted.

"Any titles I might recognize?"

"Goodbye, Lucy."

"Haven't seen that one."

He hung up laughing. Talking to her had improved his mood considerably.

Melina was the first to leave the bed. Without once glancing at him, she picked up her underwear and retreated into the bathroom. Seconds later, he heard the shower running.

Chief laid his forearm over his eyes and filled the silence with muttered swear words. Of all the things that could have happened to him, who would ever have guessed *this*? When he had walked out of The Mansion and saw Gillian Lloyd for the first time, could he have imagined that within days he would be embroiled in her murder investigation and sleeping with her twin?

"Sleeping with"? Nice euphemism, but grossly inaccurate. He, Colonel Christopher Hart, astronaut and public figure, signer of autographs and hero of schoolchildren, had fucked Gillian's identical twin, an exact replica of her, and had relished every goddamn carnal heartbeat of it. He had lost himself in her the same way he'd lost himself in Gillian.

Which made him one very sick individual.

Well, didn't it?

The bathroom door opened and Melina came out fully dressed. In a very businesslike manner, she asked, "Is Longtree back yet?"

"I thought I heard some activity in the kitchen."

She crossed the room and reached for the doorknob. "Then as soon as you're ready—"

"I usually don't make a woman cry, Melina."

Without even turning, she pulled open the door and said, "I'll be waiting for you," then closed the door behind her.

"Shit," he hissed, throwing off the sheet.

Five minutes later, he joined her in the kitchen. She was sitting at the table sipping a glass of water and talking with Longtree. She didn't acknowledge him, but Longtree asked if he would like something to drink.

"Water's fine."

"Chief Longtree has graciously agreed to loan us his pickup," Melina said, still managing not to look directly at him.

"That's very generous."

The older man passed him a glass of water. "I thought you might need it. It's got a full tank of gas. I also picked up a map for you and marked the roads I advise you to take. It might be best to stay off the main highways." He pushed the folded map and a key ring across the table.

Chief accepted them with a terse thanks.

"I don't know when we'll be able to return the truck."

"Jed will take me wherever I need to go."

Melina glanced at the wall clock, then came to her feet. "We appreciate all you've done for us."

It was while she was shaking hands with Longtree that Chief noticed it. "Gillian's pendant."

Melina rubbed the ruby heart where it lay against her throat, saying to him, "I just put it back on."

"I thought you threw it away along with your handbag."

"We checked it," she reminded him. "Besides, I hated to part with it. It's probably the last thing she touched before going to bed that night."

He thought about it for only a split second before extending his hand. "Let's take a closer look, Melina. The light's better here than inside the plane."

She hesitated only a moment before removing the pendant and passing it to him. He dangled the charm close to his face, holding it so that he could see light coming through the translucent stones. That's when he noticed a dark spot in the dip of the heart right against the gold mounting. It was barely discernible. One would have to be looking, as he was, and even then it could be mistaken for a flaw in the small stone or in the gold mounting. "Do you have an ice pick?" he asked Longtree.

Within seconds he was applying the utensil to the spot. Longtree and Melina peered anxiously over his shoulder. Before any of them expected it, a small chip popped out and landed on the oilcloth that covered the dining table. It was the color of a pencil lead and smaller than the head of a pin. Chief poked it several times with the sharp tip of the ice pick. "Hennings's love gift isn't so lovely, is it?"

Melina bristled. "That bastard. I'm sorry he's dead. I'd love an opportunity to tell him what a despicable human being he was."

Chief explained the GPS tracking system to Longtree. "The technology has advanced even more than I'd heard. I'm sure a transceiver this minuscule hasn't been approved for commercial use yet. Which means that criminals are the only ones with access to it."

"Oh, my God," Melina exclaimed. "This means we've led them straight here. I'm so sorry, Chief Longtree. After the kindnesses you've extended us, we've repaid you by putting you in danger."

"Don't worry about me."

"She's right," Chief told him solemnly. "These are bad men. They killed two people yesterday. They're on somebody's payroll, probably Brother Gabriel's, and they're good at what they do."

"You've managed to escape them."

"By the skin of our teeth. Even if we've disabled the transceiver, this will be the last place it transmitted a signal. They'll try and pick up our trail here. Is there someplace you can go, hang out for a few days?"

The older Indian smiled. "American Indians have been pushed off their land for three hundred years. I couldn't look myself in the mirror if I let a couple of thugs run me off my place. I can take care of myself."

Having said that, he moved to a drawer and took a pistol from it. "Take this with you."

"You may need it more than we will."

"I insist." He passed both the pistol and a box of bullets to Chief. "Do you know how to load it?"

Chief wanted to decline the loan of the

pistol, but he only had to remember Hennings's fate to change his mind. He asked Longtree to load the revolver for him. "As a safety precaution, I'll leave the first chamber empty," he explained. "You'll have to pull the trigger twice in order for it to fire."

"I can't go, leaving you here without a weapon or transportation," Melina told him.

"I'm not afraid. My destiny isn't in the hands of hit men." Seemingly amused by the notion, Longtree motioned her toward the door. "If you want to arrive in Lamesa before dark, you'd better leave now. The sun sets quickly behind the mountains."

At the door, Chief gripped the other man's hand. They looked hard at each other, and the understanding that passed between them made words unnecessary.

C H A P T E R 3 5

Making love to me usually doesn't make a woman cry, Melina."

She couldn't keep her back to him and walk out of the room as she had at Longtree's place. Unless she wanted to leap from the cab of the pickup, she couldn't escape. At sixty miles an hour, it was doubtful she was going to do that. She could, however, ignore him. It was so long before she answered, he thought she'd exercised that option.

Finally she said, "It shouldn't have happened, Chief."

"But it did. So let's talk about it."

"Why not just forget it?"

"Because it's like a giant wart on the end of somebody's nose. You wish you could ignore it and pretend it wasn't there. You even know that's what you should do. But it's impossible. It's there and you see it."

"And you accused women of always wanting to talk things out," she muttered, turning her head to gaze out the passenger-side window.

"You were crying, Melina. I'd like to know why."

"Because it was a bad idea."

"For a bad idea, it felt awfully good."

She gave him a look before quickly fixing her gaze on the horizon again. "I never said it didn't feel good."

"So we agree on that. Which only makes my original question more pertinent. Why did you cry?"

Minutes passed. Again he thought she intended to ignore him, but eventually she spoke, and of all the things she could have said, he never would have anticipated her next statement. "Gillian told me you didn't kiss her until after you'd made love."

Startled, he turned his head toward her. "What?"

She was looking at him now. "She said you told her it was like saving the best for last. Was that just a line?"

Ill at ease, he returned his eyes to the road.

"You didn't kiss me," she continued. "Not on the lips. Not once."

"It's no big deal."

"It wouldn't be if you had. That you didn't is significant, I think. Especially in light of what you said to Gillian."

She'd struck a chord, so, in self-defense, he copped an attitude. "You know, I think it's sick, the way you two discussed our lovemaking in such intimate detail."

"Like it's perfectly healthy to use one woman as a substitute for another."

"That's not what today was about."

"Wasn't it?"

"No." He flashed her an angry glance to match his rising volume. "It could be that I didn't kiss you afterward—saving the best for last—because afterward you were crying! Did you think of that? Or maybe I didn't kiss you on the mouth because I was involved with other parts of you."

"Parts, yes. But you weren't involved with *me.*"

"I wouldn't have made love to you if I hadn't wanted to."

"Oh, you wanted to," she said, laughing a soft but mirthless laugh. "I saw that. I felt that. Biologically you were into it one hundred percent. But it was Gillian you were emotionally entangled with."

His jaw tensed. What could he say? If he said, *You're right,* it would wound her pride. If he said, *You're wrong,* he'd be oversimplifying it. And if he said, *Hell, I don't know, Melina,* he'd be telling the God's honest truth. Ironically, it was the truth she was least likely to believe.

Would it make her feel better or worse for him to explain that up until a few hours ago, he'd been able to keep her and Gillian separate in his mind? Now, having made love to her, felt her, tasted her, experienced her moves, and heard her sighs, the distinctions between them were blurred.

It was a damned dirty trick for his mind and body to play on all of them. It was unfair to Melina, whom he had come to like and respect. It was equally unfair to Gillian, who had first attracted him and indelibly stamped herself onto his memory. And it was unfair to him, when he was trying to do right by both women.

"Never mind trying to come up with a graceful answer, Chief. I know Gillian was the one you were thinking about this afternoon. It was her name you called." Again, he looked at her sharply. "You didn't realize?" she said, noticing his surprise.

He shook his head.

"You did," she said quietly. "You called her name. Passionately."

"Oh, God, Melina, I'm sorry."

She smiled wanly. "No reason to apologize. Anything spoken during . . . at that moment, is brutally honest."

That she had forgiven him for such a dreadful gaffe made him feel even more like a shit. To salve his conscience, he felt that now was the time to come completely clean with her.

Before he could think about it too long and possibly talk himself out of it, he steered the truck off the road. It bumped over the hard, rocky ground and eventually rolled to a stop about thirty yards from the road. He cut the engine and turned toward her.

"I lied to you, Melina."

He had her undivided attention. She was looking at him with perplexity, her mouth slack. Her eyes were wide, still, focused intently on him. He applied the same intensity of concentration to her eyes as he did to the markings on the runway when he landed the shuttle. It seemed that important that he get this exactly right.

"You read me right. From the moment we met in Lawson's office, you nailed me perfectly. I wanted to distance myself from the whole mess. I mourned Gillian, but I wanted to do so privately, not in the glare of TV lights, which I was afraid my involvement would attract.

"And frankly, I was pissed that one night out of my life—as great as that night was—had the potential of ruining everything good I had going. That one, random, romantic encounter had the capacity to wipe out everything I'd worked so damn hard for.

"But even after Lawson told me that the case was wrapped and I was free to go on my merry way, something kept nagging at me. That unnamed something caused me to stick around. It wasn't until the evening following Gillian's memorial service that I figured out what it was." He paused to signal that this was the heart of the matter. "When Dale Gordon killed Gillian, he might also have killed my baby."

He saw her swallow, but before she could speak, he rushed on.

"Do you remember when I came to your house that night, battered and bleeding, you asked me why I'd changed my mind? Why I was getting involved?"

"Because someone had tried to kill you," she answered huskily. "You figured the attack on you was related to Gillian's murder. That's what you said."

"That was true. But only partially. In that same conversation, you asked me if I had used a prophylactic when I was with Gillian. I told you I had."

She nodded.

"That was a lie. I didn't. Not once."

"Oh." She lowered her eyes to her lap, where her hands were tightly clasped. "Not today, either."

"Which was totally irresponsible of me."

"You've got nothing to worry about with me."

"You misunderstand, Melina. The reason—the sole reason—I brought this up was to explain why I got involved, why I was willing to risk my reputation and career and, as it turns out, my life, to get to the bottom of this."

He reached for one of her hands and pressed it between his. "It was the prime time in Gillian's cycle to conceive, right? Hennings remarked on it in Lawson's office, but I didn't really think about the significance of it until later. She was ovulating. That's why she was artificially inseminated that day."

"Yes."

"So chances are very good that she could have conceived by me that night. You said so yourself when you asked me about the condoms."

His chest was suddenly filled with a surging emotion; the density of it stunned him, as it had that night in the Greenville Avenue bar, when it finally occurred to him why he couldn't let the matter drop and forget he'd ever spent a night with a woman named Gillian Lloyd.

"See, Melina, because my dad practically disposed of me, I vowed that if I ever had a kid, I'd be there. I'd be a constant presence in his life. He would know me and rely on me to be his parent every day of his life. I would protect his life with my own." He squeezed her hand tightly. "So if there's even a remote chance that Gillian conceived and that my child died with her, I want the son of a bitch who's responsible."

She reached for him, and he allowed himself to be drawn against her chest. She hugged him tightly, and stroked his head, and whispered words of consolation. Her breasts were softly comforting, and so was her soothing voice.

It felt good to relinquish control to someone else for a change. One by one, he knocked down all his defenses. He ceased to be a military officer, or a commander, or a celebrity. He was just a man. Not even that. He was little Christopher, seeking the comfort and consolation he'd never permitted himself to seek.

After a time, she set him away from her. Tears streaked her face, and when she spoke, her voice was barely audible. "No one would have known but you. You could still have walked away."

"No. No, I couldn't."

Even more tears overflowed her eyes and slid down her cheeks. "Chief, did you fall in love with Gillian? In the space of those few hours you were together, did you fall in love with her?"

He had been dodging this question ever since he had first asked it of his reflection in the shaving mirror the morning he woke up and discovered she'd left. He had asked himself again when he was informed of her murder and it had hurt so badly to realize that she was lost to him forever. And again, when he sat in that bar and realized that their lovemaking might have created another life. Every time he had felt stirrings of desire for Melina, it was that haunting question which, until today, had stopped him from acting on that desire. And it was why he felt so guilty now for having yielded to it.

He was tired of trying to outrun the answer he knew, the answer he'd known all along. "Yeah," he confessed gruffly. "God help me, I did."

Sheriff Ritchey shifted his weight in the uncomfortable chair. According to his wristwatch, he'd been waiting for over half an hour. He had followed protocol and called ahead. A time for the meeting had been set, and he had arrived promptly. Making him wait like this was unforgivable, especially since he'd made it clear that it was urgent he see Brother Gabriel this evening.

"How much longer, do you think?"

Mr. Hancock turned away from the computer terminal where he'd been working since Ritchey's arrival. "I wouldn't know. Can I get you anything?"

"No, thanks." Then, with an edge, he said, "This is very important."

"Yes. You've said that, and that's the message I conveyed to Brother Gabriel."

Which was in no way an apology or an explanation for the wait. It was another fifteen minutes before the massive gilded double doors opened and Brother Gabriel emerged from his bedroom.

He was wearing a bathrobe, although it was fancier than any Ritchey had ever seen, even in catalogues. It was made of silk. The belt Brother Gabriel was tying around his slender waist had long fringe dangling off the ends.

"Good evening, Sheriff Ritchey."

Forgetting his pique, Ritchey shot to his feet and nervously threaded the brim of his hat through his fingers. "How are you, Brother Gabriel?"

"Extremely well, thank you. I'm having a brandy. Would you like one?"

"I'm on duty."

"Of course. Something else?"

"No, thank you."

His feet and legs were bare. They were tanned and muscled, beautiful feet and legs for a man. Ritchey stared at them as the preacher unselfconsciously crossed the room. The silk robe didn't conceal much. Ritchey tried not to notice the obvious bulge of his sex or the crack between his buttocks when his back was to him. The man was as naked as a jaybird underneath that robe, but his immodesty astonished Ritchey more than it offended him.

Brother Gabriel took the snifter of brandy from Hancock, who'd had it ready for him and carried it to his desk. He sat down behind it and indolently crossed one long leg over the other. "You dragged me from my bed, Sheriff Ritchey, so I hope this is as urgent as you let on."

"I didn't think you'd be in bed this early. I apologize for waking you up."

"You didn't. I was in bed, but I wasn't

sleeping. Now what couldn't wait until morning?"

Ritchey's face was hot with embarrassment. "I wouldn't have bothered you, only I didn't think this should keep till morning."

Brother Gabriel took a sip of brandy, savoring it for several seconds before swallowing. "That was the agreement we reached seven years ago, wasn't it? You'll have the job of sheriff for as long as you want it. In exchange, I receive firsthand information on any matter that should arise concerning me or the ministry."

"Yes, sir, that was the agreement. I'm upholding my end of it."

"So, what's of concern this time?"

"The same as last time."

Brother Gabriel shot Mr. Hancock a quick glance. The assistant left the elaborate computer setup and moved to stand at the edge of Brother Gabriel's desk, apparently deeming Ritchey's business more important than what he'd been working on.

Hancock made the sheriff even more jittery than Brother Gabriel did, if that was possible. How could you trust a man who wore a flower in his lapel? The only other man in Lamesa County who did was the undertaker. Associating the two made Ritchey uneasy.

"I assume you're referring to the murder of the young woman in Dallas," Brother Gabriel said, returning his attention to the reason for the visit.

"Unfortunately."

"You spoke to the investigating officer?"

"Just as you told me to. Soon as I got back to my office the other day."

"You conveyed to him my regrets that a man claiming to be a follower of mine had been involved?"

"I repeated your words verbatim."

"You reported back to Mr. Hancock that the detective was satisfied with your explanation and that the case had been closed."

"That's what I was told." He stopped fiddling with his hat and set it on his knee. "Then this afternoon I had a visit from that homicide detective, Lawson. He had an FBI agent with him."

"Special Agent Tobias."

Taken aback, Ritchey glanced quizzically at Hancock. The man could have been carved from marble. Turning back to Brother Gabriel, the sheriff asked, "How'd you know?"

"Because he made an appointment with me for tomorrow. You don't see me in a panic, do you? Your urgency was uncalled for, and you've interrupted my evening for nothing."

"They came here looking for the murder victim's twin."

"Melina Lloyd," Brother Gabriel said blandly.

Ritchey was surprised to learn that Brother Gabriel knew about her, too. As though reading his thoughts, the preacher added, "You aren't my only source of information, Sheriff Ritchey."

"No, sir. Apparently not."

"Now, what about Ms. Lloyd? What did Tobias tell you?"

"He figures she's on her way here and that she might try something crazy. Get revenge, something like that."

Brother Gabriel chuckled. "Revenge? On me? What for? Surely she doesn't hold me responsible for what a madman did to her sister."

"She's been turning over a lot of rocks in Dallas hunting for answers. It appears that Dale Gordon didn't pick Gillian Lloyd at random. He knew her through an infertility

clinic where she'd been artificially inseminated. And last night Gillian Lloyd's fiancé
was shot and killed. To Tobias it looks like a
professional job. Melina Lloyd is shook up
about it all and thinks the answer lies in you,
or with the ministry, because both Gordon
and Hennings, the fiancé, had connections
to it."

Brother Gabriel took several moments to
digest all this. His long fingers stroked the
sides of his cut-crystal snifter. Finally he
said, "I'm curious as to why the FBI came to
you first. If Tobias honestly thinks this
woman is out to get me for her own illogical
reasons, why didn't he come directly to me
with the warning?"

"Because . . ." Ritchey had dreaded this
part of the meeting, and now that it was
here, he felt himself sweating under his
arms and around his testicles. He cleared
his throat, but his voice still sounded thin.
"Because he thinks her deductions may be
right."

Another long silence ensued. Brother
Gabriel didn't move or show any outward
signs of distress. Only the cold glint in his
eyes revealed that he was experiencing
some inner turmoil, and Ritchey figured it

was rage. Millions of followers regarded him as a saint, a prophet, a savior. Allegations that he might be involved in several murders hadn't set well.

"Tobias said that?"

Ritchey felt it was safe to resume breathing. "Not directly. But he asked a lot of leading questions. It was easy to tell what he was getting at."

Brother Gabriel propped his elbow on the padded arm of his chair, cupped his chin with his hand, and laid his index finger along his cheek. He was waiting, listening, and Ritchey took his cue. He repeated his conversation with Lawson and Tobias word for word.

When he finished, he wet his lips anxiously. "I have to tell you, Brother Gabriel, with all due respect, that I'm a little nervous when it comes to the FBI."

The preacher signaled his assistant to refill the snifter. Ritchey waited while Mr. Hancock retrieved the decanter, then watched the golden liquid trickle from decanter to snifter. It was so expertly poured, it didn't even splash. Brother Gabriel rolled the snifter between his palms to warm the brandy.

"What exactly do you mean by that statement, Sheriff Ritchey? About being nervous when it comes to the FBI."

"Well . . . what I mean is . . . that I can't go too far out on a limb without risk to myself. I can't be as . . . as vague with government agents as I've been with some other people who've come snooping around and asking questions about life inside the compound here."

Brother Gabriel held the snifter up to the desk lamp and appreciated the color of the brandy with the light shining through it. "In other words, your loyalty to me would be tested."

"No. No, sir. You've got my loyalty. You know that. But . . ." He squirmed beneath Brother Gabriel's searing gaze.

"But what?"

"But we're talking the Federal Bureau of Investigation here. Those guys don't mess around. If they thought I was protecting . . . What I'm saying is, if push comes to shove, I'd have to protect my own interests. I'm sure you understand that."

Brother Gabriel smiled. "Of course I do. I understand that very well. Because I have my own interests to protect." He looked over at Hancock, who immediately responded to a silent order. He crossed the room and entered Brother Gabriel's chamber through the golden double doors.

"Tell me about Tobias," Brother Gabriel said conversationally. "Is he a smart fellow or a dullard?"

"Very smart, I'd say. Soft-spoken. Observant. Snazzy dresser."

"And Lawson?"

"Looks and acts like a retired boxer. Not as refined as Tobias."

Smiling complacently, the preacher stroked his chin. "I'll bet they're fit to be tied, wondering where Melina Lloyd will pop up."

"They seemed anxious about her, all right. I've got my deputies checking every motel in the county to see if she checks in anywhere."

"She's incredibly bright. She'll be in the last place you'd expect. Did Tobias and Lawson mention Colonel Hart?"

Ritchey shook his head. "Who's that?"

"Aw, Mary," Brother Gabriel said. His gaze had moved to a spot beyond Ritchey's shoulder. "Come here, sweetheart."

CHAPTER 36

Turning, Sheriff Ritchey recognized her instantly—the same girl he'd seen earlier in the week. It was clear that she'd come straight from Brother Gabriel's bed. Also evident was that she was the reason the preacher had retired so early this evening. Her dark curly hair was tousled, her cheeks flushed. Her robe was white, much plainer than the one Brother Gabriel was wearing, but it was apparent that she was just as naked as he underneath.

The robe made her pregnancy more obvious than it had been in the school uniform she was wearing when he was last here. Her breasts were heavy. Her stomach was so stretched that her navel was distended and made an impression against the cloth.

Brother Gabriel drew her down onto his lap. "You see why I was reluctant to leave my bed tonight, Sheriff."

Ritchey couldn't respond. Not even a nod. The girl's lewd appearance and what it suggested appalled him. He wanted to bolt. He desperately wanted to cling to his illusions about Brother Gabriel. He didn't want to be here, didn't want to experience this total destruction of his self-delusion.

Brother Gabriel stroked the girl's rosy cheek. "Because Mary came to me when she was so young, I was able to train her properly. It's paid off for both of us. Hasn't it, Mary?"

"Yes, Brother Gabriel."

"Actually, she got a little upset with me tonight." Playfully he tapped her sulky lips. "I had to be very careful with her, very gentle, because the pregnancy is so far advanced. Nothing must endanger the child. Isn't that right, Mary?" He smiled beatifically at the girl. "Of course, Mary wasn't her original name. I gave her the name Mary after she came to the Temple. What was your name before that?"

She raised her shoulders.

"Mr. Hancock, do you remember?"

"Oleta."

"Oleta?" Brother Gabriel barked an ugly laugh. "A hillbilly name. An unpleasant reminder of my youth. No wonder I changed it to something more fitting." He played with one of the girl's dark curls, then his stroking fingers moved down to her chest. "Can you imagine what a lovely sight it'll be to watch the baby suck at these breasts?"

Ritchey was incapable of speaking. His hat had fallen to the floor, but he hadn't retrieved it because he hadn't even noticed. With rising revulsion, he watched Gabriel fondle the girl. Blindly obedient, she never protested or showed any sense of shame. In fact, she purred like a kitten. He and Mr. Hancock might just as well not have been there. She had acknowledged neither of them, centering all her attention on Brother Gabriel.

"Of course, there is a drawback to Mary's being here for so long," Brother Gabriel remarked casually. "Her life in the Temple would be misunderstood by the unenlightened. They would revile her. Who would comprehend the life she's had here? I look at her and see a sacred vessel that should be cherished and honored.

"But enemies of the ministry would see her in a totally different light. They would call her ugly names. Horrible things would be said of her. After being here for so long, she would be an outcast anywhere else." He interrupted his preoccupation with Mary's engorged breast to look across his desk at Ritchey. "Would you have this lovely girl thrown to the wolves? Think about that the next time you're stricken with conscience or feel an obligation to assist the FBI."

He splayed his hand over the girl's stomach and caressed it affectionately, but his eyes never drifted off Ritchey. "You said you must protect your interests. I promise you, Sheriff, that I shall protect mine."

Then he tilted Mary's chin up and kissed her passionately. The girl's tongue darted in and out of the man's mouth. Her small hand disappeared between the folds of his silk robe and began to caress him vigorously.

Chuckling, Brother Gabriel removed her hand and kissed it. "Off you go, now. Back to bed. I'll be in momentarily. Tell the sheriff bye-bye, then scoot."

She slid off Brother Gabriel's lap. "Bye-bye, Sheriff," she repeated mechanically. Then she turned and walked back into the bedroom.

Ritchey was in the grip of nausea. He had broken a cold, clammy sweat, and his head was loudly buzzing. He was thoroughly revolted but incapable of registering his revulsion. And even if he were inclined to, the preacher obviously didn't give a whit about his opinion. If he had, he wouldn't have flaunted his sexual relationship with the girl.

Brother Gabriel, watching her go, sighed. "Such an adorable child. Such a sweet disposition. And such a talent for fellatio." He then rubbed his hands together briskly. "Now, what were we talking about? Oh, yes. The pesky Melina Lloyd. Let me assure you, Sheriff Ritchey, that there's nothing for you to fear on that account. As we speak, that problem is being resolved."

The car topped the rise, then decelerated and coasted down the hill.

Dexter Longtree had been waiting and

watching. Melina and Hart had feared that the transceiver would bring the bad men here. Apparently they had arrived. Only an occasional vehicle traveled this lonely stretch of road after dark. And who coasted downhill with their headlights off?

The Army had sent Longtree to Vietnam when it was still referred to as a conflict and battles were called skirmishes. He'd seen combat and, although he deplored the idea of war, he had been a good soldier. A decade later, he'd fought stateside in a different kind of battle, participating in American Indian Movement demonstrations against the federal government. He'd been arrested and jailed many times for his participation in protests that had started out peacefully before turning ugly.

Now he felt the familiar adrenaline boost he'd felt during battle, either in the jungles of Southeast Asia or in the halls of U.S. government buildings. It wasn't fear. He was too old to fear death. He didn't want to embrace it, particularly. But when it came, he wouldn't resist overmuch. Death was only a passing, not an ending. Besides, as he had told Melina, his destiny wasn't in the hands of hired killers.

His heartbeat increased slightly. He had missed this tingling sense of anticipation, he realized now. Old men were rarely allowed to take part in contests of valor. Even if one proved to be a good strategist, he was relegated to the role of advisor. Hand-to-hand combat was reserved for the younger and stronger. It felt good to be on the battlefield again. These men may have high-tech equipment. They may have the razor-sharp instincts and skills required to be professional assassins.

But he was an Indian. Sometimes it really paid to think like one.

The car slowed down as it approached his gate, then drove past. "Good tactic," he murmured.

The car went approximately a quarter mile past his gate before it came to a stop. Longtree could no longer see it, but he heard the motor die. There was no wind tonight to mask the sound. But even if it had been blowing a gale, it wouldn't have mattered. He had lived on this property all his life. He knew the night sounds and could distinguish them.

He waited with the patience of eroding rock. He was gifted with excellent night vision, a definite asset on a night when the moon was a mere sliver. In a matter of minutes, he saw shadows shift near his gate. He focused sharply and made out two men. They hesitated, then ran in a crouch, darting from shadow to shadow to conceal their approach to the house. Longtree had left every light inside burning. The cold electric light coming through the windows in the living room indicated that the TV was on. He could hear the muffled sound track of a medical drama.

But these men wouldn't be going to the house. Not at first. Not if their tracking device was as sophisticated as Hart suspected it was. They would be looking for Melina in the shed about two hundred yards beyond the house.

As Longtree watched from his hiding place, they conferred quietly in the shadow of a water trough just inside the horse corral, then moved off in the direction of the shed where he'd left the transceiver. Thoughtfully, he'd left a lantern burning inside the shed to help them locate it in the darkness.

They moved within ten yards of him, never knowing he was there, but he got a better look at them. One was black, the other white. These were the men. When they were well past him, he crept from his hiding place behind the cord of firewood and set out after them.

Because of their stealth, it took them almost five minutes to cover the distance from the house to the shed. Longtree was short of breath by the time he reached the spot he'd chosen earlier for his vantage point. But as he leaned against the boulder, he'd never felt more alive. He breathed deeply but quietly.

He watched the two men flatten themselves against the exterior walls of the shed and scoot along them until they were flanking the door. At a signal from one, the other kicked open the door, then, with pistols in hand, they barged inside.

Their surprised exclamations and shouted profanities filled the quiet night. They had expected to find Melina Lloyd and Christopher Hart inside the shed—not ripe piles of manure that Longtree kept stored there before selling it for fertilizer.

Choking and gagging, trying to stamp the manure off their shoes, they stumbled back outside, where they were leapt upon by the men who'd been lying flat on the roof of the shed, waiting for the opportunity to pounce.

The black man managed to get off a few aimless rounds from his semiautomatic handgun before he was knocked to the ground by a young man emitting a blood-curdling yell that startled even Longtree. Another fired his rifle into the night sky as he landed hard on the white man.

The boys were having fun.

Once the two were disarmed, they were jerked upright. Their hands were cuffed behind their backs and they were shoved forward. A lance sailed out of the darkness and found earth inches away from their feet. It swayed menacingly before coming to rest.

"Holy shit," the white man said in a quavering voice.

"Shut up," ordered the black man.

Longtree stepped from behind his boulder and strode forward. He'd put on his ceremonial war bonnet. Just for show. Just for the hell of it. As he approached, he saw that the intimidation had worked. Even the black man had lost some bravado.

Longtree stood before the pair, saying nothing for an impossibly long time. Eventually the black man guffawed. "Who the fuck're you supposed to be, Geronimo?"

One of the boys jabbed him in the kidney with the stock of his rifle, not hard enough to do any real damage, but hard enough to get his attention and let him know that they would tolerate no disrespect.

Longtree spoke to them in his native tongue. He repeated the sentence three times.

"What's he saying?" the white one asked his partner in a high-pitched, frantic whisper. "What's he saying?"

Longtree glanced down at their soiled shoes. "I said, 'You're in deep shit.'"

Most of the children in the dormitory were already asleep, but Brother Gabriel enjoyed touring the facility when they were in bed. Tonight he had elected to visit the nursery. Being with Mary, delighting in her ripe body, had put him in the mood to make contact with his babies.

The nursery was as sterile as a science laboratory, but nothing had been spared to make it a cozy, comfortable environment. The temperature and humidity were con-

stantly regulated. Brightly colored prints il-
lustrating nursery rhymes decorated the
walls. Mobiles and other interactive toys
were attached to the cribs. Classical music
wafted from hidden speakers. He had entrusted the children's mental development
to experts who knew best how to stimulate
their young minds and increase their learning capacities.

But he personally oversaw every aspect of
it and was pleased to note that occasionally
the music was interrupted by his voice.
Tapes were played of him reading a nursery
rhyme or singing a lullaby. A brilliant touch,
he thought. He wanted each baby to grow
up with his voice being an integral part of its
subconscious.

Unfortunately, despite his best planning
and the meticulous screening process each
mother was put through, an occasional genetic deficiency would manifest itself in a
child who proved to be not as brilliant or
physically superior as hoped.

Coincidentally, those children also had a
propensity to contract pneumonia, to which
all had tragically succumbed.

But he didn't dwell on those misfortunes
any more than he mourned the deaths of

Dale Gordon or Jem Hennings. When someone's usefulness to him had expired, he expunged that person from his mind.

He moved from crib to crib, dispensing love and caring to each child. Actually, he chose to tour the nursery when he was certain that most of the babies would be asleep. He liked them best when they were clean and silent and he wasn't being subjected to dirty diapers or spit-up or wailing for no logical reason.

He enjoyed watching them while they slept. Moving up and down the rows of cribs, he lovingly touched each one, reminding himself of the Sistine Chapel ceiling fresco that depicted God extending his hand to his most awesome creation, Adam.

He liked to feel the softness of their baby skin, to compare the size of his hand to their small bodies, and to envision them growing into youths with strong limbs and handsome faces.

He liked thinking of them growing up to be reproductions of him.

When he came to an empty crib, he turned to the attendant nurse, who'd been hovering ever since he came in. "It's for Mary's baby," Dorothy Pugh explained in a reverential tone. "She's having a girl. She's due in two weeks."

"So I hear."

"This crib is ready for the baby whenever she's delivered."

Dorothy Pugh had been serving as a nurse for a South Dakota school district when Brother Gabriel heard of her devotion to his ministry. Her mission work was impressive; she'd brought in numerous converts. He contacted her and offered to finance her advanced training in neonatal care. She'd leapt at the chance to live and work at the Temple. After her training, when she heard that her job would be overseeing the care of the babies born to the Program, her gratitude had been so effusive it had embarrassed him. At least to the others present he had pretended it had.

Her dedication to the Program was unquestioned. He felt comfortable leaving his children in her care until they graduated to the next level, joining those who could crawl and toddle.

"I want to be notified as soon as Mary goes into labor."

"Of course, Brother Gabriel."

"And should you have to evacuate the children's dormitory in a hurry—"

"We've rehearsed many times, Brother Gabriel. If ever our enemies threatened to invade us, the children could be relocated immediately."

"You're doing an excellent job." He stroked her cheek. She blushed, her eyes radiating naked adoration and making her look prettier than she actually was. She was too old for the Program, but perhaps he should reward her loyalty and thereby instill even more. He must remember to have Mr. Hancock send for her one evening soon. She would be desperately anxious to please him. The thought made him smile.

"Brother Gabriel." Mr. Hancock had approached in his usual unobtrusive manner. "Forgive me. I know you dislike having your rare time with the children interrupted, but I thought this was important."

Reading the strain in Mr. Hancock's voice, all thoughts of an erotic evening with the nurse vanished. He motioned his assistant out into the corridor. During the day, the wide hallway was bright with sunlight streaming in through the ceiling skylight. It echoed with the sounds of children and the voices of the staff who nurtured their bodies as well as their minds. Now it was dim and deserted.

Mr. Hancock had a two-way radio in his hand. "Was it your understanding that Sheriff Ritchey was leaving the compound?"

"Of course. I gave him his marching orders. He's supposed to be keeping an eye on Tobias and Lawson, as well as watching for Melina Lloyd and Hart to show up." Joshua had already informed him that they were indeed on New Mexican soil. He was awaiting word of their containment and wondered now what was taking Joshua and his partner so long.

Mr. Hancock frowned. "The sheriff's patrol car is still in the parking area."

"But he left at least an hour ago."

"He left your quarters. He never passed the guard at the lobby desk."

"Then where is he?"

"Security guards are checking all the men's rooms."

"Men's rooms?" Brother Gabriel exclaimed with increasing acrimony. "It doesn't require an hour to take a leak. Besides, there are cameras in all of them.

They could tell at a glance if he's using a men's room."

"I'm sure there's nothing to worry about."

"Of course there's something to worry about," he snapped. "What's the matter with you, Hancock?"

"All I'm saying is that—"

"An armed man is unaccounted for."

He wasn't afraid of Ritchey. The man was a coward, a snail. He had no backbone whatsoever. He wouldn't know the meaning of pride if it bit him in the ass, and he had proven himself corruptible when he accepted Brother Gabriel's deal. But he had picked a damned inconvenient time to pull a disappearing act when he had important duties to attend to.

"I want him found."

"Yes, sir." Hancock motioned two guards forward. "Just as a precaution, I've ordered these men to stay with you and not to let you out of their sight."

"That's not necessary."

"Please, Brother Gabriel. Indulge me."

"Oh, all right," he agreed impatiently.

He headed back toward his private quarters with the two burly guards flanking him. He was in a thunderous mood. Alvin

Medford Conway was on the brink of achieving greatness. He was going to make history. His name would be immortalized, and he didn't have to be martyred to achieve it.

An entity of his stature shouldn't have to be worrying about crackpots with grudges against him. He was beyond the Melina Lloyds of the world. Even homicide detectives and FBI agents and astronauts were pissants, flyspecks, compared to him and what he would mean to the future of mankind.

Sheriff Max Ritchey was so low on the food chain as to be negligible. But he had managed to spoil Brother Gabriel's evening, and that was untenable.

CHAPTER 37

They hadn't made their deadline to reach Lamesa before dark, but there wasn't that much to see. Downtown was comprised of a few commercial buildings strung like laundry on a clothesline along either side of the state highway.

Chief noticed that among them were the requisite bank, post office, supermarket, and a pharmacy that doubled as a barbershop. A mobile home had been converted into the public library. The ladies of Lamesa could get their hair and nails done at Marta's, who also sold Indian fry bread out of her kitchen. There was one motel, where a blinking red neon sign informed travelers of a vacancy. This evening only one car was in the parking lot.

The public school campus, which served grades K through twelve, occupied an acre on the outskirts of town. Small clusters of houses, scattered intermittently here and there, constituted the residential areas.

"Have you ever had fry bread, Melina?"

"What is it?"

"Delicious. Which reminds me how hungry I am." Without even consulting her, he stopped at a carry-out food stand. The structure was barely wide enough to accommodate a stove, but it advertised burgers, chicken, and tacos. "Longtree's breakfast has worn off."

Melina nodded, but he could tell that her mind wasn't on food. She was focused on the mountain that loomed out of the desert on the west side of town. At its peak was their destination, the Temple.

Chief tried to shake off a feeling of foreboding and asked Melina what she wanted to eat. "Anything's fine."

He got out and walked up to the window.

Not surprisingly, it was a one-man shop. The cashier who took his order also deep-fried breaded chicken strips and sliced potatoes, then served them to Chief through the window. They ate in the cab of the pickup, from which they had an unrestricted view of the mountain.

"Ketchup? Salt?" He offered Melina pillows of each.

"Thanks."

Chief was using his straw to break up the ice in his drinking cup, when it squeaked against the plastic lid. It was a rude sound that caused him to laugh.

"What?" she asked.

"Nothing. Guy humor."

"Are you laughing because it sounded like a fart?"

"Melina, such language! I'm shocked."

"You? NASA's poet laureate of vulgarities and obscenities?"

He grinned. "I like that you're not too prissy. You can appreciate a man for behaving like a man."

"Like a boy, you mean."

He grinned wider. "You'd be fun to go on a date with."

"What?"

"A date. You know, dinner. In a restaurant."

"Oh."

Each was suddenly struck by the absurdity that they'd been as intimate as two people can be, but they'd never been on a date. That was a territory best left unexplored.

She must have thought so, too, because she kept the mood light. "I remember restaurants," she said as she licked ketchup off her fingers. "I even know how to use cutlery."

"So do I. On a good day." They smiled at each other.

But the mountain loomed. Despite their attempt at banal conversation, the mountain was a presence they couldn't ignore for any appreciable amount of time. Even from a couple miles away, the compound on the crest seemed to be aglow with security lighting.

Chief hated to admit even to himself how daunting it was. He and Melina had been prepared for the Temple of Brother Gabriel to be imposing, but now that they were actually here in its shadow, he wondered how in hell they would ever breach the security. Whether they succeeded or failed, there would be serious consequences.

Strangely, before going to Dallas, he'd had a cavalier attitude toward his postretirement future. But now, having met Longtree and seen how he lived, having listened to the man's quiet but persuasive convictions, he felt an urgency to do something quickly to improve the lives of the Native Americans who were still ensnared by poverty and despair.

He'd never been passionate about his Indian heritage. Longtree had changed his attitude, infusing him with a spirit of kinship. Or had it been there all along, lying dormant while he denied it, waiting for him to acknowledge and accept it?

And then there was Melina.

What about Melina?

It was fair to say he was conflicted. Was he attracted to her solely because she was Gillian's double? He had thought so. For a time. Now he was no longer sure that's all there was to it. He wanted to be with her again. He wanted to discover what he'd missed by not kissing her mouth. But how could he desire her and still claim to have fallen in love with Gillian? And he had. That was indisputable.

What a mess. All he knew for certain was that when it came to his emotional state of being, he was fucked up—to put it in the vernacular. He was accustomed to handling problems in a strictly pragmatic manner. You had a problem, you got to the source and solved the problem. Easy. No emotional element to consider. Not so this problem.

But before he could confront his future or his emotional condition, he had to deal with Brother Gabriel, who lived in a veritable fortress. "NASA doesn't throw that much light on the shuttle during a night launch," he remarked as he tossed their debris into a trash bin, then turned the pickup around and headed back toward the center of town.

Even if he and Melina went through the proper channels and got an audience with the evangelist himself, they wouldn't be allowed to roam freely about the Temple, poking into corners and closets. They would see only what Brother Gabriel wanted them to see. And if they went up there without the sheriff's sanction and managed to sneak past security . . .

He could envision the world's headlines now: ASTRONAUT ARRESTED FOR TRESPASSING. NASA DISCLAIMS DEEDS OF FORMER COMMANDER. SHUTTLE PILOT'S MENTAL STABILITY IN QUESTION.

That's how they would read, and they would be right. This was nuts. It wasn't too late to back out. He could call Tobias and let the feds take over from here. He could disassociate himself.

Screw that, he thought, dismissing the idea before it was fully formed. No. Hell, no. He was committed. He was going to see this through.

The sheriff's office, which they'd spotted earlier on the main drag, was a freestanding adobe building. Chief wheeled the pickup into one of several parking slots and cut the engine. "Now what?"

Melina drew a deep breath. "I don't know. I guess we should just go in, spill our guts, and see what kind of reaction we get from him."

"That's your plan?"

"Do you have a better one?"

He pushed open the door and stepped out. He went around to help her from the cab, but she was already standing beside the truck, chafing her arms. The tempera-

ture was much colder at this higher eleva-
tion than it had been at Longtree's property.

"Want my jacket back?" he offered.

"I'll be fine inside."

Scotch-taped to the office door was a
handwritten note from the sheriff informing
anyone who came looking for him that he
would be back shortly. He had thoughtfully
jotted down the time he left. Chief glanced
at his wristwatch. "He's stretching the
'shortly' part. He's been gone almost three
hours."

"What kind of sheriff leaves his office unattended?" Through the window they could
see that no one was inside. "Doesn't he
have any deputies?"

"They could be out on patrol, too."

Clearly Melina was annoyed by this unex-
pected delay. "I guess we have no choice
but to go inside and wait."

The door was unlocked. They went inside.
The sheriff had apparently anticipated the
night to turn chilly because he'd left the
central heating on. "Well, you won't be cold.
That's for damn sure." Chief shrugged off
his jacket and hung it on a peg near the
door. "You could bake cookies in here."

The office was small and square, with a

hallway extending from the center of the back wall. It had the usual wanted posters tacked to a bulletin board. A large detailed map of the county covered almost one whole wall. There were three tall filing cabinets, but from the appearance of Ritchey's desk, the office generated little paperwork. The top of his desk was inordinately neat.

Chief remarked on this atypical tidiness to Melina, but when he turned, she wasn't there. She had wandered down the hallway and was exploring the other rooms. "What's back there?" he called.

"A small room with a coffeepot, carelessly left on. Rest rooms."

Then a scream and, "Oh, no!"

Chief charged into the hallway, banging his elbow on the doorjamb as he went through the opening. It hurt like hell, then caused his forearm and hand to go partially numb, but it didn't slow him down. His long stride covered the length of the hallway within seconds, so that when he pulled up short in front of the single jail cell, his boots skidded on the tile floor.

Melina was crouched on the floor just inside the cell. She was holding something close to her chest and keening noisily.

"What the hell?" He knelt down beside her and placed his arm around her. "Melina?"

"Oh, Chief, Chief," she sobbed. "I'm so sorry."

Then she flung her arm wide and swung it toward his head. Whatever she'd been holding connected with the spot on his cheekbone where the skin was just now closing over the original wound. He fell back, landing hard on his ass, legs spread. He pressed his palm against his cheek, which was exploding with pain, and roared, *"Fuck!"*

Melina surged to her feet and ran through the cell door, dragging it closed behind her. It slammed and locked with a loud metallic clang that echoed in the empty building. She flattened her back against the opposite wall and dropped her weapon—a brass paperweight in the shape of New Mexico, which she must have taken from the sheriff's desk.

Sparklers were dancing behind his eyeballs, but Chief managed to pull himself to his feet. His face was bleeding, but he didn't even realize that until he gripped the bars of the cell and noticed that his right hand was red with blood.

"What the fuck are you doing?" he yelled.

She was breathing rapidly through parted lips. Her eyes were wide and unblinking as she stared at him with apparent horror over what she'd just done. "I'm going up there. T-to the Temple."

He shook the bars like a demented inmate. "Let me the hell out of here, Melina."

She shook her head no and began inching along the wall toward the exit door. "Together, they'll never let us in, Chief." She bit her lower lip, but the gesture couldn't contain her sob. "I'm sorry for hitting you. Oh, God, I'm sorry."

He gripped the bars tighter. "Melina—"

"No." She squeezed her eyes shut as though that would also close her ears to his pleas. "I need to do this alone. She was my twin. Revenge is up to me, and . . . and I don't want you to suffer the repercussions. There are sure to be some. You don't deserve that."

"Listen to me," he said in his most imperative commander's voice. "You'll get yourself killed if you go charging—"

"He won't hurt me. You, yes. But not me."

"You don't know that. Now let me out of here!"

"He won't hurt me," she repeated.

"What makes you so damn sure?"

She swallowed dryly, then turned and ran down the hallway, shouting over her shoulder, "I have a secret weapon."

Tobias was feeling the effects of the last couple days. If required, his body was conditioned to function on no more than a few hours' sleep. But the past two days had been exceptionally arduous. He was exhausted from the travel alone. Couple that with the complexities of this case—and maybe the scotch he'd drunk earlier—and it was no wonder that he was having trouble keeping his eyes open.

This case was so damned multilayered. The outer skin had been the murder of Gillian Lloyd. The next layer had been Gordon's suicide, the next the attack on Melina. Another, Linda Croft's murder. Followed by the discovery of Jem Hennings's duplicity and his eventual assassination.

Tobias strongly suspected that once all the layers had been peeled away, he would find Brother Gabriel at the core. And if even a few of their conjectures about him proved to be true, this case would have a ripple effect on the scale of a tidal wave.

An hour earlier, he had dutifully pulled Gillian Lloyd's murder case file onto his lap and opened it. But his eyes could barely remain focused, and several times he'd caught himself nodding off.

If he knew what he was looking for, it would be like going on a treasure hunt. He'd be motivated by knowing that a search would result in a prize. Instead, he wasn't even sure there was a treasure to be found. Chances were very good that none existed, that there wasn't a clue that had gone undetected. Surely either Lawson or he would have found it by now.

Desultorily, he flipped through the tabs that separated the particulars of the case into categories and, for the umpteenth time, reviewed the facts he already knew.

Crime scene.

Dale Gordon's background and personality profile.

Statements from Melina, Christopher Hart, Jem Hennings, and the neighbor who'd discovered the body.

The autopsy report.

Information on the Waters Clinic.

He had to give the national chain credit for being so cooperative, from the chairman of the company on down. Personnel were assisting Agent Patterson to locate sperm donors and urging them to facilitate the investigation in lieu of being subpoenaed. The staff at the clinic seemed genuinely incredulous and outraged by Dale Gordon's misconduct. Tobias believed that the establishment's involvement was purely innocent.

He leaned back against the headboard and closed his eyes. The TV was tuned to a *Cheers* rerun. He listened to the dialogue, smiling at something that Sam said to Woody. But soon, even the snappy comedy writing couldn't keep him awake. His head listed to one side. His conscious mind gradually shut down its circuit board. He drifted toward unconsciousness.

And in that free-falling state of mind, something sparked. Something he'd recently read.

He was jerked awake by the alarming realization that if he didn't grab hold of that flicker of a thought now, it would burn out.

It had been like the blink of a firefly on a very dark night. There one second, gone the next, as though it were a trick of the eyes and had never been there at all. Almost too elusive to have been real.

Yet he knew that it had been there, and that it had been real, and that it was important. Vitally. What was it? What was it?

"Think, dammit." He closed his eyes tightly and pinched the bridge of his nose so hard it hurt. "Think."

Then suddenly it flickered again and burned brighter, longer. He sat up and frantically flipped through the tabs in the notebook until he came to the one he was looking for.

Rapidly he scanned the top sheet, then nearly ripped it from the silver rings of the binder in his haste to leaf to the second page. He missed the notation the first time, retraced the path his eyes had taken, stopped, read. Reread.

He flopped back against the headboard and stared blankly at the TV set. Carla said something snide to Diane, but the catty remark didn't register with Tobias. Methodically he assimilated this tiny but monumental fact, which up till now had been obscured by seemingly more important information.

When his mind finally made sense of it, he bolted from the bed, yanked open the door, and raced down the motel breezeway toward Lawson's room.

CHAPTER | 3 8

When the road became so steep as to be unsafe, it resorted to switchbacks that snaked up the mountainside. She took the curves carefully. The road was dark and narrow, made more hazardous by the nervous sweat keeping her palms slippery on the steering wheel. She was also unfamiliar with the truck. It seemed as bulky and large as a tank, not nearly as easy to drive as her car.

Thankfully Chief had left the keys to the pickup in the pocket of his jacket. She'd snatched it from the peg near the door as she'd dashed out. It turned her stomach to think of how she must have hurt him. She could still feel the impact of the paperweight against his cheekbone, could feel again his skin splitting open.

But even striking him, she knew, wouldn't have hurt him as much as her tricking him. It had been a horrible thing to do, but necessary to protect him. She didn't know how this night would end, but she had to be prepared for the worst. The Lloyd twins had inflicted enough damage on Christopher Hart. She wouldn't be responsible for inflicting any more.

She came upon the gate before she expected it, which was probably a good thing. If she'd seen it beforehand and had had time to reflect on what she was about to do, she might even then have chickened out, despite her resolve.

As it was, she rounded a bend and was required to brake immediately or risk crashing into the gate, which was illuminated by floodlights. Inside the gatehouse she saw a man in a dark blue uniform with Brother Gabriel's ministry logo embroidered in gold on the breast pocket. He stepped out and approached the pickup. She rolled down the window.

"Peace and love," he said.

The greeting sounded idiotic, since he was armed and the gate and adjoining fence were topped with concertina wire. The irony seemed to have escaped him. "Can I help you, ma'am?"

"I'm here to see Brother Gabriel."

He smiled indulgently. Apparently it wasn't unusual for a devotee to arrive unannounced asking for an audience with the holy man.

"Brother Gabriel has retired for the night. You can hear a taped message from him by calling 1-800-—"

"Tell him Melina Lloyd is here to see him."

"I'm sorry, ma'am, but—"

"If you don't call immediately and inform him that I'm here, you won't have a job tomorrow. It would be a dreadful misjudgment that might also cost you your position in the new world order. If I were you, I'd risk disturbing him before I'd gamble with my place in the hereafter."

His complacent smile turned a little sickly. He retreated to the gatehouse, where she watched him lift a receiver and speak into it.

He waited, keeping his eyes trained on her. Eventually he seemed to snap to attention. He spoke into the receiver again, then bobbed his head and hung up.

Stiffly, and with an air of authority, he said, "You'll have to leave the pickup here."

Was Brother Gabriel afraid of car bombs? If he was smart, he would be. Especially if it got out that he was sabotaging infertility clinics by using his sperm in place of designated donor sperm.

She had arrived at that conclusion on the drive from Longtree's place to Lamesa. She'd had over a hundred miles to think about it, and that was the only logical conclusion. Sickening but logical.

If Brother Gabriel was creating a "new world order," he wouldn't want a physically unattractive, emotionally unstable, socially outcast individual like Dale Gordon fathering its future denizens. Jem was sterile. They, and no doubt others like them, had been brainwashed to believe in his twisted doctrine and were dedicated to bringing it about. They weren't instigators, they were facilitators.

Brother Gabriel was the egomaniac. It was he who had the god complex. Using handpicked women, he was propagating himself. At least he had been up till now. His nefarious enterprise stopped tonight.

She climbed out of the pickup.

"The key stays with me."

She dropped the key ring into the guard's extended hand. "Do I go the rest of the way on foot?"

"Someone's coming to take you up."

She waited in front of the gate. The guard didn't invite her inside the gatehouse, which didn't surprise her. He was probably miffed because she'd shown him up. He had egg on his face.

She'd slipped on Chief's leather jacket, but it was even colder up here on the mountaintop than it had been in town. She hugged her elbows while she waited on her transportation. Her teeth chattered, but she didn't know if that was because of the temperature or fear. A fear that increased when she saw headlights approaching the gate from the other side.

The electronic gate opened. But it wasn't her ride into the compound that drove through.

"Step back, please, ma'am," the guard ordered.

As soon as she was safely out of the way, three tour buses rolled through the gate and started down the mountain road. They weren't marked with any insignia. The windows were opaque. It was impossible to see who or what was inside, but it struck her as odd that they were leaving the compound at this time of night. "What are the buses for? Where are they going?"

The guard failed to answer and instead motioned her toward the gate. "There's your ride."

She hadn't seen the sedan's approach because of the buses. Now it was waiting on the other side of the gate, the back door standing open.

She walked through the gate and approached the car. As she did, a man leaned out of the open rear door. "Ms. Lloyd? Please get in."

His manner was neither friendly nor hostile, but neutral. Calling herself every kind of fool for going willingly into the lion's den, she slid into the back seat beside him.

"I'm Mr. Hancock, Brother Gabriel's personal assistant."

Two security guards were in the front seat. The driver turned the car around and headed up a curving road lined with aspens and evergreens. Nothing more was said. She was relieved not to have to make conversation because she knew her voice would quaver and give away her fear. Mr. Hancock's appearance wasn't particularly sinister—the carnation in his lapel was a dandy touch—but she mistrusted him instinctively and would be reluctant to turn her back to him.

The compound was unarguably impressive. It was pristinely maintained, architecturally magnificent, exceptional in every way. They pulled to a stop in front of the main building. The security guard seated in front of her alighted quickly to open her door and assist her from the back seat. She ignored his offered hand and got out unassisted.

"This way."

She followed Hancock up a flight of shallow steps to a wall of glass through which she could see a marble foyer.

"Password, please."

She jumped at the disembodied voice that boomed at them from hidden speakers.

"Gabriel's horn," said Hancock. Immediately the door was electronically unlocked. He pushed it open and motioned her through.

"You have a password?"

"Not always. Only when we feel it's necessary. If I'd been under any kind of duress, I would have given the code word for that, and the guard would have refused us entrance."

"You feel a password is necessary tonight?"

"We've had cause to take extra precautions. The number of guards on duty has been doubled."

Indeed. Armed, uniformed men were stationed at several points within the massive foyer. She wondered if she was the cause for the extra precautions. If not her, then what, or who? Tobias and Lawson? Had the compound been placed on alert because the FBI was asking questions about the ministry?

With so much security in evidence, she feared she would have to pass through a metal detector, but there were no more checkpoints between the door and the elevators. On the ride up, she asked Hancock how long he'd been in Brother Gabriel's employ.

"I don't remember when I wasn't in his service," was his oblique reply.

On the third floor, at the end of the corridor, was a set of double doors at least twenty feet tall. Hancock opened one and ushered her through. None of what she had seen beforehand had prepared her for Brother Gabriel's private quarters.

First she was struck by the amount of gilt. Royal blue velvet curtains had been drawn against what she supposed was a wall of windows. The fresco on the ceiling was borderline lewd. It was especially offensive since the messianic figure at its center bore a striking resemblance to the blond evangelist.

"Melina." Mr. Hancock held a chair for her.

"No, thank you."

"Is it all right if I call you Melina?"

"I don't give a damn what you call me."

"Would you care for something to drink?"

"Cut the crap, Mr. Hancock. I didn't come here to socialize. I came here to accuse this egomaniacal son of a bitch of murdering my sister."

"Delightful."

At the sound of the familiar voice, her impulse was to turn quickly. But rather than give him that satisfaction, she took her time coming around.

Brother Gabriel was moving toward her with the powerful grace of a tiger. He seemed to know the most flattering spot in the room because he stepped into a pool of mellow light cast by a camouflaged, recessed fixture in the frescoed ceiling. It poured a butter-colored light over him that only enhanced his own remarkable golden coloring.

"I expected you to be an exciting woman. One with a fiery spirit. Tremendous courage." His eyes moved over her in an unmistakably sexual appraisal. "You haven't disappointed me. Welcome, Melina, my dear."

He was the most gorgeous individual she'd ever laid eyes on.

For at least half an hour, Chief cursed everything—the jail cell, the woman who had locked him inside it, the throbbing pain in his cheek, his own stupid, goddamn gullibility.

He swore out loud as he paced from one side of the cell to the other, stamping impatiently, frequently returning to the bars, gripping them and shaking them furiously but futilely, shouting down the hallway unheard.

Finally he threw himself onto the hard, uncomfortable cot and forced himself to calm down. Having a temper tantrum wasn't going to get him anywhere. He had walked in space, for chrissake, flown three successful shuttle missions, commanded one. He was smart enough to think himself out of a jail cell in Nowheresville.

But his resources were limited. He couldn't squeeze through the bars. He couldn't dig out the floor because it was concrete. There was no window. Light fixture? Ceiling-mounted with a wire cage around it. Tinkering with that could easily result in electrocution, which was definitely a means of escape, but one he would rather avoid. Air-conditioning vent? It was a six-by-three-inch rectangle at best, although it was doing a hell of a job pumping hot air into the cell.

The heat was why he'd removed his jacket. In its pocket was the key to the pickup, which could possibly have been used to jimmy the lock or saw at the bars. He knew he'd probably seen too many movies in which jailbreak had been made to look ludicrously easy. He was grasping at straws. In any event, the point was moot. He didn't have his jacket. Consequently, he didn't have the key, or his cell phone, or the pistol—

Oh, shit. Melina had the pistol. She'd taken it with her to the Temple.

Thoughts of her and the danger she was placing herself in were enough to make him go stark-raving mad. Either she was the most courageous woman he'd ever had the privilege of knowing . . . or she was a complete imbecile with delusions of invincibility.

Was the pistol the secret weapon she had referred to? No doubt. What else could it be? But did she really think she could sneak a weapon into that compound? And if she did succeed in getting it in there, would she use it? Would she commit murder?

Revenge wouldn't fly as justifiable homicide. Not with most juries anyway. Especially if there was no concrete evidence connecting Dale Gordon to Brother Gabriel and therefore to Gillian's murder.

But he was becoming sidetracked. How the hell was he going to get out of here? He could shout and yell, but that would be a waste of breath and energy. The building stood alone and, as well as he remembered, it didn't have any neighbors within hearing distance.

Finally he resigned himself to being a captive. He was only squandering energy that he should conserve for when the sheriff returned and let him out. And where was that conscientious upholder of the law, anyway? He'd been away for almost four hours.

Muttering another litany of profanity, he placed his forearm across his eyes. He tried to ignore the persistent pain radiating from his cheekbone to all points inside his skull. Melina had been mortified by what she'd done. Her expression as she pressed herself against the wall and gaped at him through the bars of the cell had revealed the level of her disbelief. She had astounded even herself with her capacity for taking extreme measures. To get vengeance for Gillian, she was capable of doing what would otherwise be unthinkable, which wasn't a comforting thought considering her destination.

But she could be tender, too, he thought, remembering their lovemaking. He liked that she had made no secret of wanting him.

She hadn't played coy. She had been bold enough to touch him first. You had to admire a woman who could be that uninhibited without any sacrifice to her femininity.

He could still feel how her fingertips had glided over his face when they'd conducted that tentative exploration. When she touched his lips, he'd almost lost control. He'd almost lowered himself over her right then. But it had gotten even better when she touched his chest. She'd raised her head and flicked her tongue across . . .

"Dammit," he groaned. It had been great. Why did it have to end so unhappily, with so much tension between them?

He wondered: If he hadn't met Gillian first, if it had been Melina who'd escorted him that night, would the course of everything have been different? When they went for tacos, Melina would probably have said to Dale Gordon, "I'm sorry, you've obviously mistaken me for my sister Gillian." They would have laughed over the mistaken identity. Gordon wouldn't have freaked out, and Gillian would still be alive.

Would he have slept with Melina that night? Who knew? Maybe. Probably. Because the two of them were so damned much alike. The same characteristics that had attracted him to Gillian then, attracted him to Melina now. She continued to stoke his vivid memories of Gillian. Like today when she—

His train of thought came to an abrupt halt.

He rewound the recollection like a videotape in his mind. Hit play again. Closed his eyes. Watched the scene replay against his eyelids. And again. *There! That!* Involuntary. Unmindful. Natural. Seemingly unimportant. But incredibly significant.

Chief sat bolt upright. "Oh, Christ." The realization had floorboarded his heart. It was beating hard and fast. His breath was loud in the otherwise soundless building.

Easy, easy. Don't launch yet. T-minus ten seconds. Look at it again. Think it through.

He did, calmly and rationally.

The rockets fired. Liftoff.

Chief bounded from the cot and practically threw himself against the bars of the cell, shouting, "Somebody get me the hell out of here!"

At that precise moment, the door to the sheriff's office burst open.

"Hey, whoever you are!" Chief yelled. "Back here."

When they rushed into the hallway, Lawson was in the lead. A handsome black man was hot on his heels.

Lawson read Chief's expression instantly. "You know what she's done."

And Chief said, "I know she'll kill him."

C H A P T E R | 3 9

I'm so glad you're here, Melina."

Brother Gabriel was beautiful. It was easily understandable why people were drawn to him. He exuded vitality and seemed to glow from within, as though even in a dark room, he would radiate light.

But the most beautiful reptiles had the deadliest venom. As he moved nearer to her, she recoiled, a reaction that seemed to amuse him. Smiling, he *tsk*ed her. "Melina, Melina. Why do you shrink away from me?"

"Because I don't want to be contaminated."

"Then it's true. You do plan to do me bodily harm with that ridiculous six-shooter."

Surprise being on his side, he reached into the pocket of Chief's jacket and removed the pistol, which he then tossed to Hancock. "There's an X-ray machine—the kind used in airports, except much more sensitive—mounted inside that doorframe," he explained to her, pointing toward the double doors through which she and Hancock had entered.

"It registers on monitors in my bedroom, in Mr. Hancock's computer cabinet over there, and in the security center. So you see, there was no way you could possibly sneak it in." He touched her cheek. "Did you really think it would be that easy to kill me?"

She swatted aside his hand. "I didn't come here to kill you. I want you to live."

"Really? I thought for sure you had it in for me. Now I'm intrigued. Do go on. Please."

"I want you to be publicly exposed for the fiend you are. I want to see you convicted of your crimes, and then I want you to live a long time behind bars, so that you'll have thousands of days to think about the evil things you've done."

Chuckling, he hitched one hip over the corner of his desk and indolently swung his foot back and forth. "That's an awfully harsh sentence, Melina. What have I done to deserve it?"

"You ordered my twin's murder."

"Ah, sweet Gillian. I'll concede that her death was a terrible waste. I've seen pictures of her."

"Gordon's disgusting photographs?"

"Along with snapshots of her that Jem Hennings took. I was particularly fond of one in which she was clowning for the camera. She was wearing a wide-brimmed straw hat, which I thought was very fetching."

Frustrated by his seeming unflappability, she shouted, "You killed her!"

His gaze was steady and mildly reproving of her raised voice. "That was her doing, not mine, Melina."

"You're saying she chose to be brutally stabbed?"

"To her wretched misfortune, your sister's moral character didn't equal her outward beauty."

The same could be said of him, but she didn't want to sidetrack him by pointing that out. "You killed her because she spent most of that night in Colonel Hart's company."

"How delicately put," he said with that same belittling hint of amusement. Then, all trace of a smile disappearing, he added, "Gillian made a bad choice."

"Choice? Okay, let's talk about choice. Where was her choice when she was inseminated with your sperm?"

"What difference did it make to her? She was using an anonymous donor anyway."

So her conjecture had been correct. She'd clung to a thread of hope that she had been wrong. It nauseated her to think of the women he had debased. She almost envied their not knowing. Knowing made it worse. Perhaps.

She wanted to strike him, hurt him. Badly. Her hands balled into fists at her sides. It was only by an act of will that she contained her fury. "Dale Gordon. You're responsible for his death, too."

"I regret losing him. His devotion to me was unshakable."

"Which you exploited in order to talk him into killing himself."

He waved his hand negligently, as though

the life of that pathetic man was of little or no consequence outside the context of what it had meant to him.

"You hoped the investigation into Gillian's murder would stop with his suicide."

"You wouldn't let it lie, Melina," he chided gently. "While I admire your tenacity and your devotion to Gillian, you've made a real pest of yourself this week."

"Those goons you sent to my house—"

"Joshua and his assistant."

"Who are they?"

"Loyal disciples. Good soldiers."

"Not that good," she scoffed. "Chief and I managed to escape them. More than once."

He didn't take the derisive criticism well. His leg was still lazily oscillating, as though he didn't have a care in the world. But the muscles of his face looked less mobile than they had earlier. His smile had gone a little stiff, his eyes several degrees colder.

He said, "You got lucky. Especially Colonel Hart."

"Why the attempt on his life?"

"Why do you suppose, Melina?"

"As punishment for sleeping with Gillian."

"Punishment which he deserved. Gillian was honored—"

"I'd hardly call it an honor," she said scornfully.

"She had been chosen for greatness."

"Meaning that she had been selected to bear you a child?"

"Precisely," he said.

"But Chief was intimate with her."

"He desecrated her."

"He cared for her."

"He *fucked* her."

That first chink in his armor, which she had noticed moments ago, widened even more. She could use that jealous anger to her advantage. She would prod it like a sore tooth.

Leaning toward him, she smiled. "And she loved it," she whispered. "She told me that she couldn't get enough of him. His mouth. His penis. He was strong, hard, virile. She said that he was the best lover she'd ever had, that he knew how to give a woman pleasure. She couldn't wait to make love with him again. She said that if she did conceive that day, she hoped the father was Christopher Hart and not the sperm donor."

He came off the desk like a shot, his face now ruddy with wrath. "She deserved to die."

"Do you kill them all after they've borne you a child?"

"Only the ones who turn out to be cunts like Gillian."

"And the rest?"

"They continue living their lives, never knowing."

"Candace Anderson."

"For one."

"And it doesn't bother you that the Andersons grieve for their son and pray for his safe return?"

"How selfish of them."

"Selfish?" she exclaimed incredulously.

"Their son is thriving here."

"Without his parents."

"*I* am his parent."

That was going nowhere. She took another tack. First she had used his jealous anger to get answers. Now she would appeal to his monumental ego. "How did you devise such a brilliant plan?"

"By accident, actually." Composure restored, he resumed his place on the corner of the desk. "For years the Program was limited to women who came here to the Temple to live and work. But the numbers weren't large enough. Then I happened on

to an article about the use of artificial insemination to propagate endangered spe-
cies. Of course, it's been successfully used
for decades to breed livestock."

She thought she might be sick right there
on his expensive Oriental rug. "So you applied the technique to human beings."

"The technology was there. I just had
to find among my followers the personnel with the knowledge and skill in androl-
ogy."

"And the depravity to switch sperm."

He didn't contradict her, adding, "Along
with enough cunning not to get caught."

"How many women have been . . ."
Unable to complete the question, she swallowed hard.

"Inseminated by me? You would be staggered by the number. Not all conceived. Of
those who did, not all went to full term and
delivered. But our percentage of miscar-
riages is agreeably low. We've got a dormitory of healthy children who attest to our
success."

To hear him boast, one would never guess
that he was referring to human beings. "Do
you do it all from here?"

"We have two other compounds, one in

Europe, another in Asia." He winked at her. "Of course, the semen is collected wherever I am."

"How is it preserved? Shipped?"

"Expertly. It's all very scientific, I assure you."

"If Gillian had lived to have your child, you would have kidnapped it like you did the Andersons' baby?"

"It would have been brought here, nurtured, loved."

"That's what a mother is for."

"We have wet nurses, Melina. The babies aren't deprived anything, not even breast milk."

"They're deprived of their mothers, their true identities, their families."

He was shaking his head. "I become their family, and I am sufficient to meet all their needs. The women who bear them are biological necessities. Nothing more. When my scientists are able to successfully replicate the uterus outside the body, the mothers will become obsolete. That would streamline the Program considerably."

He assumed a wistful expression. "I'll confess to developing a fondness for the mothers, because they perform an essential service. But the children don't belong to them. They belong to me, to the ministry."

Except for his extraordinary good looks, he appeared as normal as any other man. His voice was distinguished by its remarkable resonance, but it was otherwise normal. His mannerisms were polished but not so different from those of anyone else. But he wasn't normal; he was deranged. He didn't rant and foam at the mouth. He didn't screech like a fanatic. But every word he spoke was absolutely insane.

"You are a lunatic."

Rather than take umbrage, he smiled ruefully. "That's been a misconception about most men of greatness, Melina. Can you think of a single historical figure who made a breakthrough in science or medicine or architecture or religion or politics who wasn't ridiculed? Name a single genius who wasn't initially misunderstood and labeled a lunatic. I can't let the skepticism of small minds dissuade me from my purpose."

"Which is what? To people the world with little Brother Gabriels?"

He laughed. "My dear, you have a wonderful way with words. Your phraseology oversimplifies, but you've captured the essence of the plan."

"Your new world order."

"I see you've listened to my sermons," he said, looking pleased. "In a few years, my children will be ready to assume their positions in the world. They'll have unlimited power and means, the likes of which have only been dreamed of by previous world leaders. Governments will be ruled by them. The world economy will be theirs to manipulate. They'll direct global commerce. Communication will be under their control.

"Art and culture will be molded around their ideas and creations. They will determine what the general public reads and sees and hears and thinks. They will dictate where wars are waged, who thrives, and who is vanquished. Coinciding with this movement, there will be a spiritual upheaval, a universal revolt against established religions."

"Ah! That's where you come in."

"Out of that ecumenical chaos, there will arise one world religion."

"You."

"Me."

His self-confidence was so unmitigated it

was chilling. "You actually believe that you're capable of bringing about this new world order?"

"I *am* bringing it about," he said complacently. "Masses of people are impatient for it. They're eager to embrace it, to embrace me. But it's not yet time. And until the time is right, we must work toward our goal in secrecy, Melina.

"Can you imagine the worldwide bedlam that would erupt if my plans were exposed prematurely, before the children are old enough to assume the positions for which they're being so carefully cultivated?"

"Couples like the Andersons would storm this place."

"You see my point."

"Women who had conceived by any means of artificial insemination would panic."

"Exactly."

"They'd be terrified of the risk of accidental incest."

"Not a possibility yet," he said. "The first generation of children haven't reached puberty. But we've prepared for it. There's already in place a tagging system that will prevent brothers and sisters, or sons and mothers, from coupling in the future."

Closing her eyes briefly, she shuddered. "My God."

"In any event," he continued blandly, "no good purpose would be served by informing the public before the optimum time."

"Except that it would stop you."

"And I can't allow that to happen." He clasped his hands on his knee and, sighing, said, "Consequently, I'm faced with the dilemma of what to do with you."

She squared her shoulders. "You won't kill me."

He arched one golden eyebrow in a silent query.

"As you've demonstrated, you're not stupid," she said to him. "Too many people know that I was coming here to confront you."

He cracked a wide smile. "Not a problem. We've got a contingency plan for that. Right, Mr. Hancock?"

"That's correct, Brother Gabriel."

Nervously she glanced at Hancock, who stood between her and the door.

"You see, Melina, like Gillian, you made a serious miscalculation. A bad choice, as it were. That unfortunate choice ordained your dispensability."

"What about the Program?"

"In what regard?" He was being deliberately obtuse. Furthermore, he was enjoying it.

"I thought you planned for me to take Gillian's place."

"That was the plan. But, to my great sorrow—genuinely, my *great* sorrow—we've discovered that you and Gillian were not, in fact, identical."

"But we were."

"No," he said, drawing out the word. "There was a difference. And, as it applies to the Program, that difference is immense, I'm afraid." His beautiful eyes turned sad and sympathetic. His mouth turned down at the corners. "You, Melina, are of no worth to me whatsoever. You, my dear, underwent a hysterectomy."

CHAPTER | 4 0

Jem Hennings didn't know about that, did he?" Brother Gabriel continued with the same taunting inflection. "Like a good sister, Gillian never discussed your medical history." Lowering his voice to a confidential whisper, he said, "Your female problems."

She kept her expression impassive, although his insulting tone made it difficult.

"Gillian never told Mr. Hennings about those pesky ovarian cysts that beset you when you were only twenty-seven. Thankfully they turned out to be benign. Following the surgery, you were no worse for wear. Except, of course, that you no longer had reproductive organs."

"How did you . . . how . . ."

"How did I know? Hennings was a good man, but on this one point he failed to do his homework. He was so eager to replace Gillian, you see. Mr. Hancock conducted a more thorough background check on you."

He reached for her hand and pressed it between his own. "I assume you barged in here believing that you could barter your life for a contribution to the Program. You reasoned that I would be reluctant to harm you since you had been selected to bear one of my children in Gillian's place. Unfortunately . . ." He raised his shoulders in a sad, sympathetic shrug.

"When Agent Tobias arrives—and we know he soon will, probably accompanied by the Dallas homicide detective, possibly even Colonel Hart—they'll find the compound in an uproar. A crazed woman, erroneously believing that I was somehow connected to her sister's murder, managed to breach our security.

"Although misguided and emotionally distraught, this young woman was extremely resourceful. She got as far as my private quarters, where she threatened my life with a firearm far too large and unwieldy for her small hand. But determination gave her strength and, for several terrifying minutes, enabled her to hold me at gunpoint. However, when she was ultimately cornered and ordered to relinquish the pistol, she put it to her own head."

He let all that sink in before continuing.

"After the mess is mopped up, the authorities will be given unrestricted access to the Temple. If you're very nice, Melina, I'll let you in on a little secret. Mr. Hancock has recorded every document in a code only he can decipher. Shh, don't tell." He even held his finger to his lips and winked at her.

She was in the company of madness.

"But to the FBI and anyone else who peruses the records," he continued, "they will seem to be those of a law-abiding American with no criminal tendencies whatsoever. We don't take the allowed tax exemption granted to churches. We pay our taxes. The ministry is not anti-government. As you see, I advocate patriotism." He motioned toward the American flag in the corner of the room.

"Yes, they'll find children and their mothers living together happily in a communal setting, which is of their choosing and which breaks no laws. They'll see that our school is fully accredited and indeed is superior to most public schools. Within the compound is a medical facility.

"I, of course, will lament Dale Gordon's descent into insanity and grieve over the tragic chain of events that a former disciple set into motion, which, to my horror, culminated in your ghastly suicide."

"Peace and love," she said quietly.

"Precisely, Melina."

Again, his complacent smile made her want to strike him. Instead she withdrew her hand from between his and took a step back. "You've forgotten a few things."

"I don't think so, but I'll be happy to listen to your observations."

"Tobias and Lawson know that you were in close contact with Dale Gordon. Chief heard Jem admit that they worked for you."

"Explainable. Hennings and Gordon devised this plan themselves. They had warped my message, perverted it to fit their vision of a new world order. Joshua and—"

"Joshua?"

"The man who impersonated Tobias. He

was hired by Hennings. I knew nothing about it. Obviously they had a disagreement, probably over his fee. He turned on Hennings and killed him."

"Joshua may tell a different story."

"Joshua is uniquely skilled to transform himself and avoid capture. He has before. He will again."

"Say Jem and Dale Gordon had hatched this plan," she said. "They could hardly implement it without your cooperation. You had to send them sperm."

"I had sent specimens to Gordon for analysis."

"To—"

"Check for genetic abnormalities I didn't wish to pass down. He was doing tests in his spare time, at my request. I'm speechless to discover what was happening to these specimens once I sent them."

She tugged on her lower lip. "The children here."

"The mothers will truthfully claim that I sired many of them. Fathering children outside of wedlock might be considered a sin by some, but I consider it a holy responsibility. It's certainly not an indictable offense."

"But they'll run DNA tests on the others that will prove they're yours."

"What others?" he asked innocently.

"The Andersons' baby. The other kidnapped children who were brought here. The—" She stopped suddenly. Then, remembering, she said slowly, "The ones on the buses."

He glanced at Mr. Hancock. "Is she referring to our production buses?"

"It would seem so, Brother Gabriel. They're the only buses I know of."

Brother Gabriel looked back at her as though to say, *Anything else?* "By the way, I've been remiss. I haven't thanked you for having Gillian's body cremated, thus eliminating DNA testing on intrauterine tissue. It wouldn't have proved that I knew anything about Gordon inseminating her with my sperm, but it could possibly have lengthened the investigation, and my schedule is already so demanding as it is. I really didn't have time for any of this. I'm relieved it's almost over and I can get on with my work."

"Don't pat yourself on the back yet. The other woman you had killed days after she conceived? Tobias is having her remains exhumed. They'll test the fetus."

"And it will match my DNA. Fortunately, I donated sperm to the sperm bank that supplies the clinic where she was a patient. There would be a logical explanation for any mixup."

She held his gaze for several moments, knowing with certainty that he was in the grip of unmitigated insanity. "You seem to have everything covered."

"We strive to be thorough. We couldn't be successful if we weren't. Years of . . ." To his utter astonishment, she started laughing. "Melina?"

"I hate to dash your record of successes, but you *have* missed something, *preacher.*"

He liked neither her terminology nor her disparaging tone. Brusquely, he motioned toward her. "Mr. Hancock. I see no benefit in further delay."

Hancock grabbed her arms from behind. She submitted without a struggle, which came as another surprise to Brother Gabriel. Even when Hancock pushed the barrel of Longtree's pistol against her temple, she didn't flinch.

"So now I commit suicide, is that the plan?"

"That's the plan." Brother Gabriel came to stand within inches of her. "I'm terribly sorry it had to end like this, Melina." His fingers trailed over her cheek, her neck, her breast. "Truly I am."

His touch revolted her, but she didn't give him the satisfaction of cringing. "You don't know how sorry you're going to be if you order him to pull the trigger."

"Why is that?"

"Because it's easy to issue an order and have someone else kill for you. It's quite another to look a woman in the eye and kill her yourself."

"You'll have to do better than that."

"All right. If you kill me, you'll destroy yourself."

He smiled. "Riddles, Melina?"

She would never know which puzzled him most—her soft laugh or her softly spoken answer to the riddle.

He reflexively retracted his hand. The facade crumbled. All pretense vanished, and it was no longer Brother Gabriel looking at her with abject hatred. It was Alvin Medford Conway.

And it was he who angrily gestured for Hancock to get on with it.

Penetrating the Temple turned out to be easier than Tobias had anticipated. It wasn't without its obstacles, but it wasn't the fiasco it could have been. He had dreaded a full-scale standoff or shoot-out with cult members. The bureau didn't need the negative publicity, and, if it went the way of similar incidents where people were wounded or killed, his career would be put on hold for the years required to conduct a thorough investigation.

But when he flashed his ID at the guard in the gatehouse, the young man was awestruck by Tobias and the men accompanying him. Because it would have taken too long to summon other agents from Santa Fe or Albuquerque, even if they'd come by chopper, and since the local sheriff was AWOL, Tobias's backups were policemen from the Indian reservation that incorporated a portion of the county.

Also with him were Lawson and Hart. If Tobias had known that Hart was going to insist on coming along, he would have left him locked in the jail cell. As it was, he was there, looking like he'd already fought in one battle tonight.

Swallowing a knot of apprehension, the Temple's young guard asked, "Did somebody do something wrong?"

"Did you admit a woman into the compound this evening?"

"Yes, sir. About an hour ago."

"Then it's you who's done something wrong. She's a threat to Brother Gabriel. Open the gate."

"Can I call my supervisor?"

Shortly, a Jeep roared up to the opposite side of the gate. A man stepped out and came toward them, his bearing defensive and suspicious. He was backlit by headlights, which he'd failed to turn off. "Baker, chief of security," he said through the iron pickets. "What's the problem?"

"Special Agent Hank Tobias, FBI."

Baker seemed singularly unimpressed with Tobias's credentials. If anything, his hostility rose a notch. "I say again, what's the problem?"

When he was informed that Brother Gabriel's life was in danger, he was only marginally more receptive to the idea of letting them inside the compound. "My men know that the woman in question is here. We'll take care of it."

"Look," Tobias said, "I don't care if you're dancing with snakes and biting the heads off live chickens in there. I'm only trying to keep Brother Gabriel from getting killed tonight. And just in case you don't think the threat is serious, look what this woman did to him." He hitched his thumb in Hart's direction and Baker took in the nasty, unattended cut on his cheekbone and the streaks of blood that had dried on his face. "And he's supposedly a friend of hers.

"Now, if you want to go on TV tomorrow and explain why we were delayed and thereby prevented from saving your boss's life, then fine. I'm not a big fan of his. I have no vested interest in this except to uphold my duty and do my job, which tonight is to apprehend an armed and dangerous woman who's threatened the life of a public figure.

"I don't need your permission to blow this gate all to hell in order to do that job. I'd just rather not have to go to the time and trouble. All boiled down, what I'm telling you is that the only choice you have in this matter is how difficult or easy to make it."

Lawson was a little less diplomatic. He drew his nine-millimeter. "Open the fucking gate."

The gate was opened, but Baker balked at Tobias's first request. "Shut down the security cameras."

"I can't do that without Mr. Hancock's authorization."

"Who's Mr. Hancock?"

"Brother Gabriel's personal assistant."

"Where is Mr. Hancock?"

"In Brother Gabriel's private quarters. With him and Ms. Lloyd."

Hart stepped forward and asked, "Are there cameras in there?" Tobias didn't rebuke him for asking. He'd been about to ask that himself.

"That's the only area of the compound where cameras aren't allowed," the security officer told them.

"But they could see us?"

"If they're watching the monitors."

"Then unless you want to alert Ms. Lloyd that we're here and cause her to do something reckless, I'd ditch the cameras."

Baker spoke into his walkie-talkie and ordered that the cameras be disengaged. Then he returned to his Jeep and told them to follow him.

"I'm riding with him," Lawson said. "Don't trust him as far as I can throw him."

Three minutes later, with Baker acting as their escort, they were admitted into the lobby of the main building. The number of armed men patrolling the building made Tobias uneasy. It was a disaster waiting to happen.

"What floor are the private quarters on?" he asked.

When Baker didn't answer immediately, Lawson poked him in the spine. "Have you gone deaf or what?"

"Third. I'll show you."

"No, you're staying here." At a signal from Tobias, one of the reservation cops quickly relieved Baker of his weapon and walkie-talkie. The man went ballistic, but Tobias threatened to put him in restraints if he didn't calm down and shut up. "This is for your own protection." Which was bullshit, and Baker knew it. He continued to grouse but was smart enough not to assault an FBI agent during the performance of his duty. Tobias ordered three men to stay downstairs to monitor the activities of Baker and his security guards.

"You stay, too," he told the astronaut as he crowded into the elevator behind everyone else. "Help keep an eye on Baker."

"Not on your life."

"It's your life I'm thinking about."

"Which I'm responsible for."

"Not tonight, you're not. I don't want a national hero getting himself killed on my watch. Now step out of the elevator."

As Chief backed out of the cubicle, he made eye contact with each of the reservation policemen. One by one they stepped out of the elevator and joined him.

Tobias knew when he was beat. He'd needed the manpower, and the reservation police force had been his only resource. He knew the story of how Brother Gabriel had acquired the property for his Temple. That's why he had been surprised when the reservation police chief had been reluctant to loan him some officers for the night. The man's excuse was that he was shorthanded, that several of his officers were out on another detail and he had none to spare.

Tobias didn't know whether to believe him

or not. Native Americans had a general mistrust of and dislike for federal agents, an inherent suspicion that was justifiable and had been generations in the making. He'd thought that as a black man he would have an edge with the Indians.

But not as sharp an edge as Christopher Hart had. If not for Hart, his request would probably have been denied. As it turned out, when Hart asked the police chief to grant him this personal favor, a team of eight men had been immediately assembled.

He also recognized leadership qualities in Christopher Hart that were admirable and enviable. With nothing more than a look he had commanded the eight men, and he knew before testing it that Hart's authority over them would supersede his.

"We can take the stairs," Hart said.

"Get in," Tobias said tightly.

As they rode up, they checked their weapons. The group alighted and silently approached the double doors. Just as they reached them, they heard, "If you kill me, you'll destroy yourself."

Then Brother Gabriel saying, "Riddles, Melina?"

"No. Answers. If you kill me, your baby will die, too."

Christopher Hart had heard enough. He barged past Tobias and thrust open the door. The men surged into the room, weapons drawn and ready to fire. In an instant, Tobias assessed the situation and shouted, *"Drop the weapon and release her!"*

The Indian policemen fanned out to form an arc along the perimeter of the room. Some of their weapons were trained on Brother Gabriel, others on the armed man, whom Tobias assumed was Hancock.

Chief was unarmed, but his voice posed enough of a threat when he strode up to Hancock and said levelly, "If you hurt her, I'll kill you."

Tobias knew he meant it. "Let me handle this, Hart."

Hart seemed not to have heard him. "Gillian, are you all right?"

"Gillian?"

That from Brother Gabriel, whom for the time being Tobias ignored. "Let her go!" he ordered the man still holding a pistol to Gillian Lloyd's head.

Brother Gabriel spoke again, this time with

remarkable composure, considering the shock he had suffered. "Mr. Hancock, it's safe to release her now. She's not going to shoot me in front of so many witnesses. You men arrived in the nick of time."

Hancock looked indecisive for a moment, but at a gesture from Brother Gabriel, he lowered the pistol, then dropped it to the floor.

The reservation policeman nearest him kicked it out of his reach. Christopher Hart stepped forward. He and Gillian Lloyd reached for one another. Hands clasped, he drew her out of harm's way. They exchanged a look that tweaked the heart of even a confirmed bachelor like Tobias. It lasted no more than a millisecond, but it was potent.

Then she pulled her eyes away from Hart and addressed the evangelist. "I'm Gillian."

"You're lying."

"It's been nearly a week since I was inseminated. A simple blood test will show whether or not I conceived."

"It's true, you son of a bitch," Chief said. "She's Gillian."

"Believe them," Tobias said. "I read the autopsy report tonight. Read it, not skimmed it as I had before. The body the coroner autopsied didn't have a uterus or ovaries."

"I missed that," Lawson admitted. "Melina Lloyd had had a hysterectomy."

"He knows," Gillian told them. "Hancock discovered that when he did a background check on her."

Brother Gabriel smiled pleasantly. "Well, well, what a surprise. You're Gillian. Pleasure to meet you."

"Go to hell." Turning to Hart, she said, "If Longtree hadn't left the first chamber of that pistol empty, I'd be dead. He'd pulled the trigger."

Hart took a threatening step toward Hancock, but Tobias spoke his name sharply and he stayed where he was. Although it might not have been his order but rather Gillian's hand on his arm that kept him where he was.

Tobias looked from them to Brother Gabriel and was surprised to see that he was smiling. "We haven't been properly introduced. I assume you're Agent Tobias."

"That's right."

"Our appointment isn't until tomorrow. Why'd you come tonight?"

"On the pretext of saving your life."

"Pretext?"

Lawson said, "I'd like to question you about the murders of Melina Lloyd, Linda Croft, and Jem Hennings."

The preacher turned to him. "And you must be Lawson." His eyes took in Lawson's mismatched wardrobe and rumpled appearance. "Your reputation precedes you, Detective. I can't fathom why you'd want to question me. I wasn't anywhere near Dallas when those people met their demise."

Lawson practically growled at him.

Brother Gabriel dismissed him and looked back at Tobias. "Ms. Lloyd—Gillian, as I find out—talked her way in here tonight, issuing accusations and threats on my life."

"He's lying," she said quietly.

"She pulled a gun on me. Mr. Hancock had just divested her of it when you burst in."

"Three busloads of children left here as I arrived," Gillian said. "I'm sure you'll find the Anderson baby among them."

"Video and broadcast equipment," Brother Gabriel explained with a helpless shrug. "We transport it in buses when we telecast from a remote location."

"There's also a dormitory full of children," she said.

"There is indeed," he conceded, laughing. "They belong to the men and women who live and work here at the Temple. She's delusional. Her twin's death has—"

"Shut the fuck up," Lawson snarled.

"Lawson," Tobias said. Then, to Brother Gabriel, "Why were you holding a gun to her head? Was that necessary to subdue her?"

"Mr. Hancock thought so. She, along with Colombo here, is entertaining a crazy notion that I'm somehow responsible for her twin's murder. Mr. Hancock was merely restraining her until our local sheriff could be summoned."

"I don't need to be summoned."

At the new voice, all eyes turned to the uniformed man who stepped from behind the heavy velvet draperies. He was clutching a service revolver between his hands, and it was aimed at Brother Gabriel. "It's not this lady's word against yours. I can tell them all they need to know about you."

"Sheriff Ritchey! So that's where you disappeared to."

"The last place you'd expect," the sheriff sneered. "To quote you."

"How'd you manage?"

"I came in while you and Hancock were out. The so-called bodyguards that came back with you didn't even search behind the drapes."

Brother Gabriel looked over at Hancock, who was glaring at the sheriff. "Those men should be replaced." Then, turning back to Ritchey, he said, "Can you explain why you've been lurking behind the draperies?"

Ritchey gripped the extended pistol tighter, but his hands were as unsteady as his voice. "I want to hear you say it."

Tobias was thinking, *Shit, shit, an element I hadn't foreseen.* "Easy with that weapon, Sheriff Ritchey."

But Ritchey was impervious to anything except Brother Gabriel. Tears had filled his eyes, but he was unmindful of them. "I want to hear you say her name."

"Who's name?"

"Oleta's name," he fairly screamed. "Her name isn't *Mary.* And she wasn't a whore when you got her. You turned my sweet, curly-haired little girl into a whore! You said if she came to live here, she'd be treated like a princess. That she'd have a better life, get a better education than I could afford to give her. But all you taught her is how to . . ." His voice cracked. He was unable to finish.

"Sheriff Ritchey, holster your weapon and—"

"No. I'm not letting him smile and fancy-talk his way out of this."

"If he has charges to answer to, he'll answer to them in court."

But Ritchey gave a hard shake of his head, rejecting Tobias's calm arguments.

One of the reservation policemen took cautious steps toward him, but he caught the motion out of the corner of his eye and warned the man not to come any closer. "Stay back! This is between him and me. You can shoot me if you want to, but I'd kill him anyway. At this range, I wouldn't miss."

Brother Gabriel glanced frantically at Tobias. "You're the FBI, for God's sake. Do something."

"Who's Mary? What's he talking about?"

"I traded my little girl for a badge," Ritchey sobbed. "A badge. You convinced me it would be good for her. Her salvation, you said. You said it would be best for everybody. But you took her innocence and turned her into a whore."

The man was rapidly unraveling. Tobias was desperate to prevent bloodshed. Anybody's. "Ritchey! Put down your weapon. Now!"

"Sheriff, you heard Agent Tobias," Brother Gabriel said silkily. "Stop this nonsense. Mary's nature was never innocent. She was born to do what she's doing. I never forced her to do anything. Ask her. She'll tell you how much she loves loving me."

Suddenly the sheriff's congested features cleared. He sniffed his nose. He blinked away his tears. And with amazing calm, he said, "You're going to die."

He knew what he was doing."

Agent Tobias was addressing the group that had assembled in the sheriff's office, for lack of a more convenient place. Chief had readjusted the thermostat to a tolerable temperature. The deputies, who'd been summoned back, had made coffee. They were operating like robots, shocked that their boss, Sheriff Ritchey, was occupying the jail cell. He was under suicide watch. The door between the front office and the hallway leading to the cell was closed.

Gillian was glad she couldn't see down

the hallway. It brought back bad memories, although she only had to look at Chief's face to be reminded of what she'd done to him. *Part* of what she'd done to him. But not nearly the worst.

Tobias continued. "He shot Conway—Alvin Medford Conway, a.k.a. Brother Gabriel—in the gut. Two rounds before we were able to stop him. He didn't want to take Conway out right away. He wanted him to think about dying."

The medical facility at the Temple had been inadequate to handle a traumatic injury like the one Brother Gabriel had sustained, so 911 had been called.

"He succumbed in the ambulance a half mile short of the emergency room," Tobias told them. "He lived a long half hour in excruciating pain, watching himself bleed out, knowing that he wasn't going to make it. Ritchey got what he wanted."

Lawson snorted with what sounded like satisfaction, then took a hefty swig of his Dr Pepper.

"What about Ritchey's daughter?" one of the reservation policemen asked.

Tobias shared what Ritchey had told him. "He'd had a series of unsuccessful jobs. He was in debt. Conway approached him and they struck a deal. They staged Oleta's abduction, which is still on the books as an unsolved crime. Mrs. Ritchey will soon be reunited with the daughter she thought had been kidnapped when she was ten years old." He looked down at the floor between his tasseled Bally loafers. "I understand the girl is about to deliver Brother Gabriel's baby."

Gillian heard Chief swear under his breath. "He sold his own daughter into sexual slavery?"

"Essentially," Tobias replied. "Although I believe him when he says he thought he was doing best by her. He didn't learn until recently what her role at the Temple actually was. Brother Gabriel used her to guarantee Ritchey's silence and continued cooperation. Tonight his guilt caused him to flip out. He's glad Conway is dead and will corroborate your statement, Ms. Lloyd."

"Call me Gillian. Please."

He had no time to acknowledge her request. A commotion outside drew their attention to the door. Two men were pushed into the room, their hands handcuffed behind them. Gillian and Chief recognized them instantly.

They were in the custody of several strapping Indians, all heavily armed but smiling. One's cheeks sported two stripes of war paint. It was he who detached himself from the others. "Agent Tobias?"

He came to his feet and extended his hand. "I'm Agent Tobias."

"We're reservation policemen, working undercover. We arrested these men on a civilian complaint for trespassing, but their car turned out to be a rolling arsenal. Besides illegal automatic rifles, we found black market surveillance equipment and a box of contraband prescription drugs from Mexico." He glanced over at Gillian and Hart. "We have reason to believe they're connected to your case here."

"He's the one who impersonated you," Gillian said, identifying the black man for Tobias. "Brother Gabriel referred to him as Joshua, but that's probably an alias. They were tracking Chief and me."

"With this."

She hadn't noticed Dexter Longtree until he stepped from behind a taller, younger man. In his hand lay the ruby pendant and the tiny transceiver they had removed from it.

"Thank you," Tobias said deferentially, obviously impressed by Longtree's regal bearing. He deposited the evidence on the desk, then turned to the two men in restraints and looked balefully at the one who had dared to pass himself off as him. "What's your name?"

"Fuck you."

"Middle initial?" Lawson asked.

Everyone laughed.

"Later," Tobias said to Joshua, making it sound like a threat. Along with his unnamed partner, Joshua was remanded to FBI agents who had recently arrived from Santa Fe. The pair were led back outside, where they were placed in separate cars for their trip to the city.

Chief left his seat and approached Longtree. Gillian joined them. The two men shook hands. Chief thanked him.

"I was glad to help," Longtree replied. "Actually, it was fun."

After they all shared a smile, Chief said, "I'd like to hear more about NAA."

The older Indian regarded him for a long moment. "You don't owe me anything."

"Maybe not. But I owe it to myself."

A light flickered in the old man's eyes. "I'd

be pleased to arrange a meeting at your convenience."

"I'll be in touch."

After they shook hands again, Gillian took Longtree's hand in hers. It was rough to the touch, strong, warm, confidence-inspiring. "You've been awfully kind. Beyond that, you risked your life for my sake. I'm grateful." She hesitated, then, acting on impulse, gave him a hard, brief hug. Not seeming to mind, he patted her shoulder before releasing her. "Thank you, Chief Longtree."

"You're welcome, Gillian."

Respectfully, the reservation policemen let him go first, then they filed out behind him. It wasn't until after they had disappeared through the door that Gillian realized Longtree had called her by the correct name. She looked at Chief. Their eyes met. "When did you tell—"

"I didn't."

"So how did he—"

"I don't know. He seems to know a lot of stuff the rest of us don't."

Lawson's voice broke their long stare and drew them back into the discussion. "Where does the investigation go from here?"

Tobias explained. "A task force will arrive

sometime tomorrow. In the meantime, agents from Santa Fe and Albuquerque are at the Temple making sure that nothing is destroyed or altered. All activity has been suspended at the ministry's installations abroad, too. The task force has their work cut out for them. It's going to be a chore just to sort through all the data on Hancock's computer systems."

Gillian said, "Brother Gabriel told me that everything had been entered in code and that only Mr. Hancock could decipher it."

"Our experts have cracked tough codes before. It might take them months, but I'm confident they'll crack Hancock's, too."

"Maybe he'll cooperate," Chief said.

"Doubtful. Our own government trained him not to. Hancock was a CIA operative. The day he retired, he joined ranks with Brother Gabriel." Reading their shock, he added, "Ms. Myrick informed me of that not a half hour ago after she ran a background check on him."

"Frightening," Gillian said softly. "And significant. We may never know how pervasive Brother Gabriel's influence is."

"Let's hope that influence dies with him," Chief said.

"We'll probably experience a backlash from diehard followers," Tobias warned. "We must be prepared for some unpleasant repercussions. How severe they are remains to be seen, but many will think we've destroyed a man that God Himself had ordained."

"Brother Gabriel wasn't speaking for God," Gillian argued fiercely.

"Let's hope they'll conclude that when all the charges against him are made public."

They reflected solemnly on that for a time. Gillian recalled that Chief had a colleague who had sent her daughter to school at the Temple. How would people respond when they learned how consummately evil Brother Gabriel had been? Legions of followers would feel bereft. Others, refusing to accept the truth, might react violently. When Dale Gordon saw her with Chief, she never would have imagined the far-reaching consequences of that encounter.

She asked, "Did they locate the buses?"

Tobias nodded. "Intercepted on a direct route to Mexico. They were packed with TV production equipment. And forty-seven children."

Gillian released a long sigh of relief.

"All appeared to be in good health, although they were frightened to be taken off the buses. They were turned over to New Mexico CPS. The state agencies, acting on orders from the governor's office, have been exceedingly cooperative. A sidebar. Among the caretakers who'd hustled the children away tonight were Dorothy Pugh and Hennings's sister. Two of the children were hers."

"Fathered by Brother Gabriel?"

"We're assuming. She spat on the arresting officer who asked."

"The Andersons' baby?"

"There were several boys in that general age group. It'll have to be determined which one he is."

"Chief and I promised to call them as soon as we knew something. I have their private cell number."

Tobias shifted uncomfortably and coughed behind his hand. "There's an ugly aspect to this that obviously hasn't occurred to you." Gillian, along with the others, looked at him expectantly. "The Andersons might not want the boy now. In fact, I'm guessing that most of the couples whose kids were kidnapped will reject them once they learn who sired them. It's one thing to conceive by an anonymous donor of your choosing. When you know your baby was fathered by a maniac . . ." He left the remainder unspoken.

"Jesus," Lawson said, "I hadn't thought of that."

Gillian had. Thinking about it had consumed her ever since it was first alleged that Dale Gordon was switching sperm in his lab. The thought of it had sickened her enough to make her throw up on the side of the road.

Thinking of it now made her ill. Shivering, she raised both hands to her lips and blew on them to warm her cold fingers. She stared sightlessly into near space. When at last she cleared her vision, she realized that the conversation had flagged and that everyone was staring at her.

Tobias cleared his throat. "I guess I speak for everyone. Why'd you do it? Why'd you pretend to be Melina?"

She looked from him to Lawson and then from Lawson to Chief. But she couldn't hold Chief's gaze for long, so she addressed Lawson. "It was something you said."

He nearly dropped his can of Dr Pepper. "Me?"

"When the two policemen came to Melina's house that morning, they didn't address me by her name. Or if they did, I didn't catch it. I'd been awakened from a deep sleep. All that registered was that my twin had been murdered."

"Why were you at Melina's house in the first place?"

"After leaving . . ." She hesitated, and instead of saying Chief's name, she said, "After leaving The Mansion, I drove home. Melina was already asleep. I woke her up. We talked for a while. That's how I knew about Jem's coming to my house with his gift of the pendant. I left it there on the nightstand. Melina spared no details of their encounter, so when the time came, I was able to make Jem believe that I was the woman he'd seen the night before."

"Jeez, this gets confusing," Lawson remarked.

"For me, too," she admitted with a wan smile. "Melina prevailed upon me to let her finish the night in my bed, since she was already there. It made sense. So I drove to her house and spent the night."

For a moment she was buffeted by the horrible memories of that first half hour after hearing that her sister had been stabbed to death. "When I rushed into my own house, you, Mr. Lawson, prevented me from going into the bedroom. Remember, you held me back? You warned me against contaminating the crime scene and said, 'You want to know who killed Gillian, don't you?'

"And that question was like a slap in the face. I came to, so to speak. That's when I realized your mistake. Melina had been identified as me. Apparently the killer had made the same mistake. When I saw the words written on the wall, I knew that I had been targeted to die because I'd been with Chief. But who even knew? And why would I be killed for it? I decided not to correct the mistake until I knew more.

"Then Jem arrived, and things really took a bizarre turn. Initially he didn't know that I—Gillian—had spent the night with Chief, so he didn't know that Brother Gabriel had ordered the murder. Up to that point, his shock was genuine.

"But when I announced that Gillian had gone with Chief in Melina's place, and after

Jem saw the words scrawled on the wall, he realized why Gillian had to be killed. He probably even suspected that Dale Gordon had been the one to do it. That's why—when we were in Lawson's office—he kept interrupting when Chief began to describe Gordon.

"But even before then, I suspected that he was involved on some level. Why did he lie about the engagement? Why did he claim that he was against artificial insemination when he had encouraged it from the time I first advanced the idea? Until I knew the answers to those questions, I had to protect myself. And in order to do that, 'Gillian' had to remain dead.

"Jem never suspected. I know that. I couldn't conceal my aversion, but he and Melina had never gotten along. Tricking him into believing that I was her was easy. It wasn't so easy to pretend to others." She couldn't resist glancing at Chief. His eyes were riveted on her.

Quickly she continued, looking at Lawson. "I confessed to our switching places the night before, and then let you assume that we'd switched back when the evening ended. We didn't."

"I never asked you when you'd switched back?"

She shook her head. "You only asked what time Gillian had returned home from The Mansion. I did return home around two-thirty that morning, but went on to Melina's house after our brief visit. She slept in my bed and died in my place."

She had to clear her throat of emotion before she could continue. "It was hard for me to endure everyone's grief over me, when it was Melina they should have been grieving. Often I nearly cracked under the pressure of it. The only thing that kept me going was the determination to find the person responsible for her death."

"How long did you figure the switch would last?" Lawson asked.

"How long would I continue being Melina? For as long as necessary to avenge her death. I didn't think past that. I suppose I committed a crime, didn't I? Impersonating someone?"

"I'm looking into it," Lawson mumbled.

Tobias said, "You exposed Brother Gabriel's crimes. That's my focus."

Gillian turned to Chief. "I was so afraid you were going to forget that we had seen Dale

Gordon. That day in Lawson's office, when we supposedly met for the first time, I was prompting you to remember running into him at the taco restaurant. I had to let Lawson know that Dale Gordon was a lead, but I couldn't reveal it myself."

"You recognized him that night?"

"Immediately, although I couldn't place where I knew him from. Not until he said he worked at the Waters Clinic. Then I remembered seeing him there. He'd spoken to me a few times. And . . . and other things, apparently." She shuddered, thinking of the photos taken of her when she was unaware.

"That's when I learned she had a twin," Chief told the others. "She told me that Gordon must have mistaken her for her sister Gillian."

"But you *were* Gillian," Lawson said with some confusion.

"Pretending to be Melina," Chief reminded him.

Lawson scowled at her. "You're sure you're Gillian now?"

"Yes," she said with a weak smile. "I am."

"She is," Tobias said, looking abashed. "The autopsy report confirms that it was Melina who was killed."

"I was terrified that you would discover the discrepancy," she told Lawson. "Why would a woman with no female organs be artificially inseminated?"

"That's why you rushed to have the body cremated."

"Yes. Then when you, Mr. Tobias, told me that Lawson had given you the file on the murder, I was afraid that you would find it."

"I didn't. Not until tonight. I ran to tell Lawson, and we came rushing over here to enlist Ritchey's help to locate you, and instead found Colonel Hart locked in the cell, fit to be tied."

She turned to Chief. "They told you?"

He was about to speak when Lawson spoke for him. "We didn't have to. He had figured it out on his own."

"You had?" she asked huskily. "When?"

One of the deputies who was monitoring Ritchey chose that moment to open the door and interrupt. "Agent Tobias, he's asking for you. Wants to know if he has to see his wife. Says he can't face her or his other kids."

"Be right there." Tobias stood, officially adjourning the meeting. He told her and Chief that he had reserved rooms for them at the motel. "There'll be a chopper here to-morrow at ten to take us all to Albuquerque. From there you can fly on to Dallas." He glanced at Chief. "Or wherever. Just make sure you leave me a number where you can be reached. There'll be a lot of details. Paperwork."

His cell phone rang. He opened it and an-swered, "Tobias. Oh, yeah, Lucy. Thank you for calling me back. No, nothing else tonight. Go home. Rest. You can resume to-morrow. I just called to tell you again what an outstanding job you did on this case. Truly outstanding." He turned his back to them, but Gillian heard him say, "And to ask what kind of flowers you like. That's right. Flowers."

I should have planted one of those transceivers on you myself."

Gillian had opened the hotel room door to find Chief with a hand on either side of the doorjamb, forming a human barrier. He was frowning deeply. "I've been knocking on this door for five full minutes."

"I was in the shower." Which should have been apparent, since she was bundled up in a white terrycloth robe, courtesy of The Mansion. Her wet hair had been combed, but the ends were dripping water onto her neck.

"For three days I've been leaving messages at your office and on your house phone. Why haven't you returned my calls?"

"Who told you I was here?"

"Tobias."

"He caved?"

"When I threatened to sic NASA's PR department on his ass. He's got enough to worry about."

"I couldn't go back to my house, Chief. I never want to step foot inside it again. And Melina's house . . . it seemed like another violation of her for me to be there. I hated myself for being there before."

"Are you going to keep me out here in the hall?"

She stepped aside and closed the door behind him. "I talked to Candace Anderson this afternoon."

"They got their kid back, I know. Tobias told me. They were giddy. Said it never occurred to them to reject him."

"He's only seven and a half months old. Hopefully if there's been any emotional damage, it will be minimal."

"They'll fix it."

She was as confident of that as Chief. "Have you checked on Pax?"

"Bandit's fine. He's fine. We're going for a beer together next week. Everything's bloody fine. Now—"

"Would you like something to drink?"

"No!" he said impatiently. "The trip back to Dallas? I thought you were going to be on my flight."

"How's your face?"

"Stitches."

"How many?"

"Seven, I think. I went to the men's room in the airport, and when I came out and didn't see you, I assumed you'd already boarded the plane."

"It'll scar."

"It'll make me look dashing and dangerous."

"It already does."

"But you weren't on the airplane, and I was stuck sitting next to Lawson. Who, by the way, has a crush on you."

"Lawson?"

"Hates my guts. Snorts every time he looks at me."

"I took another flight."

"To avoid me?"

"I had something important to do, Chief."

"What?"

"Get a blood test."

His chin went up as though someone had yanked a string on the back of his head. "Oh." He didn't have the courage to ask, but his face looked so anguished she didn't keep him in suspense.

"Negative."

He swallowed thickly. "It could have been mine."

"I thought of that."

She noted a small spasm at the corner of his lips that might have been caused by regret.

"But it could also have been his. And if it had been . . ." She closed her eyes, but that didn't trap the tears. They leaked out her eyelids and rolled down her cheeks.

He spoke her name softly and cupped her face between his hands.

"I'm sorry, Chief."

"Sorry?"

"For so much." She opened her eyes. "I didn't know I was going to meet you that night. I didn't know how I was going to feel about you from the moment I saw you. When I went to your room, when we started—"

"Shh."

"I didn't even think about the artificial insemination. It never crossed my mind. I swear it didn't."

"I believe you."

"Do you?"

He nodded. "Because I wasn't thinking about anything else, either."

She reached up to comb a strand of dark hair off his forehead. "Do you know how difficult it's been for me not to melt every time I looked at you? That afternoon in Lawson's office, it had only been twelve hours since I'd left your bed, but I had to act like a complete stranger. I thought I was going to die from wanting to hold you and wanting to be held. I'd seen Melina lying there dead, viewed the bedroom and all that blood. I was stricken with grief. Afraid. I needed to be held, and I wanted to be held by you."

"Do you know how depraved I felt, wanting Melina every bit as much as I'd wanted Gillian?"

"When did you figure it out?"

"When I was in the jail cell."

"How?"

"I couldn't help comparing Melina to Gillian. Each time I did, I wound up with a thousand similarities but no differences. Not one. And I started thinking about Gillian eating the tacos that night. How she'd sucked on her finger when she got salt in a paper cut. It was sexy as all get-out. It was just as sexy when Melina did it that afternoon."

Her eyes widened with sudden recollection. "When I was eating the french fries in Longtree's pickup. I had reopened the cut and the salt stung it. I didn't even realize I was doing it."

"Me either. Not until I started thinking about it. The two images merged in my mind. Same finger. Sucked on in the same manner. I started piecing it together, and all of it fit."

Tears came again. "I've done you so many injustices. Put you through so much. Can you forgive me?"

He backed up to the bed and sat down on it, then guided her to straddle his lap. He shrugged off his jacket and unbuttoned his cuffs, then pulled his shirt, still buttoned, over his head. By then she had released him from his jeans. He untied the belt of her robe and parted it. Neither could wait. She impaled herself on him.

"I knew it," he whispered into her neck. "I knew I couldn't be wrong, knew this couldn't be duplicated. This doesn't happen twice in a lifetime. Not within a few days."

They hugged one another tightly and remained like that for a long while. Then he pushed his hands into her robe and smoothed them over her back and hips, finally settling on her waist. She nuzzled her face in his hair and lightly kissed his bandaged cheek. He gently touched the nasty bruise on her collarbone.

"How is it?"

"It doesn't hurt anymore."

"I should have killed the bastard."

He lowered his head to her breasts; his tongue caressed her nipple. She whimpered in response.

"Incredibly sensitive," he murmured, sucking her gently. "Here, too." He wedged his hand between their bodies and touched her in a way that caused her to catch her breath.

"Did you talk to Melina about this?"

Momentarily unable to speak, she shook her head.

"You didn't?"

"No, Chief. I didn't confide anything. It was too personal. Too special."

"But you shared everything."

"Not you." Her fingers skimmed over his chest and down his belly. She withdrew his hand and lifted it to her mouth, kissing it lightly. "I wanted to keep you all to myself."

"So everything that 'Melina' told me Gillian had said was actually—"

"My feelings. My own words. Things I couldn't tell you, but wanted you to know."

He covered her breasts with his hands, gently rubbing their raised centers against his palms. "Why did you cry after we made love?"

"Because I wanted to tell you how I felt, and couldn't. When you said my name— Gillian—my heart shattered. With joy. And with despair."

"As you said, when a man says something at that particular moment, it's brutally honest."

"Isn't it?"

"It was then," he said gruffly.

She began to rock her hips slowly. Forward, then back. Barely any movement at all, but enough. Each subtle motion coaxed a moan from him. She squeezed his hips between her thighs. "I can feel all of you."

He managed to gasp, "Yes."

Possessively he splayed his hands over her hips. His fingers made deep impressions in her flesh as he guided each erotic undulation. They were close, close . . .

So she was stunned when he said, "Wait!" and lifted her off him. He turned her quickly and pressed her down onto the bed. With no wasted motions, he finished undressing, opened her robe completely, and stretched out above her. When he reentered her, she thrust her hips toward him.

"No, be still, be still," he groaned.

"But—"

His mouth sank onto hers. It was a long, deep, and hungry kiss. Their mouths melded in an honest admission of mutual desire, need, and vulnerability. Then it changed character. As they smiled against each other, their lips and tongues barely touched. They tantalized, teased, flirted. He sighed her name and she responded in kind. The kiss then became a very sweet, tender, and heartfelt expression of affection. But ultimately passion flared again, and the kiss grew blatantly sexual. Their roles were clearly defined by the manner in which his tongue made love to her mouth.

At last he pulled back and looked down

into her face. "You are incredibly beautiful," he whispered.

Although she was unadorned and without makeup, she felt beautiful. Her cheeks were flushed. She could feel the flattering fever in them. Her lips felt full, bruised, and suggestively wet. She dragged her tongue along her lower lip and tasted their kiss.

"And sexy as hell."

Looping her arms around his neck, she said, "Don't hold anything back."

He didn't, and neither did she. Afterward, damp and deliciously spent, they lay as they were for a long time. When he finally levered himself up, he kissed her forehead, her nose, her cheeks, finally her lips, using his own to lightly rub the words into them. "I'm in love with you, Gillian."

"I know. You told me."

"Doesn't count. I thought I was talking to Melina."

She shook her head and whispered, "But I was the one listening."

Lincoln Township Public Library
2099 W. John Beers Rd.
Stevensville, MI 49127
(269) 429-9575